The Harbor of Ill Will

by
Phil Locascio

An environmentally friendly book printed and bound in England by
www.printondemand-worldwide.com

This book is made entirely of chain-of-custody materials

FastPrint Publishing

www.fast-print.net/store.php

First published by BeWrite Books of Canada, 2012
This edition published by Fast-Print Publishing of Peterborough, England, 2012

The Harbor of Ill Will
Copyright © Phil Locascio 2012

ISBN: 978-178035-435-4

All rights reserved

No part of this book may be reproduced in any form by photocopying or any electronic or mechanical means, including information storage or retrieval systems, without permission in writing from both the copyright owner and the publisher of the book.

All characters are fictional.
Any similarity to any actual person is purely coincidental.

The right of Phil Locascio to be identified as the author of this work has been asserted by him in accordance with the Copyright, Designs and Patents Act 1988 and any subsequent amendments thereto.

A catalogue record for this book is available from the British Library

This book is sold subject to the condition that it shall not, by way of trade or otherwise, be lent, resold, hired out or otherwise circulated without the publisher's consent in any form other than this current form and without a similar condition being imposed upon a subsequent purchaser.

Phil Locascio is the author of three novels, *The Sins of Orville Sand*, T*he Sorcerer of Hooterville* and T*he Restoration of Josef Mundt*. He is also the author of a collection of short stories titled, *Howling Hounds.* Phil has had dozens of short stories published in magazines and anthologies. Several of his tales have received Honorable Mention in *The Year's Best Fantasy and Horror*. He welcomes comments at: *Lucysdad2@comcast.net.*

To all those, too numerous to mention, who have unknowingly demonstrated to me, through their actions, perseverance and sacrifice, what true bravery is.

The Harbor of Ill Will

Prologue

November 13, 1928
The Yugoslav/Romanian Border

The wind had found its voice, skipping through the thorny shrubs and shivering the nearly naked branches with its low moan. The whirl funneled through the woods scattering leaves along a downtrodden path leading to a weathered, rickety wagon. Along its side, the words read "Zarpello the Great". The two black mules, whose job it was to pull the rig, stood tied to the limb of a withered oak that shielded them from the autumn breeze. An impending rain storm rolled forward in the distance. The animals snorted and bobbed their heads in foreboding. It was not the advancing clouds that stirred them, but a rustling in the brush.

Something was not right.

Whispers signaled danger to the mules. The noise, dancing on the edge of the wind, was imperceptible to their master, the not-so-great Zarpello. Shielded by the sound of the swaying limbs, a branch snapped, leaves crunched under a boot and a "hush" quieted an unruly voice.

In the wagon the big-bellied Zarpello rested in his cot shuddering at the enormity of his discovery. His beleaguered thoughts would not allow him to sleep.

Virgillio Zarpello came from a long line of gypsies who made their living on the fringe of legitimacy. Deception, fraud, misrepresentation, and slight of hand had served him well through the years. However, unlike some of the former family members who had handed over the trade to him, Zarpello actually had a heart buried deep beneath his barreled chest. He viewed the filling of elixir bottles with stream water and selling it as a panacea for everything from baldness to sterility as an innocent malfeasance. In fact, he had many times witnessed the sure belief of a cure that his bottles promised providing that exact result through the power of suggestion. The shell game he had become so adept at, he viewed as a lesson to those who thought gambling was a viable pursuit. He used his so-called fortune telling skills, provided at a modest fee, for a variety of benevolent purposes: easing the mind of a wife troubled by her husband's infidelity, relieving the anxiety of girls fearful that the right man would never come along or pacifying a grieving parent that their recently departed child had found peace in the loving hands of God.

His broached ethics never caused him any concern. But now?

Zarpello threw back another swallow of his Chianti and stared at the wooden box where the subject of his fears resided. The vision of the old gypsy woman who had given it to him crystallized in Zarpello's mind: the wrinkled lines on her brown face; the thin, bent frame; the scraggly, dark rags that draped her body. She had said that all she wanted was her son returned to health. As was his custom, he sold her a bottle of snake oil and promised her the potion would deliver her son from the brink of death.

It was all she wanted, she had said. Miraculously, somehow, the child regained his health.

And it seems when her son recovered, the gratitude she felt found its release in the gift she had provided Zarpello.

Zarpello remembered her words when she had returned the next day with that dark sack in her hand, the pouch that leaked odd sparkles of light.

"Now you can have whatever you desire." But most unsettling was the glare in her eyes when she placed her gnarled hand on his arm and spoke: "It will grant one good thing, one worthy demand. And then no more. But be warned for a granted wish, a price is paid. For good, good: for evil, evil. You must not let greed or jealousy shape your request. It must be a selfless desire you choose, a noble cause, virtuous and worthy, one not made in sin or selfishness. For those will warrant recompense too. You will reap what is sown. Be mindful then ... of unrighteous wants. For it takes in measure what it gives."

Zarpello leaned forward toward the box, his hands shaking in anticipation of something he could not quite understand. The thing in the black sack that leaked rays of colored light out along the seams had been so mesmerizing, so hypnotizing that he had tried to deaden its allure by putting it in a wooden box. But still it drew him like a magnet, the way sin nags the mind of even the most virtuous of monks. He had only looked at it for a short time, but the way his thoughts had twisted both frightened and tempted him. Urges he had never felt had arisen in his brain. Impulses imploded in his mind. Devious, dark thoughts not only arose in his consciousness, but an overwhelming desire for those things began churning into plans and designs that seemingly only needed his consent to crystallize. He had slammed the cover on the box with the last effort of his conscious will before submission occurred.

But now the temptation was drawing him again.

In all of his travels, Zarpello had witnessed many curiosities and through purchase, chicanery, trickery and bartering had acquired a great many of them, all now part and parcel of his traveling road show: mummified remains from ancient Egypt, deformities floating in glass jars, a two-headed snake, jewelry with supposed mystical powers, shrunken heads, relics of saints, medicinal herbs and more. But nothing carried with it the aura of wonderment and awe as did this oddity.

"Eee-awww"

Outside one of the mules stamped its foot and bobbed his head. Whispering came from the side of the wagon.

"Who is that?" Zarpello asked.

A voice spoke just low enough for him to be unable to discern the words.

"I warn you to answer!"

Suddenly someone pulled the back tail of the wagon down. Two men stood in the dim light, their faces obscured by handkerchiefs. Immediately Zarpello realized their intent. Quickly he reached behind him and grabbed the hatchet he kept for just such purposes as one of the men giggled and began climbing into the bed of the wagon.

"He's got an ax, Yanko!"

Yanko had pulled himself up into a standing position hanging on to the back trying to solidify his balance when Zarpello swung the weapon at his thigh. The weight of the hatchet's head buried itself into the man's leg.

"Ahhhhhh," he screamed. His grip faltered and as he clutched his thigh now spouting blood he fell off the edge of the ramp. Zarpello lost his grip on the weapon as the second man crawled in and grabbed him by the collar. The man wrestled Zarpello up and flung him out of the wagon. As he did, Zarpello's foot caught the edge of the wooden box and accidentally kicked it off the edge of the shelf. The thief jumped down on the big man and they began wrestling in the dirt. The stench of the vagabond's clothes and body nearly overpowered Zarpello as he tried to use his massive weight to pin his rival down.

The robber squeezed out from under the big man's grasp and leveraged the advantage. With his knee buried in Zarpello's chest, he raised his dagger high above his head and plunged it down.

The boy turned his face away from the smoke. Plumes drifted up from the heap of burning embers that consumed the trash he and his father had accumulated from their two-room shack. Behind the boy on the edge of the woods the dwelling leaned up against the side of a hill. The fifteen year old shuffled back a few feet and rubbed his eyes when he heard a half scream, half-shout emanate from deep in the trees off to his right. A quiet pause followed and then the thumping of slammed wood. The youngster turned his head toward the house where he and his father lived. His father had been lying in bed an hour before when he had screamed at his son to get to the chore of burning the trash. The man would no doubt be fast asleep now, nearly unconscious as usual from the wine he had consumed. He would not be pleased to be awakened because of idle, nonsensical noises drifting through the trees.

The boy disregarded the sounds and went back to raking the papers and refuse into the flames.

Again an odd noise pierced the darkness and seemed to ride the swell of the breeze off into the distance. A kind of rustling screech and moaning followed and then a muffled shriek and the banging of wood once again. An animal screeched.

And then silence.

The boy stood staring into the darkness down the wagon path that many travelers used to negotiate the hilly forests. Leaves skittered across the trail, crackling in their dryness. The scent of the coming rain tickled at his nose.

An animal whinnied in the darkness. An agitated donkey perhaps?

Earlier in the day, he had seen the fat man with the curious wagon roll past the house and plod the rig's grinding wheels down into the hollow beyond. Had he bedded down for the night beyond the sloping tree line?

Once again the braying of an animal rose in the distance. The boy leaned the rake against a tree and stared off down the path. The smoke from the burning trash swirled in the air and curled around his head causing him to cough and draw further back from the fire. Once his vision cleared, he turned back toward the house. The hesitancy he felt at investigating the nature of the noises registered only slightly less than that of waking his father. Cautiously he moved off toward the trail that led around the bend in the woods and down into the flattened valley where the strange sounds had now gone eerily silent.

Chapter 1

October 2, 1984

A fine mist hung low over West View Cemetery. The only sound was the lull of traffic from Parkridge Highway that filtered down along the winding frontage road. An occasional car sped down the pot-holed country blacktop bordering the graveyard.

Andre Haskim sat quietly in his parked car and gulped down the last swallow of his beer. As happened at times, his misshapen lips caused some of the alcohol to trickle down the side of his chin forcing him to use his sleeve as a napkin. Haskim could not have been in a place more acclimated to one whose features so resembled a decaying corpse. He had been there earlier in the day, moving mysteriously, hiding his distorted face, searching through the headstones until he found the right grave. It had taken him some time to locate it because he could not risk asking information from anyone who worked there. The following day there would be an investigation of a macabre event and someone who looked as he did would have immediately been put under scrutiny.

What he had decided to do did not in any way offend his sense of decency, because he had no such sense left. One thing did bother him though. The gravesite was just a short way down a curving lane to where a dilapidated house sat on the property. The home belonged to the cemetery's caretaker, a crusted-over, gray-haired ancient who may very well have looked more at home in a cemetery than even Haskim. Haskim would have to be as quiet as possible in carrying out his task. There was too much at stake.

The night was cool and damp, the graves themselves seemingly seeping fog from some unholy place. Not even a gentle breeze stirred the branches of the trees interspersed in the graveyard. It was 1:22 am and all was still. Morning would not come for at least four more hours. Hopefully, he would be long gone before the pale light of dawn revealed his hellish deed.

When he pushed the button that popped the trunk, the noise seemed to scream across the expanse of pavement and race through the graveyard to summon the dead. Dressed all in black, Haskim got out and retrieved the shovel he had brought with him. In his other hand he carried two cans of beer still secured to their six-pack plastic holder. He would need some refreshment to help him through this night.

In the distance two headlights warned of an approaching vehicle. He scampered across the asphalt and nearly tripped in the gravel shoulder where it sloped drastically down into a shallow ravine bordering the black rail fence that ran along the perimeter of the cemetery. Haskim stayed low in the grass and waited until the car went by. In the driver's seat of the passing vehicle, a stone-faced gray haired woman stared straight ahead oblivious to the grotesque figure peeking out through the tall weeds. Satisfied the coast was clear, the thief pitched his shovel over the fence. A brick pillar gave him sufficient foothold to mount the barrier and within moments he was traipsing through the graveyard trying to orient himself to his destination.

In his black garb, Haskim was like a shadow drifting in the dark. Only an occasional flash of moonshine lit his silhouette as he darted through the head stones lurching along in that hobbling limp his condition demanded.

In the dim light, the marble stones glowed chalky white. Farther ahead the tall mausoleum Haskim was searching for stood tall against the sky.

The would-be-thief found the grave he was looking for and set up his flashlight so it pointed directly on the area where he would be digging.

Fear began to well up inside him. For some reason the past flashed through Haskim's mind, all the things that he had been through, and now this, the plundering of a grave. But it would all be worth it if he found what he sought. Haskim put on the heavy gardening gloves he had brought with him for protection. No doubt the amount of shoveling he would need to do would tear at the thin skin covering his deformed hands.

Down the curving lane sat the caretaker's house, a sloping cabin with a short porch surrounded by a dilapidated picket fence. The shack stood bracing a hillside as smoke trailed from the crumbling brick chimney that rose from the roof. All the lights were out except for one dim bulb illuminating a curtained room. Suddenly a German Shepherd came racing around from the back of the house and began barking in the intruder's direction. Haskim quickly sat down and waited for the dog to quit. A sharp voice from inside the house turned the dog's attention for a moment. The animal got the message that he was to stop, but his gaze remained fixed toward Haskim, his frustration revealed by a low growl.

Haskim fretted over what to do. It appeared that the slightest irregular noise would be detected by the dog and its incessant vigilance would soon reveal Haskim's presence. A sudden gust of wind approached from the west and spread across the grounds like a wave. The breeze filtered through the trees before the intensity waned.

As quietly as he could, Haskim rose and began digging. Unfortunately the dirt forced him to thrust hard with the shovel head to break the ground. It only took two jabs against the earth to arouse the dog once again. The German Shepherd resumed its loud barking forcing Haskim to hide behind a tree. Perhaps he would have to abandon his effort that night and return the next day with a poison steak because he would not be able to carry out his task with so vigilant a sentry on duty. The dog raced along the fence line barking as he went.

"Willy, shut the hell up!" a voice from inside the shack yelled.

But this time Willy would not be silenced. His barking continued as ferociously as ever.

Panic began to engulf Haskim. Just as he was about to withdraw, a man came out from the house shouting once again at the dog. He came to the fence and grabbed Willy by the collar bringing the dog up short before staring out over the graveyard toward the area where Haskim remained hidden. For a few moments the man held his gaze trying to detect what had frenzied his dog into such a state. Haskim peeked from the side of the tree and held his breath. The dog's owner was dressed in shorts and was not wearing any shoes. Haskim reasoned that the man would not be interested in traipsing through the graveyard barefooted looking for a rabbit or deer whose presence so infuriated the animal.

The caretaker mumbled something unintelligible and then pulled Willy with him back to the house. To Haskim's relief, the man forced the dog inside and shut the door.

Haskim went back to work. The top layer of the ground was easy to remove due to the heavy rains of the previous days. After the first foot or so however, he met with more thick, pasty clay. Every scoopful required heavy exertion. By the time he had dug down two feet, he had to stop and catch his breath. He leaned against a nearby headstone and popped open a beer.

Haskim's hands ached terribly. The flesh was especially susceptible to tearing at the creases due to the lack of its elasticity. At the base of his thumb the skin was already bleeding from a seam that had opened up. Haskim gave himself a few moments of rest beneath a tree.

The idleness, he soon discovered, allowed macabre thoughts to enter his head. What could he expect to find in the casket? What does a body look like after such a long time? What was the stench going to be like? But most of all he wondered whether the thing he was after would really be there. He admitted to himself that he did not have much to go on, only a vague suggestion.

Well, what did he care? If it wasn't there, it wasn't there. After all he'd been through, digging up a corpse was a relative picnic. He could do that.

He was prepared to do a lot worse.

Haskim finished his beer and returned to his task. His nervousness and the alcohol running through his veins fueled him on. Scoopful after scoopful the hole widened. His hands and shoulders began to ache more than ever and he needed to take another break. Every once in a while he heard the muffled barks of the German Shepherd from inside the caretaker's house. The dog refused to give up. As he progressed deeper and deeper into the pit, the hole he found himself enclosed in made him more and more panicky. Haskim's bravado faltered. He trembled as much from the exertion as the dread running through his head. The one saving grace of being in the pit was that the walls of the enclosure deadened any noise he made.

As he took a break, he examined his progress. The hole was approximately four feet deep. Haskim wondered just how deep coffins were actually buried. He imagined that it most likely was not the typical six feet everyone assumed.

With waning energy, he resumed his digging. Suddenly the shovel clanged, stopped short by a solid object. Through the hole left, he saw glistening metal.

Reaching the casket energized Haskim. He began digging frantically now that he was so close. Quickly he exposed the top of the coffin and clawed with his hands trying to find the latch. He finally located it and pulled as hard as he could, but it would not give way. He shook the casket and beat on the side of it and still the latch would not give. The pounding alerted the dog once more and this time he would not relent. Haskim pressed on. Filthy, dirty and sweating profusely, he stood on top of the casket and jumped up and down trying to dislodge whatever dirt might be blocking the path. When he returned to the latch, it finally gave way. The lid popped open slightly. A small gushing sound, like a lover's whisper, emanated from inside the coffin.

The hinges creaked and groaned, but the wall of the hole was not dug out far enough to allow the lid to rise to a sufficient height. Lying over the coffin, Haskim clawed desperately, digging away the earth that blocked his progress. After clearing the space, he tucked the flashlight under his arm and began raising the heavy metal hood. As the lid reached chest level, he shifted the position of his hands and began pushing up with his palms. A terrible stench rose up snatching his breath away. With a powerful last thrust, the last mound of dirt blocking the opening gave way. The lid swung open and rocked back and forth on the rusty hinges.

Haskim shone the flashlight down into the box.

In the cabin the caretaker's patience had worn thin. Willy would just not give it up. Something was disturbing the dog and it was obvious that his master wasn't going to be able to get to sleep until the matter was investigated. Most likely some nocturnal rodent was making a ruckus. Perhaps two animals were vying for territory among the marble head stones snarling or growling at one another. It was not unusual for deer to invade from the woods on the far side of the cemetery, especially at night. But something about Willy's persistence alarmed the grave digger.

Could it be possible some raucous teenagers intent on vandalism had returned to the cemetery?

The year before in the middle of the night, two troublemakers had come through knocking down headstones and spraying graffiti on others. Their shenanigans had caused him a lot of work and didn't endear him to the cemetery owners either. He had learned a lesson from that debacle. He had ways of dealing with critters or vandals who wanted to do damage to the cemetery. The caretaker lumbered over to the corner where he kept his shotgun. Willy stopped his protests for a moment and froze in his spot alerted that finally his master was going to act.

The withered corpse rotting inside her lovely sky blue dress leered up at Haskim. A huge diamond brooch sagged from above her breast. The stench of decay rose from the coffin encircling him as he gazed down. The woman's head was shrunken, the remains melded into the silky pillow. The face was almost entirely skeletal except for a few black patches that clung, here and there, to her skull. Her left eye, set in a blackened recess, glared out. The shriveled orb seemed locked on Haskim. The unpleasant smell and the vision of the emaciated body unnerved him.

The corpse's wedding ring, now oversized on the bony finger, glistened in the glow of the flashlight sending prisms of yellow sparks all about the soft white padding. Haskim searched around the coffin but did not find what he was after. He cursed and pulled the body up to check beneath it. The remains sagged beneath him falling in on itself like stiff gelatin. By now Haskim was panting furiously. He swung around and reached his hands down into the bottom part of the coffin. He shivered as his hand ran along the side of a bony thigh.

It was no use. His hunch had proved wrong. It was not there.

Haskim swore. He pried the ring off the finger and pulled the brooch off the dress. *Their value would be some reward for all his hard work.*

His thoughts scattered now. He felt himself losing control. He had to get out of there. The combination of terror, smell and claustrophobia was becoming overwhelming.

He climbed out and rolled sideways to escape the hole. Down the road a flashlight illuminated the front door of the cabin. The dog's incessant barking suddenly increased in volume. The door to the cabin opened and the flashlight flickered in jiggling swirls at the cabin's doorstep.

A voice rang out: "Who's there?"

Haskim hugged the ground and waited. The dog continued barking and the man moved a few steps out from the doorway. This time Haskim noticed that the man wore boots.

"What is it, Willy?"

The man flashed his light out into the night, but he was too far away from Haskim to observe anything. The dog ran along the fence line now back and forth barking furiously. The man retreated into the house, but the door remained open.

What now? Haskim thought. Should he make a run for it or wait it out? He decided to wait and see what would happen next. A few moments passed and the dog calmed slightly resorting to interspersed growling between bursts of barking.

The man came back out of the house this time with a jacket on and something in his hands. He closed the door and with the flashlight shining before him made for the gate entrance. Willy began spinning around in his spot anxious to get at his prey.

Haskim had seen enough. He got to his feet and ran for the fence.

The caretaker spotted him. "Hey ... hey you!"

Haskim didn't know if he could make it to the fence before the dog got to him, but he was just as concerned about the shotgun he had seen in the caretaker's hands. By the time he made it to the stone pillar he had climbed to enter the grounds, the barking had stopped and Haskim knew the reason. The dog had been released from the yard and was expending its energy chasing his prey. Haskim's hands hurt terribly from all the shoveling he had done. That and the heavy panting his run produced made him nearly helpless for a moment. His hands would not grip the rails and he could not catch his breath.

A small burst of barking gave Haskim a clue as to the dog's progress. He still had some time. He collected himself and began climbing. When he reached the top of the pillar, he looked back and saw the dog, its form illuminated by the moonlight in sporadic flashes as it peeled through the shadows of the trees and then open ground.

"You hold on there!" the man screamed from a distance beyond the dog.

Haskim jumped down and fell into the fence just as the dog arrived. Haskim's shoulder took the brunt of the fall and for a moment he sat immobilized. Before he could react quickly enough to pull away from the fence, the dog locked its jaws on Haskim's left hand. Haskim screamed and pulled his hand free but not before the dog had managed to tear at his hand.

In the distance the caretaker was advancing. Haskim ran to his car. With his mauled hand he tried to pull the keys from his pocket. His bleeding fingers would not work. Finally he managed to retrieve them. As he got in, the caretaker had reached the gate and opened it allowing the dog to escape the grounds. By the time Haskim got the car started, the dog was at the side of the vehicle jumping up at the window scratching furiously. The road forward was a dead end forcing Haskim to turn the car around. As he quickly circled, the man reached the car and banged on the window. Haskim turned his head and stared directly at the caretaker just before he was able to floor it and peel off down the street.

The caretaker had seen a lot of stiffs in his time. He had cleaned them, dressed them, powdered them and buried them, but he had never seen one climb out of its grave before and drive off.

Chapter 2

October 5, 1984

Demetri Davos tapped his cane on the slick floor and waited for the elevator that would take him down to the lobby. Beside him a stiff looking executive, with black horn-rimmed glasses and blue silk tie, checked his watch and shifted his feet before needlessly pressing the already lit down button twice more. Demetri remembered a past when time cramped him as it did this up-and-coming business man. Now Demetri had nothing but free time, but it was not endless. His time was grinding down like the second hand of a watch with a worn out battery, clicking forward until that final moment when the next second's lurch would prove too demanding.

The old man tried to dispel the desire that lurked beneath his easygoing appearance. Those feelings were trying to distort his will the way the thrust of a hammer on a hot anvil shapes the edge of a sword. Each pounding clang curled his willpower just a little more, threatening to weaken his self-control even more than it had already been compromised. A spike of anxiety shuddered through Demetri. Now it was his turn to react to the elevator's delay by strolling over to the window.

Before him the overcast sky grayed the Chicago River as it rippled past the two pillars of Marina City standing across Wacker Drive like two large ears of corn. Below him swarms of Chicagoans pressed down the wide sidewalks, darting in and out. Some trudged on wearily while others bounced along merrily, those being the tourists, perhaps from Japan or Europe awestruck by the tangle of vertical structures, some of which in their magnificence rose to such heights that clouds obscured their tops.

Ding!

Demetri and the executive squeezed into the mirror-walled elevator and like the rest of the riders made every attempt to stare at some obscure point in the ceiling or floor where their eyes would not be forced to connect with someone else's. Everyone holding to an anonymity that allowed them to hide their inner most thoughts from the surveying glances of the other silent riders. All held to it but the little boy who gripped his father's hand with his right while his left wiggled the green army man up his side as if the soldier were climbing a wall. He made a "puff" sound indicating the soldier had fired his rifle and looked up at Demetri for his impression.

Demetri smiled as he wondered what it might be like to live in the mind of that little boy, obsessed with nothing more than army men, his next meal, perhaps already dreaming of the Halloween candy that was soon to come.

Staring down at the child brought the stomach-churning anxiety once again to the old man's bowels. It had been with him in a less muted version ever since age began tearing down the walls of youthfulness as it invariably does to all human kind. Age had done its best to sag his belly, slump his shoulders, and enlarge his double chin. His continual sour stomach however now reaffirmed to him the results of the latest tests performed by Doctor Goldman. The stomach pains would get worse and there was little that could be done.

What did a seventy-one year old man expect? All the riches in the world could not halt the slow, inevitable crawl to the grave. Nothing could ... except ... And that scared him more than even the consequences of an inoperable cancer.

The doors opened at the lobby and the more industrious of the elevator's inhabitants, including the impatient executive, funneled quickly out fanning into the throng of hustling businessmen and women. Quickly they dissolved into downtown Chicago. Demetri held back and let them all shimmy past him. His needs did not dictate a hectic pace or require anything more than a stoic stroll helped along by his wooden cane.

The vision of Doctor Goldman's eyes came back to him, the way his blinking increased and he seemed to find excuse after excuse to look away from his patient. It had taken three or four requests from Demetri before the doctor finally came clean: there was no cure, yes, his colleagues agreed with his diagnosis, the pain would get worse, time was running out. Demetri sighed deeply as he buttoned up his overcoat and fitted his leather gloves to his arthritic fingers. He moved aside of the hustle and bustle and stared out the door. A Wendella tourist boat slowly cruised past on the Chicago River, its mast just visible above the stone bridgework.

Demetri made his way through the revolving door and found the stiff breeze that accosted him to be quite welcome. He wanted to feel everything now, to be absorbed with everything, to have his brain filled with anything at all just as long as it muted that incessant temptation that continually haunted him. It had been getting stronger as the weeks went by and his sour stomach had ached and cramped. But he knew it was nothing compared to what would be coming. It would be dangerous now, extremely dangerous, but not necessarily for him. His weakness might make someone else pay, something inflicted ominously on one of his own.

It was odd. At some moments what the doctor had told him sent a chill through him shrouding out all his senses, nearly suffocating him with fear and uncertainty. He was not an overly religious man, but he had always considered himself an honorable one. That had always been an enigma to him. If he wasn't overly concerned about what the Almighty might consider a fair retribution for the things he had done, why would he not follow the route of conceit and self-gratification regardless of how hollow and shallow they might be? Would not his world exist within the confines of grab for all you could, dog eat dog? It must be that civility and fair-mindedness were in themselves goals that in some way were pursued as a natural by-product of the motives of selfishness and egotism.

So even in that, was the self-restraint he had demonstrated for much of his life simply, in actuality, another demonstration of his self-centeredness?

And why, when he had already suspected what the team of doctors' final verdict would be, did he mumble prayers into his pillow like a little boy who first realizes that his parents cannot solve all of his problems?

Had that been what he had turned into, a sniveling child, tucked under the covers of his huge bed, in his fashionable bedroom, in the second story of his spacious manor house? That was fine, he supposed, *except for the naked exposure it brought, the fright, that could so easily turn into desperation and despair which of course could be so easily remedied, so effortlessly relieved, with so tragic of consequences.*

The old man's stomach began once again to stir.

It might be better to put something in it, he reasoned.

Using a pay phone, he called his driver, Nigel Quimby, and told him he was going to stop and grab a bite to eat. They arranged a pick up time. Demetri chose the Greek restaurant off Randolph Street. They generally had a large menu and served good, tasty food. He went through the revolving door and was greeted by a young blond-headed hostess in her midtwenties who seated him at a booth toward the back against a window. Through the glass he witnessed scores of people headed up and down the street bustling through their busy lives.

The old man sighed and opened his menu.

Across the street standing in the doorway of an office building was a man fifteen years younger than the one he had been following. His overcoat was tattered in several sections. In its time it would have been considered an elegant coat, one that might be worn by an elite class of executives who didn't punch a clock for their daily bread but instead worked their own hours, mixed pleasure with business over extravagant lunches, and were very unconcerned as to whose turn it was to pick up the check. A day in which a wave of his hand would get his cigar lit, a time when the waiter would address him as, Sir, and would make a point of knowing what the customer's 'usual' was.

But that seemed so long ago now, before the accident, the operations, the endless stretching exercises during his months of recovery. Now his presence was as welcome as that of a coughing tubercular patient in a roomful of children. The man pushed up the sun glasses on his face, but they simply slipped down once again to the edge of what constituted his nose. A small child being led by the hand by her mother could not help but stare up at the figure slumped in the doorway. Although the man wore oversized sunglasses and his black hat low over his face, the girl could see the man's cheeks and chin and the gnarled tip of his nose. Perhaps in later years maturity and age would combine to impose the rules of common courtesy upon her, but for now there was only the half-open mouthed, stunned expression on her face.

The man had seen it so many times that his mind no longer registered the scorn and slump in spirit that had for a period been a by-product of such obvious, yet innocent and understandable, stares. Andre Haskim had last conversed with Demetri months before on the occasion of Demetri's last visit to the convalescent center where his former friend recuperated from his ordeal. Andre's pleas, no matter how decidedly just he felt they were, had fallen on deaf ears. When he persisted, Demetri became more and more obstinate in his refusal. He had done what he could to alleviate Andre's bills, but he would not agree to the real wish his former partner asked of him. Together they had made a mistake, together they wished upon a star and together they now suffered in their own way, Andre in the physical and Demetri in the mental and spiritual. Both had wrestled the demons of depression and emotional turmoil.

It had turned one vengeful and the other mournful.

The dissension between the two men had become so pronounced that Demetri would no longer agree to see Andre.

The injured man had begun to scare him. In the permanently swollen socket that held now a discolored, misshapen eye, Demetri saw only intolerance for anything that would not satisfy him. Revenge and resolute conviction indicated a kind of unbalanced reasoning, a scary unreasonable thing, like that of a paranoid schizophrenic who is so certain of the veracity of his beliefs that any disagreement only gives added impetus to the realization that he was indeed correct. Yes, there were plots against him, his suspicions were valid, and he was right to be scared, very scared. And he would need to protect himself.

Andre Haskim pulled a pack of Pall Malls from his coat pocket, cupped the lighter and lit up a cigarette. His thin, almost non-existent lips gripped the cigarette crookedly to the side where his misshapen mouth contorted into a type of half-sneer in order to hold it. He had let it be known to the doctors that he was back to smoking and they recounted the risks and advised against it, and he told them to stuff it. The joys of his life were few and spaced too far apart. He would not deny himself, his health be damned.

What had the doctors done for him anyway? Only his steel will had pulled him through, only his callous self-centeredness had given him the will to pull on those cables and stretch the skin of his forearms through the pain and the tearing burn. Only his insatiable desire to obtain what was rightfully his gave him the courage to endure through surgery after surgery. A lesser man would have left himself for dead and gone and not risen to the status of a mutated, scarred monstrosity.

Besides if his plans came to fruition, his health, vigor and appearance would be changed to those of a handsome young prince.

Andre Haskim did not believe in a benevolent God. With everything that had happened to him, how could he? There was nothing left for him to do but follow the trail of his motivations for as far as they would go. He would kill Demetri if he had too, but only if he could get away with it and still that would not console him because he didn't care about Demetri. Vengeance was the lesser of his motives. Payback, if it happened, was fine, but what he really wanted was something only Demetri could give him. And if Demetri's will was stronger than his, he might not get it. And that scared him. So he might need a trump card, a wedge that would separate the man from the thing. He would not hesitate to find one and use it, if necessary.

Andre flicked the cigarette down to the ground as a bus pulled along the curb in front of him and shrouded him in shadow. He tilted his fedora further down along his forehead and made his way across the street. He did not want to take the chance of Demetri seeing him before Andre could force him to listen. The walls of the manor, the security of Demetri's grounds, and the absence of any solitariness on the part of the old man had limited Andre's ability to confront him. Only by tenacious surveillance and some conveniently placed bribes, was he able to pin down a time when the old man would be alone, unguarded, and vulnerable to Andre's brand of reason.

Andre had taken a wild chance in the cemetery and come up empty. It was on now to the next tactic.

Andre entered the restaurant as a waiter made his way toward him. For the first instant of his recognition the same old wariness appeared on the face of the employee, that almost involuntary hesitation so many people displayed when they were confronted by his appearance. It was human nature and Andre understood it. Any animal, man included, was designed to pull back from anything foreign, uninviting, odd, or out of the ordinary.

Andre waved the man away as the waiter mumbled something. The deformed man pointed down the aisle indicating that he did not need to be seated but was in fact meeting someone already there. The waiter nodded vaguely and turned back. Andre moved quickly, his head down until he reached the table where Demetri sat staring down at the menu.

Demetri looked up and of course immediately recognized his old partner. For a split second, almost instinctively, he made a move to slide out of the booth and avoid the confrontation. Then he stopped, paused, and even let a glint of a smile come to his face. There was no real danger here in a crowded restaurant.

Maybe after all this time, he owed the man something.

"Andre ..." Another pause before he waved his hand toward the empty side of the booth. "Please ..."

Andre stared down at Demetri and a wave of relief came over his face when he realized his old friend would not run from him. He would get his opportunity. That was a start.

"Your security and secretiveness required lengthy surveillance, Demetri, but I managed to break through your wall of resistance. I would apologize for the inconvenience, but I'm not sorry and we've been through too much to stand on ceremony, eh?"

"I suppose so," Demetri sighed.

Andre slid into the other side of the booth as the waiter came up to the table. "May I ... get something for you, Sir." The awestruck stare was there, but muted this time.

"Coffee, for now."

Andre removed his hat and unbuttoned his overcoat displaying the gnarled, knotted scarring along his upper chest beneath his neck. Demetri noticed Andre's bandaged left hand. He wondered what had happened.

"What'd you do to your hand?"

"Oh that," Andre chuckled. "Believe it or not, I was attacked by a dog."

"Really? What happened?"

"Long story for another day, perhaps."

Demetri stared at the bandaged hand and then brought his eyes back up to the face. The toupee Andre wore was obvious, the color of the hair much too dark, the edges too thick, but that was the least of the problems with his looks. No one was going to tell Andre Haskim that he needed a new hairpiece to improve his appearance.

Demetri folded his menu in front of him and clasped his hands together on top of it. "I've heard that you are completely ... how should I say ... healed. You look good. In a way, I can say I am almost happy to see you."

"That's odd coming from a man who has done everything he can to avoid me all this time, no?"

Demetri nodded in half-agreement as his brain took the moment to evaluate Andre's features. The last time he had seen the man this close they had had that unfortunate row. Back then Andre did not have the toupee. He was still in treatment. There had been more facial reconstruction since then, Demetri could tell.

Andre's forehead was nearly normal looking. Patches of skin, Demetri reasoned, from his buttocks or legs must have been used to create the seamless texture from the bridge of his nose to just beneath the area where the wig hid the deformity on his skull. The look was not entirely natural, one could tell that there had been repairs made, but it certainly was an improvement. The skin of the forehead was almost blanched, unnaturally pale, bleached looking and bland, missing the obvious features that an adult's forehead would normally display: the curled outline of the skin as it went around the eye sockets, the curved wrinkle lines of the brow, the symmetry of one side to the other. Unfortunately, the rest of the facial features had not been brought into any semblance of what one would consider normality. The entire effect his face displayed, beyond the obvious stark deformities of discoloration, unnatural thicknesses, and rivers of raised skin lines, was that of a bland, featureless landscape, one in which the normal wrinkle lines, creases and contours were absent.

Haskim's left eye was like a black hole. The socket was misshapen, seemingly shrunken down by the permanent damage which had distorted the spatial proportions making the eye appear as if it was in a continual squint. The absence of eyebrows and eyelashes served to accentuate the unnatural appearance providing no camouflage whatsoever for the deformity. Meanwhile, the black patch that covered the right eye leant an air of malevolence to Haskim's entire visage. In comparison to the rest of his facial deformities, Demetri wondered what the orb under that eye patch might look like now. He had seen it early on and knew that it had been damaged almost beyond recognition. Perhaps a level of acceptability could not be achieved and the only accommodation possible was to hide it from sight.

Most prominently askew were the nose and the ears which the fire had nearly incinerated totally. The outer ridges of the ears including the lobes were no longer there having been completely consumed by the heat and flames. What was left were abrupt stubs of discolored flesh curled in at the edges and highlighted by dark holes that seemed overly large in comparison to the remaining gnarled cartilage. In an attempt to conceal the damage, longer hair on the edge of the toupee draped over what remained but only served, by its obviousness, to bring more attention to the disfigurement. Two nostrils, one larger than the other, seemed to stare out from the middle of his face because skin no longer existed on the very tip of the nose. In its place was a skin-toned prosthetic designed to recreate the flesh which had been lost. To Demetri it appeared to be a light plastic of some sort. He could not fathom the method used to fasten it. The untarnished flesh tone of the piece contrasted with the rest of Andre's face which was spotted with patches of brown, darker bronze, and rosy red areas.

Demetri felt the sickening rumble in the pit of his stomach not so much because of the gruesome spectacle in front of him but because of the guilt he felt in considering the role he had played in creating it. Regardless of the hatred he knew Andre held for him, Demetri felt sympathy and empathy for all the man had gone through.

This is what greed brings, he thought. A scripture verse came to Demetri's mind – *the wages of sin is death*.

In Andre's case, death may have been a more charitable end. Something for nothing brought only misery and despair and now Demetri knew that Andre would want to continue that pattern. And what would come of that? More tragedy and calamity, perhaps not for him or Andre, but most likely someone close to one or the other of them.

Andre let out a long sigh as he picked up the menu and knowing now that Demetri was going to allow him his time, began skimming through it, his parched, gnarled hands fumbling with the plastic.

"You know I was always partial to soup, especially when I was young. My grandmother, she made a great lentil soup, you know thick, pasty, almost like a mush but a deep flavor ... you know, the kind of a soup kids wouldn't like. But me, ahhhh ... Of course now, since I spent all those months unable to chew, sipping my meals through a straw ... well ... I've lost my urge for soup. I like to chew my food now. That's one thing my condition has profited me – new dentures." Andre opened his mouth spreading his lips apart to display a perfect set of teeth, white, gleaming, and perfectly aligned. A waste really in such a fouled head.

The waiter returned and the men ordered: Swiss steak for Andre and tuna salad for Demetri. When the waiter filled their water glasses and let them be, Andre folded his hands together in front of him and aimed his one good eye in Demetri's direction. With the way the light beamed down from above and the sliver of space from which his gaze emanated, the only thing visible to Demetri was a glint of watery fluid in a dark bubble.

"You'll have to forgive me for getting personal, but I see that you were coming from your doctor's office. Anything serious?" The stiffness of the skin surrounding what was left of Andre's lips and the unnatural spacing around his mouth that would not allow his lips to articulate words successfully caused his *s*'s to have a kind of watery edge to them, as if they were being funneled through spittle.

"I commend you on your spying capabilities, Andre. But you always were a Snidely Whiplash type, weren't you?"

Andre brought his right hand to his forehead and flipped it away in scurrilous type of salute. Only the tips of his fingers were visible because Andre wore a fingerless glove on his hand. It was black with plastic supports that ran along the back and the inside of his wrist. The fire had so severely ravaged the muscles of his wrist and forearms that the brace was needed.

Demetri returned to the original question. "My condition ... nothing serious. I'm quite healthy as a matter of fact," he lied. "And you ... how are you?"

"They've done what they can now. They've taken all the good skin they can from virtually every place on my body possible. I don't know what hurts more, the damaged areas or the healthy ones that have been stripped."

As Andre said the last sentence, the gaze of his left eye drifted toward the ceiling and for a moment he dropped his guard and his look displayed a kind of wishful sanguinity. When it did, Demetri found himself feeling pity for Andre, something that was not entirely foreign to him. Misery and heartache were a shared commonality for the both of them, so joined were they now in the tragedy of what had happened.

"Patchwork job, you know. They're quite astounded, the doctors. They've never seen anyone survive such drastic burns, nearly 80% of my body. Even damage to my lungs, the breathing in of the heat you know ... and the smoke. Well ... you know all that. I suppose I should be grateful. You know they have discovered that the one true factor that allows for longevity of life is when the body is given just a wee bit less than the normal amount of food it needs to survive. They've found that the body then goes into this type of ... survival mode and in that state the body's immunities are on added vigilance and are more on guard to protect the body from cancers and other diseases. So all those months when I could barely slurp my food, and all of this ..." he waved his left hand in front of his face "gives me a one up, eh?" The catty smile was off center. A normal person would have needed an extra moment's time to even realize the man was attempting one.

Demetri nodded. "You've been through a lot, Andre. No one knows that more than me. How's Geoffrey?"

Andre rolled his head slightly. "He visits. My son used your help to finally get himself situated. He's off drugs now, but, well, we'll see."

Demetri sensed sadness in Andre's words, a moment he had given him that wasn't permeated with hatred, scorn or contempt. It brought back more pleasant times when the partners had shared a profitable enterprise, worked side by side to raise their printing business from its meek beginnings to its heights before the financial decline and the mismanagement and all the rest.

As if he sensed the momentary lapse of resolve he had showed, Haskim's stare took on a look of malice. "You know, I would like nothing more than to reach over this table and strangle you with my bare hands, but I won't."

"And why not?"

Andre bent in over the table and his one good eye widened. "Because you're going to give –"

The waiter's arrival disrupted the stream of discontent that was about to cross the table from Andre's mouth. The Swiss steak went in front of him and the tuna to Demetri. Demetri could not help but witness the manner in which the waiter's quick stares appraised the facial features of his customer.

When the server left, a pall fell over the table, broken only when Andre picked up his fork.

"You know that won't happen, Andre. If you are here to ask me, plead with me, I am not going to do it. We've been all over that. Do you want to endanger your son?"

"We don't know that," Andre replied, as he shoved a slice of steak into his mouth.

"No, we don't know that do we. Other than the fact that it is true, and you know it. If not him, someone else. You have a niece don't you, somewhere, a sister?"

"Bitch hasn't talked to me in fifteen years. She's turned her daughter against me anyway." Andre's mouth worked not like a normal mouth but like a machine, like a food mixer, mechanical, automatic. Dribbles of juice escaped from his lips and trickled down his discolored chin. The destruction to the nerves of his face made it quite likely that he could not even feel the drips. Haskim brought his napkin to his mouth and wiped away the spittle. Most likely his experience with eating real food had taught him that he might not always be aware when morsels of food escaped his mouth. He used the napkin repeatedly as he ate.

"We made a mistake," Demetri continued. "Look at what it has cost. My daughter, my wife. You were not always so bathed in discontent and scorn. Lord knows each of us has our share of character faults. Hell ... greed and business savvy were what brought us together once. I know that. I don't hold myself out as some damn saint. I feel just as much shame as I can drag through the day with me. The temptation to ... to do something stupid is always with me. But I have the sense to know now that I can't let that happen. Too many people have been hurt already."

"Too many people have been hurt, eh? You have the effrontery to bring that up to me? During all that time, all that hell I went through, you know what kept me going? Knowing that once I got through, I would have a reward, compensation, what I'm owed. And at the end of this rainbow, what do I find? The one person who I would have thought would do whatever he could to make up for all of my suffering is now the only thing standing between me and what is rightfully mine. And whatever scruples you have, I don't care. What's that saying, 'To make an omelet, you've got to break a few eggs'?"

Andre bent low over the table so that Demetri could smell his harsh breath. "You talk about somebody getting hurt, let me tell you this. Somebody is going to get hurt if you don't play ball. I've got little left in this world to grant me any solace. Through all of this, I'm financially solvent. We got what we wanted, both of us. But now I have only this repayment left. And if I don't get it, then I am going to make a point of hurting somebody. Oh, you can rest assured it won't be you. I know that that is a sacrifice you would almost welcome at this point, you and your precious guilt. But there are others."

Demetri shot his hand out and grabbed Andre by the collar pulling his head closer. "You listen to me, Andre. I'm not playing games with you. The answer is no and if you try to hurt Isabelle or anyone else in my household …"

"Or you're going to do what?" Andre spat back as he tore Demetri's hand from his collar and shrugged his shoulders. The anger he felt displayed itself in a flush of color that swelled in his cheeks turning the pale, mottled skin an odd shade of purple. The burned man feigned a degree of insult as he readjusted the twisted collar of his shirt. "This is it, Demetri. I'm giving you an honest chance to do the right thing."

Demetri lowered his eyes to the table. Maybe the prognosis the doctor had given him earlier had been a good thing. He had nothing much left to hold onto. If he was gone, and took the accursed thing with him, that would be the end of it. There would be nothing Andre could do. He could rant and vent, but he would know that his mission would be thwarted. There would be no purpose in hurting anyone else because it would be useless in terms of achieving his goal. Demetri was glad he had not disclosed to Andre the degree of his illness. It could not come quick enough now. But there were problems with that too. As his physical failure progressed, there was an increasing danger that his resolve would be compromised, his willpower placed in jeopardy.

But what could he do?

Lies ... he was lying to himself and he knew it. He knew what he needed to do.

But the truth was he didn't have the courage to destroy it or toss it into the river because in the back of his mind the slippery tentacles of temptation were still there clawing at his resoluteness. He found the courage he needed to deny Andre's request. That was easy enough, but the rest of his mentality was bathed in cowardice. Lack of willpower, the easy way out, that is what had brought him to the position he was in now and there was no denying that he was still susceptible to that whispering voice that lurked beneath the noble principles he clung to with all his might. His plight was not dissimilar to that of an alcoholic who everyday faced the same demons shaped in brown bottles and quart containers. Except for one difference. If those people slipped there was no great loss other than the setback to the person's own progress down the road to sobriety. The damage would be self-inflicted and self-absorbed. Not necessarily so in the situation Demetri found himself. He could deliver to himself whatever gain he wanted. There would be a price, but who knew who would pay it.

And therein lay the most troubling aspect of the enticement. The principles of honor, courage, and nobleness were pitted against the selfish desires of greed and want and twisted by the uncertainty of moral weakness and human frailty. A man of contestable volition could very easily find himself dismissive of the honorable option. It had not taken much for Adam to succumb to Eve's imploring and Demetri knew he was in great danger of abandoning his ethics and the lessons he had learned so disastrously in the past because he was weak. So fallible that he couldn't find the courage to do what he should have done long ago, destroy the thing or if not that, taking the not so easy option of destroying himself.

"Well ...? I won't wait forever for you to make up your mind. I've waited too long as it is."

"I can't," Demetri mumbled.

As if he had read the uncertainty, fear and hesitancy in Demetri's mind, Andre leaned in once again. "You're weak Demetri. You've always been weak. I can see the confusion and timidity in your eyes. You're like some ... naïve little boy who just wants everything to be all right, everybody to live in peace. You're gullible and pathetic, a Chamberlain waving your damn piece of appeasement in the wind. You can't stand up to people like me. Give it up and go on your pitiful way. Save yourself this wretched little display of bravery."

As Andre spoke, Demetri realized he was not far from the truth. He felt sorry for himself now too, another of his weaknesses that he was so prone to dwell on. It was all closing in on him. The stress bore down on him like a lead weight. His hands now shook, his thoughts spinning dangerously, his willpower stretched to its limit. The pressure rose against the bricks in the dam testing their vulnerability. He had to corral this thing now. Somehow he muscled up the guts to raise his eyes to Andre.

"How do you know I haven't destroyed it already?"

Haskim's look sharpened. The thought shot through his mind like a runaway train. Then the panic eased. Demetri had tried this ploy before.

Demetri noticed the glint of panic and followed up. "It's gone, Andre. I told you before. I knew it would bring no good to anyone. When Sophie died, that first night, terrible ideas began coming to me. You can imagine the things that went through my mind. I was terrified, unhinged. I feared I would do something ... something macabre. I was at an impasse. Something had to give ... so I buried it. I told you I would. When she went in the ground, so did it. Now I can't be tempted. It's in a place where no one will ever be able to be tempted by it again. No matter how much they want it."

Andre pulled back and leaned into the leather booth trying to ascertain what his next step should be. Demetri had indeed told him before that he planned to bury it with his wife. He had told him that when he visited him in the hospital while his wife was near death at home being cared for by a live in nurse and Quimby and Amanda.

Demetri knew it was a lie, but he thought it possible that he could build on it seeing that he had told him once before that he intended to dispose of the globe in that manner. And he had intended to bury it with his wife. But when it came right down to it, when it actually came time for him to slip it into her casket, he couldn't bring himself to do it. To shut the door totally to the possibilities the globe provided was too much for him. He just wasn't strong enough for that.

He didn't really expect Andre to believe him. But then again ...

"It's of no use to either of us now. Gone forever. I couldn't risk the temptation any further. Even now, aging as I am, who knows what I might be coerced into doing by my own cowardice and insecurity."

Andre fumbled for something to say, something he could do to advance his position. He didn't necessarily want to admit to Demetri that he had dug the grave and knew it was all a lie. He didn't know what kind of crime he may have committed and the last thing he needed now was trouble with the law. "You haven't done that. Trust me, I know. You're not strong enough to have done that. You haven't got the balls. You're forgetting, I know you. Know you as well as anyone. Even more than Quimby, I dare say. You're too much of a coward to have done that."

Demetri tried hard to hold fast to an advantage he imagined he had. Much of what Andre said was true. He was a coward, weak. He did know him well. Dismissing it seemed the safest and best move. "You think what you want, do what you want. But it's gone. I buried it with Sophie and now no one will ever reclaim it."

Andre detected the bit of improvisation in Demetri's words. His will was stronger than Demetri's and he knew that

Demetri could not stand up to a stern inquisition. He could sense the hesitation in Demetri's voice. Andre gave Demetri an unrelenting stare as he slowly slid out from the booth and began buttoning up his coat. Then he bent in low so that the only thing in Demetri's field of vision was Andre's glaring countenance. "You're pitiful."

When a man tells a fib and is brought on the carpet for it, the claim generally carries with it little or no staying power. Not like the truth does in a direct confrontation. Demetri made a valiant attempt to rival the strength of Andre's stare even as he smelled the sourness of the man's breath in his face. But the lingering tug of insecurity forced him to make an attempt to brace his contention. It was important to him now to convince Andre of his sincerity.

"When she went, it went. She's gone and so is it. And that's that. Buried forever, just like her."

Andre held Demetri's gaze for a few moments more before the swirl of his thoughts distracted his attention and inadvertently led him to drop his gaze to the table almost as an afterthought. Andre realized the criticalness of this moment. He needed desperately to get some clue as to where Demetri might be holding the prize. The whole point of the torturous rehabilitation he had gone through was to someday garner the reward he was owed.

Sensing the upper hand, Demetri gloated. "Buried forever ..."

Andre turned away from the table and then made his move. He turned back suddenly and glared at his old partner. "You're a liar, a sniveling, bald-faced liar. You and I both know you didn't bury it with your wife. So get off of it. Give it up, Demetri. Give it up."

"It's gone ... gone." Demetri clung to his words fiercely trying to hold onto a defiant stare. Confidence suddenly came to Andre. If he played along with Demetri perhaps he could make the man at ease. Better for him if his old friend thought that he really believed Demetri. Then he would relax a little and Andre could follow another avenue for getting what was rightfully his. He already had another plan in mind.

A snicker came to Andre's malformed lips as he leaned back away from the table and clamped the final button to his jacket. His stare never left Demetri though. Acquiescence for the time being seemed his best approach. "Very well ... If you can turn your back on me, then to hell with you. I'll get by. You seem to forget one thing though my friend. No amount of ... recompense will save you from damnation. There's one big difference between you and I. I've already been to hell."

Chapter 3

The black Cadillac pulled up alongside the curb and Quimby got out and opened the door for his employer. Demetri was already waiting for the car when his driver arrived. He knew that Quimby would be on time, as he always was. Using his cane to guide his steps, he folded himself into the back seat and let out a long sigh as the driver climbed back in and slid the Cadillac into the traffic along Clark Street. If there was one constant now in Demetri's life, it was his loyal servant.

Quimby was a butler of the old school. He had formerly been employed by the widow Narmont whom Demetri had known for years from his dealings with her late husband. She had lived in a large rambling country place in Barrington Hills amid the exclusive posh homes where the prospect of visiting your next door neighbor required a car ride or a lengthy walk through forested hills.

The widow, before her demise, had taken to welcoming Demetri for tea occasionally so that she could fancy herself staying abreast of the latest business news. Demetri had always been impressed with Quimby's formal manner and efficiency. The Narmont house was kept immaculately clean. It was always well appointed with that touch of class that the upper crust appreciated: the fresh flowers in the vases, the symmetrical arrangement of the magazines on the coffee table, the polished silver. Quimby carried himself with dignity also: the creases in his black suit sharp as razors; his hair slicked straight back, frightened, it seemed, to dare have a strand out of place; his shave impeccably clean; and always that light scent of cologne trailing his footsteps. When the final days came for the widow, Demetri made a generous offer to Quimby to come into his employ. He graciously accepted. Since then Demetri's home had run like clockwork: smooth and regular, precise and tight.

"I hope your visit to the doctor was a good one, Sir."

"Yes, well ..." he mumbled. "One thing I want done Quimby. More emphasis on the security of the house and the grounds. Speak to Victor will you? I know Isabelle likes to sneak out and ride Whisper in the middle of the night sometimes." Demetri sighed. "I hate to take that away from her though," he mumbled almost to himself. "I can't say no to the girl, the way she is."

"Yes I know. Is there cause for alarm?"

"Let's just say that Andre has made an appearance," Demetri said.

"Well, we knew that would come, didn't we?"

Demetri looked down at his fingernails and started to pick at them. That feeling was coming back over him, and he cursed Andre for resurrecting it. Since he learned that he was dying, he found himself slipping into the throes of a frightful depression he had trouble negotiating. The depth of his feelings was dangerous on more than one level. A man facing his own demise would be downright irrational not to consider what lies ahead. Invariably his mind went to what the ramifications of some of the actions he had taken in his life might be.

There was guilt on his soul. That he could not deny. Many things haunted him from his past: his father and his victims, Estrella, Antoine, the tragedy that had befallen Sophie. Even the problems with Isabelle, although technically not his sin, would not have occurred had he done the right thing a long time ago.

And then, of course, there was Andre Haskim. The guilt there was more his than Demetri's, but Demetri shared in it. His lackadaisical attitude toward the business, his naïve trust in Andre's managerial abilities and his failure to adequately monitor the cash flow were inexcusable. Although he had his hands full at the time with his wife and daughter, he should have been more vigilant.

Through the years Demetri had learned to control his drinking, but liquor had been a lifelong struggle for him. Often at those times when he had fallen susceptible to that accursed globe, booze had weakened his willpower. Alcohol had a way of fueling desires that every rehabilitated alcoholic knew only too well. The stories he had heard at the AA meetings he had attended bore the same outline: things going smoothly, bills being paid, responsibilities maintained, temptations held in check.

Then came the inevitable fall.

When it did come, the fact that the person had brought alcohol to their lips, in and of itself, was not the problem. It was what the alcohol did to the mind that was the real trouble. The bars of maturity which confined the allure of temptation to a weak urge were loosened. Enticements formerly easily controlled found an added thrust of desire. Lusts that sobriety held in check crept out of their shells and bloomed in colors not so easily dismissed. Rationality had its sharp edge dulled. The prohibition arising from knowing the risk of repercussions lost its strength, flushed feelings destabilized reason and dragged it from its normal rank as the main director of actions. Marriages dissolved, finances ruined, relationships forever tainted by distrust.

And always at the finish, the long regrets came. That pitiful bemoaning of "if only" was muttered and lamented upon, sometimes for decades.

In Demetri's case, his weakness for liquor worked in combination with the character flaw of helplessness and cowardice that unfortunately were part of his make-up. Together these traits meshed and broke his will, if only occasionally. But that was enough to bring temporary satisfaction and long-lasting misery.

The despair Demetri felt, combined with the warmth of the car and the monotonous hum of the rubber against the road, lulled him into a light sleep. When he got home, he made his way upstairs, disrobed and prepared himself for a proper nap.

The fact that it was just late afternoon alarmed Demetri somewhat because he realized the bottoming out of his feelings left him barely enough energy to even get himself into bed. Sitting on the edge of the mattress, he examined himself in the dresser mirror. At seventy-one, he had still had vigor and energy until the cancer had begun to whittle him down. The combination of the disease and the culpability and self-pity he felt weighed on him like a great boulder. At five foot eight, his slumping shoulders and moderate pot belly made him appear older. His head no longer displayed the thick black hair that had once been so prominent. It had thinned considerably and what was left was now gray. His skull was oblong-shaped protruding forward with a pronounced chin. The curved nose displayed large rectangular nostrils which exposed an obvious view of the fleshy inside cartilage obscured slightly by gray hairs protruding out wildly. The trifocals he required finished the portrait of a fading, listless codger.

Shockingly, it dawned on him that his life was over. The inoperable tumor was growing and there was every reason to believe the tentacles of the disease could soon begin altering his thought processes.

Odd, he thought. *The very symptoms signaling the end was coming represented an avenue of escape via the tortured, twisting of his will.*

He let himself dwell on that option and for a moment pleasurable thoughts came to him: a bristling young man on a beach flexing his muscles, a shapely blond chasing in his splashes, a yacht gliding across a glassy sea, fine wine, money ... youth.

How dangerous those thoughts were.

Demetri pondered the irony of life. It was not all that hard to be a responsible, mature person. Most men did it without even realizing it. But no man had ever been faced with the temptations that made Demetri's position so vulnerable. He realized how strong the urge of that wish was now that the end was in sight. It had been growing ever since the first indication of his disease. Even before that, when time started to slump his shoulders, ache his joints, and diminish his strength. It had been easy to dismiss those idle whims back then because the severities of age and his inevitable doom had not yet arrived. Though he sometimes lay awake at night and wondered about it, the depth of his desire had never reached the level that made that option a real possibility.

But now?

Demetri lowered his head. There was no denying that he was weak. One way or the other he would have to maintain his courage ... one way or the other. And it would have to be soon, before his mind started to go, before he was unable to plot things out logically. In the last several months he had noticed his memory slipping. All the usual signs had begun to appear, but in marked increase: misplaced keys, forgotten appointments, and general absentmindedness. If dementia or senility began to encroach on his senses, if his ability to resist became more fragile than it already was, a breakdown in his willpower could be inevitable. If the pain became too unbearable, it would only work against him. Fear, desperation ... these were all down the line for him. It terrified him to think of it. He might not be able to withstand an onslaught of all those dreadful certainties that sometimes loomed ahead for a terminally ill man. Not when escape was just a wish away.

His thoughts confused him now, a bundle of garble and puzzlement. He had trouble focusing on the implications of his discussion with Andre.

He couldn't possibly believe Andre would just go away and forget the whole thing, could he? Would Isabelle be safe? Did the impression he gave Andre, that he had buried the infernal thing, come out the wrong way?

Something ominous about that whole discussion bothered Demetri.

What had Andre taken from that conversation? If he really believed Demetri buried the thing with Sophie, would he be crazy enough to dig up a grave? No. It was too nightmarish for even Andre to contemplate. Demetri pushed it out of his mind.

Tears came as Demetri realized what he needed to do.

Only one truly safe way out existed for everyone involved. He would leave instructions for Quimby. Quimby could be trusted, of that he was sure.

If he did away with himself, Isabelle would be safe. If he did away with himself, no one else would be hurt by his weakness or cowardice.

If only he could find the courage.

He laid back and drew the blankets over him. He slept.

Demetri awoke sometime in the night with an excruciating headache and an upset stomach. He sat up in bed and held his hand to his belly. A severe depression gripped the whole of his being and once again the possibility of salvation tempted him.

He could not go on. The end must be now. He had to do it now, he knew, *before he lost control of his will.*

Tears rolled down his cheeks. Pity, fear and terror held control of his thoughts. He mumbled a prayer to God. In the last several months when the futility of it all had became more obvious, he had become more devout. He viewed it as just another example of his cowardice. His prayer was that his self-sacrifice would serve as atonement for the wrongs he had inflicted on innocent people through the years by his actions and inactions, his vanity and carelessness.

On spindly legs, he made his way to the door of the balcony and opened it. A brush of cold wind rushed past him chilling him to the bone. He walked to the edge and stared out over the ledge. Off to the far right sat the horse barn and through the panes of a window he could see a portion of the room where Isabelle chose to sleep. His shivering lips mumbled a goodbye to her. If there was anything good in his life, truly pure, it was her.

With a degree of trouble, Demetri climbed the stone ledge. Beneath the balcony a row of burning bushes stood tall against the night. Tranquility loomed over the great house in the early morning hours. Amanda and Victor were no doubt in bed now. The light from Quimby's room was out also.

Except for the occasional swirl of wind that danced around the mansion's high columns, the night was still. The gloom seemed poised for some tumultuous event or sound to break the hush. The old man looked up at the heavens sprinkled with sharp pinpricks of starlight glistening in the purple sky. Two doves nestled in the crevice of a parapet below turned their heads up and gazed at the odd sight above them. They poked about for a moment, bobbing their heads, seemingly annoyed by the interruption in their rest. One cooed, craning its neck even more, turning its black eye above before becoming convinced the disturbance was sufficiently removed from its immediate presence as to be ignored. It snuggled its neck down into its feathers and tried to reclaim the sleep that had been disrupted. After all, it was cold.

Demetri's legs wobbled causing his frame to sway dangerously. Tears filled his eyes now blurring his sight.

It had come to this then, had it?

He had become wealthy, and yet the gold weighed heavily.

He had become a revered man, and yet the recognition paled in comparison to the torment of knowing the underlying means which had sustained his rise.

He had gilded his life, unknowing at the time that any alteration to his initial wants would not be recognized. The outcome of his wishes would proceed: unalterable and irrevocable. Even now the realization of how that was to proceed through the years terrorized him. None of his stature or wealth could alter the course of events that might follow.

His will had been broken. There was no energy left in him to try to restructure events for the good. When maturity and age finally allowed him to corral his irresponsibility, only guilt and humiliation kept him company. He had tried to put away the accursed thing, but its suggestive pull was always there gnawing on his sleeve, beckoning for him to surrender. The soft, tempting whisper invariably held the magnetic allure of unspeakable sin. It presented itself in those moments when his spirit was low or his courage at its weakest or his emotions depressed. And then took wind when he drowned his confusion in liquor.

If only he had never come upon it? If only he would have found the courage to destroy it.

The good intent of his soul was only strong enough to remove the possession to a place of safety away from his immediate surroundings, but not far enough that if the temptation became too strong he could not reclaim his prize, stare into its hypnotic core and make a wish.

Now he was only too aware that age had decayed the potency of his willpower. His disintegrating memory was blocking out the rational, valid reasons why he had to avoid the glass, but seemingly did not garble the range of possibilities open to him by the sheer wanting of it.

What would happen if he gave in and wished to be granted that which any curdling, half-senile old crow would not desire: to be young again, to live again, to love again?

That's why there was only one way out for him now.

To delay any further would raise the risk of his stamina slipping and his resolve wavering. Already the suggestion tickled his consciousness like a feather, begging him to scratch. The temptation was colossal in its magnitude, pulling him like a magnet, breaking down the fields of resistance.

The terrible truth was he didn't know how much longer he could hold out. And if he gave in, the price to be paid was too horrible to consider.

The old man's arm, leaning on his cane, trembled in the dim light. He stared down and remembered back to that night so long ago when his innocent concern had brought him to such a dazzling discovery: the moaning down the rutted path into the woods, the broken down wagon, the dying Zarpello, his hands clutching the velvet bag with shafts of glistening light streaming out through the fabric.

Zarpello's last words as he reached it out to him were: "Bury it, bury it!"

If only he had. Even the conniving, devious fat man who had made a career out of swindling innocent folks recognized a true threat, a temptation so dangerous and perilous that even the most evil of men needed to beware.

Demetri flicked his wrist disgustedly sending the wooden cane to the grass below. The pigeons below him cooed and tilted their heads in anticipation. When the old man finally stepped forward, his eyes closed, his hands trembling, and fell to the grass below, one of the pigeons turned his head to follow the path of the body as it tumbled head over heels. When it struck the bushes and slid to the ground, the pigeon locked onto the sprawled figure for a moment and then turned his head and buried his face into the feathers of its back.

It was cold after all.

Chapter 4

Isabelle awoke with a start. Above her head the crossbeams of the barn hung just barely visible in the light of the lantern she always lit before going to bed. The blankets lay heavy on her keeping out the chill of the fall night that was trying to seep in through the gnarled bedding. In the stall next to her came the sound of Whisper snorting and thumping his hoof against the side of his enclosure.

That must have been the reason I awoke, she thought. *It was time for their evening ride.*

Whisper had gotten used to their nightly trot, but Isabelle also knew about his aches and pains. A soreness in his right rump had been bothering him now that he was getting up in years and a shooting pain sometimes ran down his left fore leg when he galloped. Isabelle understood, as truly no one else ever could, how much the horse missed his old companion, the mare, Mattie. Mattie had passed away in the spring. Isabelle made a point of moving her cot into Whisper's shed the night it happened and for several nights after that she slept there to console the beast. She managed to fool Victor for awhile by pulling the cot back in before the barn keeper made his rounds in the morning. To Isabelle's surprise however, when Victor caught her one morning, he just smiled and patted her on the head, mumbling sounds that Isabelle of course could not understand. As it turned out, Victor was not mad. Maybe he comprehended Whisper's need for some comforting. Since then she had slept in the barn on many occasions. She felt more contented there than in her own room.

If there was one person Isabelle understood somewhat, it was Victor. Victor was a hired hand who worked on the grounds doing all kinds of odd jobs. Of course, tending to the animals was one of his most important tasks. Isabelle always thought of Victor as an old man, but her perception was greatly exaggerated. He was a Mexican, the son of immigrant field workers who had come to America to pick corn and beans in the summer months. He had always loved the country life especially those farms that raised horses. One year when his family was to return to Mexico after the autumn harvest, Victor stayed on getting a job at a horse track cleaning stalls and tending to the horses. His short stature and natural riding ability lent himself to training horses and eventually to jockeying as a profession. He made a living, but soon found that he liked caring for the animals more than the racing itself. Eventually he wound up working on Demetri's estate where he made a home for himself.

Demetri, in days gone by, had kept up to seven horses corralled on the property, but as the years went by the numbers dwindled through attrition until now only Prado and Whisper remained. Demetri would have never parted with either of them because of the affection Isabelle held for them. A connection with animals was something that kept Isabelle in tune to her environment and although her ability to communicate with humans had broken down, the link the animals brought to the girl seemed to keep her focused to some degree. The child had a bond with all the animals on the grounds: Blackie, the dog; the barn cats that came and went; the trio of goats; and of course, most of all with Whisper and to a lesser degree, Prado.

Demetri had always hoped that somehow that connectivity would blossom out to people as it once had. The presence of the animals brought the girl a degree of pleasure that nothing else seemed to provide. As long as it did, Demetri would keep that association available to his child.

Isabelle peeled back the covers and put on her clothes. Shivering from the feel of the chilly garments, she took a moment to examine herself in the small mirror hanging on the wall. She was short in stature with pale skin. Her hair was blond, short and curled around her face like a helmet.

In contrast to her light colored hair, her eyes were wide and intensely blue. Her nose and ears were petite and to many people her overall appearance was almost pixie or elf like.

Isabelle went to Whisper's stall and dressed him in a bridle and saddle before leading him out through the door on the far side of the barn ensuring that Victor would not spot them.

Whisper tromped along and informed Isabelle that the neighing she heard from the other end of the barn was only Prado complaining about being disturbed. Prado kept most of his feelings masked not because of a secretive nature but as a byproduct of a dense and nondescript intellect. His thoughts and feelings stayed, for the most part, dull and lifeless. The monotonous drone only rose to a higher degree when Victor prepared his meal or incessant flies got his dander up. He rarely displayed curiosity or indulged in thought conversation the way Whisper did. Isabelle often tried to prod through that humdrum mentality and learn more about the horse, but her prodding could not loosen very many secrets from the beast.

Prado's disposition was generally disagreeable. He did not get along well with any of the other animals that came and went through the barns and pens, except perhaps for Blackie. His toleration of the black lab may have had more to do with Blackie's continual snooping than anything else. Prado had simply come to realize that the dog represented no threat or concern to him. Blackie, who could only be described as hair-brained, really didn't fixate on his thoughts too much either and therefore provided little insight into why Prado accepted him. The dog basically ignored everyone except for Victor who was in charge of filling his bowls daily.

The night was clear and the deep sky glistened with sharp sparks of light. Orion had risen over the trees now, distinct and bold. Whisper clomped to a stop and waited while Isabelle opened the gate. From there the trail curled down to a ravine before finally leading up to a broken prairie where Isabelle liked to get the horse galloping.

Isabelle communicated to Whisper through their subconscious dialogue that it was a little cold tonight. A noise came from back up at the house, too faint for Isabelle to hear but not for Whisper. He turned his head and listened again.

Whisper told Isabelle that something was amiss at the house. Isabelle turned and listened but could hear nothing. She waited a moment longer and then gave up. With a smile curling on her face, she closed the gate and quickly climbed aboard her mount. Together they trotted down the trail. The only bad thing about riding after dark was that the night critters were apt to be darting about. Many times they would spook Whisper by scampering out in front of the horse disturbed from their business by the sound of his clomping gait. She had tried many times to prepare the horse for these sudden disturbances, but for some reason the animal was not able to process that information into any kind of plan against becoming flustered when it happened. It just seemed to be one of those things that made a horse a horse.

When they circled around a wide patch of tall oaks, they came to a break in the foliage. The spot provided them a view of the thin creek and brought them the trickling sound of the water streaming across the rocks. Whisper walked forward and Isabelle knew that he wanted to drink. The horse found a secure spot, bent his head and began to slurp at a small pool before him. Isabelle slid off her saddle and stood by the side of the horse. She slipped her hand along Whisper's mane and then brought her nose right up to the horse's skin to take in the scent of the huge beast. It was a miraculous thing that musty, bristling smell, one of the best things she liked about being so close to Whisper all the time. She was closer to this animal than to any other living thing in the world. There existed a bond between the two of them that surpassed in depth even her relationship with her father or Victor. Isabelle squeezed Whisper's neck a little tighter as she felt the discouraging despair and loneliness that often came upon her. At fifteen years old, she was for the time being safe and protected. Between Amanda, Quimby, Victor and her father, she received all the care and protection she needed. For now she was safe. Her fear and uncertainty was for her future, the years ahead when her aged father might pass away. What would happen to her then? She had already lost her mother and that had been a crushing blow to her.

The tears began once again. In her own mind she felt capable and intelligent, but she could not communicate any of this inner knowledge to the humans around her. She had seen a movie called *The Miracle Worker* years before when she had been a normal child. The story of Helen Keller showed how she had been as a child before her teacher had calmed her inner demons and helped her understand how to communicate. The child had been unresponsive, uncommunicative, combative, and unreachable. Isabelle was not combative or totally unreachable, but she could not understand normal English language. Also she was not able to respond to people in a way they could understand. Human contact for her basically consisted of some gesturing that she understood and common knowledge learned strictly through repetition and duplication. Those who met her and the numerous professionals who had examined her all agreed that she was not unintelligent or slow. Most of the doctors were baffled. They concluded that either she had suffered some brain damage or had contracted some mysterious late-blooming autism of some kind. Her ability to communicate with humans remained stunted. Attempts to improve her condition through tutoring did not benefit the child. Eventually Demetri accepted Isabelle's condition and did his best to ensure her safety and keep her as comfortable as possible. She lived on the property like a released spirit, free to come and go, under the protection of Demetri and his employees.

With animals it was much different.

The creatures that surrounded her on the grounds were all her friends. With most of them she could communicate silently, intuitively, almost subconsciously, thought to thought. It was odd about animals, how they communicated with each other, unlike, in many ways, the way humans interrelated to each other. Most of the time only those of the same species could directly interact with each other, kind of like the way an Englishman could only freely communicate with someone else who spoke English. But unlike humans, their ability to communicate with other species was not as easily accomplished as say an Englishman could use gestures or common words or phrases to make himself understood to a German. Animals were not as intelligent as humans and this ability to express themselves across species was lacking. There was also a reticence to even attempt such a thing. Suspicion was high and most animals preferred to keep to themselves, reliance being on caution, something Isabelle could understand. Some of the animals around her were harder to communicate with than others. Most, like Prado, kept deep within themselves either locked in by a limited intelligence or a stubborn, intractable hardheadedness.

With others, like Whisper, Flip the cat and Nattie the goat, the communication was free, uninhibited, and clear.

Whisper knew Isabelle as no other animal had ever known a human. For whatever reason, the old thoroughbred's thoughts came to Isabelle in a comprehensible, logical format that she had no difficulty interpreting. She was sure too that her responses to Whisper also made their way back to the horse. There was clarity there and she wondered why. Perhaps she would never know, but she worried what might happen if Whisper was taken from her. Since Whisper was only ten, he hopefully had some years ahead of him. As far as Isabelle knew, aside from the few aches and pains Whisper related to her, the animal was in good health. But you never knew. He could easily become sick for any number of reasons. Since he really performed no great function on the property, his value was limited and she feared that even the most trivial of illnesses could be used as a final nod to consider eliminating the animal. Isabelle did not want to think about the possibility of losing Whisper. He was her only real contact ever since that dreadful night when she lost all the communicative powers she had taken for granted.

She thought back to that day and those before. Animals had always been her one true fancy, above the piano her father made her practice, her school work, or her friends. Isabelle had always felt a kinship to those critters that pranced around the property, some who were a vital part of the landscape like the horses, and some who just became citizens of the manor by simply hanging around long enough to qualify for squatter's rights.

Several stray cats and two dogs, one of them Blackie, had come to the manor unexpectedly, roamers of the countryside who simply made themselves at home on the grounds. One of those cats was a tabby named Flip. From Flip she learned quite a bit about how a cat thought and what motivations really drove their behavior. She understood now that cats were actually quite intelligent, but their aptitude was generally confined to cautiousness. They had a guarded view of the world, smart enough to know danger and remarkably well-equipped to avoid it. Flip had the habit of suddenly, from a stationary position, jetting off at fast speed. The best Isabelle could tell was that at times his pent-up energy suddenly overflowed and the urge to take off was simply irresistible. Cats felt most comfortable at night because they were natural hunters. That's why Flip was always prowling around after sunset. Isabelle tried to communicate to Flip that it was unnecessary for him to hunt because his food was always provided him by Victor.

Although Flip understood that, he could not be dissuaded. To him, skulking around at night, searching out cracks and crevices, staying attuned to any swift movement by a nocturnal rodent was reward in and of itself. The fact that the hunt was unnecessary did not alter his delight in the chase.

Whisper had been Isabelle's horse from an early age. Her father had bought the horse after its racing days were shortened at age three by a leg injury. Together on their romps over the property and the neighboring woods, even before her change, she had felt their interaction as if she could almost talk to the animal. Of course, that last obstacle that always came between man and animal prevented her from truly understanding how the horse thought or how it sensed things. She yearned to know how information was processed through its head, those guarded patches of knowledge garnished who-knows-how by senses humans knew nothing about. To her it was a great mystery.

When Whisper got to galloping, his mind would go to his greatest victory as a racehorse: a stakes race at Arlington Park in Chicago. Whisper, whose actual racing name had been Whisperwind, had ridden against Caesar's Tomb once before and had lost by two lengths, but at the head of the stretch a horse by the name of Troubled Kid had boxed him against the rail for several seconds causing Whisper to pull up just enough to lose any chance at the end. Caesar's Tomb had been haughty about his victory though and made a point of reminding Whisper of his superiority.

On a Thursday afternoon four months later though, Whisper found himself on the outside of Caesar's Tomb on a muddy track with Javier Couras on his back. Once they came around the final bend, Javier took him a little wide to keep him safe from the splatter of the mud and then began bearing down on the leaders. Both Caesar's Tomb and Whisper went to the front with an eighth of a furlong to go. At that point Javier let him go and Whisper knew he had his competitor. They were pounding down the track together until the final few lengths when Whisper put his neck ahead and blistered past.

At those moments when Whisper relived that race, Isabelle could almost feel as if she was on Whisper's back pounding down that stretch: thought to thought, feeling to feeling, sensation to sensation. The communication was miraculous.

While she was still in school, others of her friends dreamed of boys, movie stars, and the latest fashions. Isabelle imagined herself in front of a great throng of scientists, doctors and professors describing to them the mental processes of dogs, cats, and horses. She dreamed of demonstrating to them how she could communicate in a personal, intimate way with animals, something only she could do because she had discovered the mystery, a gift she unfortunately could not dispense to others. A talent she alone possessed. It was a nonsensical idea, a silly fantasy, but still it did not dispel the admiration she felt whenever she watched TV and saw a herd of giraffe springing across the savannah or a whale lurching in a choppy sea. Even on the grounds when Blackie's inquisitiveness presented itself or she fed sugar cubes to Whisper, she wondered at the quiet brilliance going on in those unapproachable minds.

And then ... well ... had it been worth it? She still wondered that often, all she had lost. In the house and on the grounds now she was like Helen Keller had been in the movie, unable to converse with others, lost in confusion and inability when it came to communicating in any meaningful way. Isabelle could come and go as she wanted, but the language she had spoken before the change was gone to her. She found it difficult to even understand the simplest of hand gestures or motions. The eating regiment of the house and the regular workings of the grounds were known to her and allowed her the ability to find her way around and remain safe, but she was like a severely autistic child when it came to communicating with fellow humans.

In an effort to regenerate her daughter's former skills, Demetri had hired several different tutors and even sent Isabelle away to a school where autistic children and kids with other similar communication disorders were housed. But Isabelle could not endure it. For reasons she could not even put her fingers on, she had no tolerance for being touched or manipulated. She never thought herself a disobedient child, but for some reason any effort to corral her, educate her, or cultivate the communication skills she formerly had provoked in her a wrath and a combativeness that defied control. Cooperation escaped her. It was almost like a form of mental illness that frightened her and kept her pinned in an isolation in which loneliness and solitude were ever present. They had tried various different drug regiments on her also and although those dampened her normally inflexible ire, it also dulled her senses to such a degree that concentration was nearly impossible. At night in her bed at the home, she would curl up with the home's cocker spaniel who always sought her out to the dismay of all the other children who loved the dog, and tried to understand what it all meant. How she had come to such an odd and frightening end.

And it all went back to that night several winters before when she had awoken and saw the odd fluctuations of light shimmering off the hallway wall. A muffled snoring came from her father's room. Quietly she had made her way down the corridor and peeked into his bedroom. He was lying across his bed on top of the covers sprawled out asleep. At the edge of the bed just out of reach of his right hand a glass globe sparkled and shone with lights of various colors. The aura it threw off was hypnotizing. It drew Isabelle like a magnet. Each step she took that brought her closer to the globe also seemed to sharpen her senses. With both hands she picked up the ball and took it back with her to her room where she sat and gazed into it.

Inside of her the things she most desired in life seemed to well up so strongly that she could hardly think past the almost insatiable longing she felt. Some of her thoughts were modest and shallow like the desire to be more popular in her class and the urge for a new saddle. Others ran deeper like the wish she had for her mother to be well again. But the most exciting and sensitive need she wanted satisfied was that odd desire she had always had to be able to communicate with animals.

The globe seemed to hypnotize her as she stared into it. She could get lost in the vibrating streaks of light and visual images that ran through her head. Her imagination ran uncontrollably into realms of thought that before had only been passing fancies. A deep relaxation fell over her and the visions that flowed through her head held a presence similar to dream sequences. Isabelle felt as if she was asleep and dreaming while she was still awake. She saw herself talking to animals of all different types, walking through the woods, conversing with birds, squirrels and deer. A view of the woods flashing before her as she trampled down a trail on the back of Whisper came to her while the horse communicated to her in some unconscious way as if its thoughts just magically appeared in Isabelle's mind.

Isabelle's yearning became almost an insatiable desire and with her whole heart and soul she wished for it to be. And it had. But for some reason, her ability to communicate with animals came at a terrible cost. For some reason she could no longer convey herself to humans as she had before. She lost the ability to put together words. She could not make herself understood to others. Language became a confused garble of sounds and inflections with no pattern discernible to her anymore. It was staggering. Her ability to communicate with humans had transferred to animals only.

She had gotten what she yearned for at a horrifying price.

Isabelle climbed back atop Whisper and turned the animal back toward the mansion. As she plodded down the trail through the woods, she heard a siren screeching out into the night. It sounded like it was coming closer and closer. Whisper bobbed his head reaffirming to Isabelle what he had indicated to her before. Something was not right. As a view of the mansion finally showed itself through the edge of the woods, she saw flashing lights streaming against the west side of the house. An ambulance had driven up the drive and circled around through the grass right up to the side of the house.

Isabelle soothed Whisper. The siren and the lights had the animal stirred up. Isabelle turned her eyes back to the mansion. There was a bustle of activity going on. The siren had silenced but the lights from the top of the vehicle were spinning red, blue and white light in a circle around the walls of the house. The activity alarmed Isabelle. She was confused and frightened. It was all like a bad dream.

Had something happened to her father? A wave of terror ran through her mind. *What was going on?*

Tears began to well in her eyes. Whisper had regained some of his composure and slowly Isabelle led the beast down the bottom of the trail toward the barn. Whisper hobbled along making odd grunts and groans.

As they approached the house, Isabelle saw two men loading a gurney into the back of an ambulance. One of the men jumped into the back while the other climbed into the driver's seat. The siren's scream began again and caused Whisper to startle and stop in his tracks, bucking his huge head in fear. Isabelle prodded him forward but not before the vehicle took off and raced down the winding drive back toward the main road.

Quimby stood next to a row of bushes beneath the balcony to her father's bedroom staring up toward the roof. He appeared agitated and confused. When he saw Isabelle approaching, he moved forward and quickly grabbed Whisper's lead.

Quimby yelled toward the barn, but of course Isabelle could not understand the words he spoke. Victor came running out and took the reins, slowly guiding the horse back to the barn. Isabelle wanted to follow, but Quimby grabbed her by the arm and led her into the kitchen of the big house. Amanda made Isabelle sit at the table and petted her hair.

Isabelle could sense that Amanda was terribly frightened. Quimby went to the phone and made several quick calls. Amanda began to cry. When Quimby finished the calls, he quickly dressed. Amanda led Isabelle upstairs to her room and laid her down in the bed.

The sound of the garage door opening and the squeal of tires racing down the drive came next. It appeared Quimby had some urgent business to attend to. Once Isabelle felt the coast was clear, she got back up and went back out to the barn. She would be much more comfortable in her little bed with the smell of Whisper close by.

As he sped to the hospital, Quimby tried to understand what had happened. He ripped open the letter he had found on the dresser addressed to him in Demetri's hand. He turned on the dome light above his head and shifting his gaze from the road to the letter and back again, read the message: Bury it when I'm gone.

Chapter 5

November 19, 1928
The Yugoslav/Romanian Border

Although dawn was nearly an hour away, Demetri Davos could not sleep. He had been rousted from his bed, as if heralded by some tempting siren.

Lying in his bed, the boy could see specks of colored light falling to the base of the wall to his side. His fascination caused him to reach under the bed and bring up the black bag. Pinpricks of light leaked through the fabric faintly illuminating his hands. Quietly he rose and moved silently through the house to the fire. His father had come home late, drunk as usual, and with that glare of anger dancing in his eyes, flopped onto the rack in his room. At times like these, Demetri knew it was wise not to disturb the thin, reedy man. To wake him now would be to invite harm to himself in the way of a fierce beating. Demetri still nursed several welts along his back from his father's strap for some imagined transgression that the boy could no longer even remember.

Demetri pulled the three legged stool closer to the light and slid the globe out from its bag. The ball glowed softly as if filled with luminescent smoke. Almost immediately, streams of emotion flowed through the boy's mind like the tentacles of lightening bolts: sharp, flashing, sporadic. Images in the glass swirled in unfixed designs and colors weaved in hypnotic swirls that fluctuated in intensity and brightness. The globe did not always shine as elaborately as it did now. With every glistening shape and curling outline, Demetri's brain sparked and fumed. The effect was exhilarating. Looking into the glass seemed to draw desires and impulses out of his subconscious. Things he had wished for or hoped for, perhaps only in passing, now jumped out of their languid existence and became suddenly equipped with a restlessness and impatience he could hardly contain. Idle wants became irrepressible needs. Non-essential frivolities suddenly seemed to take on a singular importance.

Demetri never considered himself to be selfish or vain, but a strain of self-centeredness seemed to take center stage in his thoughts now. The urge to fulfill his desires and wants intensified whenever he gazed into the glass. Alongside it was the realization that his suddenly rash impulses embarrassed him somewhat. Notions of good, productive changes in his life that would be best for both himself and his father made their presence known also. If only his father would stop drinking. If only the bitterness he seemed to be constantly burdened with could be redirected into self-restraint and positive results. If only somehow his mother could return, all forgiven and forgotten, and they could together begin a new, more wholesome life together.

These idle, winsome desires, both selfish and beneficial, never presented themselves so strongly or urgently as they did whenever his eyes locked on the glowing glass. Not only did the notions present themselves to Demetri, but his thoughts seemed to crystallize and focus down, weeding through the assortment of options and opening some sort of door for him to send one single desire of his choosing through. That irrepressible selfishness made it hard for him to give more than a passing acknowledgment to any positive possibilities. He had suffered too long under his father's authoritarian rule to not want for instant gratification. His thoughts sharpened down into one piercing stream of malcontent and with a last stab of menace, he gave into the spiteful, unpleasant wave of dissatisfaction that he had lived with for so long.

He made a wish.

In an instant the glass flushed with color. Reds, greens, and blues flashed through the ball in waves of explosive shudders that pirouetted, spun and curled in on themselves. A surge of heat suddenly came from the globe as if it were on fire. Demetri dropped the glass onto the rug and watched it roll off to the corner of the room as if it was self-propelled. The orb became jammed between a chair and the wall and vibrated as if angry that it could not release itself from the corner. Demetri rose and backed up fearful the ball would explode. The quivering reached a crescendo and the lines of color became so bright that it made the boy turn away. And then suddenly the glass went dark except for a yellow spark deep within its core. The ball somehow found escape from the position it was in, rolled out into the center of the room and, as if guided by a magnetic force, lodged up against Demetri's right foot and came to rest.

A flush of concentrated dizziness rushed through Demetri's mind and then just as quickly passed. Peace returned to the room. Through the window to his right, he saw the wind rustle the branches of the pine trees that shrouded the hills in the upper elevations. Demetri went to the window and stared at the spindly canes and rickety wooden fencing that held the grape vines in place along the hillside. The night bathed the area in a wave of solemnity; a marked contrast to the upheaval and turmoil Demetri had just experienced.

Demetri's focus shifted slightly.

What had just happened? He felt as if he had awoken from a turbulent nightmare. All the rush, surge and upheaval drowned in silence, calm and tranquility. Demetri reached down and put his hand to the ball. The warmth had dissipated. Feeling somewhat uncertain, the boy returned the globe to the black bag from which it came and tucked it in its hiding place.

Demetri felt drained and sat down on his bed. A feeling of revulsion crawled through him as he strained to understand what had come over him. His emotions had subsided in their intensity now, but there was no denying the strength and forcefulness they had held when he gazed into the crystal. The embarrassment that normally would have prevented him from ever venting the desires that had risen in him returned now softening the edges of his anger and disillusionment. A wave of depression filled the void previously occupied by his wrath and urges.

Demetri sighed. Today was Saturday and Father Sesco would be visiting their village as he normally did.

Perhaps, Demetri thought, *he could purge the shame he felt by letting the priest hear his confession.*

At fifteen, Demetri had begun to feel the changes that maturation brings to a young man. Was this just part and parcel of what he was to expect in the future? He had heard from teachers and others he respected that he would begin experiencing both emotional and physical changes in his mind and body as he developed from a gangly youth to a man. He had dismissed most of their talk, but now found himself genuinely frightened. Never before had he felt so pushed and prodded by his emotions.

Was the maturation process promised him going to require him to ride out more waves of turmoil like he had just experienced?

Demetri closed his eyes and tried to relax.

Perhaps there was nothing for him to be concerned about.

The tender somberness delivered on the wings of the soft night breeze reassured him that he was safe now.

Zarpello, he knew, *was a conjurer and a trickster. The man made his living by illusion and craftiness. The ball was simply some illuminated trick from the magician's store house of deceptive devices, gimmicks and gizmos.*

Demetri recalled the time he had seen a gypsy wizard produce flaming balls from beneath her gown in the town square and the oohs and aahhs it had brought forth from the assembled crowd of gawkers.

The odd deviations in his thoughts and the intensity of his desires were only the direct result of a ... magic trick ... on the mind of an unworldly, gullible adolescent. Who knew what other oddities Zarpello had tucked away in his wagon.

Demetri rolled over, exhausted and confused, until finally sleep reclaimed him.

Demetri awoke to an odd noise. He rolled over and stared across the room toward the fire where his father sat mumbling to himself. The man must have stoked the pile considerably because the glow from the pit lit up the room. This surprised Demetri because several times he had received a beating from his father for just the same reason, wasting wood in the middle of the night when an extra blanket would serve the same purpose.

Sislau Davos busied himself by polishing one of the rifles he had secured during the war. The unmistakable scent of gun oil hung in the air. The look on his father's face alarmed Demetri. He stared into the fire wide-eyed, intensely focused. His hands worked methodically rubbing the metal barrel of the weapon as it lay across his lap while his lips moved mouthing words and phrases so low Demetri could not make them out.

There was only one thing worse than Sislau Davos when he was drunk and that was when Sislau woke up with a hangover and discovered he had nothing left to drink. Sislau had been drunk now for going on three days straight. He had slept little except for the times in which he passed out in front of the fire succumbing to the calming effects of the roast scraps of pork his son was able to provide him. Demetri assumed his father had emptied all the wine bottles he had in the house and that his words were in response to the anger he felt at having nothing to drink.

But this seemed different. There was an odd glow in his father's face as if he were attentive to some distraction not obvious to the boy.

Recently Demetri had come to a final realization. He no longer wanted to endure further beatings from his father. Demetri had grown bigger and broader in the last few months, shooting up like a weed in spring. It had become obvious to him that he was not as afraid of his father nor as frightened at the prospect of not pleasing him in every way as he had been before. The fear of his beatings with the leather strap or the wooden rod which his father customarily used on him for imagined transgressions no longer filled him with dread and terror and would no longer incapacitate him into inaction if the blows began reigning down on him. This surprised Demetri because usually his cowardice and timidity dissuaded him from such thoughts.

Demetri's mother, Delia, had taken it as long as she could before she could bear it no more. The night before she left, Sislau had beaten her unmercifully for some frivolous reason his warped, drunken mind had imagined. That was six years earlier when Demetri was only nine. It was rumored she had taken up with a group of magicians, jugglers, acrobats and clowns, a traveling troupe of entertainers reported to be off to Nice for a carnival. Demetri had never seen her since nor heard from her either. It was days like this, when the sun was cold, the food scarce, the dread of another impending winter and his father's anger so imminent that would make Demetri stare off into space and wonder about his mother.

Had she really loved him? He remembered when she had woken him in the middle of that night, wondering why there were tears in her eyes and why she was lavishing kisses on him. He had been too sleepy for his concern to rouse him from his stupor into any form of realization and he just rolled over and went back to sleep not knowing that might possibly be the last time he would ever see his mother.

Not a letter, not a word, not a note since then.

Why hadn't she taken him with her? Perhaps the desperate need to get out was too strong and the only avenue available to her was closed to her young child. Perhaps she was too ashamed now to ever attempt contact.

The conscious portion of his mind, the part that could think things through logically, worked hard to try to dispel the anger he felt toward his mother. His age and maturity had certainly allowed him to see the desperation that must have driven her to abandon him. Though love and longing were the strongest emotions he felt for his mother, Demetri could not help but feel disappointment with her. Once she left, Sislau's unwillingness to provide for his son combined with his inability to care for him due to his constant state of intoxication forced the boy to leave school and devote his energies to earning whatever pittance he could to put food in the pot and to provide his father with liquor money to sustain his insatiable need for alcohol.

It had not been fair, none of it.

Since that day it had all been a terrible nightmare for Demetri. The boy suffered the beatings normally reserved for Delia, and the burden of housework became his to master. And through the long years that followed he struggled on trying to make sense of a world turned bitter and cold while Sislau's anger festered daily fueled by the cheap alcohol he consumed.

And the hatred Demetri felt for his father grew.

These last few months the urge to pick up and leave had blossomed in Demetri as never before. Somehow that passage of time had opened his eyes to the realization that his father's life and his were separate entities, two lives which could be parted. His mind dawdled more and more on imagining what life might be like if his father were somehow ... gone. Demetri had made several friends in the village, namely Cyrus, the baker, whom he helped with the sweet cakes, bread and biscuits for the Sunday morning crowd. Without the overpowering presence of his father, he could possibly earn a living sufficient to entice a lovely, like Estrella, the winsome girl from the village who had struck his fancy.

Perhaps life would not have to be such a burdensome weight.

But never before could these idle imaginings be given the ability to fly as they had now that he had come into possession of the globe he had found in the outstretched hand of Virgillio Zarpello. Some of these same sentiments had been with him during the night when he had been so focused on the crystal. And then at a weak moment, he found himself uttering that vengeful wish that now brought such fear to him and yet an odd type of satisfaction.

"All liars, boy ... all liars and thieves ..." Sislau muttered the words without turning his head to his son. His eyes remained focused on the flames. His father's voice cracked when he spoke. "Liars and cheats ..." He drew his gaze away from the fire and concentrated more intensely on the barrel of the rifle, wiping it down meticulously, almost caressing it. A log from the fire sparked and crackled. Sislau paused and shifted his attention toward Demetri. Slowly he put down the white rag and grabbed the wine bottle at his feet draining the remainder of the red liquid. Somehow the man had found a last bottle.

"Damn bastards, the whole lot!" Sislau stood quickly and smashed the bottle down into the flames. The fire erupted and bits of burning embers sprayed out onto the rug at his feet.

Sislau just stood there immobile and unconcerned with the sparks that were even now beginning to ignite the filthy carpet.

"Father ... the fire!" Demetri sprung into action racing to the flames and quickly thumping down on the burning embers trying to put them out.

As if awakening out of a trance, Sislau backed up and stared at his son. Demetri was so busy with the scattered coals that he did not notice his father repositioning the rifle in his hands and aiming the weapon squarely at him.

"You're a no good ... worthless son. You're no good to me just like your mother." Demetri looked up and saw the rifle leveled directly at his face. "I should send you to hell boy ... do you understand? 'Cause you ... everyone ..." His father turned as if guided by some unseen voice. More mumbling, more incomprehensible muttering spewed forth from him.

Then his father stumbled out of the cabin. Through the window, Demetri spotted him mounting their mule, Mooka, and kicking it viciously until it brayed, bucked and finally chugged out past the gate toward the road. Across Sislau's arms lay his rifle.

Demetri had seen his father viciously drunk, terribly hung over, and even at times when he managed to sober up for a few days, almost mournful and apologetic. But never before had he seen him so ... phantom-like, so menacingly driven.

Then he remembered the globe and what had occurred in the middle of the night, the intense desire that had led him to put into words that terrible wish.

No ... he would not think of that now. No child, however bitter or unhappy, could mouth such a thing and really mean it. He had not really meant that he wanted to be rid of his father.

Demetri raised the ax above his head and brought it down on the end of a thick branch from a tree he had felled the day before. The wood would provide many hours of warmth to the cabin in the coming winter, but not before the mighty limbs were splintered and broken down into useful size chunks to fit in the grate. Even though autumn had hardened and a stiff breeze bit down on the clearing where he labored, sweat had coated his inner garments to such an extent that Demetri was forced to lay down his tool and remove his outer jacket. Above him the wind swirled the tops of the beech and pine trees so prevalent in the hilly area where they lived. Short, wispy white clouds curled in the sunlit sky above his head, whipped and shredded no doubt by the high winds.

The boy paused when he heard the tromping of hooves coming around the curve in the path. Two mules lugged methodically forward pulling behind them a flatbed wagon of gnarled wood. Tied to the back of the wagon chugging along on a long lead was Mooka. Seated at the top of the wagon guiding the lead mules was the local village magistrate, Adam Viteazu. Viteazu was part of the civic guard whose job it was to ensure the security of persons and property and maintain order in the nearby village. His uniform consisted of a brown, single-breasted tunic-like jacket with collar, with two upper pockets and two sideways, each with a flap, trousers, and a headdress which showed the country emblem framed by a wreath of oak leaves.

Demetri could not remember ever seeing the officer so formerly dressed, as if he was on some mission. The officer noticed the boy far ahead and dropped his head in response. Only when the wagon turned slightly in the road to avoid a massive oak stump did Demetri notice that something was lying in the wagon's bed covered by a heavy woolen blanket colored with brown and red plaid patches. Viteazu pulled the wagon off to the right as he approached the boy and pulled back on the reins. The tightening of the leather straps creaked and in response to the bite of the line in their mouth, one of the mules bobbed its head cantankerously.

"Woooo, Jandy now," Viteazu said. The mules stammered to a stop and the magistrate loosened his grip on the reins. His gaze came up and met the boy's and he nodded his head. As if waiting for a signal, he paused before climbing down from the wagon and walking around the mules to where Demetri stood.

"Hello, boy," Viteazu mumbled. His mouth twitched and the end of his huge bristled mustache above his lip fluttered slightly in the breeze. He removed his hat and passed his wrinkled hand through the thin, stringy hair left on his head straightening the locks that had been pressed out of shape.

With a bowed head he said apologetically: "I've some bad news for ya' now, Demetri."

Demetri noticed then his father's rifle propped up against the seat where Viteazu had been seated. He felt the chill in the air press down upon him. It flashed in the boy's head what the blanket-covered thing in the bed of the wagon must be.

"Your father ... he came into town and ... well there's no way to tell ya' than to tell ya'. For no reason it seems, he shot Marcel yelling something about how the man had cheated him out of money. When his wife fell upon him, he shot her as well.

Cyrus, the baker, had been out repairing the window to his shop and went over to see what the row was about and ... well he was shot too. Cyrus's wound appears mild, but I'm afraid the others ... They're dead."

Demetri turned and looked toward the back of the wagon. A wave of nausea swept through him and the taste of the stale biscuits he had for breakfast rose in his throat.

Demetri began moving toward the rear of the wagon when Viteazu cut in front of him. "I had to shoot him, son. I didn't want to do it. He was ... crazy, mumbling. I've seen your father drunk, wayward, but this was something ... else. As if he was just ... I don't know." Viteazu's hands shook fluttering the feathers in his cap. A tear had come down his cheek and Demetri felt a wave of sympathy for the man.

Viteazu stared off into the distance with a stunned expression on his face. "I've never had to kill a man," he mumbled.

Without hesitation, the boy went to the back of the wagon and flipped the blanket aside. His father's head lay crooked at an odd angle and a splash of blood smeared a spot up under his chin. A wound in his chest had bloodied his shirt and a mass of blood trailed down onto his trousers. Viteazu gave Demetri a moment and then came back to join him.

"When I heard the shots I grabbed my shotgun and went out to the street. Your father was walking past the general store ... just mumbling. I don't know what he was saying, but when I came toward him, he leveled his rifle at me. He fired once missing and then trained his gun on an old woman holding her dog cowering behind one of the posts in front of the livery stable. I ... I had to shoot him. I ... tried to make him ... I'm sorry Demetri but ... there was nothing I could do."

Guilt flushed through Demetri's mind obscuring for a moment the shock he felt. The wish he had made the night before haunted him.

How could such a thing ...? His wish had come true.

He had vented his misery and frustration by giving voice to a terrible want and now he felt a horror more chilling than any emotion that had caused him to air his desire. Part of his feeling of culpability was diminished by the realization that somehow he had not been totally responsible for what had occurred. Some power beyond him, some potency in the globe had accentuated his desires to an almost unquenchable degree.

He had wished himself rid of his father. Now he was, but not without the imposition of a terrible price.

"I have to ask you son. Did you and your father quarrel this morning? Or do you have any idea what came over him?"

Demetri pulled the blanket back over his father's face and stared down at the ground. "He's been drunk for the last few days. This morning ... he acted strange, mumbling. He even pointed the gun at me at one point. But then ... then he just ... left."

Viteazu rubbed his index finger against his bristling mustache and sniffled. He had still not come to grips with what happened. Demetri had known the magistrate his whole life and knew him to be an honest, good-natured man. If he shot his father, he knew he must have had good cause to do so. Demetri regretted the possibility that he was responsible in some way for bringing sorrow and lament to the man.

Viteazu ran his sleeve up along his brow and squinted up at the sky. "First this ... thing with Zarpello. Two dead there and now ..." Viteazu stared up at the sky. "Must be a bad wind passing through. Sometimes ... there's no explaining things. Lord help us." He sighed.

Viteazu stayed with Demetri for a few hours, helping him carry his father to an area at the back of the property and providing most of the muscle necessary to dig a decent grave. Demetri chose a spot at the top of a hill that looked down on a ravine where a trickling stream wound through the dense vegetation. The spot below served as a watering hole for some of the shy woodland creatures like deer and rabbits who found security in the camouflage.

Later Demetri followed Viteazu back to town where the local villagers stared at him with awkward glances that revealed the various shades of emotion the terrible events of the morning had produced: pity, disgust, horror and shame. The widow, Constanti, embraced the boy without apology. Her husband had died of the drink a few years before and Demetri could not help but wonder if perhaps only that woman could truly understand the ordeals that had weighed on him because of his father's failings.

Eventually some of the other residents resolved any ill feelings they had and by the time he made his way back home, the wagon was weighed down with food and supplies necessary to keep the boy's belly filled for days. The emptiness and weariness that shrouded him in depression went with him providing him only enough energy to fix a fire and stare into the flames. During the busy day, he had not had much time to revisit the issue that had so frightened him when he saw the grimaced face of his father in the bed of the wagon. Although now with the weight of his unhappiness leveraging itself against a feeling of relief that he found himself too shamed to freely admit, Demetri thought once more about the globe and the odd occurrence of the night before. As time passed, his mind seemed less and less seduced by the possibility that he bore any guilt at all in what had happened. Although still uncertain, he could not accept the fact that the crystal had any mysterious power to affect the future or that his wish in any way could have produced the madness of his father's actions.

Demetri went to his room and retrieved the globe. In front of the fire he stared into it, but now it shed no light except for the yellow spark in the center. In the orb, he saw the reflection of his face. He placed it back into its bag and returned it to the spot beneath his bed.

Exhausted, he fell back and tried to rest. His thoughts raced as he tried to imagine what he would do now to maintain his existence. Some of the villagers had offered their homes to him if he wanted to live with them instead of staying alone at his cabin where now his only company would be birds, mice and the occasional timid deer.

He closed his eyes and let his mind wander through the realm of obstacles ahead of him.

When he slept, he dreamt of two things: the darkened orb beneath his bed and Estrella.

Chapter 6

October 6, 1984

Amanda came out to the barn and retrieved Isabelle early in the morning. From the way she fretted and mumbled to herself, Isabelle could tell she was terribly upset about something. At the driveway at the front of the house, a police car sat and when Isabelle was led into the kitchen through the back door, she heard people talking in the dining room around the table.

Amanda sat Isabelle down in a chair and fixed her some breakfast. While Isabelle ate, Amanda went to the dining room door and listened in on the conversation. Isabelle could not understand what was happening, but she knew enough not to give Amanda any trouble because the heavy set woman was quite upset. She kept dabbing her nose and eyes with a tissue and mumbling to herself. She was acting very strangely with Isabelle too, trying not to show her how upset she was.

Amanda had always cared for Isabelle, even when her mother, Sophie, was still alive. When she was younger, before she lost the ability to communicate, Amanda coddled and primped Isabelle and treated her as if she was her own daughter. She cooked for her, helped her bathe, and read her stories at night. Once Isabelle changed, Amanda pampered her even more as if her caring could instill in Isabelle the powers she had lost. Frustration got in the way for both of them through time and though Amanda still spoke to Isabelle as if she could understand, she never expected a response.

After Isabelle finished eating, Amanda ushered her out of the kitchen and let her go her own way. Isabelle went back to the barn and watched as people came and went from the house. She passed the time brushing Whisper who had grown a little nervous with all the added commotion. Whisper asked Isabelle in his way about what was happening, but Isabelle had no answer for him.

The morning was overcast and cool, but Isabelle felt the need to take a little jaunt around the grounds. Whisper was still upset and Isabelle felt the thing she needed to do was to take the animal for a little ride.

Perhaps it would wear the horse out a bit and calm him down.

Isabelle saddled up Whisper and mounted him. They walked down the trails that led back into the woods and clopped along unhurriedly. A fox crossed the path in front of them and Isabelle read the concern the animal had. Its den was just off the trail to the right and her cubs were hungry. The fox had not had any luck searching for game during the night and worried about whether she could risk hunting a little longer this morning. The fox stopped off to the side of the trail and stared at Isabelle as she went by. The fox had no fear or urge to run as it sensed a kinship with the girl. Isabelle hoped she would soon find a mouse or rabbit to help feed her cubs. Later she might bring some food out to the area. Isabelle learned through her thoughts with the fox exactly where its lair was located.

The girl dismounted when they came to the large pond beyond a grove of trees about a half mile behind the house. She wondered again about all the commotion at the house. Obviously something was wrong. Usually her father rose early in the morning and had his coffee in the kitchen while he read the newspaper. Today however, she had not seen any sign of him. She knew sometimes if his hip was hurting him badly, he might stay in bed a little longer and take his breakfast in his room, but Isabelle noticed that the tray Amanda always used to carry his meal was still on the middle island in the kitchen and had not been used at all that morning.

Well, perhaps he was still sleeping, she thought. *Still, it was odd ...*

Heavier clouds had begun moving in and Whisper began to get panicky. The horse had never done well in storms.

Thunder and lightening scared him terribly. Isabelle had tried many times to ease Whisper's fears whenever weather closed in on the property, but many times the horse could barely be consoled.

In the distance a wave of thunder rumbled. Whisper stamped his foot and then backed up a couple of feet in a sudden lurch. Isabelle rubbed the animal along its neck to help soothe him. She mounted and turned the horse around to follow the trail that led back to the barn. A sharp bolt of lightening streaked the sky off to the west where the darker clouds seemed to boil. Whisper reared up and shook his head trying to get Isabelle to let go of the reins, but Isabelle held tight. She let the animal trot lazily but communicated to him that there was no need to run. This part of the trail was narrow and overhung with low-lying branches that she would have to negotiate around.

A soft rain began to fall and Isabelle pulled the hood of her coat over her head. Whisper clopped along, but Isabelle sensed the tension in his thoughts and in his taut muscles. The horse turned his head several times as if trying to peer through the dense brush to see what the sky was doing. Suddenly a burst of lightening cracked almost directly above their heads. Whisper reared up as the thunder came crashing down upon them. The horse spun quickly to its right as he came down. The left side of his body buckled and Whisper ducked his head as he lurched forward, lost his footing and slid down toward the ground. Isabelle could not control herself on the saddle and fell forward across the horse's right shoulder. She landed roughly on her side onto a pile of branches from a long fallen oak tree. The bed of limbs broke her fall to a degree so that she did not hit the ground beneath very hard.

She lay for a moment on the ground getting her bearings until she heard Whisper's rasping neighs. The horse had fallen on its left side onto the side of the trail and was now trying to get back up but could not seem to get his legs underneath him to support his weight. The animal screeched and neighed in a panic.

Isabelle ran to Whisper and tried to calm him. Her presence quieted the horse for the moment, but he kept struggling to get up. Isabelle told him to stay down and finally succeeded in coddling Whisper's head so that she could examine his legs and try and determine if he was injured. She immediately sensed the problem from Whisper's thoughts. Whisper had sustained an injury to his right hind foot. The bone was not exposed, but the leg was contorted in a way that did not look normal. Swelling was already beginning at the joint.

Isabelle began patting Whisper's head to reassure him while she desperately tried to figure out what to do. The horse sensed the chill running through the young girl. The fear that ran in Isabelle ran in Whisper too now. Together they tried to comfort each other as the rain intensified and seemed to swallow them in a swirl of wind and water.

To her left the fox stuck her nose out into the clearing. She stepped forward and stared at Isabelle as if trying to understand the situation. Isabelle spoke to her and told her to go on her way. The fox tilted her head for a moment and then jumped back into the brush and disappeared.

Chapter 7

October 7, 1984

Andre Haskim entered the Rossetti Italian Supper Club with his fedora bent low over his face. In front of him in the dim light stretched a long, wooden bar lined with red leather-topped stools. High in the corner the light from a TV set shone down on a gray-haired woman who busily ragged down a portion of the counter. Beyond the bar was the dining area broken up into several different rooms where an assortment of tables sat draped in red and white checkered table cloths. From the juke box, The Velvet Fog, Mel Torme, crooned softly in the background.

Since it was after nine, most of the dinner crowd had already moved on. A scattering of patrons still lounged here and there nursing a cup of coffee or finishing up their spumoni. A couple of them looked up in response to the door opening, paid a dismissive glance to the new arrival and turned back to their table. Only one woman in the low light noticed the peculiar features of the man who entered the restaurant and held her gaze for an inordinate amount of time before the realization she was staring dawned on her and forced her eyes back to her table. She could not resist however, another quick, furtive glimpse when Haskim walked to the bar and addressed the bartender.

"I have an appointment with Mr Mizetti. I was told to meet him here."

The woman could not hide the hesitancy she felt when the man's features became obvious to her as he moved forward into the brighter aura surrounding the bar. Sprinkles of light sparkled off the numerous liquor bottles lining the mirrored wall behind her. As the woman stared at Haskim, he could not help but realize that this woman had no doubt seen every type of undesirable, dishonorable and corrupted form of humanity there was in the world and probably never displayed the look she now held in her eyes as she bumbled for something to say.

"Yeah ... he's ... Does he ... Is he expecting you then?"

Haskim leaned on his best behavior. "Yes, if you could tell him I'm here please."

The woman nodded and strode hurriedly around the end of the bar and disappeared into the far back room. She quickly reappeared at the entrance to the room and signaled for Haskim to come back. As he approached he heard the chatter of several voices. Someone made an unintelligible comment and several men gushed out in laughter. The last tentacles of that laughter continued until Haskim turned into the room and the individuals present immediately silenced at the stranger's presence.

The room was a make-shift kitchen, approximately thirty-five feet long and twenty wide with an old-fashioned white sink lining the side wall. A back door with a window through which Haskim could see a small deck with a table and chairs stood against the back wall. Two other shut doors led to other areas and faced the sink on the other side of the room. In the middle of the room sat a circular card table sprinkled with beer cans, ash trays, poker chips, half-filled glasses and a half-eaten bag of pretzels. The five men seated around the table immediately came to attention when their eyes caught the face of the man who entered.

Haskim recognized two of the men, Jimmy Vitello and the one they called Freddie. They were part of Mizetti's muscle. They had squeezed Haskim before his accident. The others were hangers-on with whom he had no concern. Vitello had been helpful in setting up his meeting with Mizetti.

An older, heavy-set man with gray hair and a stained white shirt was unable to hide his shock at seeing Haskim and turned his gaze abruptly to the man to his right as if asking for guidance. The man he looked at was the leader of this crew of thugs, Leo Mizetti.

Mizetti sat leaning back in his chair with his huge hands grasped around his cards which he was just in the process of examining when Haskim had entered. The stub of a large, dark cigar protruded from the corner of his mouth. Mizetti was a heavy man, but not excessively so, more to be considered large than overweight, the bouncer type. In a fight, Haskim could not imagine how anyone could defeat him. All he would have had to do was lean on you and you were toast. His biceps and triceps nearly tore through the arms of the striped shirt he wore. His chest was wide and well-defined. If you looked at him from the sternum up and not been witness to his belly, one would have sworn that he was a body builder. His facial features consisted of dark, shiny black hair, greased back beyond his large forehead. Dark brown eyes stared out from beneath a lowered brow. Heavy facial hair displayed a prominent five o'clock shadow. The cheeks were slightly puffy and a double chin surrounded his neck like a fleshy scarf.

All in all a good-looking man in that larger than life mode except for his marked nose which was bent and flattened slightly with a small scar at the bridge as if it had been broken by a hockey stick or perhaps a baseball bat.

An awkward silence fell over the room.

Mizetti's expression initially appeared to be one of amusement, as opposed to surprise. Haskim's disfigurement was known to him, so he was not overcome with shock. The mobster had seen a lot of things in his life, even murdered two men in his early years. It took a lot for fear, even when brought about subconsciously through shock, to take root.

"Mr Andre," Mizetti blurted out as if in retort to the silence.

"Yes," Haskim replied as he scanned the table. "I hope I am not disturbing your card game."

"No. I'm out, Joe," Mizetti said as he pitched his cards into the center of the table. He stared up at Haskim and shook his head almost in absurd unbelief. "Come on back," he chuckled.

"Gentleman ..." Haskim said as he removed his hat and smiled. He enjoyed, sometimes, the effect his looks produced in people, especially those with whom he normally would find himself a bit leery. It was an odd sort of gloating, born out of his own jealousy. If he had to live with his deformities, it helped to know he could impose a certain discomfort in those whom he normally considered to out-rank him.

Mizetti rose from his chair, grabbed his drink from the table and went to the closed door to his right. The door opened into a smaller office containing a desk in the middle of the room, a beige file cabinet wedged against the corner, and a TV set perched high on top of the cabinet. Behind the desk hung a calendar containing pictures of voluptuous women in various suggestive poses. An autographed picture of Dick Butkus, squatting in his navy blue Bears uniform smudged with grass and mud, wearing an expression of wide-eyed expectation, graced the far wall.

Mizetti stepped aside allowing Haskim to enter, before closing the door and going to his chair behind the desk. "Please ..." he motioned to a seat across from the desk. Mizetti seemed to be on his best behavior, another involuntary effect Haskim's appearance caused in people sometimes. Even those with a reputation like Mizetti's.

"Can I get you something?"

Haskim chuckled slightly. "You know a beer might be nice."

"Nicky ... bring me a beer" Mizetti yelled loud enough to be heard outside the door.

It took only a moment before Nicky, one of the younger guys at the table, came in and responded to Mizetti's finger which pointed at Haskim. Nicky placed the beer in front of Haskim and quickly left.

Mizetti took another moment to size up his guest. "For what's it worth, your score has been settled. What your partner paid me is good enough. After I heard about your ..." Mizetti circled his face with his index finger. "I figured what you went through is enough." Mizetti smiled widely. "Just to show you we ain't all heartless bastards around here."

"Yes I understand that ... and I appreciate it too," Haskim responded.

Mizetti rocked back on his chair a little. "So I says to myself 'We're square, so what's Haskim want with me now, social call?' Jimmy said it was business that you were eager to talk to me about."

"Yes, it is business."

"I heard you and your partner, what's his name, is it Demetri?"

"Yes that's right."

"He told me you ended up doing quite well on the fire although ... I can see you paid a heavy price."

"Financially fine. Settled us up anyway."

"Yeah well ... I hope in the future less painful methods of compensation can be had."

As if to squelch any further discussion on that point, Haskim took a sip of his beer, quickly wiping the side of his mouth where a drop had dribbled.

Haskim placed his fingers in the indentations of his fedora where it was pinched in the front and set it down in front of him on the desk.

"I am interested in having a burglary done, retrieval of an item, if you will." Haskim bent his thin lips into a curl. "You see there is something I am owed ... and ... well I want it done right. I'd do it myself, but I'm afraid I'd botch it."

"What makes you think that I can ... meet your needs?"

Mizetti and Haskim both knew that this was just the preliminary round of the bout. Mizetti denying he knows anything at all about such things, Haskim prodding him more, the possibility listened to and evaluated, maybe Mizetti did know of someone who might be able to help, and then of course the inevitable discussion of money.

"Your friend Vitello," Haskim flicked his left hand with his thumb cocked to indicate the boys in the other room. The sharp move agitated the fragile skin between the thumb and the index finger which still had not healed from his graveyard mission. Haskim stared at the raw spot before dipping into his pocket for the jar of skin cream he always kept with him.

Mizetti watched as Haskim applied the cream to his hand. Noticing he was being observed, Haskim said: "You won't believe it, but a dog bit me. Plus the fire, the skin is no longer pliable. Breaks easily, terribly dry. The cream helps a little."

"A dog bit you, eh? Seems like you ain't had much luck lately." The ice in Mizetti's glass clinked as he brought it to his lips and took a sip. "A burglary you say?"

"Yes, I'll pay quite well. As I said, I want this done right. No foul ups. Your burglar may take whatever he wants, I could care less. The home he is to rob is very well appointed. There is only one item I am interested in and a small request."

"And …" Mizetti brought his right hand out in an open palm as if holding out a platter.

Haskim knew it would come to this. He would have to explain what it was he wanted and what it was for and his odd little request. Lies would be needed now. He had to be concerned about who might be in possession of the thing once it was stolen and for how long. It was important that he be given the item immediately upon its being stolen.

"The thing I want is of no earthly good to anyone but me. It's a globe, a crystal ball so to speak. It was stolen from me and now I need it back." Two of his three statements were outright lies. He might need to tell more before his discussion with Mizetti was over.

"Is it a family heirloom? Some kind of gemstone, what?"

"Oh no … It's much too large for that." Haskim held his hands in a circular shape to show the relative circumference, as big as a softball, the size peculiar to the type of game played by thousands of kids in the Chicagoland area.

Mizetti frowned. "So what is it, a magic globe, tells the future, what?"

Haskim did his best to pshaw that with a juicy chuckle and a wave of his hand. But that didn't put off Mizetti.

"What?"

Haskim let the smile fizzle slowly from his face. The look Mizetti gave him indicated that some answer would need to be provided before the discussion could continue. Haskim toyed with the idea of telling him exactly what someone in possession of the globe could do because it would be Mizetti's turn to pshaw Haskim with a chuckle. But the risk was too high. The skin beneath the patch on his eye began to itch. Haskim used the edge of his right index finger to scratch at it before turning his gaze back on Mizetti.

One thing Haskim had discovered since his accident was that few men could outdistance him in a staring contest. People became too ill at ease whenever they were forced to hold eye contact with him. Between the black patch over his right eye and the distorted orb of his left, a sustained gaze was seemingly impossible to hold because of the awkwardness it brought, discomfort that even the most unnerved observer could not endure for any length of time. Invariably when the loser dropped his gaze, a certain level of his tenaciousness fell too. Haskim found that he could use the method to his advantage when a battle of wills presented itself, such as was happening now.

Haskim locked his eye on Mizetti until the man looked away. The moment he dropped his gaze, Haskim said: "I'm afraid I must simply have it, and that will have to be enough."

Mizetti shot a glance back up at Haskim as if realizing he had been had but was willing to surrender the point. "And this small request of yours ..."

"That is simple enough. I want to be very close when the globe is retrieved, so that it can be put in my possession immediately. Simple enough, eh?"

Mizetti wondered about this peculiar request also. But since there was no perceivable loss to him, he did not belabor it.

"And you would want this done when?"

"As soon as possible. Tomorrow night, if it can be arranged."

"And whom are we robbing?"

"The home of Demetri, of course."

"Your former partner?"

"The same." Haskim took a moment to observe Mizetti's confusion. "No need for you to be perplexed, Mr Mizetti. Just a simple job. He lives in a stately, fashionable home in Long Grove. Quite exclusive. Somewhere a person of my, how should I say, physicality would stand out. And now as far as price is concerned."

Mizetti held up his hand. "Wait a minute. I haven't said I'd go along with this little ... masquerade. Something don't feel right about this."

"Well, when I tell you the price I am willing to pay for the globe, you will most definitely be willing to entertain my request."

Chapter 8

April 23, 1929

The sixteen year old Demetri Davos stood on the stone bridge and stared down into the rushing river below him. He had not quite come to grips with what Estrella had done. An ominous pattern had developed, one he did not want to recognize, because it would complicate greatly the plans he had for the future.

Beneath him the waters churned rapidly over the rocks. There had been a heavy snowfall that winter and the mountains were beginning to release the snows they held. Demetri tried to imagine what it must have felt like to go over that bridge: the long tumble through the air, the icy cold of the water, the sudden thud of the body striking the shallow, rocky bottom. He couldn't imagine the level of depression and desperation that could drive a person to that.

Viteazu had confided in him that Estrella's body had struck head first on the rocks and her face had been nearly obliterated in the process. When her body washed downstream and was found, the mangled facial features and the bloated corpse had made it difficult for even him to recognize who it was. The funeral had been quick and solemn. Several times during the graveside service, Demetri had met the gaze of Estrella's father and mother. Their piercing glare had made it perfectly clear that they blamed him, at least in part, for what had occurred.

Estrella had been a cheerful, fun-loving girl. She made friends easily and rarely ever pouted or became moody. Even when her monthly womanhood came to visit, she did not suffer the discomforts, mentally or physically, that other girls did. Things had begun to change just before Christmas when she seemed to suddenly become entranced with Demetri. Her parents and friends had never known Estrella to become attached to any one boy before. Her giddiness and immaturity had led her to several relationships in the past with some of her male school mates, but most of those had frizzled as fast as they had developed. She simply was too consumed with a general cheeriness and unstructured gaiety to be held down in any one general direction. However, prior to Christmas she told her friends of a sudden unrelenting infatuation she found with Demetri. Her parents became aware of it and at first did not object. They had found a place in their heart for the boy because of the unfortunate events that had left him orphaned.

Estrella and Demetri spent many long hours together after school stealing away to the woods or to Demetri's home where they could be alone. In a short period of time, Estrella became deeply attached to the boy. Prior to the sudden shift in her feelings, she had not treated Demetri any differently than any of her other school mates. They had belonged to the same set of loosely attached friends, but Estrella never displayed any specific attachment to Demetri. In fact any discussion she had with the timid boy seemed, at best, awkward and strained.

No one could understand the sudden obsession that overcame her. Demetri and she became inseparable. She no longer had time to spend with her other friends because she wanted to devote herself to Demetri.

Demetri thought back to the times he spent alone with Estrella. At first he fell wildly in love and reveled in becoming the single source of her affections. As the weeks went by however, he began to feel cramped and claustrophobic. As happens with many affairs, the pining Demetri felt when Estrella was merely an unobtainable idol, proved to be less sensational once the allure of the girl's inaccessibility disappeared. As with many adolescents, just when he seemingly had captured the girl of his dreams, he found others to be more captivating. Demetri's immaturity proved to be too unsettled to handle the deep foundations of a relationship that suddenly obsessed Estrella. He soon began to realize that the desire he felt for Estrella prior to their relationship was much more entrancing than the actual thing.

As Demetri became disillusioned, Estrella became more and more desperate to secure his waning affections. Unfortunately, as immature boys are inclined to do, young Demtri disclosed to his friends the extent of his and Estrella's escapades. The giddy friends, incapable of controlling the urge to broadcast their juicy gossip, spread the secret inappropriately until the entire village became aware of it. The news, although a smudge on Demetri's good name, in no way measured up to the immoral slur weighted against the poor girl's reputation. Such a slight could be forgiven a young, bustling boy, but the stain forever cast on Estrella's character caused the villagers to view the ill-fated girl's behavior as contemptible. The local parson did not hesitate in making an example of the situation in order to demonstrate to the faithful the shameful immorality of today's youth. The irretrievable scourge became unbearable for the outcast girl.

Alone, frightened, bewildered and despairing, the broken-hearted girl threw herself from the bridge on a chilly morning as the birds chirped harmoniously in anticipation of a burgeoning spring day.

Now gazing down from the same height Estrella had leapt from, Demetri struggled to understand it all. Several deer came out of the woods poking their nose down among the sprouting ferns searching for berries when they caught sight of Demetri standing on the bridge. At first they started, but then sensing no danger existed, ignored the boy and went about foraging through the brush. Demetri sighed and wiped the tears from his eyes as he leaned against the stones.

There was no doubting what had occurred and the boy cringed in regret. He didn't want to accept the culpability he bore in Estrella's death. After his father died, Demetri struggled to dismiss the notion that the wish he had made into the crystal ball had nothing to do with the insane actions of his father. He had wished to be rid of his father and it had happened, but the two could not possibly have been linked. It had simply been a coincidence, an innocent happenstance and nothing more. Nevertheless he had made a point of putting the globe away, hesitant to tempt fate again.

He thought back to the time he had seen Estrella at mass, sitting with her family. He made a point of positioning himself near the door of the church after the service so that he might possibly engage the girl in discussion. Her parents had approached him after the service asking him how he was doing and if there was anything they could do for him. Estrella seemed nothing more than polite and understanding, standing off behind her father and offering only a gracious smile when Demetri caught her gaze. There was no hint from the beautiful girl that her feelings for Demetri were any different than those she felt for any of her other school mates. When her parents finished with their greeting, the girl walked off with them. Demetri gazed after them hoping Estrella would give him some sign that her feelings were in any way in line with his. The girl never looked back.

Later that night, frustrated by his inability to get any response from Estrella, Demetri laid in his bed unable to sleep, the vision of Estrella's blue eyes holding court in his mind. The winter night was dreadfully cold. Demetri got up and attended the fire in the hearth piling on two more logs that would see him through until dawn. The boy was nervous about the coming winter. His supply of chopped wood had diminished at an alarming rate due to the excessively cold autumn days. He might need to resupply his stock sooner than he thought. In addition, there were repairs to the cabin that needed to be made. Without his father to help him, Demetri worried about how he would sustain himself. He would have to hunt more on his own and, once the weather changed, tend to the garden to ensure he had sufficient vegetables to carry him through. The baker had assured Demetri that he could continue to work for him. However, Demetri would have to make a point of being very careful with his funds. He knew he could count on the pity of some of the women in the village to ensure he had sufficient food and supplies, a benefit he had no shame in exploiting.

Somehow he would get by.

But now there was another problem he was facing that his longing for Estrella only exacerbated and that was his loneliness. Even though his relationship with his father had been contentious and strained, there was a certain comradery it had provided which kept him from feeling totally isolated as he did now. Demetri's mind turned to the globe hidden beneath his bed in the black sack. Caution tugged against the urge he felt, but he found himself unable to resist. Demetri rationalized that viewing the globe could not possibly do any harm. When he pulled it out and brought it over to the fire, he could not help but notice a soft glow emanating from the middle of the ball. As he stared into it, a vision of Estrella came through, her eyes sparkling. His desire for the girl increased markedly as he stared into the crystal.

If only he could win her love. What a difference that would make. Any hardship he was due to suffer could be endured if he had her to lean on. The crystal grew brighter as the urge within him rose. It was as if the globe was exhorting him on.

Almost hypnotically focused, Demetri found his resistance waning. The ball became brighter. The urge inside him blossomed. Any hesitancy he felt before became obscured by the sentiment that nothing harmful could possibly come from such a grand request. The world went away and there was only Demetri and the globe and Estrella. He made his wish. The globe radiated colors wildly, peaked in brilliance, flooded the room with eye-piercing light and then slowly faded back on itself until only the dim yellow flicker remained.

Exhausted, Demetri returned the globe to its black bag, stuffed it under his bed and went to sleep.

Meanwhile in her village home, Estrella abruptly awoke from her sleep. For some reason her mind began dwelling on Demetri. She had never paid much attention to the boy before ... but now ... suddenly and inexplicably, she saw him in a completely different light.

Chapter 9

October 8, 1984

Isabelle sat on a couch across the hospital room from a bed where her father lay. Seated next to Demetri, Amanda held his hand and spoke softly to him. Behind Amanda, Quimby stood with a concerned look on his face. Isabelle, of course, could not understand what Amanda was saying to her father, but it also seemed that her father was not hearing what the woman was saying. Demetri had not spoken nor moved since they had arrived. His head was bandaged and tubes ran up his nose. Another tube ran from a hanging bottle to the outside of his hand. He looked like he was sleeping.

Things were swirling out of control in Isabelle's mind. Amanda had brought her in the car and led her into the hospital. Together they rode up an elevator and made their way down the hall past a desk full of nurses. Quimby had been seated in a chair near the window looking frazzled when they came in. Amanda had let Isabelle sit next to her father for awhile and coaxed her to kiss him. Obviously her father was not well, but Isabelle did not know exactly what the problem was. Heavy bandages were wrapped around his head so she couldn't see his face clearly. There was also a cast on his right arm, the one opposite the one in which the tube was attached. His right leg was elevated, strung up on a cable.

Whatever was wrong with her father, it was serious. Monitors showed jagged lines and gave off an occasional beep now and again. A nurse had come in and spoken to Amanda and Isabelle noticed how the housekeeper dabbed at her eyes and nose occasionally as the nurse spoke to her. From everything she had observed including the ambulance that had pulled away from the house three nights before, her only guess was that somehow her father had fallen from the balcony outside his bedroom though she could not imagine how that possibly could have happened because of the stone wall that surrounded it.

But her father's condition was not the only thing troubling Isabelle. She was desperately worried about Whisper. The wound that Whisper had suffered in his fall was serious and Isabelle knew enough about horses to know what a broken leg, if severe enough, could mean.

Isabelle's safe, comfortable world was suddenly beginning to crumble around her. Since the change that had come over her, a terrible hesitancy took residence in her heart. She was always a happy, buoyant child, never self-conscious or worried, always eager to please. Her heart was happily displayed on her sleeve. She kept no secrets and gave her love to her father, mother and those others who cared for her not out of insecurity or fear but out of a true blush of sentiment.

But then the change had come all in one night, that one fateful night.

Her world suddenly became defined by those things she knew how to do for herself. Her inability to communicate with others forced limitations on her. New tasks became nearly impossible to learn. Her reliance on others became more and more essential. As long as father, Amanda, Quimby or Victor was around, she had no worries. As long as she could continue her intimate relationship with Whisper, she could feel safe and needed and a part of something. But she knew that father was the source of it all. She was wise enough to realize that all things came from him: the house, her meals, and her safety. The servants relied on him just as much as she did. His wealth allowed them to continue in his hire and provide for her needs. What would the future hold for her if something were to happen to father?

And what of Whisper? The vet would be coming to check on the horse surely. She remembered what had happened with the old mare they had before, Teedee. She had come up lame one day also, they bandaged her up, but she had no patience for the brace. She kept kicking it off and reinjuring it. The panicked look in her eyes never left. And finally when the damage became too much ...

Was it possible her father was not going to survive? Was Whisper not going to understand that he had to wait to heal? The thoughts filled Isabelle with dread. She could not allow the ones she loved to die.

Isabelle knew she had little time to debate the issue in her head. She had to act quickly.

A doctor came into the room and both Quimby and Amanda went to him. As they began talking, Amanda looked down at Isabelle and then came over to her. She led her into the hallway and sat her down in a chair outside the room and with her finger indicated for her to stay there. Quickly she hurried back into the room.

Isabelle looked down the hallway to where a nurse's station lay bathed in bright light. There was a nurse seated at the desk jotting notes onto a clipboard. Another nurse came by and leaned over to talk to the other woman. Just then a large black man wearing all white came down the hallway pushing a large cart containing all kinds of supplies from towels to toilet paper. As he passed Isabelle, he gave her a big smile and said something to her. When she did not respond, he smiled again and went on his way.

From the next room a young boy in a wheelchair slowly rolled himself out into the corridor. He was pulling alongside him an IV stand. His head was shaved. His features looked gaunt and pale. When he saw Isabelle he gave her a half smile and then moved his chair out a little further into the hall. Isabelle wondered what could be wrong with him. He caught her staring at him and smiled a little more brightly this time. Then he just sat back in his chair and in boredom looked around.

For a few minutes they both silently sat there about eight feet apart each in their own separate worlds. Occasionally a noise or voice from the nurse's station would rouse their attention and they would look over at it and then just return to their own thoughts.

As Isabelle sat there, she noticed something very curious. When she was at home, Whisper and she were generally always in communication. The stream of consciousness between the two of them was pronounced even if there was nothing much going on at the time. With the other animals like Prado and Blackie, the communication was spottier. In tranquil times their worlds did not mingle much. Isabelle may have had a general sense of what they were thinking, but their innermost thoughts were not as pronounced and available to her. However, in times of crisis or excitement, the level of communication would increase substantially. For example, whenever Victor began preparing Blackie's dinner, the dog would get extremely energized swinging around in circles barking up a storm. In that heightened state, Isabelle could perceive his thoughts much more clearly. When the bowl was finally put down and Blackie started eating, she could read his mind very readily. It was almost as if the higher the emotional state, the more open to reception was their communication. She knew that it was true for the dog too because it was at those moments that the animal seemed to recognize the thought exchange more and would converse back to Isabelle via his thoughts. Of course, with Blackie, who Isabelle knew was not the most intelligent of animals, conversations were usually limited to only the instinctual habits that pressed on the dog's consciousness: when would he eat next, his fixation on chasing rabbits, or his endless desire to track scents.

There would be times when Blackie suddenly spotted a rabbit and gave chase and no matter where Isabelle was, his eager agitated state would immediately become known to her in loud raucous screeching that would almost give her a headache. Once the chase was frustrated with the rabbit escaping, the dull thudding numbness of his normal plodding mind took over and again the communication became hazy and lackluster.

But now, for seemingly no particular reason, Isabelle sensed the thoughts and feelings of the boy in the wheelchair. The patterns coming through were not exceptionally strong, but there was no mistaking the fact that she could actually sense what he was thinking. This had happened to Isabelle only once before and that had been when Quimby had been driving her home from somewhere and they came upon an auto accident. While they were waiting for the police officers to wave them through, Isabelle started receiving communication coming from one of the cars lying on its side in the ditch. At first Isabelle assumed there was a dog in an agitated state trapped in the car. But then she realized that the thoughts were coming from a young girl. Her arm was bleeding and she was upside down wedged tight to the door by her seat belt. She was being told to relax by two men who were working to free her, but there was no mistaking her anxiety and panic. They were just beginning to wedge the door open and pull her out as Quimby was finally motioned through. As they sped away from the scene, the communication became fainter until it dissipated totally.

Isabelle stared at the boy and quietly digested the thoughts that were coming to her. He sat calmly staring down at his hands almost mumbling in his mind to himself. For some reason the image of a bird's nest kept coming through and Isabelle couldn't figure it out. The boy's emotional state at the moment was fragile. He seemed to be arguing with himself about something. A high level of fear emanated from him, but it was not necessarily fright for himself or his condition. Self-pity did not rule his thoughts. A heavy sadness laced with fear was definitely on display. A vision of a woman kept popping up too and immediately when it would, a spurt of guilt would follow it. A mixture of emotions rolled through his head: helplessness, guilt, sadness. But mostly it was shame. Then that bird's nest again and for a quick moment the vision of an infuriated sparrow.

A doctor came down the hall and when he saw the boy, came up to him, leaned down and spoke to him. Almost immediately the boy's fear level decreased and because it did, the volume of the transmissions coming from him diminished in strength. Fortunately, she could observe the two of them and gather what they were saying to each other from their actions. The doctor was very intent with the youngster. He had his hand on his shoulder and seemed to be reassuring the boy. The boy nodded in agreement and then some vague thought came dancing through: something about tickets to a Cubs baseball game. The doctor patted the boy on his head and went on his way.

Almost immediately the boy's emotions became aroused again. This time there was shame but also a heightened desire that seemed to swallow up all the other emotions there. The boy brought his hand to his eyes and wiped away a tear as he watched the doctor make his way down the corridor. For the first time Isabelle sensed a deep desire come from the boy. It had to do with the doctor. He wanted to help, to be like him, there was that darn sparrow again pecking at a squirrel. The strength of his feelings was profound now, almost bottomless. A yearning came from his very soul. In a way it was wonderful to see and at the same time heartbreaking.

Suddenly the boy turned and looked at Isabelle. He had a curious look on his face like he couldn't figure something out. His mouth started to move to say something, but he never finished. A wave of confusion came through to Isabelle from him.

"Did you ... say something ...?" the boy asked, but he wasn't really asking that. He just didn't know how else to interpret what he was sensing.

Isabelle just looked at the boy, unable to answer him.

A moment later, Quimby came out of the room and indicated to Isabelle that it was time to leave. The activity distracted the boy and the communication came to a halt. Quimby was about to lead Isabelle back into the room, but Amanda came to the door and shook her head. For some reason she did not want Isabelle to go back in the room.

Quimby talked to Amanda for a few more seconds and then grabbed Isabelle and began leading her down the hall directly past the boy. As she passed him, Isabelle's and the boy's eyes locked and a wave of confusion rolled into Isabelle's head. Before she had any chance at all to respond or do anything, they were half way down the hall heading around a corner to reach the elevator.

On the way down and all the way home Isabelle tried to figure it out. It was so wonderful those few moments when she actually felt as if she was able to communicate with another human being. She sensed that the boy felt something too, but what exactly she didn't know. What she did know was that the boy was sick, seriously sick. He was scared to some degree, but the biggest thing she got from the whole exchange was how sorry and rueful he was. His fright was due to his perception that a marvelous opportunity was slipping through his fingers.

Quimby brought Isabelle back to the house. It was very late, but the girl could not sleep. She routinely woke every few minutes out of her own worry over her father and because Whisper's restlessness continually interrupted her. In addition, that whole communication with the boy at the hospital nagged at her, but she didn't have time to worry about that right now. Tonight she had a mission to accomplish.

Quimby had left Isabelle in her bedroom in the house, but as soon as she felt safe enough, she made her way down to the barn to stay near Whisper.

The horse was half-panicked by the bandages on his leg and needed reassurance. He had related to Isabelle that he was not in any great pain, but the animal's nerves were frayed by the abnormality of it all. Isabelle had tried several times to explain it to the horse and it had helped calm Whisper down somewhat, but Isabelle had learned that even though she could communicate with animals, some more intensely than others, there was sometimes a wall that she could not totally cross. In this case it was the inherent nature of a beast not wanting to be bound in any way. It would not bother Whisper to be penned into a corral or to be tied to a post. That limit on his independence did not produce panic. However, the bandages on his leg were too strange for him to comprehend. It created great anxiety in the beast, almost borne out of a self-conscious intolerance to such a thing, that words or actions such as a heavy brushing, which Whisper loved, could not soothe. Her repeated attempts to calm the animal only bore limited results. Isabelle had learned there were some things foreign to an animal that no amount of reassurance could remedy. It was simply the nature of the beast.

Isabelle had learned that panic in an animal was different from panic in humans. With animals it was all consuming. In humans, reason can be present in the mind along with fear and excitement in a stressful situation. The reason can eventually modulate the panic to bring reassurance and finally a stabilizing calmness. However, with animals, the panic blots out any semblance of rationality. As long as pain or fright is present, the animal seeks immediate release. It was all part of the animal's nature. They lived in the here and now. There was no past, no future, there was only now. And if pain or terror was prevalent, it called for immediate escape. Only when Victor had tended to the wound and relieved most of the piercing pain, was Whisper able to quiet down and rest.

But Isabelle had not wanted to leave Whisper's side. She knew what happened to horses that were sickly or old or had a wound that could not be mended. The fright and panic had moved from Whisper's mind to Isabelle's.

The only good thing about Isabelle removing herself from Whisper's presence was that the animal would be able to perceive easily the worry in Isabelle's mind and that concern may have inflamed the horse's uneasiness even further.

Isabelle rose and went to her friend. She tried to give the animal a carrot from the sack hanging on the wall, but Whisper just threw his head away. For the horse to refuse a carrot spoke volumes. She patted the horse's flank, rubbed his ears and whispered sounds to him for nearly a half an hour before she was able to ease the animal's restlessness somewhat. She finally coaxed him into eating a few carrots and that seemed to help also.

Isabelle went to the barn window and stared up at the big house. Her eyes followed the bricks up until they rested on her father's bedroom window. She wondered if the globe was still where she had last seen it. She still could not quite grasp what had happened to her to so drastically change her nature, but she knew her wish upon the globe had to have been the cause. That fateful night she had made a wish and it had come true, but at a terrible cost. The two had to be related. They had to be, but that didn't matter now. The fear she felt was overriding any sense of judgment she might be able to discern.

Whisper thumped a hoof and neighed several times when Isabelle left the barn and headed toward the house. The child went in through the side door that was always left open for her and climbed the stairs. Quimby's room was toward the back of the house, so Isabelle knew to be quiet. Quimby had that uncanny ability of a good servant to never be caught off guard by any activity in the house. By nature he was a light sleeper and anything the least bit curious would no doubt awaken him. She went down to his room and through the closed door could hear the cadence of his snoring.

The night light from atop the west barn was always left on at night to serve as a faint sentry over the estate. Its dim beacon through a high window served to guide Isabelle's path back down the hall. It was advantageous for Isabelle that Amanda was at the hospital with her father. Nothing ever got by that woman and Isabelle's presence regardless of how quiet and sly she would have been would not have gone unnoticed by the maid servant. Now that she reached her destination without arousing Quimby, Isabelle felt more secure.

She entered her father's room. The bedroom seemed creepy now that he was not in the house. She felt as if she was intervening into an eerie, unnatural world. Isabelle tiptoed about as if to avoid scarring the sacred ground.

The closet lay off to her right and she quickly made her way to it. Isabelle had no idea if the globe was even there or if her father had moved it somewhere else. The last time she had ever seen it, it had been secured away on the top shelf. She hoped her father had not moved it because she feared that what she was about to do represented the only possible way he could recover.

Isabelle pulled a chair into the closet and stood on top of it. The shelves led back in the dim light where the sloping ceiling made it more and more difficult to see, but there was no need for more light. A faint glow leaked out of a wooden box where the brass hinges secured the top. Now that she had found it, Isabelle had to be very careful in extracting it. She remembered the weight of the thing and that, combined with the wooden box and the location of it on the shelf, would make it very tricky to extract it silently. Isabelle did her best to clear the area leading to the box which she then slid down closer to her. Using all of her strength, she managed to get the box onto her shoulder before lowering herself to the ground. On the last step she stumbled to the ground but held onto the box. She quietly made her way out of the closet and placed the box on the bed.

Isabelle thought for a moment as she observed the sprigs of light emanating from around the hinges. She wondered about the ramifications of what she was about to do. The last time she had encountered the globe and made a wish, trouble ensued.

Had the granting of her wish, in and of itself, been the cause of her inability now to communicate normally with her family?

She couldn't be absolutely sure, *but there had to be a connection.*

What was this globe? Why was it here? Where did it come from?

Did she dare risk tempting fate again?

Isabelle opened the box and looked inside. The globe lay in a black velvet bag that cinched at the top with a draw string. Shafts of colored light escaped from the puckered end. Isabelle's hands shook as she reached in and brought the sack out and laid it on the bed before her. She pulled back the string and the ball seemed to roll out of its own accord gently lodging up against her right thigh. The light transfixed Isabelle. Inside the glass, swirls of color danced and jittered in a smoky white haze that distorted the shapes and angles. Its effect was mesmerizing and any thoughts that Isabelle had of resisting the globe were swallowed up by its spellbinding allure.

There was only one thing more captivating in Isabelle's mind than the curiosity surrounding the globe: fear. The worry however was not for what might occur if she made another wish. What was of concern to her was what might occur if she did not make the wish she was contemplating. She could not imagine life without the reassurance of her father's presence.

What would become of her if he died?

Her condition made it impossible for her to make any type of stance on how things should go for her. She would be at the mercy of choices made by any number of other people. Those decisions would be totally out of her control. Isabelle knew father had money and she was wise enough to know that money did strange things to people.

How could she be sure her needs would even be considered? In the tug of war that might ensue who knew where she would wind up? Perhaps the house and stables would have to be sold. What then? Where would she go?

Besides her father's condition there was Whisper to consider now. She could not lose her friend. That was as unthinkable as losing her father. But if her father died, even if Whisper recovered, all might be lost anyway.

There were several people in her father's confidence that she did not care for, one of them being Alvin Rothman, his attorney. She had noticed how the man avoided her whenever she was around. The oddity of Isabelle's condition and behavior did not sit well with him and there were times when she could feel the reluctance and hesitancy on his part to even greet her. His demeanor made Isabelle feel as if he regarded her as no more than the family dog. One he was not inclined to pet. Isabelle knew that if that man had any say in her father's business, it would all be dollars and cents and he would show no aversion to making drastic changes based solely on the financial worthiness of the option. Something as important as Isabelle's well being could easily be swayed by other interests. Regardless of what Isabelle thought, an option that made sense financially could most assuredly be shown to be "what was best" for her.

Isabelle realized just how vulnerable she was. Up until now her living situation made her ability to communicate with animals an extremely pleasurable part of her existence. The fact that she was just as intellectually smart as ever and in some cases more intelligent than those around her like Victor and Amanda could be overlooked and adapted to because all her needs were met. Of course her inability to communicate with other people often led to lonesomeness, discouragement and depression, but she could always talk to her animal friends and withdraw into that world. Since it was not explicitly necessary for her to communicate with others around her or to carry on any business of any kind, she had found a certain level of contentment that blotted out the negative repercussions of her existence. However that could all change in a heartbeat, or rather her father's lack of one.

It suddenly occurred to Isabelle that although she loved her father very much, she had been almost totally consumed with how his present condition might affect her. It dawned on her that concern for his actual well-being had hardly entered into her thoughts. She had been pushed and prodded up to this point by apprehension for her own well-being only. A certain level of shame overcame her and she became more alarmed than ever. This was another price her condition exacted on her. It had forced her to view people in light of what they could do for her. Since she could no longer converse with them or share ideas, she had become isolated, a prisoner of her own mind. Fear and insecurity had twisted her vision of people into objects she learned to use for her own safety and needs. The change had happened almost without her realizing it. She knew this now, but it made no difference. That precondition was forced upon her. It was the only way she could survive. And wishing it were any different wasn't going to change it.

The globe, almost in recognition of the depth of her worry, began to glow brighter. Isabelle stared at the glass more intently. There was no running from it now. Whatever reasons made up her will, it always brought her back to the same point. She could not allow anything to happen to her father. She lied and told herself that she was doing it because of her love for her father. She placed her hands on the globe and wondered again if something bad would happen as a result of her wish.

What would it matter if it did? There was no other recourse, no other option.

Could she just not make the wish and hope for the best for her father? Maybe he could recover.

The shimmer from the globe grew more intense as Isabelle realized the folly of that notion. No, it was obvious. She had seen him in that hospital bed, the look on the nurse's face, the reactions of Amanda and Quimby. There was too much at stake.

Isabelle could feel heat coming off the globe now, prodding her on. Tears welled in her eyes. Regardless of the repercussions, she had to do it. She had to ensure that her father would recover.

Suddenly she was pulled away from the globe. Standing there, silhouetted by the hallway light behind him was the figure of Quimby. He had a stunned, menacing look on his face.

He pulled Isabelle up roughly and pointed toward the door. The stern look on his face was impossible for the girl not to understand. She was shaking terribly as she meekly turned and followed the hallway back down to her bedroom. Quimby followed closely and shut the door once Isabelle had entered.

Isabelle walked to her bed and laid herself down. Did Quimby know what the globe was all about? There had been times, especially in those first days after her ability to communicate was lost, that her father had taken her to his room and tried desperately to communicate with her. He had taken out the globe once and showed it to Isabelle who simply stared at it. Isabelle felt that her father was trying to see if he could get any type of reaction from her. The times he had showed her the globe, it had glowed meekly, not as vibrantly or brilliantly as it had the night she made her wish to communicate with animals or even just now when she had been so close to wishing for her father's health. But above all he let his child know in no uncertain terms that she was never to go near the orb, never play with it or handle it. There were some emotions in the thoughts and actions of the ones she loved that carried so much weight to them that it was even able to pierce that impenetrable shell around her consciousness.

On one occasion after her father had dismissed her, she thought she overheard him whimpering in his room. She went and peeked through the keyhole. He was seated in his chair staring at the globe. This was before her incapacitated mother had passed away. The ball's intensity rose and subsided, the light spiraling around the room in a dizzying whirl. The look on her father's face was the most puzzling thing of all. It appeared as if he was wrestling with some great question in his mind. He would turn away from the orb and then back, stare at it attentively and then draw his eye away. Finally he shouted "No" and quickly returned the globe to its sack and back into its box.

When he finished he put his hands to his face and began crying.

Isabelle went back to her room, frightened and bewildered. Whatever power the orb had, whatever its allure, she realized its use was dangerous for all involved. She had herself as proof of that. What she did understand was that her father was wrestling with some great desire he wanted met, some wish he wanted satisfied. But he was too afraid, too haunted by what the cost of that fulfillment might be.

Isabelle could only wonder now exactly what Quimby knew. Her father, she knew, trusted the man unequivocally. She could only assume that he understood the globe's possibilities.

However, there was nothing she could do about that now. She laid her head down, closed her eyes and prayed.

Quimby returned to Demetri's room and closed the door. The crystal was barely glowing at all now, no doubt due to the man's stern discipline and self-control. He returned the globe to the bag and its box and placed it back up on the shelf in the closet. Then he turned and went to the door. As he opened it, he turned and stared back toward the closet. For a moment that strict self-control and emotional mastery that separated a good servant from a great one faltered a bit. For a moment Quimby allowed his mind to drift from servitude to egotism. In that short time, he saw the faint glow from inside the closet swell just slightly at the base of the door.

Quickly he regained his composure and left the room making sure to lock the door securely behind him.

Chapter 10

11:45 pm, October 8, 1984

Vince Passetti pulled up at the curb and peered through the rain-splattered glass for the man he was to pick up. The entrance to the café he was looking at was dimly lit. It was a storefront-type restaurant on Chicago's west side that held several tables for its customers. In the doorway, standing underneath the awning, a darkly clad figure with a fedora bent low across his face raised his head. The man stood with his hands buried deep in his pockets and a cigarette dangling from the corner of his mouth. Recognizing his ride, the man flicked his cigarette down to the ground and moved across the pavement toward the passenger's side door.

A chill ran through Vince as he caught a passing glimpse of the cadaverous face. Mizetti had warned him about the man's features, but he found himself apprehensive at the thought of riding deep into the night and embarking upon burglary with such a menacing figure.

Vince Passetti had been a sneak thief his whole life and had also worked with Mizetti's gang on other jobs which ran from shaking down store owners, leaning on late debt payers, and rousting local thugs who tried to move in on his boss's territory. Competition always had to be kept at bay where drug markets, gambling games and prostitution rings existed. But Vince's attributes were not really on the muscle end of things. Although he had to bloody-up some goon occasionally, it really was not his cup of tea. He was a second-story man. That's where his talents lay. Actually roughing-up some loser and drawing blood made his skin crawl. He really didn't care for that end of the business. Some other things could make his skin crawl too and Haskim's ghoulish presence was one of them. It didn't ease his apprehension any that his instructions, should he succeed in his endeavor, were to deceive the stranger and not follow through on the supposed arrangements the man would be expecting.

The stench of cigarettes greeted Vince as the man seated himself in the passenger seat. For the first time he saw the man's features clearly in the dim glow of the streetlights. Vince found himself leaning back as if unconsciously trying to place more distance between him and that scarred mug.

"Hello, I'm Andre Haskim." Haskim held out his gnarled hand and Vince hesitated for a moment before shaking it.

"Yeah ... I'm ... Vince Passetti."

"Vince eh ... That's good. You've been briefed then I take it? On tonight I mean?"

Haskim had seen the hesitancy in Vince's eyes, one he had seen before many times and he did not wish to be bothered with it.

"Yeah I ... I was told the deal. Sure," Vince replied

Haskim's look altered, but it took Vince a moment to understand that the crinkled lines and irregular fissures on his face actually were meant to be a smile. Haskim held his grin for a moment before turning and securing his seat belt. Vince thought it a bit ironic that a man so marred would be concerned enough to belt himself in.

Haskim sat back in his seat and faced forward making an odd noise that Vince took as a clearing of his throat. It took a moment for Vince to gather his wits and realize he needed to drive the car now. He placed the vehicle in gear and pulled away from the curb.

"I was told you are very reliable, Mr Vince."

"Yeah reliable, that's me."

"I was told you are very accomplished in the ... shall we say ... art of burglary."

Vince grunted. "Huh ... I've never been accused of being an artist. Done a few jobs in my time though."

"Good," Haskim replied. "So ... I know I am not dealing with an amateur."

"Do I look like an amateur to you?" Vince asked sarcastically.

"No ... no. You appear to me to look like a thief."

Vince didn't like the way that came out.

Isabelle had been unable to sleep because of worry. Even after Quimby had sent her back to her room, she felt restless. She was still worried about Whisper and decided to sneak out and visit him in the barn.

Quietly, so as not to let Quimby hear, she made her way out the back door and went to the barn. Whisper heard her coming and his agitated state relaxed a bit. He simply would not stop stepping back and forth in his stall however. Isabelle spoke to him softly and patted his neck. The horse was still panicked and Isabelle had only limited success in breaking through that terror. Whisper could not reason out his injury.

Eventually Isabelle's presence calmed Whisper down. In his own way, the horse began to cry to Isabelle. There was no future, no past for Whisper, only the pain he felt and the confusion of his bandages. Whisper had not drunk or eaten much since the accident, but Isabelle convinced him now to drink some.

Maybe when the vet came the next day he would be able to provide Whisper with some type of sedative to ease his suffering.

In the meantime, Isabelle yearned for her late night ride. She made her way to Prado's stall and began saddling him up. Immediately he displayed his annoyance. He was crabby and tired and Isabelle understood that he was not interested in going for a jaunt, but the girl simply ignored his stammering and wagging of his head and tightened the straps below his girth.

She guided the horse out of the barn, mounted him and led him down the path toward the end of the property.

The night had begun to mist and the flicker of the windshield wiper kept time as Vince drove out onto the expressway to the west. As they drove through the night, Haskim made small talk with the driver. Vince sensed a subdued elation emanating from the man, a kind of bustling excitement almost the way a kid would react on his way to an amusement park. His actions indicated that he was certainly looking forward to something.

Vince tried to make sense of it. Mizetti had told him what it was the man was after, a crystal globe of some sort, supposedly as big as a cantaloupe. He had no interest in money, jewels, artwork or anything else of any consequence that a normal thief would concentrate on in busting into a well-to-do home in the far suburbs. What was confusing was Mizetti's response to it. From what he could gather, Haskim was paying Mizetti a hunk of change for providing him a reliable thief to do the job right. Haskim had insisted that he be allowed to come along to ensure that he received the goods. That was odd. You were paying big dough to have the job done, but there was always the chance of being caught. Why put yourself in harms way? Mizetti had told him that the globe was a sentimental item. That had to be bullshit. There were a lot of reasons why a person would want to commit burglary, but for an item of sentimental value?

Vince's mind wavered as Haskim went on about the design styles of today's cars. He remarked how he longed for the days when you could tell whether a car was a Buick, Chevy or Cadillac immediately. Not like now when all the cars held the same boxy, undistinguished lines.

Vince grunted in response and thought some more. From what he gathered from Mizetti, he was being paid more to circumvent the supposed plan and bring the globe back to Mizetti instead of giving it to Haskim. He wasn't sure how he was going to accomplish that deception. Mizetti had left that up to him. He didn't seem to care how Vince executed that objective. Vince had killed a man once and it had brought him a great deal of distress. The man had been a drug dealer who just wouldn't pay what he owed. Vince and another man had paid a visit to the man for the expressed purpose of trying to reason with him. They had approached the man in a parking lot and Vince immediately recognized the wide-eyed, drug-induced stare in the man's eyes but never expected him to pull out a gun and start blasting. Vince's cohort was shot in the chest before Vince brought the man down with his pistol.

Vince escaped the scene and did not necessarily blame himself for taking the chump out because he had little choice. However, the whole thing had left an uneasy feeling in his mind. He did not want to repeat that experience especially with such a cadaverous looking subject. If he did get his hands on the globe, his plan was simply to pull his gun, make the man get out of his car and drive off.

That would be easy enough to pull off, Vince reasoned.

What he didn't know was that Haskim was taking no chances on securing his prize. He had a gun too and he had analyzed the possibility of a double-cross carefully. Mizetti had seemed especially curious about the item Haskim was after, perhaps a bit too curious. He might just want to inspect the prize before allowing Haskim to have it. Of course, Haskim could not let that occur. The danger was far too great.

Haskim found Vince to be unusually edgy as he made small talk. Of course, not everyone could relax in Haskim's presence because of his deformity. Both the nature of their quest and Haskim's looks certainly could make anyone a bit nervous, but if Vince was truly a professional, he had most likely been in many untoward situations in the past. Haskim didn't know quite how to read the situation. Perhaps his uneasiness was unnecessary, but one could never be too careful.

Haskim relayed to Vince where he thought he might find the globe. Haskim had been to Demetri's house many times and had enough conversations through the years with him to know that he did not have a safe, but that he kept many of his valuables in the corner of his closet up on the shelf. He suspected that it had probably been stored there on that ominous night when Demetri had first introduced Haskim to the secret. He was hoping that Demetri had not changed his ways or his method of securing things since then.

Haskim had followed his instinct on digging up Sophie's grave. At the time, he hadn't known that the globe would be there. He had risked it because of something Demetri had once said to him when he visited him at the hospital during his recovery period. Haskim knew the possibility had been remote, but he would dig all the way to China if it meant getting his hands on that glass.

Now that that possibility had been eliminated, Haskim relied on the fact that by nature Demetri had a certain naïveté and was set in his ways. He felt that as long as Demetri's security measures through the years had not met with any breach, he just might be fool enough to assume they never would. It was very possible that the globe was not in Demetri's closet and that perhaps the man had actually hidden it somewhere where Haskim could never get to it. Haskim did not want to think about that possibility though because he could not face the idea of never getting his hands on it.

However, if indeed their burglary attempt failed tonight and he was left empty-handed, he knew what his next step would be, where Demetri's weakness laid. And he would not hesitate a moment in pursuing that option.

The drizzle had stopped by the time Vince pulled onto the road leading to the estate. They had entered an area where the homes were scattered haphazardly with property sites sometimes measuring several acres. They pulled onto the acreage from the back by accessing a side road that led between the estates. Off to the right along a row of tall trees, the outline of the Demetri's home sat in stillness. Further to the left a large barn stood off amongst a scattering of trees.

Vince dimmed the lights and eyeballed their situation. They were about two hundred yards from the house swallowed in the shadows of the trees around them. The property was not gated. It would just be a matter of walking up to the back of the house.

"I'm gonna hide the car back behind those trees and I'll walk up," Vince muttered. His persona seemed to intensify now that the game was afoot. A shallow ditch forced Vince to ease the vehicle slowly down the embankment and back up. He positioned the car so that it was hidden behind the trees but at an angle that would provide for a quick getaway if one was needed.

Vince reached in the back seat and grabbed hold of a black cap which covered the top of his head. He was now dressed totally in black with only his face exposed.

"You know what you're looking for right?" Haskim asked.

"Yeah a globe, crystal globe. Mizetti told me."

"It may be in a black sack inside a wooden box. I don't care about any other items. If you want to take something for yourself, fine. But bring me back the globe."

As they had gotten closer to the grounds, Haskim's mood had turned bullying and dictatorial. The intensity of the job and the nearness to his prize had sharpened his ambition, but Vince was not used to being talked at like a dog.

"Remember go for the globe first," Haskim directed. "If you want anything else, that's after. Do you understand?" Haskim grabbed Vince's arm as he began to exit the car. "The globe comes first." His tone was downright heavy-handed now.

Vince had enough. "Listen you freak. I'll do the job the way I see fit. It ain't you risking your ass on this deal. I take my orders from Mizetti and this job follows through the way he says it follows through. You got that?"

Haskim backed away into his seat. "Sure ... sure Vince. I understand."

Vince got out, leaned down and grabbed the crowbar he had behind his seat and gently closed the door without letting it slam. Haskim watched him move off toward the property.

Alarm rose in Andre Haskim. He didn't like the way Vince had said that business about following through the way Mizetti had told him.

Was there some altered plan going on here? Would Vince not turn over the globe if he got his hands on it? Maybe Mizetti's curiosity had gotten the best of him. Maybe he wanted to see first hand what this mysterious item was all about that Haskim was willing to pay so much for. Had he made a mistake in involving Mizetti?

He already knew that he did not have the amount of money he had promised Mizetti for the job. But he wasn't worried about that. If he got his hands on the globe, money would no longer be a problem, ever.

Haskim pulled out his gun and checked it once again. He stuffed it back in his pocket and waited nervously.

His mind was going a mile a minute. If that globe came out of that house, there was no way it was going anywhere without Haskim. Haskim clutched the gun again and practiced pulling it out swiftly and pointed it at the driver's window. If he needed to make a move on Vince, he wanted to practice getting the drop on him.

No way that globe was going anywhere without him.

Vince approached the back of the house by crossing an area beside the large barn. The grounds were quiet and still. Only a dim light from the kitchen area shone inside the house. The late hour made it impossible for Vince to be sure whether anyone was at home or not.

Vince reached the back door and checked it. Surprisingly it was unlocked. Quietly he opened it and stepped inside.

The furnace hushed air out from a vent near the entrance breaking the stillness. A nightlight burned above the stove casting the kitchen in a dim yellow light. Vince waited and listened to hear if his arrival had disturbed anyone. Through the far door that led into the dining room, the sound of a swaying pendulum ticking inside the case of a standing grandfather clock measured the night into seconds. The burglar moved quietly through the kitchen until he was able to gain sight of the winding staircase that led up to the second floor. Again he waited until he was sure he had not aroused anyone.

Vince took a moment to look around. From his vantage point he could see the dining room, upper stairwell and living room.

The thief tiptoed to the staircase and took the steps slowly until he wound his way up to the second floor. He listened for snoring but heard none. Was it possible he was lucky enough to be robbing an empty house? Vince was about to move when he thought he heard a sound, perhaps the faint creak of a floorboard. He listened for a moment more but hearing nothing made his way down the hall to where the door to the master bedroom lay. Haskim had provided him with an outlay of the house, so he knew which one it was.

He turned the knob. The door was locked. He wedged the crow bar in between the door and the frame. Slowly he wiggled it further so that he knew he had a good strong leverage point to spring the lock. He made sure his gun was handy. If someone was asleep, the noise just might awaken them. That was why he wanted to burst the lock with one swift forceful jolt.

Vince braced himself securely and then with all his might pulled back swiftly on the bar. The door exploded open in one shot. It sprung back against the wall jamb and slowly halted.

Quickly Vince scanned the room. There was no one there. He had gotten lucky. He closed the door behind him, turned on the light and began searching.

Isabelle had heard enough of Prado's complaining. They had gone through the woods down the paths in the forest, but Isabelle had not raced the animal. She began tromping along the tree line back to the grounds proper when she saw the car parked beneath the trees. A man was seated in the passenger seat. Prado ignored the whole thing prodding Isabelle to let loose so he could go back to the barn, but Isabelle pulled him up tight.

Now who was this? she wondered.

Quietly she dismounted and tied Prado to a tree. Then she snuck around back beneath a shroud of low branches so she could get a better view.

Suddenly the man opened the door of the car and stepped outside. He moved toward the front of the vehicle, leaned against it and lit up a cigarette.

In the glow of the flame Isabelle saw the disfigured face and the odd eye patch and nearly cried out. A wave of horror swept through her. She had never seen such a monster as this. Just the look of him made her squirm. The way he kept looking up at the house and pacing nervously made her all the more fearful.

What should she do? she wondered. *Should she wake Quimby?*

She could do that easily enough if she was in the house, but she would have to go past the car to get there. She did not want to be seen by the man.

Vince made his way quickly to the closet and opened the door. The shelves led back into the dim light where the sloping ceiling made it more and more difficult to see.

That was odd, Vince thought. In the corner there was a faint glow coming from the sides of a wooden box where the brass hinges secured the top. The box was in the farthest reaches of the closet and Vince had to pull aside many of the clothes that hung on hangars in his way. He moved aside several items as quietly as he could until he was finally able to reach the box. Cautiously he slid it out until he got a grip on it and pulled it down. He half-stumbled his way out of the closet and laid the box on the bed. As he reached to open the lid, the light which had been glistening from inside seemed to go out.

A strange feeling came over Vince. Something was odd about this whole scene and a chill crawled up his spine. A noise broke the stillness. Did he hear someone in the hall? The sound had been so faint that he couldn't be sure. His attention returned to the box and he gently opened the lid. Inside was something round contained in a black velvet bag. Vince lifted it out and pulled open the drawstrings. It was the globe. He had found it just like that.

This may be my lucky day, Vince thought.

He returned the globe to the box and closed the top. He tucked the prize under his arm and made his way to the door. He paused for a moment and hearing no sound walked out into the hallway.

"Who are you?" a voice said from behind him.

Vince turned around. Standing in the hallway was a tall figure in a maroon bathrobe. Fortunately for Vince his hands were empty.

Vince made a dash for the stairs and Quimby quickly intercepted him. In the circular stairway Quimby grabbed at his shoulder as the stairs turned below him, but he was unable to stop him. At the base of the stairs Vince tried to transfer the box to his other arm and dropped it to the floor. Hurriedly he picked it up, but the delay allowed Quimby to reach him. The huge butler grabbed him around the waist and threw him up against the foyer wall. A porcelain statue was knocked to the ground and splintered in a thousand pieces. Quimby bent down to gather up the box. But when he looked back up, it was just in time to see the intruder's boot coming for his head. The blow landed beneath Quimby's jaw and sent him reeling.

Vince scooped up the box and ran for the door. He made his way outside and crossed the grounds toward the car. Haskim saw him coming clutching the box in his hands.

"Did you get it! Did you get it!"

Vince slowed as he reached the car gasping for breath.

"I think so. Is this it?" Vince handed the box to Haskim and bent over his knees to try and catch his breath. "I had to take on some guy. I think I knocked him cold with a good kick though."

Haskim paid no attention. He placed the box on the ground and quickly opened it. He scooped up the bag and looked inside. It was the globe, the center faintly showing a yellow spark of light.

"Yes this is it. This is it! I must thank you, Vince, on a job well done." Haskim was near delirious with excitement.

Vince had regained some of his composure. "Don't get too excited pal. The globe goes back to Mizetti first."

"But ... but that is not our arrangement. The globe is my property. I have a deal with Mizetti. Cash basis. He does not need the globe." Haskim had a worried look on his face. He sharpened up. "The globe is mine," he said sternly.

"Don't try to get cute with me. I take my orders from Mizetti, not you."

"But what does he want with this? He knows nothing of it. It is nothing to him."

"Look, I don't know shit, except I am to bring him the goods. Whatever you got to work out with him, you work out with him."

Haskim took a step back. Panic was starting to rear its ugly head.

Always complications, always complications, he thought.

"Come on, let's go," Vince said.

Haskim's brain spun.

What to do? It was very possible that Mizetti would not understand the globe and simply hand it over as agreed.

But Haskim had led him on to believe the globe had some very special importance.

That was foolish, Haskim thought. *Why had he done that? Mizetti might not hand over the globe unless he was given a satisfactory answer and the ball being an old family heirloom or some sentimental item from Haskim's past wasn't going to cut it. That kind of an explanation would never fly.*

Could he risk placing the globe in someone else's hands, someone as powerful as Mizetti?

No, he could not. If Mizetti were ever to discover the significance of it, there would be no getting it back, ever.

But if he didn't play ball with Mizetti, what would happen then? Mizetti might use all at his disposal to hunt him down. With his features, that might be accomplished quickly.

However, with the globe, his features would soon be much more appealing.

What to do?

If he was going to act it had to be now. But was he to kill Vince?

Vince noticed the hesitancy in Haskim's manner.

"Let's go friend. In the car."

Isabelle had crept closer to the vehicle while Haskim waited for Vince. When the man returned, she was able to overhear their discussion. She saw Haskim bend down and pull the globe from the bag. A chill ran through her. They had stolen the globe! But she needed it. She needed it to make sure her father regained his health. She couldn't allow them to run off with it.

But what could she do?

Quimby pulled himself up from the foyer floor as blood dripped from his mouth. Struggling to gain his wits, he went to the gun cabinet and pulled out a shotgun. It took a moment for him to load it. Then he made his way outside to try and find the burglar.

Haskim took a step back.

Vince sensed trouble and moved toward him. As he did, Haskim made a move for his gun but before he could get it out Vince was on him. The box went tumbling to the ground. The two men began wrestling around, turning one around the other as they each tried to gain the advantage. Isabelle saw her chance. She ran from out of the thicket where she was hiding and scooped up the box. Vince saw her first and let go his grip on Haskim so he could get up and stop the girl. His arm free, Haskim raised the gun and shot Vince point blank in the gut. Unfortunately for Haskim Vince fell directly on top of him and it took him a moment to free himself from the entanglement. The shot had alerted Blackie and now he came running across the grounds toward Haskim from the barn where he had been sleeping.

Isabelle turned and ran as fast as she could into the woods. Haskim rolled Vince off him and got to his feet. Suddenly he heard yelling from behind him.

"Hey stop!"

Quimby was running toward the vehicle with a shotgun in his hands. Suddenly the butler became woozy and he had to stop. He had not yet fully recovered from the blow he had taken to the head and the added effort of running with the gun had not helped. He stopped for a moment to catch his breath. He looked back up in time to see the man rise up and look to the woods. Quimby raised the gun and fired one barrel, but he was too far away for the shotgun to have any effect.

"Son of a bitch," Haskim swore. He had seen the girl run off with the globe, but what could he do. "Damn it," he muttered.

Quimby was moving again and getting closer. Haskim had no choice. He jumped into the car and peeled around in a circle making for the way out. Quimby had one more opportunity as the car spun around and the driver's side window came into view. He immediately recognized Haskim. The shock of seeing him caused Quimby to hesitate. As the car finished its spin,

Quimby almost let go with the shotgun again, but the fact that he knew the man made him waver. The car weaved back and forth several times before Haskim, uninjured in the entire incident, regained control.

Isabelle had heard the shotgun blast, stopped running and looked back. Through the trees she could see the vehicle spinning around and making its way off the property. She wondered if Quimby had seen her before the woods had hidden her from sight. After the car pulled away, Quimby turned and began moving quickly back toward the house, calling for the dog to follow him.

For the moment she was safe. She waited until Quimby had returned to the house before she mounted Prado and went the long way around to get back to the barn. She knew Quimby would be looking for her to make sure she had not been injured and she had to make sure he did not know she had the globe. At the barn she quickly dismounted, took the saddle off Prado and returned him to his stall. She ran back to her shed and wrapped the box in a blanket before shoving it under her bed. Just as she finished she heard the shuffling of feet coming from the house. Quimby entered the barn and quickly found Isabelle. He was holding a towel up to his face and Isabelle could see it was spotted with blood.

He quickly grabbed Isabelle by the hand and led her back to the house. He brought her upstairs and took her up to her bedroom. Isabelle could tell he was angry. The butler looked at her and wagged his finger. Through the years that communication was obvious. She was to stay in her room.

When he left, Isabelle heard sirens in the distance. A short time later the driveway was lit up with red and blue lights spinning wildly as police cars haphazardly parked this way and that on the grounds. Isabelle leaned back in her bed and watched the spinning lights weave in circles on the ceiling in her room. Haskim's face kept coming back to her in her thoughts. She had never seen such a person in her life. *What was he, some sort of monster?*

But now the monster knew she had the globe. This monster was a killer too. She had seen him shoot the other man down. Fear began to course through her.

Now he might be after her. The monster might be after her. Did he know who she was? Isabelle drew the covers up over her head. She was scared to death. Never before had she felt such anxiety. So many different terrifying things were going on all at one time: her father, Whisper's injury, the sight of that man being shot right in front of her, and now some killer might be after her.

Isabelle's hands shook as she held her blanket.

Maybe she just needed to stay put for right now. She would be safe in the house with the police there.

But she couldn't wait too long to get back to the globe. Her father might be dying. She had to get back to the globe.

Isabelle rose and went to the window. Two more police cars had arrived and were now parked in the circular drive, their lights flashing. They were talking to Quimby near the front door before they actually came into the house. Victor had joined them now.

Toward the back of the property an ambulance had arrived and there was a bustle of activity where the man had been shot. A police car was there too

Isabelle could hear voices downstairs now.

The lights from the police cars and the ambulance swirled around her ceiling. Isabelle returned to bed. For now she had to wait. When she closed her eyes, all she saw was the disfigured face of the killer. It was obvious from what she had witnessed that the monster knew the power the globe had.

What did he want with it? How did he know about it?

Whatever happened now, she knew she must do whatever she could to keep the globe from him. But he knew she had it and Isabelle knew deep in her heart that he would never stop looking for her until he had it.

Chapter 11

France 1939 - 1940

Spring 1939 brought the rumor of war to Europe. For twenty-six year old Demetri Davos, the years had been flying past. Once his father died, he lived in the cottage in the woods working in town, growing vegetables on his land and basically trying to find a way to get by. The depression in America had spawned equally troubling times throughout Europe. Through those desperate years, the young man's dreams began to blossom even as he slaved away to simply survive.

Many times in weakness and despair he had thought to use the globe to alleviate some of his torment, but he had been lured twice in the past and both times it had resulted in death and dishonor. He dared not tempt fate again although many times the enticement was almost too much to bear. To keep himself from falling prey to temptation, he buried the globe in the ground above his father's grave. His father's body served as a constant reminder to the inherent peril that could come from a moment's weakness. Anytime he found himself in danger of giving in, the thought of digging at his father's grave to retrieve the orb brought him up short.

Finally Demetri came to an age where the small farm and the tiny town could no longer contain his imaginations and ambitions. The boy was not only a quick learner, agile and strong, but he possessed the spirit of adventure.

When a local land developer offered to buy the property from Demetri, he quickly obliged. The money he received was sufficient to allow him to make his way to Saint-Nazaire, a coastal town on the western edge of France where his intention was to seek passage on a steamer headed for either England or America. Saint-Nazaire, based on its location on the right bank of the Loire River estuary, had a long tradition of fishing and shipbuilding. The town had become the base for passenger steamship travel. Although the depression had hurt the economy of shipbuilding in the town, the French government commissioned the ship builders of Saint-Nazaire to erect a dry dock sufficient to construct large passenger ships. Demetri felt that making his way to the port town would be the best way to ensure that he could somehow book passage on a steamer.

However, he could not have picked a worse time to try and leave France on a ship. Jews from all across Europe were departing in droves to reach the new world. With the panic in the air, the steamships were able to demand a high price for passage even in third class or steerage. For many of the Jews, price was not an object. Those with means recognized the danger in not grabbing what opportunity they could to leave and were more than happy to pay the fee.

Demetri simply did not have enough money to pay his way. He had gone through most of the meager funds he had obtained from the sale of the farm. For a while he took a room in a cheap hotel and spent his days looking for work with the hope that somehow time, finances and opportunity would combine to offer him the chance to sail away.

Demetri began to frequent a café along the waterfront where sailors and stewards off their ships for brief respites drank wine, smoked cigarettes and discussed the topics of the day. Demetri's English, as well as his French, were adequate at best. Many times he conversed with the men who worked on the ships to try and figure an angle how he might find employment on one of the vessels. Times being what they were, jobs on the ships were hard to come by. However, just maintaining a presence there helped him improve his skills in English and French and kept him abreast of the local events and news of the day.

One day while he was seated outside, the owner came bustling out of the door pulling one of his waiters by the scruff of the neck. He threw him down on the pavement and gave him a harmless boot to the backside intended not to hurt the fellow so much as to reiterate to him that his services were no longer required. From the words spoken, it seemed the owner had caught the man with his hand in the till and had now summarily dismissed him. The proprietor was a huge barrel-chested man by the name of Claude Dupier. The waiter rose to his feet, whipped his apron off and flung it at Claude mumbling in French what he thought of his former employer. When Claude took two more steps toward the man however, he quickly darted away sniveling and grumbling his discontent.

Claude turned about and stared at the patrons who had witnessed the little show. He had a smug grin on his face as if to say "no one messes with Claude". Once the air of boastfulness ran its course, his features quieted and a look of slight puzzlement replaced it. Now that he had dismissed his waiter, he needed a replacement. He noticed Demetri sitting at one of the tables nursing a glass of cheap wine. Demetri had been a patron at Claude's establishment for several months and had once asked him for a job. Times being what they were, he was unable to oblige the young man. However, an inherent trust that develops between an owner and a loyal, repeating customer had developed between the two and now Claude mulled over the prospect of trying Demetri out. The language barrier he thought might be a problem, but most of the work was obvious in nature: waiting on customers, cleaning tables, washing dishes. The trust he felt in his short experience with the lad was much more valuable to him than the slight added time communication might require.

Claude motioned for Demetri who immediately grasped the situation. The two shook hands and Claude led him back behind the counter where he gave him an apron. It was the busy part of the afternoon, but Demetri jumped right into his new role. Having seen how the café operated through the weeks he had been there, he knew what jobs needed doing. After having had his bad experience with the former waiter, Claude would not let Demetri handle any of the payment of bills or use of the register but after a few days, having witnessed the boy's industriousness, he felt he could trust him and let him handle the register also.

During some of his breaks or days off, Demetri would gaze out upon the harbor at the huge ships and wonder how he could rustle up enough money for even a third class ticket. Things were becoming even tighter and more expensive as the months went by as far as passage was concerned. Demetri was saving every nickel he could, determined to make his way on board. He figured with a little luck, he would have enough money by October to pay his way.

Then Europe exploded. The Germans invaded Poland and everything changed. Even the French themselves became fearful. Previously most of the tickets were being bought up by distrustful French Jews who fearing their fortunes would soon be confiscated were panicked into paying any price necessary to get to America or England. But now refugees from all over Europe were in a panic. Gypsies, Jews, teachers, intellectuals, members of high society, and even commoners who had sufficient funds were now all vying for a way out.

Demetri's spirits fell. Just when it looked like he might make it out, passage on one the boats seemed farther away then ever. Demetri was eager, ambitious, and driven. He felt if he could just get to America or England, there was no limit to what he could achieve. He was afraid of nothing. His attributes included honesty, diligence, ambition and a willingness to work hard to achieve his goals. He just needed that one break now to get him across the sea.

Then who knew what great future he could devise for himself.

One other thing nagged at him that he was hesitant to let anyone learn. On his mother's side, he was half-Jewish. The rumors coming out of Eastern Europe were frightening. Jews in Germany and the newly conquered lands of Austria and Poland were supposedly being rounded up. A general feeling of panic permeated west from the battlefields in the east.

As the months went by, Demetri began a friendship with Antoine Edgard, one of the other waiters at Claude's Café. Like himself, Antoine was half-Jewish and the events in the east were disconcerting to him also. Demetri's English was still poor, but Antoine spoke not only Romanian but French and English as well. He was a scholarly type who came from a reputable family whose finances had been wiped out during the depression. Like Demetri he yearned to escape across the sea, but like Demetri he did not have the funds to accomplish it.

On May 10, 1940, the Germans invaded France, as well as Holland, Belgium and Luxemburg. The hurried pace of the harbor turned from concern to outright terror. Passage on a steamer was now so expensive that the idea began to fizzle away in Demetri's mind. Not only did the cost of passage rise astronomically, but all the staples of everyday life became exorbitant in price: bread, meat, vegetables, and clothes. A depression began to drag him down. He maintained his job at the café, but the optimism and excitement he felt toward the future turned to discouragement and dismay. On some nights with his friend Antoine, their pessimism caused them to drink themselves into a stupor. With each passing day news from the east became more and more alarming.

Although over three hundred thousand British and French troops had been evacuated by sea from Dunkirk by the first week in June, many more thousands were left behind in France with little hope of rescue. Many of those flocked to St-Nazaire desperately looking for a way out. As the Germans began pushing the French lines west across the country, it was soon clear that France would not hold.

One night half drunk, depressed and fearful, Demetri went to his closet and took down from the top shelf a wooden box wrapped in a blanket. He pulled the blanket away, opened the box and removed the black sack containing the globe. When he had sold his property he had intended to leave the globe where it was, buried with his father, but the temptation had been too much. Who knew what dangers lay ahead for him? Beneath his honorable qualities and the resolve he had held to ever since the tragic events surrounding Estrella, stood a nervous, lonely boy who faced an uncertain future. He had no one to lean on, no family to support him, no real mentor to guide his way. His finances were slim.

Although he took the globe with him, he vowed he would never use it again. However, another voice whispered in his head and although he would not admit it to himself, it was there nonetheless. And that was ambition. He knew what the globe could achieve for him and he was simply not strong enough to turn his back on the possibilities it provided.

Demetri stared at the glass. It was almost dark now except for the constant yellow glow that came from its center. Demetri knew how the globe worked. It would not simply answer any wish. The wish had to have weight behind it, an unyielding desire. Demetri simply was not panicked enough yet to achieve the level of emotion necessary. Also the fear of what such a wish would cost discouraged him.

He put the globe back in its bag, returned it to the closet, went back to his bed and worried himself to sleep.

British troops flooded into town. Operation Aerial, the code name given for the evacuation of British and Allied forces from France, had begun. From every available port in western France, British troops were being evacuated back to England. At this point panic reigned. Antoine and Demetri went to the British officials trying to plead their way onto any ship that would take them out of Saint-Nazaire. But it was no use. Every available spot on any ship was taken by fleeing British troops or civilians in a much better position to obtain passage than two able-bodied, young men of little means.

The crescendo of fear reached an apex on the night of June sixteenth. Antoine and Demetri turned, in their fear and apprehension, to the bottle. In Demetri's room they discussed their options which were few and none. Demetri and Antoine had become fast friends and both feared that when the Nazis finally arrived in Saint-Nazaire, they might never see each other again. Terrible rumors floated about as to what the Nazis were doing to civilians, especially Jews. In the distance flashes of light and the rumble of artillery fire served to fuel the panic even further.

Antoine had fallen asleep on the floor with an empty wine bottle still gripped in his hand. Demetri weighed his options. His drunken state heightened his urge to turn to the one source of escape that would no doubt not fail him. He tried to reason through the horror that had resulted from the two times he had used the globe.

Rationalization began to slip into his thinking.

His first wish had been that somehow he could escape the clutches of his father's mistreatment. But had he actually wished him dead or that any other innocents would be harmed? That certainly was not what he had desired. He had only wanted to be free of the violent nature that accursed him at every turn. Was that so wrong? At that point he had known nothing of the globe's power. The urge had simply become overwhelming to him when he gazed into the ball and it became brilliantly illuminated before him. Surely he could not be held guilty for the actions of his father. The drink had done it to him. The alcohol had finally driven his terrible rage to a point of excess that there was no going back.

Perhaps his wish with the globe had not even been a factor in what had occurred. It was very possible his father may have lost control of his senses regardless of any perceived wish that Demetri had made. His father's behavior at the time had been inconsistent, volatile and erratic. Part of Demetri's fear had been due to his realization that his father was not in full possession of his faculties. His wish had been foisted as much on fear for his own safety as anything else. Wasn't a boy owed the opportunity to grow and flourish without the whip of injustice held above him?

But what of Estrella? He had wanted her fancy to fall upon him and it most certainly had immediately after he had made his wish. Again he had not directed any ill will toward the girl. In fact, he wanted nothing more than to care for her, marry her, love her, and be a source of pride for her. Unfortunately, and he saw the truth of it now, at fifteen the desires of boys and girls were as fickle as the wind, one day here and the next day gone. It could have certainly been possible that Estrella had fallen in love with him regardless of any supposed power of the globe. After all, he was not a bad looking boy. Other girls he knew, but did not care for, had found him attractive. And when his desire for her had waned, he had tried his best to comfort her and let her down gently, although he was guilty of propagating stories about their short-lived affair. He had to admit the suicide of a young girl dashed by unrequited love was certainly not a common thing. However, it was not unheard of either.

Demetri took another swig from his wine bottle and stared out the window. It was the middle of the night and there was very little activity on the streets. However, occasionally a scream or yell bellowed out from a nearby alleyway or street. A sense of dread permeated the stillness. The air was almost thick with apprehension.

Down the street a groups of soldiers, half-drunk, singing, went trudging off toward the harbor. Here and there a person went scurrying by. It was dangerous out there tonight. Law and order were certainly in disarray. Fear and panic could turn even a noble soul to do something crazy or insane. In the distance a girl's scream caught his attention. A rabble of shouts and incoherent yells broke the silence and a flurry of activity from the street beyond crackled and then fell away.

An ominous hum of panic seemed to drift down the hallways and lanes and seep out of the shuttered windows like the tentacles of some hideous entity.

Demetri's mind refocused on his plight and the globe. But what of what he wanted now? He saw that although he had not intentionally wished ill will against anyone, the results had been horrible. However, there was one difference between what he had wished for before and what he considered now. His previous two wishes were selfish. They concerned himself, his needs, and his desires. His wishes in no way truly were meant to benefit anyone but himself. Altruism had surely not factored into the equation. But now, wanting to find a way to escape from the clutches of the Nazis and saving his friend at the same time could certainly not be considered egotistical. After all, if he did not make the wish, it was a very real possibility that Antoine and he would be separated forever and that their Jewish heritage would likely bring them nothing but suffering and perhaps death.

Demetri went to the closet and pulled down the box. His mind tensed with both fear for his safety and fear for what he was now considering. His rationalizations had gotten the better of him. This was a matter of life and death for himself. People were dying all over Eastern Europe with the approach of the Nazis and soon that death and destruction would be at their very door. What options did he have? Didn't he have the right to try and protect himself and his friend? He would be a fool to let an opportunity to escape slip through his fingers because of a fear of repercussion that may not even be valid. What if he was wrong about this idea that any wish he made would be paid for by someone else?

And what if it did? There was a war on. It was a crazy world. It was every man for himself at this point. Even now the British soldiers planned their desertion of the good residents of the town.

They were saving their hides, why shouldn't he save his?

Demetri pulled the globe out of the bag. It was glowing now, the light rising and sparking in its center like shots of lightening. Demetri's mind swirled, but he had gone beyond the hope of turning back. His emotions were sharp now, his desire pointed and crisp. He began to give voice to his wish in a soft whisper as the ball now sparked as if it were on fire. He was pushed over the edge of indecision by justifying to himself that he was doing this for the good of Antoine, but he knew deep down it was a lie. This, like the other wishes he had made, was self-serving and selfish, fueled by fear, terror and his self-preservation alone.

He gave up all resistance and softly spoke his plea. As he made his wish, his mind was centered not on his friend, Antoine, but only on himself. He wanted them both to be saved, but the true depth of his emotion was on himself. His thoughts focused on his fear and need now and no one else's. The ball glowed even brighter. The aspiration he mouthed crystallized until he saw only himself, clear and away, safe from harm. The globe heightened in intensity, becoming so brilliant Demetri had to turn his head. The crescendo reached its zenith and then slowly faded away until all that was left was the constant yellow flicker in its center.

Antoine suddenly began to stir. Demetri quickly replaced the globe in its bag and back in its box. By the time he had shoved it under the bed, Antoine was wakening.

Demetri sat on the bed and tried to regain his composure.

Antoine rose and told Demetri he was going home. He was drunk, slurring his words and seemed especially agitated. Demetri walked him down the stairs and out the door.

Antoine turned to Demetri and laid his hand on his shoulder.

"What will we do now, my friend?" he asked.

"I don't know," Demetri responded. "Somehow we will find a way out. I promise you."

Antoine shook his head and stared up the street. Suddenly from the doorway to a tavern down the way, a British sailor came stumbling out onto the sidewalk. From inside the tavern a burst of laughter echoed out into the street while the door slowly closed. The sailor collapsed in a heap before sitting back on his hunches and spitting up. He mumbled something to himself before he tried to rise to his feet. Halfway up he fell back down and stared at the sidewalk below him. Finally he got up and began shuffling up the street toward Antoine and Demetri.

As he approached them, he staggered and then lost his balance and fell against the side of the building before plopping down to the walk. His head bumped against the bricks with an awful thump that sounded as if someone had dropped a melon. The sailor moaned and lay motionless.

"Goodness," Antoine muttered as they both went to the man. His head was bleeding from a nasty gash along his right temple.

"Let's get him upstairs," Demetri said. "We'll need to tend to this wound."

The boys lifted the sailor up between them and slowly plodded their way up the steps. Blood dripped now from his ear and the man appeared to be unconscious.

The boys managed to get him up the stairs and down on the bed. They put towels beneath his head to soak up the blood and washed the wound clean. Demetri had some bandages and he used them to wrap the man's head slowing the bleeding. Nevertheless they both realized the man's injury was indeed serious.

"We need to get a doctor," Antoine said.

"Where would we find one now?

"I don't know, but the alcohol makes the bleeding worse. What should we do?"

Demetri thought for a moment. The whole situation made him suspicious. He made his wish and suddenly now this sailor flops down on their doorstep. Were they linked? He could not fathom, however, what advantage the situation held for them.

The man groaned and his eyes fluttered open. His head drooped once again.

"I will go and try to find someone to help," Antoine said. "You can stay here and tend to him."

Immediately a sense of dread rose in Demetri. To venture out on this night, no matter how justifiable or righteous the intent, could easily turn disastrous. Antoine only lived two blocks from Demetri and for him to make it home would have been easy enough, but to walk the streets with an unsure destination seeking help from those who perhaps could not be trusted was an entirely different matter.

There was no denying, however, that there really was no other option. Although dangerous, the plan was a logical one. Antoine went off to find help while Demetri returned to his patient. There was really nothing much else he could do for the man other than to monitor his condition and wait for help. Demetri went to the window and watched Antoine disappear around the corner. He was most likely heading to the harbor where he could find other sailors and perhaps a doctor.

Demetri tried to make the man more comfortable by removing his uniform and covering him with a blanket, before he sat himself down in a chair. It was the first time he had really had a moment to think about what he had done. Fear of the possible consequence of his wish mingled now with the general alarm he felt over his entire predicament. He stared over at the sailor once again.

What was happening here? he thought. *How was he to react to things now? What was he to watch out for? Was this sailor somehow a part of his solution?*

The patient began to moan again. He mumbled incoherently. Then his head fell back and he was still.

Demetri waited a few minutes for him to stir again, but the sailor lay motionless. Demetri realized that the sailor's breathing had stopped. A cold, clamminess seemed to fall across the room like the shadow of a ghost. Demetri went and checked on the man. There was no response. The face lay back on the towels, the mouth agape, the eyes opened wide in an unfocused glare.

Demetri backed up stunned. The sailor was dead.

The man's injury was severe. That was true, but Demetri never expected it to be fatal.

His thoughts began to spin. *Had this been part and parcel of the wish he had cast upon the globe? Why? What purpose did it serve?*

If anything this unfortunate turn of events complicated any chance of their being able to leave town. When the authorities came, there would be questions to answer. The shock of the man's demise came to him and he held his hands to his face as if to muffle his distress.

Demetri went to the window and looked toward the harbor, but there was no sign yet of Antoine. His emotions calmed a bit as he realized that this simply had been an unlucky happenstance. When Antoine brought a British doctor or officer of some kind, they would simply have to explain what had happened. There was no one to blame. The British would gather up their sailor and dispose of him in whatever way seemed most expeditious in the crazy rush that certainly would follow the next day. This poor sailor would not be taking his spot on whatever transport was set to deliver him back to England.

Then it struck Demetri. He paused for a moment to think it through.

Of course, it was so simple! But what of Antoine? What would happen to him?

Demetri rushed to the window and looked out. There still was no sign of his friend.

Would the course of action he had laid out leave Antoine in the lurch? He didn't believe so. Why should it?

When Antoine returned with some soldier or doctor or whomever, he would wonder what had become of Demetri, but it would not alter the story he would tell. The trail of blood up the stairs certainly would bear witness to his tale. Perhaps it may even become obvious to Antoine what Demetri was planning. Demetri could wait for Antoine at his own apartment. Once this nasty business was done, he would most certainly return there.

Demetri looked again out the window. Now he could see two blocks off three men approaching. As they passed the streetlight, he recognized the coat Antoine had been wearing. There was no time to lose.

Quickly he gobbled up all the things he would need, threw them in a sack and went down the back stairs out to the alley.

Demetri walked to Antoine's apartment. Since he lived in a basement flat, Demetri checked all the low windows and luckily found one that was opened. Once he was in, he looked through the things he had brought with him. He had thrown everything he needed into a big gunny sack and lugged it through the streets over his shoulder. The bag contained the globe, all of the sailor's clothes and personal identification, all the money Demetri had in the world, and some of his own personal items. His escape through the alley had not been a moment too soon. The sound of boots tramping up the front stairs could be heard as Demetri scuttled down the back.

Now he stared down at the contents of his gunny sack. There was a splotch of blood along the back of the sailor's blue uniform, but amazingly none had gotten on the white front blouse. Upon trying the uniform on, Demetri found the bell bottom pants to be a bit too long, but the waist size was nearly perfect. Washing the top helped to remove most of the blood stain and the dark blue color disguised the rest of stain for the most part. The sailor had his identification papers in a black wallet. His name was Robert Blairman and although the face in the picture was much different than Demetri's, he hoped his disguise would still hold. From the papers in Blairman's possession, Demetri was able to ascertain that the sailor was due to report to the harbor in the morning to the HMS Highlander and ship out by the afternoon.

If he was lucky, with the amount of panic, confusion and disarray that no doubt the harbor would be in the following day, it should not be too hard to make his way aboard.

But what of Antoine? How would he be able to make his escape? They would have to figure that out the next day. When Antoine arrived, which Demetri hoped would be shortly, they could figure it out.

Demetri leaned back on Antoine's couch. It was late and the entire night's events had brought him near exhaustion.

Antoine would be here shortly, he thought. *Then together they could figure a plan.*

Demetri closed his eyes.

When Demetri awoke, he was startled to find the sun up and the streets bustling with activity. Antoine had not yet returned. Where could he be? The time was after nine. Demetri could wait no longer if he was to attempt his escape through the disguise of Blairman. Quickly he washed up, dressed himself in Blairman's uniform, loaded his gear and a change of clothes into his gunny sack and left for the harbor.

The streets were abuzz. Civilians and soldiers dashed about. Demetri walked the two blocks back to his apartment in an attempt to try and find out what had happened to Antoine. There was no one there. Cautiously he walked up the stairs, but all was quiet. His room was empty. Blairman's body had been removed. It was curious, but Demetri had no time to ponder it any further.

He returned to the street and headed for the port. When he finally reached the harbor there was almost an uncontrollable panic in the mass of people that crowded the river port. It took nearly half an hour for Demetri to make it to the loading dock of the Highlander. The ship was a destroyer and Demetri could tell the ship was being used to ferry troops from the harbor.

Demetri paused for a moment and watched the proceedings. The guards were having so much trouble with the crowd that any sailor who approached was not checked for papers or asked any questions. They were simply allowed to pass through the check point while the guards were left to try to control the unruly masses left on the pier. It was a golden opportunity for Demetri. He pushed forward. When he finally reached the front, the guard simply took one look at him and let him pass. Demetri walked up the gangplank and tried to figure his next move. Now that he was aboard, he was concerned that his limited English would immediately arouse suspicion. He searched out a spot where he could change back into his civilian clothes. He went below and found an empty washroom where he quickly made the switch before returning to the deck.

The decks were crowded with soldiers and lucky civilians who had somehow made their way aboard. Demetri wanted to find a place where he could simply sit and avoid anyone else. He looked around and noticed a ladder that led up to a gangplank that was closed off. At the top of the ladder, there was room for one person to sit. No one would come up any farther. He could be isolated and still have a good view of the harbor.

Time drifted by slowly and the ship's decks filled with more and more sailors. All the space on the outside of the ship was filled with people. Demetri could only imagine how many were crowded down below. The ship was a madhouse of humanity. Most of those on board were British sailors. Of the civilians who had managed to find passage, many were women dragging crying children along with them.

Demetri's thoughts went to Antoine. *Why had he not returned to his apartment last night? Most likely, he had been tied up with the French and British authorities investigating Blairman's demise.*

Guilt began to wind its way through Demetri's head. It appeared his wish was being granted, but Antoine may not have been part of the deal.

But what could he do?

The entire evacuation effort was mass hysteria. Rules were breaking down. It was quickly becoming every man for himself. It was hard to fathom the level of distress running rampant amongst the ordinary citizenry. Here were hard working people going through their daily lives trying to support their families, struggling to stay above the tide and now it was all for naught. A misguided, vengeful dictator and his marauding minions stomped forward delivering havoc, panic and misery upon all of Europe. Who knew where this all would end up. Who knew how many would die.

The guards at the gangplank now began clearing the area. People started screaming and shoving to try to board at the last moment, but the authorities would not allow it. The ship was finally going to depart. Every aisle, passageway, platform and cabin was filled to bursting with soldiers. Bodies occupied every available space. The ship could hold no more. Out in the deeper part of the harbor the HMT Lancastria lay anchored. The Lancastria was a former Cunard cruise liner now converted into a five-decked troopship. Its draft would have been too deep to come to the dock. It sat waiting in the harbor being loaded to overflowing with as many soldiers and civilian escapees as it could hold.

As the ship began to pull away from the dock, Demetri could not help but look upon those still left behind. Would there be other ships available to ferry these people out? Small fishing boats were crowding the harbor making passage away from the dock slow and methodical.

Suddenly Demetri saw Antoine. He was standing amongst a group of French gendarmes outside of a shop along the waterfront. The authorities were discussing something while Antoine simply stood there with his head down. As the ship pulled out further, one of the officers grabbed Antoine by the arm and started leading him along. Demetri saw his friend's hands shackled together in front of him. The group began moving off down the lane before turning a corner.

There it was. Somehow the authorities held Antoine to blame for what had happened to Blairman. It was the only explanation that made any sense. Demetri looked again and saw one fleeting last glimpse of his friend as the group disappeared among the masses. In his heart Demetri knew that he would never see him again. He was most certainly lost to the madness. Sadly he realized that most likely he would never even know whatever became of him. Demetri sat stunned staring across at the throngs of people on the dock. Various thoughts came to him, a mingling of different emotions: thankfulness for his escape, guilt for what his responsibility might be for Blairman and Antoine, and fearfulness for the uncertain future that most certainly lay ahead.

Air-raid sirens in the port city began to go off. The level of noise and panic in the harbor rose. Voices cascaded through the air and people began pointing up into the sky. In the distance came the rumble of engines. Demetri looked up to the east and saw German planes advancing on the harbor. Several zoomed directly over his head and a sudden explosion ripped through the end of the dock. Several bombs landed in the water amidst the boats sending huge plumes of water cascading into the air.

The planes proceeded past the harbor and began diving on the Lancastria. With no opposition against them, the bombers were free to line up their target calmly and deliberately. As Demetri's ship made its way toward the liner a huge explosion ripped through Lancastria's main deck followed almost immediately by another. The German planes basically ignored the port itself and concentrated its efforts on the troopship.

Within minutes the ship was listing terribly while the barrage only increased in intensity. Demetri had seen before the attack that the Lancastria was loaded to overflowing with soldiers and refugees. It was obvious that hundreds had lost their lives immediately in the blasts. Soldiers on the upper decks opened fire at the attackers, but it soon became apparent that the Lancastria was doomed.

The liner began to turn in the water now lying on her starboard side. Hundreds of troops stood on the steel plates of the Lancastria as she began to slide beneath the gentle swell. As the German bombers strafed men in the water and on the turning hull, a plume of fire encircled the vessel making it almost impossible for those who could attempt to jump off the sinking vessel to avoid being incinerated in the flames.

As the vessel lay listless and turned in the water, the Germans continued to attack, dropping incendiaries into the oily sea and machine gunning the thrashing, struggling throng. Demetri's vessel soon became a makeshift rescue ship trying to pick up survivors floundering in the water, but already its decks were packed to overflowing. Demetri had never witnessed anything so terrible in his life. That scene would forever haunt his nightmares: the sinking vessel, the screaming voices, the stench of burning flesh, the floating bodies, the horror of knowing that hundreds perhaps thousands below Lancastria's decks in the cabins and bowels of the ship were drowning in pitch darkness.

Demetri went to the railing and tried to help in whatever way he could. Some of the survivors they fished out of the water were hideously burned and maimed. A sailor to Demetri's right lifted what appeared to be a bag out of the water and hoisted it back behind him into Demetri's hands. Only then did Demetri realize that it was the upper torso of a young child who still held in her gnarled hand the burned remnant of a small doll.

Chapter 12

October 9, 1984

Tommy woke to find himself staring out the hospital window. His mind was swirling in that dreamy place again, weighed down by a heaviness that made him both dizzy and nauseous at the same time. He couldn't quite remember when he had fallen asleep. His last memory was of the nurse coming in with that sack of candy she always gave him and replacing his drip bag.

It was always like that though. He had gone through the experience enough times now to know how the pattern went. Once the treatment was over, a wave of fatigue followed sometimes strong enough to make him fall into a deep slumber. The sleepiness was not unwelcome, however, because many times he would be sick to his stomach.

From the amount of light coming in through the window, Tommy guessed that morning had just broken. He must have been asleep for a long time and found that now, although he felt drained, he was not sick to his stomach. His eyelids were heavy though and he kept his head right where it was pointed out the window. From his viewpoint he could see the tops of trees across the street. Seeing those trees reminded him of the huge oak outside his bedroom back home and the rotted out indentation in the trunk just above the fork of two branches that had been converted into a sparrow's nest.

Ever since he had discovered the nest in the spring, he had monitored the comings and goings of the mother and the number of babies she cared for. The most trivial and commonplace of all of nature's doings, a bird carrying for its young, Tommy had found astounding. The nest itself had been a bundling of brown twigs, sticks, grasses and some kind of white fuzz Tommy was unable to identify. The hole in the trunk seemed almost too small for the mother to go through though he had seen her do it many times. When the mother was absent, the chicks had remained absolutely silent. Somehow nature had made it clear to the young ones that they were highly vulnerable at this point and that only by caution could they hope to remain alive. But oh, how that silence turned to boisterous, impatient squawking when the mother landed on the limb and fluttered once or perhaps twice to the front of the nest. Even before the mother stuck her beak in the hole and subsequently hopped in, the chicks had seemed to sense her presence.

It would excite Tommy when the mother would make her appearance. She would land in her favorite spot, hop once to a branch just beside the nest and vault through the hole to the clamorous exaltations of her young. There had been at least three and perhaps four different chirps that came from out of the nest.

The sparrow would jump back out of the hole and once again the yapping would begin in earnest. Of course birds did not have facial expressions that could be interpreted to know what they were thinking, but there was something there that Tommy had admired. It was the determination, the doggedness, a solitary state of mind bent on one end and one end alone, raising her chicks. There was no hesitancy, no self-serving motives, nor any detour of effort. There was a mission to be carried out with no questions asked, no praise expected, and no personal gain to be had. The mission constituted serving up of its strength, resources and wisdom to keep her babies safe, secure and fed.

This aspiration was held to even at the risk of her life. It had happened one day that a squirrel had come wandering down the branches toward the nest, innocently enough. Suddenly the mother appeared and stood her ground on the edge of the opening as the bigger animal came bounding down the limb. The bird began chattering incessantly at the intruder and flittering above the squirrel's head nipping and crackling at the animal. The squirrel had wanted no trouble to begin with and simply skittered on its merry way.

However, the sparrow had not known the squirrel had no interest in her chicks. There was only the suggestion of a threat and her mission could not be compromised. There would be no disruption in this bird's objective. All was in subjugation to the ultimate goal as long as she had a beak to peck the eyes out of anything that got in her way.

Tommy Silver was twelve years old. He had just had his birthday and he wondered if he would ever see another one. Tommy was a thin boy, reedy, with spindly arms and legs. He had an elongated head, a sharp nose and gray eyes holding a spark of inquisitiveness and intelligence that even the deflating effects of the medication could not totally mask. The hair on his head had all been shaven off and there was a large scar running in a curve around his left ear. In sports he was always one of the last chosen because he was awkward and hesitant athletically. Around girls he would shrink into a ball and around his male friends he was usually quiet and shy.

However, academically he was outstanding. He had an insatiable desire for knowledge. School for the most part was a bore to him because whatever subject matter they moved on to next, Tommy would pounce on and devour immediately like a dog making quick work of a steak. While some of his friends plowed through arithmetic problems as if their feet were stuck in quicksand, Tommy would breeze through and find himself, once again, idle and bored.

Unlike many of his friends, he didn't care for television. Though he did have some interest in science shows, he found there were too many commercials and silly ones at that. Tommy liked books especially instructive books on astronomy, science, and medicine. Dinosaurs fascinated him and he found himself obsessively preoccupied with learning everything he could about them. Many nights his mother would force him to close his books and go to sleep. To feed his insatiable curiosity and combat his boredom at school, Tommy brought books with him. Luckily his desk was in the back of the room so when the class was busy on some material that Tommy already had mastered, he would pull out one of his other books and read.

He had been ill for quite a while now and he was beginning to feel a different kind of exhaustion overcoming him, one that was beyond the normal fatigue and listlessness he usually felt. He had first gotten sick about two years before: a bout of severe headaches and unexplained listlessness. For several months he took treatment and was forced to miss a lot of school time. Then for about a year or so, things got back to normal, he returned to school and his friends had almost stopped the kidding they had given him about being sick, his thinning hair, his gaunt features, his occasional hand tremors.

Then the headaches returned: more tests, more treatments, more pills, surgery, radiation treatments, and chemotherapy. His mother had been forced to quit work to stay home with him. He had done all kinds of things that had embarrassed him: peeing the bed, throwing up, uncontrollable tremors, and seizures. And through it all his mother had sat beside him and cleaned him and fed him and nursed him and cared for him, much like the sparrow was doing: selflessly, without complaint.

Through all his discomfort and his mother's mental anguish, there was something wonderful that he beheld, both in his mother and the sparrow. It astounded Tommy to witness the selfless, undeniable fixture of steadfastness, the staunch relentlessness to the cause, the unyielding steady march forward without compromise, the tenacious will of self-sacrifice.

He had always been a good child. He had always tried to do what his parents wanted, what his teachers asked of him. However, this extraordinary example he was being provided by both his mother and the sparrow made him examine more closely just what was the root cause of that behavior. Why exactly did he try to be a good child, why exactly had he been an obedient student? As best as he could tell, there was an inherent desire inside him to please people. He knew his parents expected him to be well-behaved and so he complied. School had never been a problem for him, so getting good grades had been a snap. But when he looked at things closely, really broke it down, he saw that his behavior both in school and at home was in the end self-serving. He had been surly and defiant with his parents at times, but his father was a strict taskmaster and didn't take any huff. The punishments he had received, like his bike being taken away for a week, simply did not justify what little gratification he got from mouthing off or being disobedient. It just simply wasn't worth it. So the motivation for his good behavior was not explicitly because he favored to do the right thing, but simply because in the long run, it was more profitable.

Same with school. When he got good grades his parents rewarded him with money or some other gift. Since he was naturally good in school, there was no reason not to proceed in that manner. True he had always liked learning, but that did not alter the fact that there were other motives in place there for getting high marks. Many times he had found himself plotting what reward might next be in line for such scholastic achievement as his.

The undeniable fact that he could not shake was that there was a method to his madness, so to speak. He had selfish reasons for acting the way he did. He did not so much do the "right thing" because he valued doing good over bad, but because of rewards and punishments that behind the scene motivated his behavior. In a way he almost felt guilty about this.

However, what he learned in watching the sparrow and his mother was something totally different. Their behavior had nothing to do with selfish motives. Theirs was a commitment above and beyond any rational, contrived plan of behaving properly so that you could receive reward of some kind or so you could profit from it or avoid punishment.

A wave of nausea suddenly rolled through Tommy's stomach. It came and then it passed as he knew it would. There would have been a time when the way he felt now, drained, hollow, and sapped of strength, would have made him call for his mother, but he was beyond that now. In many ways his illness had made a new person of Tommy.

The new Tommy now thought of nothing but serious matters. He had talked to enough doctors who hid things from him, kept a smile going, and basically led him to believe things were progressing just fine. However, he had also seen the change in their expressions when they talked to his parents: the more sullen features, the hushed voices, that look of helplessness that would appear momentarily in a weak moment before the doctor or his mother would freshen it up in the presence of the boy.

Tommy knew exactly what was wrong with him. He had a malignant brain tumor and its location made surgery tricky. They had gone in once, removed what they could and closed him up. They had hoped to shrink the remaining tumor through chemotherapy and radiation and perhaps be able to attack it then. The first regiment he had gone through had worked to some degree but not entirely. The tumor had shrunk some but not enough. They decided to give Tommy some recuperation time before administrating chemotherapy and radiation again. It was obvious that the reappearance of his symptoms had caught Doctor Tim and his team off guard.

What they were doing to him now, the regiment of new drugs they were administering, seemed like a stab in the dark. He had heard his father and the doctor say so once when they thought he was asleep.

Tommy liked Doctor Tim. He had a certain dignity about him, a good bedside manner they called it. Also Tommy found him easy to read. He could tell when he was not being up front with him, if he was trying to shield something from him. Doctor Tim always came to see him when they were getting him ready for his treatments. Lately Tommy had sensed uneasiness in his behavior, evasiveness in his manner. Something was not right and Tommy suspected what that might be. The doctor was uncomfortable in the role he was playing, the stalwart rescuer. Tommy almost asked him the questions he wanted answered, but the doctor had wiggled out of the room before he had a chance too. He didn't want to ask his parents. His mother was upset enough and he didn't want her burdened with having to tell him some grim news.

He would play along until his next meeting with Doctor Tim.

Funny, he thought, *I don't even know about life yet, but I might shortly be dead.* There was something terrible there in that thought about death, something lurking under the surface, something cold, ghastly, frightful, something he couldn't quite put his finger on. He couldn't say he was terrified of death. No, it wasn't that exactly. It was the waste of it all.

The waste of it all, that's what troubled him more than anything. That and the things his mom and a tiny bird had taught him.

Tommy rolled over and tried to make himself comfortable without disturbing the IV running into his hand.

He daydreamed for awhile until he came upon that peculiar incident outside his hospital room, the girl who had stared at him from the other doorway. She never spoke a word. He said something to her, but she never responded. And yet, he could have sworn she spoke to him.

He hoped she was not as sick as he was. Maybe he'd get a chance to see her again. Then his headache came back and he forgot about the girl and the odd little encounter he had with her.

Chapter 13

The morning at the Davos Estate broke cloudy and damp. A low haze hung over the manor shrouding the brick tips of the fireplace vents that rose from the roof. Isabelle was up early. Police cars still sat at the house and strange voices scaled the staircase from the kitchen downstairs. Out toward the back of the property, two policemen roamed about looking down at the ground in the area where the fight had taken place the night before. In a way Isabelle was glad to see the police were still there. The monster man would surely not come back while they were around.

Isabelle felt certain Quimby had not seen her scoop up the globe. He had simply been too far away. It had been so dark she doubted he could have picked out anything distinctly from there. That was good. If he found out she had the globe, he would take it away from her as he had done before. However, she had to be careful now. With all the activity going on, she had to wait for an opportune time to retrieve it from the barn.

Isabelle hesitated not knowing what to do first. She did not know what condition her father was in. For all she knew he might have already died, although she doubted that. Had her father died during the night, she would have sensed it, known it somehow. Amanda would have come to her. Communication of that type would have been impossible to mistake. However, she could not afford to wait to make her wish on the globe. It may be true that he was still alive, but how long could she trust that to be the case.

The vision of the monster man came to her. No doubt she was safe from him here at the house with Quimby, Victor and Amanda to protect her, but she could not get the image of his face out her mind. That black eye patch sent an unsettling panic through her. The possibility of him returning reinforced the idea that she needed her father back healthy and well. She would never really feel safe until he returned.

She remembered about Whisper and worried about his condition also. At least for right now she could go check on him. She quickly washed and got dressed. As she went down the hallway she spotted Amanda in her bedroom, sitting on her bed. When she saw Isabelle she motioned for her to come to her. Tears were running down her cheeks and she hugged Isabelle.

Could this mean her father had died? Isabelle did not think so. Amanda did not seem to hint at that. She seemed more confused and anxious than anything, frightened at all that had occurred in the last few days. The woman looked very overwrought and Isabelle suspected that this morning was the first time she had been home since her father's accident.

Amanda was a good housekeeper, a loyal servant and very responsible about her chores and duties. What she was not, was a woman of strong backbone. Isabelle had known how stricken she could be by anxiety, how much she relied on her pills to get her through the day and to sleep at night. She was not of the adventuresome spirit. Her needs were basically those of food, clothing and shelter and little more. Isabelle had always thought that she lived fearfully as if her life consisted of pulling the covers over her head and hoping nothing bad happened.

Isabelle really did not know exactly how she had come into her father's employ, but she knew she had been with the family since her birth. She had been a great asset in caring for her mother. Amanda was Eastern European, and older than Quimby. Isabelle's father treated her very well giving her a separate bedroom on the second floor of the house and with Quimby gave them considerable freedom in the running of the household.

Although Isabelle was not able to communicate her thoughts and words to others, she still retained the ability, some times even more introspectively than most people, to understand what others were thinking, what was buried in their hearts. Perhaps it came from the fact that she relied so heavily on watching others, their actions, their movements in trying to detect what their intentions were. It was so frustrating for her, this blank wall in her mind that made it impossible for her to understand the language she had once known and this inability she had to demonstrate or exhibit what she wanted to express, the inability to form words. Especially at a point such as this where she wanted to comfort Amanda and let her know that things would be all right. She wanted to communicate to her patience. As soon as she was able to get to the globe, she would make things all right with father. He would be well and he would be home soon to keep them all safe.

Isabelle left Amanda and went downstairs. Quimby sat at the kitchen table talking to a policeman. The officer had a pad of paper out in front of him writing things down as Quimby spoke. A nasty gash rose from Quimby's chin, went past his lips and across the bottom of his nose. Part of the wound was covered in a white gauze dressing that had splotches of yellow cream oozing from its corners. Victor stood in the kitchen, slurping coffee, idly looking on in awkward silence.

When the three noticed Isabelle, they grew silent. Quimby motioned for Victor and the handy man came over to her, took her hand and walked her to the back door. From the rack he took down her rain parka and helped her into it. The officer and Quimby watched the girl quietly. Once Victor got her outside and closed the door behind them, Quimby's voice could be heard once again. They had been waiting for her to leave before speaking anymore. Perhaps they did not want her to know all that had occurred the night before.

Isabelle felt relief. Their reaction to her presence proved that they thought she knew nothing about what had occurred the night before. In reality, she knew everything including who had shot the burglar and where the globe was. She also knew her father would soon be well. It was a wonderful little secret she held amid all the turmoil going on around her.

A chilly breeze blew from the north as they trudged across the grounds to the barn. The wooden door creaked softly as Victor pulled it open. The smell of damp hay and manure greeted them as they stepped inside. Isabelle hurried over to Whisper's pen as Victor pulled the door closed.

Whisper was very excited to see Isabelle, but his excitement was laced with a degree of anxiety and panic. The horse bobbed his head up and down in consternation and impatience. Whisper kicked out with his left leg which was now bandaged snugly and fitted with an ice pack to control swelling. The bindings were something he did not understand. Confusion and fear were underlying his thoughts and now that Isabelle had appeared he demanded to have the bandages removed.

Isabelle wrapped her arms around Whisper's neck and tried to calm the beast. She offered the animal one of the carrots from the bucket on the other side of the stall, but the horse was too upset to eat it. Isabelle mentally tried to guide the horse through his panic. Once or twice the animal's impatience was too much for him to bear and he kicked out with his leg again slamming his hoof against the wooden boards of his stall. Victor came to the animal and also tried to quiet him. Once they had gotten Whisper stilled, Victor bent down to examine the bandaged leg. With his hands he gently probed the joints down to the horse's shoe searching for hot spots and swelling. Isabelle noticed that Victor had placed a different type of shoe on Whisper's sore leg. The padded shoe served to cushion the shock of his footfalls and prevent further damage.

After he examined the foot and leg, Victor rose and patted the horse on the rump. Isabelle could tell Victor had some concern for the animal but overall did not think the injury too serious. Keeping the weight off and monitoring the swelling around the joints might be sufficient. A little time and Whisper would be all right. Isabelle leaned her head against the horse's flank and reassured him. He needed to keep the ice and the bandage on for a while. It was a treatable injury. He had to be patient, but he would be all right.

Whisper spoke to Isabelle and a semblance of reason finally worked its way through the panic and fright. The bandages confused and alarmed him, but he was beginning to yield to the relaxation that Isabelle kept prodding him toward. Whisper trusted Isabelle inherently and acceded to her urging. He understood now that as long as Isabelle was not alarmed, he did not need to be either. The natural impulse to fight against the bandages and submit to the panic that the oddness of the situation presented was still there, but its strength was modulated. Isabelle could feel the animal relaxing under her hand. The petting of his mane and flank helped to ease the horse down further.

Again she offered Whisper a carrot and this time the animal crunched it down.

Victor left Isabelle with the animal and she fed him a few more carrots. Convinced that Whisper now understood things and was more relaxed, her mind went back to her father.

Victor had left the barn and gone across the grounds to one of the out sheds where much of the outdoor equipment was kept: lawnmowers, hedge trimmers, shovels and tools. He came out pushing a wheelbarrow with a rake in it and turned left toward the garden. Victor had been working that area the day before raking leaves and working to put the garden to bed for the winter. The work would certainly keep him occupied for a while.

At the house the police cars sat idly and through the kitchen window Isabelle could see Quimby standing at the sink. A squirrel climbed along the window sill, peeked in at Quimby and the policeman and moved on.

This was her chance.

Quickly she walked back to her stall and reached under the bed for the box. It was there waiting for her. She went into the corner, pulled out the globe and tucked it into her lap as she sat with her legs crossed against the wall. A soft glow beamed from the center. Flares of colored light occasionally sparked from the middle. Isabelle's thoughts began to sharpen. She did not want to hesitate, but she remembered what had happened the last time she had wished upon the globe.

In a way it had been a miraculous thing, this gift she had been given of communicating with animals. It opened up a whole different world of understanding not only the ways of animals, but to the ways of humans also.

Isabelle's ability to see into the minds of animals had convinced her, more than any church service ever would, of the reality of God. Their simplistic, general trusting nature could not possibly have been instilled in them without a governing body that would oversee to their general well-being.

But for the wonders of this gift she had, she yearned to recapture the simple ability to converse and share her gift with others. To be understood once more. This dead zone of language and exposition was something she missed dearly. It had not passed her by that when she gained the one power, she lost the other, but she did not think of it as a payment the globe required of her so much as a rearrangement of the communicative powers she did have. In other words, there was only so much communication skill available to her. Before, that had rested in the normal abilities most people had to speak, converse and express themselves in physical motion to their fellow man and to be understood by them. In her case, the wheel had shifted and those powers now fell into the realm of the animal kingdom. She had not actually lost anything. One domain had been exchanged for another.

Would there be a shift now in some way if she made the wish for her father to regain his health? Would a price need to be paid in some manner?

She did not know that answer and it hurt her head to think about it. She only knew she needed her father to get well. She needed his protection, his care. It occurred to her that in reality this wish was a very selfish one. She had not thought about her father being in pain or him dying in any other terms than how it was going to affect her. When she realized that, she felt guilty but that shame did not alter, deep down, her reasons for wanting her father to recover. She could not rectify that fact in her mind or change the reality of it. She simply forced herself to not think about it any further.

The black eye of the monster man gleamed out at her when she looked at the ball. Now it flared more brightly: sparking, flashing, beaming. Isabelle cleared all the doubts away and stared into the inferno now bursting from the middle of the globe. With ever deepening want, her fear and her insecurity pushed her on. The ball became luminescent, flooding the stall with an intense, almost breathtaking, glow.

Isabelle closed her eyes and made her wish. The globe flared one more time, the colors fusing in a tumbling whirl so brilliant it seemed as if the sun itself had burst forth from the crystal. The gush of color held for a moment more and then slowly began to recede, absorbed into the crystal as if it were a giant magnet drawing back the streams of light from every corner of the stall. The sparks fizzled, the streams dissipated, the glow wavered like the breaths of some unseen light monster.

Then the crystal went dark, save for the tiny yellow flicker, that constant vigil, coming from its core.

Isabelle opened her eyes and stared down at the globe. She felt almost disconnected from the world as if she had just woken up from some deep slumber and had yet to be able to judge where she was or what was happening. Then her thoughts settled. She placed the globe in the black sack and back into its box.

Isabelle carried the box back to her bed and shoved it way underneath. She covered the box with a blanket to prevent any light from escaping and then sat down on the soft mattress. Exhaustion flooded her body as if she had just carried a great weight for a long distance. She lay back on her bed and wondered about what she had done and what might happen next.

Suddenly Whisper began whinnying and stomping about in his stall. Isabelle could sense the panic and terror coming from the animal from across the barn. The horse lashed out wildly with its bandaged hoof so strongly that it cracked one of the boards in his stall just as Isabelle reached the gate. She burst in and watched in awe as Whisper reared up on his hind legs and then came crashing down so hard on his front hooves that he stumbled into the side of the barn. Isabelle had never seen Whisper so panicked before in all her life. She tried to break through that surge of fear that had gripped the animal, but Whisper was too deep in panic. The horse recognized Isabelle and acknowledged her presence for a moment but the level of fear he was experiencing would not allow him to relax. Whisper reversed direction and backpedaled recklessly into his hay trough. A surge of terror raced through the animal's mind. Something had frightened it beyond even Isabelle's ability to quiet it.

The horse began bucking wildly now, flailing its hind hooves violently against the back of the enclosure. The sound of the thumping hooves was like the blast from a gun: sharp and violent. Every time he kicked the animal would let out a terrible blustery snort that Isabelle knew was a cry of pain. Victor suddenly appeared and went for the reins and the bit trying to control Whisper's violent thrashing, but the horse would have none of it. The beast swung to its left suddenly and kicked out catching Victor along the thigh. The blow had not been a direct hit but was sufficient to send Victor reeling into the hay trough and spinning him to the ground.

Whisper reared up again, came down suddenly on his front hooves and shot out his bandaged leg with a kick so violent it penetrated the boards to the other stall. A sickening snap accompanied the sharp thud of the wood and the horse turned on himself, rotating swiftly to his left. With his hoof caught in the hole he had left in the boards, Whisper could not find footing and crashed down on to his belly. The fact that his foot was stuck increased his panic and he lashed out with his foot repeatedly trying to free it from the hole. A stain of blood appeared at the ragged edges of the broken boards and still Whisper would not relent. He kicked out again and pulled his leg splintering the boards even more until finally his wedged hoof was released.

Isabelle lunged at Whisper's neck and finally connected to the horse's thoughts. She hugged him tightly trying to break through to whatever reason she could find. Whisper pulled his front hooves out and went to stand but halfway up collapsed back into a heap. Pasty splotches of sweat covered the horse's neck and upper leg and thick foam dripped from his mouth. Again he tried to rise and again he collapsed bringing Isabelle down beside him in the hay. Victor was back up now and had circled around to grab the reins tight enough to keep Whisper secure on the ground. The horse tried raising his head again to make another attempt to rise, but Victor had the leverage on him now. The animal snorted and bellowed, neighing in a raspy, harsh yowl that translated pain to Isabelle.

Now that the animal was held to the ground, Isabelle was able to break through and gauge his thoughts. The animal had suffered some unexplainable fright he could not even conceptualize in his mind. His thoughts were a blur of fear, panic and confusion but now that he had been checked by Isabelle and Victor, he listened to her admonitions. Stay down she told him. She pleaded with him to remain calm. Her cautions worked for the most part to control the horse, but even still a wave of panic would suddenly engulf him and take him out of the realm of Isabelle's guidance. Victor pulled the reins tight and kept him down.

For several moments, after a last wave of panic appeared to have subsided, a clatter of activity arose from the other end of the barn. Quimby called out obviously having overheard the disturbance. He came rushing into the stall followed by two of the police officers who also must have heard the ruckus.

Quimby quickly spoke to Victor trying to get some explanation of what had happened. Victor gave an account as to what had occurred as he managed to get himself up to his feet. One of the officers came around and took over the reins from Victor as the hired hand sat back against the wall totally out of breath. Blood stained through his pants from his thigh and he held his leg and grimaced in pain.

Isabelle continued to pet Whisper along his mane as their thoughts began to finally melt together. One message kept coming to Isabelle. Whisper did not want her to leave him. Her presence reassured him and he was able to fixate on her thoughts and gentleness. Isabelle assured him she would stay. Whisper still was not totally under control. Whatever had frightened him, he could not describe. It was as if a fit of terror had overcome him about his bandaged leg. For a period of time he had lost control, but he could not remember why or how or what had caused it. He said to her that it seemed he had a nightmare while he was still awake, the terror of which he could not rid from his mind.

Isabelle continued to pet and rub his flank and head. He was all right now she assured him.

Quimby circled around the horse and knelt down at his back legs. By this time Victor had recovered enough to stumble over and kneel beside him. Isabelle turned her head, but she could not see the horse's legs because the butler's body blocked her sight. Victor moaned and suddenly Whisper raised his head, but then gently laid it down, his eyes spinning wildly in his head. Victor examined one of Whisper's feet and then he looked up at Quimby as if he was looking past him, an empty expression, almost a void of emotion. Quimby brought his hand to his face and rubbed at his forehead then he turned and locked eyes with Isabelle. The look held for just a moment and then Quimby could hold it no longer because it displayed awkwardness and ineptitude. Isabelle felt the regret he tried to disguise.

Quimby rose and then Isabelle saw Whisper's limb. The bone was completely shattered at the foreleg. The break was so bad that the hoof was curved at a near ninety degree angle, hanging together only by a cord of muscle and tendons. The mess of gristle and blood left was nearly unrecognizable as the ankle bone of a horse. A shot of panic shot through Isabelle and Whisper immediately sensed it and began again trying to rise to his feet. The animal yelped ferociously now, his mind blanketed with fear and terror. There was no mistaking the dreaded certainty that Isabelle's frightened thoughts translated to him.

The officer tugged at the reins trying to keep Whisper's head down as the horse bucked and reared up on its side only to be brought down by the leg pain and sheer force of the officer's strength.

Quimby yelled an order at Victor and he just turned and looked pitifully at the butler and then turned to Isabelle. Victor was a warmhearted, simple fellow who never meant harm to anyone. What Quimby ordered him to do left him no option. His gaze fell to the ground and then rose and caught Isabelle's. The look he gave her spoke of hopelessness. He was thrust into a position he was not comfortable with at all. His eyes seemed to plead with Isabelle in that moment for something: understanding, sympathy, forgiveness.

Quimby raised his voice even higher and Victor went scurrying off, limping as fast as he could. Meanwhile Quimby grabbed Isabelle and began pulling her away from Whisper. At this all semblance of patience or control left the beast. The officer could not hold him down any longer. Whisper rose to his front paws and lunged himself up to a stumbled crouch taking all his weight off his decimated rear left leg. The officer tried to steady the horse who now had become uncontrollably inflamed. Isabelle bellowed out a horrible sound, part scream and part wail as Quimby wrestled her away. Whisper thoughts screamed in fear to Isabelle. His hoarse, raspy shrieks reverberated around the stall.

Quimby carried Isabelle out of the stall as Victor came lurching past them. Isabelle felt cold metal brush up against her leg as she tried to escape Quimby's clutches. Now the other policeman had positioned himself in the doorway to the stall preventing Isabelle from even seeing what was going on.

A jumble of shouts from the men in the stall and Whisper's horrible shrieks rose to a fevered pitch. A hard thump whacked the side of the stall once and then again. Whisper called for Isabelle now in desperation. The poor beast had lost all semblance of patience or assuredness. Wild dread from the animal nearly drowned out Isabelle's own thoughts. Terror-stricken and panicked beyond all control, the horse shrieked, bellowed and kicked out furiously desperate for relief.

BAM!

A great weight fell to the ground inside the stall. Quimby eased his grip. Isabelle listened. Whisper's pleas had suddenly gone ominously silent. For a few moments the silence held check and then came a soft murmuring. Victor was sobbing into his sleeve.

Miles away, Nurse Wesley finished her conversation with the teenager who had been in the motorcycle accident. The kid had not seen the pothole while going seventy and lost control of the bike. Both of his arms were bandaged heavily from his wrists to his shoulders. They had already removed patches of skin from his buttocks and thighs and used them to try and mend the areas that had been chewed up by the asphalt. Although he had not been wearing a helmet, he had only a slash to his skull.

It was a miracle he was still alive.

The nurse went down the hall into room 511 and thought the same thing. It was a miracle the man was still alive. Suffering a fall from a two story height could easily kill even the hardiest of souls, not to mention a man in his seventies.

However, there was not much more they could do for this one now. The doctors felt he was in an irreversible coma. They were waiting a few days, hope against hope, that the brain swelling would go down, that somehow there could be a recovery.

Poor guy was done for, she thought. *Let him go.*

Nurse Wesley went to the drip bag and examined it. She took up his chart and entered in her notes as she studied the monitors. She half expected the poor guy to have expired even before she came on her shift. All she could do was monitor his condition and act the dutiful, sorrowful nurse when the end came.

For some unexplainable reason a nagging obsession made her go check the IV drip once more, almost like one of her attacks of obsessive compulsive disorder again. She suffered mild spells of that condition before through the years: checking and rechecking locked doors, driving back home to make sure she had let the garage door down. Mostly innocent mild instances like that.

But she had not experienced a wave of compulsion in a long time.

Odd that it was happening now, she thought.

The bag was fine, the drip set correctly.

Just before she walked away, she gave a final glance to the patient. Only then did she notice that he had opened his eyes and was trying to mouth some words.

Chapter 14

Andre Haskim woke up in the middle of the afternoon with a pounding headache. It may have been because he didn't finally make it to bed until five in the morning after ditching Vince's car in a nearby neighborhood and taking a bus home. Or it could have been due to the fact that when he did make it home, he downed about half a quart of Bourbon in a tirade of frustration knowing he had come so close to capturing his prize. However, there was something else now that superseded the lack of sleep and the drunken stupor. Not only had his plans been foiled at the last moment, but now he had murdered an associate of a mobster who wasn't the kind who went to the police to seek out justice. He most certainly would want an explanation and Haskim had none to provide that would get him off the hook. That being the case, Mizetti would look for recompense, but not through the normal channels of arrest and trial.

Haskim tried to think through the pain. He had not disclosed to Mizetti where he lived so for the time being he was safe. However, with his looks, it would not take long for the mobster to track him down if he wanted to catch up to him. Even if somehow he could be convinced it was not Haskim who had shot Vince or that Haskim was not at fault, he would want the rest of the payment for the job even if it had been botched. Then he might want to rid himself of Haskim just to ensure that the whole sordid affair could not be linked back to him. No, he would have to steer clear of Leo Mizetti.

Not only did he have reason to fear Mizetti, but the police might very well be on his tail right now. Haskim wasn't sure that the butler had gotten close enough to see his face but the girl, that miserable wretch of a daughter of Demetri, had seen him up close. He had to assume she had seen the whole fight he had with Vince and that she had seen his face and there was no mistaking his face. But the kid was some kind of mute, had some kind of affliction that prevented her from communicating effectively. Maybe she wouldn't be able to tell the cops anything. Maybe, but Haskim knew he could not bank on that.

After reasoning through all the factors working against him, Haskim's head felt like it was going to explode. Regardless of what he was going to do now, he needed to get his mind right so he could think straight. He dropped three aspirin and took a long shower letting the warm water stream down his head and face. Then he made himself a pot of coffee and drank down several cups. The shower, pills and coffee worked to clear his head somewhat.

After dressing, Haskim sat down at his kitchen table and lit a cigarette. He now found that since his headache had abated somewhat, it was desperation that prevailed. Now more than ever, he had to get his hands on that globe. All his problems would be solved if he could just manage that. He would wish for youth and for the return of his once handsome features. If he accomplished that, he would no longer need to worry about the police or Mizetti. They would not recognize the new Andre Haskim.

Haskim stubbed out his cigarette and quickly lit another. The nicotine flooding his lungs seemed to bring him back to his senses even more than the coffee and shower. Again he cursed himself for having been so close.

Why hadn't he waited until they were away from the property before having it out with Vince? And that damn kid! Where the hell had she come from anyway? It had been the middle of the night. What was she doing tromping around in the woods?

One thing was for sure. He had to clear out from his apartment. It was too dangerous to stay there. He had plenty of cash to see him through, so he thought it best he rent a room in some obscure hotel and hide out while he tried to figure out how in God's name he was going to get his hands on that globe. The element of surprise was obviously lost to him now. Also with what happened the night before, he couldn't possibly show his face anywhere near Demetri's house. Plus now that the kid had the globe, who knew what she would do with it.

Where would she take it? he wondered.

Most likely it would wind up back in Demetri's hands and knowing now just what measures Haskim was willing to go to get his hands on the crystal, who knows what Demetri might do. He might even follow through on his threats to destroy it. Haskim would not let himself dwell on that possibility. More likely he would hide it away in a safety deposit box or some other obscure place. Either way, any hope of ever reclaiming it might be gone forever.

A cold chill went through Haskim as he realized that in all likelihood he was finished. He had tried to persuade Demetri and that had failed. He had taken the best shot he would ever have at stealing the crystal and that had failed. Now not only had he blown his best opportunity, but he had to keep looking over his shoulder for not only the police but for Mizetti's thugs. And people like Mizetti had ways of finding things out that even the cops weren't privy to.

Haskim went to his closet and retrieved a suitcase. He packed it with everything he would need. For all he knew, he might never be returning to his apartment again. His next stop would be to the bank and withdraw enough money to keep him stocked for months if need be. He would go find himself an obscure roadside motel and check in. And then … then he would get himself something to eat and hope for some divine revelation to tell him what his next move should be.

Two hours later, Haskim found himself seated in a booth at the Chicken Shack out on old Route 72 in Gilberts, Illinois. His headache was almost totally gone now, but he wondered if it wasn't preferable to the despair he felt. The truth was he was a murdering, grave-robbing, hideously-looking gypsy now, on the run from not only the police but the mob as well. The young waitress came over and trying not to look too horrified took his order. Haskim ordered the chicken shack deluxe, three pieces of chicken, fries and a soda. The apprehensive girl quickly fled back to the kitchen and Haskim could hear the mumbling going on back there. Soon the cook and the other waitress would sneak a peek at the monster in booth seven.

On the wall off to the right was a sign that said "No Smoking." Haskim pulled out a cigarette and lit up anyways.

Let one of these sons-of bitches try to tell me to put it out, he thought.

He wasn't going to take shit from any of them now. He was too pissed off and depressed to worry about any of that kind of stuff now.

On the table to his right was a Chicago Tribune newspaper folded up in half. Haskim reached over and grabbed it. Of course it would have been too soon to see any report about the shooting in the paper, but Haskim needed something to do while he waited.

As he perused through the pages it occurred to him that maybe all was not totally lost when it came to Mizetti. He had not told Mizetti exactly what power the globe held. That would have been too dangerous. What if he went to the mobster and spilled the beans, told him what happened and explained to him exactly what the globe could do? Maybe he could convince the mobster to use all his influence and power to obtain the globe. After all, he wouldn't care if the mobster wished for a few things as long as he got his shot at it. Then reality set in and the more Haskim thought about that idea, the more insane it became to him.

Who in their right mind would ever believe such a ludicrous tale? Mizetti would have to be convinced of the truth of it beyond any doubt in order to commit his resources to such a dangerous venture.

Haskim had no proof to offer him other than the desperation he had shown the thug in trying to get his hands on it. Surely that would not be enough. Mizetti would simply come to the conclusion that Haskim was insane, cut his losses and then in all likelihood put the whole matter to bed with a single slug to Haskim's temple.

Nice try, Haskim thought. *Face it, you're dead meat.*

Suddenly Haskim saw something in the paper that lifted his spirits from despair to hopefulness. It was there in a small article in the second section of the paper buried on page four.

This was an opportunity, Haskim thought. *But how could he make it work for him?*

He reread the headline again to make sure he had it right: Long Grove Man in Critical Condition after Fall. The article went on to explain that Demetri Davos had been found at the base of his balcony. It was assumed the man had fallen from two flights up. The article hinted at a possible suicide attempt but that authorities were not certain. It went on to explain that Demetri was diagnosed with an incurable form of cancer and that perhaps that had been the reason for the attempt. At the present time, the man was in critical condition in the intensive care unit of West Suburban Hospital.

Haskim gnawed on his chicken and reread the article over and over. So Demetri was dying, eh. If he died, he might indeed have the globe buried with him. That was a possibility. However, if Demetri was unconscious he wouldn't have known that the girl had the globe. Then Haskim thought about the girl. They just might bring her to the hospital to see her father. Could he somehow stake out the place and snatch the girl if she showed up? In the situation he was in, kidnapping was a mere triviality. *Hell, he would kill the girl if it came to that.* Most likely he already had one murder on his hands. They could only hang him once. Besides at this point there was nothing left for Haskim to live for but that globe. Everything else was subservient to that goal: murder, kidnapping, torture, whatever. In Haskim's mind, he would either get his hands on the globe or die trying.

Now caution reared its tentative head in Haskim's mind. He had to be careful though. He was so easily recognizable that he couldn't simply hang around the hospital waiting for that damn kid to show up. On the other hand, he had to be close to Demetri at all times. Who knew when the kid might show up, if ever.

What to do … what to do? Haskim deliberated.

Maybe he had one good trick left up his sleeve. One more shot at getting this right. Quickly he swallowed down the remainder of his meal and paid his bill making a point of leaving no tip for the apprehensive waitress.

Chapter 15

July 9, 1955

Demetri leaned back in his chair and stared out over all of the guests dancing in the center of the ballroom while the sounds of the eight piece orchestra swirled around the room. To his right his brand new wife, Sophie, was being led across the dance floor by his partner, Andre Haskim.

Life is good, Demetri thought.

On his wedding day he was wearing a black tuxedo with tail, a white shirt with black button studs, a black bow tie, a red cummerbund and black shoes shined like mirrors. The five glasses of red wine circulating through his system combined with the whirl of the music made the spinning figures in front of him almost dizzying. But he didn't care. This was a new beginning, a break from the past. In his mind he had decided that from this day on he would look only forward. His past mistakes had haunted him through the years with a guilt that had been at times like a milestone around his neck, but when he met Sophie things changed. She gave him a new purpose, a new direction he had never found with any other woman. When she had told him they were going to get married, he vowed not to let the past invade their lives.

Demetri had been at a juncture like this years before when he had escaped France and made it to England and then on to America. He had vowed then that he would work hard, be industrious and make something of himself. Once in America while the war raged he moved to Chicago because he had heard it was a booming city of opportunity, a place where a man could go as far as his ambition could take him. At first things were tight. He got a job working for a typesetting firm in the downtown district of the city known as printer's row. His ignorance of the printing business itself did not deter his drive and ambition to succeed. His first job was working nights on one of the smaller presses where he would simply run off sample copies of material for the proof readers to evaluate for mistakes. One of the proof readers, Marvin Little, had been a former English teacher, now retired, who made extra money using his proficiency at English grammar to ensure that the content of the material they printed was grammatically correct.

Marvin took an instant liking to Demetri and spent extra time tutoring him in English. Demetri knew that for him to get ahead he would have to master the language first. Marvin's instruction was instrumental to Demetri fine tuning his speech and writing ability. Marvin also helped wean Demetri from his heavy European accent. Demetri was forever grateful for the help Marvin provided and when the man suffered a heart attack and things looked bleak for him, the temptation of turning to the globe to aid his friend seeped into his consciousness. However, he did not allow himself to be persuaded. Demetri felt relieved when the inevitable came. His friend had lived a good life and his legacy would not be disgraced for a few extra years of longevity that someone else's misfortune might have provided him.

The war ended and soldiers returning home from overseas flooded the cities looking for work. It was at this point in his life that Demetri made friends with Andre Haskim. The two met while working together for a small typographical business named Thompson's Typographers. Demetri had been working nights on a press and Andre alongside him on a similar machine. Andre had served in the army during the war. He had seen action in France before being wounded by shrapnel which had pierced his shoulder and upper arm. A short convalescence in the Chicago area where his mother and sister still lived allowed him to recover from his wounds without leaving him a disability. Like Demetri, Andre knew nothing of the printing business but the two forged a friendship over the months working side by side.

Andre Haskim had grown up in Cicero, Illinois during the height of the gangster era when speakeasies hid in the back of established businesses and smartly dressed hoods carved out a nitch for themselves. Andre had always been fascinated with the cavalier, high-handed arrogance displayed by the thugs who hung out in the Italian clubs and swaggered their way around the neighborhoods seemingly unconcerned with any repercussions that might befall them from the authorities for their less than altruistic endeavors. Andre was not Italian and this barred him from the inner most sanctums of the gangster hierarchy. This disadvantage did not hinder Andre's ability to make himself useful however to some of the lesser mobsters by running errands for them and keeping his nose to the street picking up any useful information here or there that might be of some value to an up-and-coming thug.

Andre's street-smarts perhaps had been one of the things that most attracted Demetri to him. Andre always had an angle to play, a scam to run that although not exactly legal, fell into that netherworld of catch-as-catch-can where no one was really hurt by the shortcuts taken or the flexible ethics employed. Upon his return from the war however, the pervasive influence of the gangland world had withered due to the end of prohibition and finally the clamp down by authorities over the more brazen and cutthroat tactics formerly considered commonplace in bygone eras. The mob still had a presence and the Chicago-way was still employed in certain neighborhoods of the city, but the ability for an uneducated, muscle man to make a living in the underworld by skirting the law through numbers running, prostitution and gambling had become more elusive and less fashionable. So Andre Haskim, like everyone else, had to figure a way to earn a living legitimately.

Post war America fostered a new spirit on the land. The country's great nightmare was over and for the first time in a long while, citizens felt safer and more relaxed than ever before. People now wanted normality in their lives. The returning soldiers found mates, married, had children and prospered. The economy grew along with their families and this new generation turned their eyes to those inventions and devices that would transform life's former chores and drudgeries into ease and simplicity through the miracle of modern technology. Americans saw washing machines and they wanted them, they saw refrigerators and they wanted them. The explosion in families resulted in spiraling demands for new furniture, new homes, and new appliances. The great dream of owning an automobile was no longer considered unachievable. The desire for new conveniences brought by the miracle of electricity became nearly unquenchable. Everything from electric stoves to electric razors was no longer deemed to be an extravagance. The boom in businesses that rose up to meet these new demands meant increased competition and in order for a company to best its competitors it needed to advertise its wares. The most economical and readily available method of advertising was through the printed word and advertising firms sprang up in big cities rallying to answer the call.

Most of the printing assignments that Demetri and Andre worked on ended up in magazines, newspaper sale flyers and trade publications. Through the years the industrious young men moved up in the company so that by 1952 both were journeymen printers and Demetri had acquired the position of day shift manager. However, Old Man Thompson was getting up in years. He no longer possessed the ability to run the business efficiently nor had the energy to recruit new business. Demetri had been frugal through the years earnestly saving as much of his salary as he could in the hopes that someday he could muster up sufficient capital to start his own business. It was no secret that Thompson was looking to divest himself of the company if the right offer came along. Demetri discussed the option with him and visited several banks in an effort to borrow the necessary funds needed. The banks evaluated his position and showed him the door. There simply was not enough meat on Demetri's bones. Without collateral of some sort or a sizeable increase in the down payment he was able to provide, the banks simply could not make the numbers work for the enterprising young man.

Demetri weighed his options. Always at the back of his mind was that damn globe. For the last seven years it had sat idly in a safety deposit box at Guardian's National Bank on LaSalle Street in downtown Chicago. Whenever he considered it though, visions of his father's grave, the rickety bridge over the creek near Estrella's home and the dead British sailor flashed in his mind. What was just as demoralizing was the shame he felt over Antoine. After the war had ended, he made an effort to try and determine what had happened to his friend. Of course, the war ravaged any kind of record-keeping in France and the fate of Antoine became one with the many millions of others cast to the winds of war torn Europe. The futility of it all soon became apparent to Demetri and he had to abandon any hope of ever learning what had become of his friend, the one for whom they had been one sailor's uniform short.

Demetri had considered asking Andre if he might be interested in becoming his partner. Andre, Demetri knew, had some funds he had acquired through the years in side jobs he had done with some mobster ties he still maintained from the old days. The money he had amassed had come from disreputable enterprises such as truck hijackings and numbers running. Always smart enough never to get into things too deep, Andre had the sense to back off once he had banked enough money to make himself comfortable. His most lucrative pay off had come when he became aware of a horse racing con being run out of Sportsman's Park on the city's south side: a sure thing, the fifth race on a rainy Thursday, Sweetsie, a 70 to 1 long shot. Andre had it on good authority that the fix was in on that race and his timidity to venture a large sum on such a risky scheme was tempered when he saw the amount of money some of the higher ups in the mob were willing to place on Sweetsie's nose. Just prior to the start of the race, the horse's odds plunged from 70 to 1 to 35 to 1, obviously in response to the heavy late money that was put down.

Andre jumped in with both feet and made a bundle that day. And there were other races on other days.

During this period Demetri and Andre spent a good deal of time cavorting with friends in the nightclubs and go-go joints along Rush Street trying to hustle women and living the carefree life of the gigolos they fancied themselves being. They had each had their share of women through the years. Andre in fact had been married and had a young son, but that marriage had dissolved unhappily a few years prior in most part due to his indiscretions and carousing. Demetri had several affairs through the years also, but he had never seemed to find quite the right match. It seemed that the more he fell for a woman, the less interested she was in him while those girls that did fawn over him had always come up short on attributes Demetri felt important in a serious relationship such as fidelity, intelligence and respectability. He had struggled long and hard to achieve some measure of success and he found himself hesitant to jeopardize his progress by forming a bond with a woman who was not equally trustworthy and responsible.

This same caution held true in his consideration of adopting Andre as a business partner. Demetri had never forged a friendship with another individual quite like the bond he had with Andre. In some ways he would have trusted Andre with his life and in others he wouldn't trust him farther than he could throw him. Many of Demetri's other friends thought the two made a strange pair.

Demetri was known to be courteous and shy while Andre's temperament contained a dash of vanity and instability. Demetri was hard working, industrious and disciplined where as Andre was more a child of vice and corruption. Both were ambitious, but Demetri was willing to sacrifice to make it work while Andre was more apt to look for short cuts, scams or down right larceny to attain his goals. Although his outward demeanor displayed civility, Demetri knew Andre well enough to know that down deep there was an egotistical core that disregarded fair play in situations where a desired opportunity presented itself.

Demetri suspected that his bond to Andre had to do with the very fact that in many ways their positions were in direct opposition to each other. Demetri admired how Andre was able to achieve results in a way that Demetri found so awkward to accomplish. Demetri usually played his cards close to the vest, stayed on the straight and narrow and operated within societal rules and norms. His original nature had not always been rooted in such goodwill and amity however. The shortcuts he had taken with the globe served, in the long run, to reign in his selfish impulses and improprieties. The sacrifices that had been made as retribution for his wishes left him feeling culpable and guarded. He was much more cautious now. His former follies had left him more reserved and calculating, but his shrewdness was not employed for the expressed intent of benefitting his social stature or finances. Although his concerns were to keep himself untarnished, safe and financially solvent, they were not particularly selfish ends borne out of a desire to get ahead in the world. Demetri's goal in becoming prosperous was to avoid ever being in a desperate situation again, especially one in which his reckless or careless behavior was the root cause. If he were ever forced into a corner either in his professional or private life, whether by his own hand or not, the globe would always be a temptation for him. He had to be careful and make wise decisions that had the most minimal chance of backfiring or jeopardizing his stance in the world. At times living under that vexing prospect wore Demetri to a frazzle, yet he could not bring himself to destroy the thing. And the reasons were basically twofold.

Demetri needed insurance. The world was a crazy place, the war had proved that. Who could know what the future might bring, what calamity, misfortune or tribulation laid in wait for even the most vigilant and attentive of men. Someday, somehow, somewhere ... he might have no recourse but to use the globe.

The second reason Demetri was not particularly proud to admit to. As realigned as his priorities now were and as learned as he was about the inherent danger in using the globe, there was always the unimaginable possibilities that whispered in the recesses of his brain. The endless array of options was just too incredible to dismiss. The lure and enticement would have been impossible for even the most righteous of men to ignore.

Demetri knew that he needed to acquire a degree of wealth and success in order to ward off temptation. He figured the best way he could do that at this point in his life was to acquire Thompson Typography. The potential financial reward was obvious. With some new blood, reinvestment and expansion, Thompson Typography could easily become a major player in the advertising and marketing world blossoming in Chicago. The time was right, the factors aligned and the reward a virtual certainty. All Demetri needed was a few more lousy dollars to make it happen. Old Man Thompson had told him there had been some interest shown by at least two other parties intent on acquiring the business, but that his wish was to sell to someone he had employed through the years, someone loyal to him whom he knew would guide the business with respectability and competence.

If he wanted the business, he had to act now. If he was to assure himself of a profitable future, he had to find the available funds now.

And that brought him back to Andre Haskim.

Andre's ethnicity was a fusion of several different European cultures with an accent on German and Bohemian.

Andre was a tall man, six foot four, with a thin frame that curved up to widened shoulders. His hair was black and full and his complexion dark. The contour of his face was oddly rectangular with a square chin anchoring the bottom. One would have never described Abraham Lincoln as good-looking, yet he had an unmistakable look about him and in that same way Andre's appearance was singular in nature. The uniqueness of his features pieced together in a way that left an indelible impression. The elongated ears, sharp nose, lean lips, thin moustache and piercing brown eyes combined to give an overall impression of strict tenacity. There was something magnetic in his persona. Women were drawn to him in the same way a traffic accident drew a crowd.

In contrast to Andre's height, Demetri was only five foot eight, medium build, and dark brown hair. He was not an especially good looking man, but his features were pleasant enough. He wore his hair short and parted on the left side. His eyes were blue and his nose long and straight.

While Andre had always been a loyal friend, Demetri had seen instances where his behavior toward others had not been so diplomatic. There were several individuals at work who Andre had rubbed the wrong way or with whom he had found fault. He was not a trusting individual with those he did not know well and apart from the occasional exception like Demetri, he kept himself at arm's length from others. He didn't like people knowing too many of his innermost secrets or his past. It was as if he intentionally kept a distance between himself and others in order to keep available to him the option of using the individual for his own advantage or self-aggrandizement without having the complication of a close friendship hindering his strategy. Although affable enough at gatherings and socially versatile, he did not have many close friends though he had a myriad of acquaintances. He was one of those people that somehow everyone knew.

Andre was not necessarily a violent individual, but he sometimes displayed an off-kilter temper that arose under situations that were not entirely obvious. An innocent happenstance like someone stepping on his toe might send him into a rage. Someone jokingly using him as the brunt of a gag might produce an exaggerated overreaction. There was a certain unhealed wound somewhere in his psyche that was especially sensitive to annoyance and harassment. For no particular reason, he found certain individuals irritating and it was not unusual for him to find reason to hold a grudge against those with whom he had differences.

Andre liked his liquor and that was a concern also.

Business wise Andre was not lazy, but he was not overly driven either. However, Demetri was not particularly worried about that aspect. Demetri's forte laid in the careful handling of finances, good business sense, a talent with a wrench and screwdriver, and those certain other qualities so necessary in entrepreneurship: self-discipline, responsibility and sound judgment. What Andre could bring to the business was something that Demetri was not good at: making connections, schmoozing potential clients, and recruiting new business. Andre's street smarts and sphere of influence, Demetri had to admit, could be invaluable to the company's expansion. His friend was one of those people who knew many individuals from various walks of life. A partnership with Andre would mean that the day to day scrutiny of the business would fall upon Demetri's shoulders, but he almost welcomed that because he wanted to be in a controlling position.

Although he recognized that the partnership might not be idyllic, Demetri felt it could work. The two men had discussed the possibility of joining forces before and Andre had been receptive to the idea. However, Demetri worried that Andre viewed the proposition as a scheme that could allow him an easy route to the good life. Andre knew that Demetri would make the business work out of sheer will power if nothing else, and was banking on that as his ace in the hole.

Demetri was wise enough to know that in every man's life there comes certain critical junctures where their entire future and the capability of success hinges on them following a particularly narrow trail at precisely the right moment before it disappears in the blink of an eye. This was that moment for Demetri, the kind of moment old men in their rocking chairs think back upon and say "if only I had ..." Regardless of the pros and cons of entering into a partnership with Andre, the truth was that Demetri was out of options and the window of opportunity was closing fast. Time, circumstance and avenue had all come together at that precise moment and if he wasn't able to consummate the deal now, he may very well never have another chance like it.

What he did not want to let on to Andre, was how desperate he was. Part of him wanted to get on his knees and plead for Andre's commitment and the other half wanted desperately to avoid placing his future in such precarious hands.

They had dinner together at LaMonte's Italian Restaurant in little Italy on a warm evening in August 1952. Old Man Thompson had promised Demetri he would give him till the end of the month before he would formerly market the company for sale.

The door to Demetri's future was slowly closing.

"Demetri, have you thought about what we talked about the other night, trying to buy the business?"

Demetri leaned back in his chair and gazed at the photograph behind Andre, a wide angled aerial view of the city of Palermo that the Sicilian proprietor proudly displayed for his clientele. They had finished their Lasagna and their dishes had been removed. Now Demetri was working on the last of his Chianti while smoking a cigar. Andre puffed on a Lucky Strike and nursed a brandy as he sat slumped in the soft vinyl.

"I've thought of nothing else," Demetri replied as he softly tapped the edge of his cigar in the ash tray. "It's not a matter of not wanting to do it, but I have to be honest with you. I know you're eager to jump in but ... I question whether you understand what we're getting into. It's a big thing. Lots of responsibility."

Andre leaned over and rested his elbows on the white tablecloth. "Yeah it's a lot of responsibility and I don't want to feel like I'm forcing you into this, but think of it this way. If you don't do this with me, what options do you face? You're nearly forty years old and you don't have any encumbrances now. The banks won't give you the time of day and there is nobody else you can go to and trust that can get you over the hump. The old man wants to sell, right? And he wants to sell to you." Andre backed off and drew on his cigarette lifting his head to blow the smoke out toward the high ceiling. He cast his glance sideways at Demetri.

"What is it? Let's not kid each other. This is no time to hide behind lies. You want this, you want this bad. But you don't trust me." Andre stabbed the air with his cigarette. "That's where it's at, no?"

Demetri let his gaze fall to the tablecloth and locked on a spot of tomato sauce to his right. He scratched the back of his head and ran his hand through his hair. Andre was right. This was no time to pull punches. If they were going to do this, they best have no misunderstandings. It irked Demetri that Andre was so wise to the spot he was in, but he could never fool Andre. Damn guy knew him too well.

"What's it gonna be, Demetri? You gonna stay a journeyman printer for the rest of your life?"

Demetri looked up. "Look, Andre, I know you. You like the good life, but you're not all that fond of actually working for a living whereas I don't mind getting my hands dirty or working long hours. You know how disciplined I can be, how driven I am, how serious I would treat this. But if you come in with me, it's all the way. I have to know that you got my back, risk for risk."

Andre threw his hands up. "What do you want me to say? I know it's a serious business."

Demetri wasn't quite sure he did. "Yeah, but I get the feeling that you're viewing this as a free ride. You know I'm stuck, you know this is a now or never thing. I wish I didn't have to rely on someone else's funding but ... it is what it is." Demetri rubbed at his moustache. "You're thinking I'm your meal ticket, don't you, Andre?"

Andre chuckled and then burst out laughing. "Okay, let's face it. I know you're a hard worker. I see an opportunity here for me and I won't kid you. I wouldn't consider this kind of a thing with anyone but you. You'll work your fingers to the bone on this. You're honest, trustworthy, and you got that ... that something that I know will bring success. You're ... what's the word ... old school. I trust your instincts, I know you'll be committed and that you'll run the business efficiently." Andre paused and stubbed out his Lucky. "But this is your shot too. My putting in with you is the only way you can swing it. You wait too long and Henry Baxter at Smolsen Type is gonna jump right on this thing." Andre saw the alert flash in Demetri's eyes. "Yeah, I talked to Tommy Caleo at Smolsen. He says Baxter's trying to line up the money himself. See I've been doing a little homework on this deal myself. Baxter wants to throw in with the Hammond Brothers. Did you know that? My assumption is together they could work out the financing, no problem."

A silence fell between the two men broken only by the faint voice of Mario Lanza over the intercom.

Andre went on: "We're friends, Demetri, but I know how much control you like. You hate the thought of having to compromise anything so close to your heart as this, especially with someone like me." Andre chuckled under his breath. "That's okay. If I were you I probably wouldn't trust a son of a bitch like me, either." Andre paused for a moment and took another sip from his brandy sniffer.

"So, the question is if I agree, where would I fit in? Let's be frank. Long hours, supervision, day to day managing of the company, I'll leave that up to you. I would insist on being a voice in major decisions to be made, obviously, but come on, let's call a spade a spade. I ain't interested in getting my hands dirty. The mundane ongoing supervision of workers, balancing books or any of that other shit that needs doing, you're better at that stuff than I am anyway." Andre leaned back and smiled at the ceiling. "No, the way I see it, I'd like my end to be strictly financial. You know I got some money. I can make this thing work for you. And I'll do my end in trying to recruit new business. Schmoozing as you say, eh?"

Demetri brought his hand to his forehead and with his fingertips pressed hard. That strain of self-interest and greed was certainly showing itself in Andre's tone. For a moment the vision of the globe flashed in his head. He didn't have to put up with Andre's brashness at all if he didn't want to, did he? Quickly he dismissed the thought.

"I appreciate your frankness, Andre. I agree that we need to be honest with each other. And to tell you the truth, I already had all of that figured out. In fact from a business point of view, I think it best you leave the day to day running of things to me anyway. I'd keep you in the loop, you know that, but respectfully, I consider myself a better business man than you, no offense."

"None taken."

"But let's get something straight. Just because you may finance more than my end, I ain't working for you. We're partners, partner. A nickel for you, a nickel for me. Right down the middle. And if we have a disagreement business-wise, you're gonna have to agree to defer to my better judgment. I mean we'll discuss everything out, no problem. But you got to make that promise to me. You know I won't be pigheaded or anything like that. I'll be fair, reasonable, all that. Agreed?"

"You're kind of getting a little haughty on this thing, Demetri. Partners yes. And partners have equal say so. I'll not try to hog the decision-making process, but that's got to be a two-way street."

"That's fine. I agree. Now your strength is the selling end. I would want you to do your part in selling the business, making contacts, bringing in customers, etc. But you can function that way. You're a better social butterfly, schmoozer if you will, than me. You know most of our clients. Even the old man recognizes your social skills. That's why he made you point person on some of the business deals lately. That's a good starting point. That's the kind of thing you need to keep up on though. Agreed?"

"I said it before. Agreed. So what else? If we get the business, what kind of long range plans you thinking about?"

Demetri turned his thoughts to the future. "Well, you know the other half of the building is vacant. The old man's got more business coming in right now that he can handle. I think we have to have more space. We buy the building or at least expand. I think the time is right for that. Some of our customers like Vandaverg and Holt Brothers are giving some of their work to other firms just because we haven't got the man power to push it right now. And that's strictly on the old man. He just doesn't have the mustard or inclination for bigger thinking. He's happy with what he's got. His two girls don't want anything to do with the business." The more Demetri spoke, the more excited he became. His enthusiasm was not lost on his potential new partner. "I'm telling you I can feel it coming, Andre. The whole country is in to this idea of bigger and better. Families are booming and that means more refrigerators, more washing machines, more television sets, more vacuum cleaners. It's the boom of the modern age and the way that business is going to deliver that to them is through advertisement and that's us. It's a direct link.

"I've been studying the magazine world too. Every year more and more magazines are being started. I think there's a lot of business coming down the pipe that we haven't even dreamed yet. I'm telling you, with a little luck we could do just fine, just fine indeed."

Andre raised his glass to Demetri. "Demetri I can hear it in your voice, my friend. You're fired on this thing and I like that."

"And the best thing we got going for us is that the old man doesn't think big. He's still living in the horse and carriage era, candle lit room days with the outhouse out back. He doesn't see the potential here."

"You got that right. Taking advantage of that old weasel is half the fun in my eyes. What about the numbers, you been working on them?" Andre had a glint in his eyes. He was excited too.

"Oh yeah. Over and over. Thompson told me he'd be willing to sell for one hundred and ten thousand. Hell the amount of work coming in right now is worth that. The bank is gonna need twenty percent, but that's just for the business. We got to work out expansion, cost of new equipment, etc. And then we're gonna have to hire more typesetters, printers and even a couple more secretaries. We're gonna need a budget for advertising our wares too. We got to take that into account. So we're gonna need a bunch more down to finance the whole project."

Andre nodded his head in agreement. "I like it. I'm with you."

Demetri lit up his cigar again since it had gone out. Then he took a sip of his wine. He was playing out the time because he had a couple more things to mention. "Andre, I want to say this so it's out there and said. I've seen this happen in other businesses, they start out great and then disagreements start, resentments build, and pretty soon the business is working against internal forces besides the normal external ones of supply and demand. I want us to vow to each other that the business comes first. Now I realize our objectives here are not exactly parallel but neither of our goals can come to fruition unless we make a concerted effort to not let disagreements bar our progress. You talked about speaking frankly. I'm speaking frankly. What do you say?"

Andre pulled another Lucky from its pack and with a snap of his lighter brought it to life. Then he turned his eyes to Demetri and held the stare for a moment. His eyes squinted slightly as if there was something in his mind that he wanted to say but that would not be productive. "I agree, Demetri. Money can do strange things to people and the pursuit of it can lead to pathways not even imagined. But you and I, I believe, are a pair. A good fit, perfect no, but a good fit. What one lacks the other has. If we keep to our roles, each hold up their end …" He let the words fall away and took one more drag on his cigarette.

Demetri stared down at his wine and swirled the glass. There was one other thing he wanted to say. No way else to say it but just to blurt it out.

"One more thing, Andre."

"Another worry?"

"I don't know how to say this, so I am just gonna say it. Sometimes, you can be an asshole. You don't like somebody and a streak of vengeance comes out of you. You got some prejudices. I've heard your rants against niggers and Japs. You can be rude and overbearing, especially when you're drinking. I don't want employees or business associates to have to deal with that. So, I am asking you to reign in your 'assholeness'. How's that for frankness?"

Andre blushed slightly and raised his glass to Demetri. "I must admit," he chuckled, "well said."

"Then I have your word on these things?"

"Friends don't need to give each other their word, Demetri. It's understood." Andre raised the last of his brandy to Demetri in a salute and quickly downed it. Then he reached over the table and held his hand out to his friend and they shook.

They had drunk on it, agreed on it and shook on it, but it was not lost on Demetri that Andre had evaded his final question.

Chapter 16

Sophie finished her dance with Andre and came over to the table where Demetri had been day dreaming about the past.

"Honey, are we going to dance?"

"I'm afraid I'm danced out, Sophie. Too much wine. Besides seems like Andre's giving you a run for your money."

Sophie scowled at Demetri as Andre sauntered over to the table. From his stagger it was obvious he was drunk.

"Demetri ... how did a slob like you get so lucky with a girl like this?" Andre wrapped his arms around Sophie and gave her a big kiss. He nearly knocked her down when he lost his balance. Sophie managed to hold him up.

"Wooo, Andre, you need to slow down."

Andre stumbled back and refocused his eyes as a friend of Sophie's came over and started telling her how much she loved her dress. Soon Sophie was surrounded by other women bent on fawning over her and they went off across the hall engrossed in conversation.

"Sit down, Andre. Take a break."

Andre grabbed a chair, pulled it back and slumped into it. He raised his glass to Demetri as if to propose a toast. "Demetri, you got it made buddy. Nice wife, lots of friends and what's more ... D & H Printing is a booming success."

"I must say in no little part to your efforts, Andre. I have to admit when we first started out two years ago I had my doubts that you'd pull your weight. But your schmooziosity has brought quite a number of new clients our way. Salute, my friend."

The two clinked glasses. Although Demetri sugar coated his comments somewhat, he had to admit his initial fears about Andre had not come to pass. The man had done as well as could be expected in keeping up his end of the deal. He was good for taking clients to lunch, wining and dining them and being the social front for the enterprise. He had managed to recruit new business for D & H. Andre had even taken a role in the everyday workings of the business. It was all Demetri could have hoped for.

However, more and more Demetri had been working behind the scenes establishing solid base relationships with their customers. Their clientele appreciated his work ethic. When deadlines got tight, a quick change in a layout was required, some snafu needed quick attention or a vital last minute emergency filled, it was Demetri their colleagues generally called. More and more, customers began to realize who truly represented the backbone of the business.

Demetri found that his social adeptness had improved and had become more crucial to the business. Although Andre still provided a certain splash by the sheer grandiloquence of his character, when people wanted to talk turkey, they sought out Demetri. When a customer referred a new prospective client to D & H, it was Demetri's name that was passed along. However, whenever crucial decisions needed to be made or an important meeting held, Demetri made sure that Andre was included. Demetri had been pleased to see that, for all practical purposes, Andre took the decision-making process seriously and actually provided some good insights into their business transactions.

Demetri knew that Andre was drinking more and gambling more, but so far his behavior had not jeopardized the business. So even when other reputable business men, knowing a good thing when they saw one, confided in Demetri that they would consider buying out Andre's end and teaming up with Demetri, he did not consider a major change. After all, a deal was a deal and since D & H was rolling along so well, Demetri did not become overly concerned with Andre's bad habits.

And the business was doing well. The infusion of cash invested by Andre had provided sufficient collateral for the bank to authorize not only enough money to buy the business but enough capital to enable them to expand and finance the additional typesetting equipment they needed. They had initially gone out on a limb hiring more typesetters and pressmen for the increase in business they anticipated. Several commercial artists were brought in to offer a more sophisticated consulting option for their customers in the advertising displays they were commissioned to work on.

For several months they treaded water keeping pace with their expenses and picking up extra business as they went along. Then they caught a huge break they had not expected. Hammond Type went out of business. Somehow even though there seemed to be enough work for a number of firms to thrive, the Hammond Brothers had gotten themselves into tax problems. Their sudden bankruptcy left a number of established advertising firms holding the bag. Both Demetri and Andre quickly made connections and to stave off other competitors, offered to complete the projects that were in midstream at no charge. Knowing that the establishment of trust was important to secure future business, the small financial loss incurred was a mere triviality.

The ploy paid out in spades. D & H Printing gained a number of new customers and increased their footprint on the typesetting industry. The amount of work they produced increased by thirty-one percent the first year and by an additional seventeen percent the second year. During the third year, they were able to start throwing some of their weight around. The amount of business they were now producing allowed them to undercut some of their competitors and gain an even stronger choke hold on the industry. Andre and Demetri in three short years had found themselves officially 'well-off' and slowly ascending to the status of 'wealthy'.

Demetri's good fortune during this time was not limited to business alone. Haymarket Advertising had an advertising executive by the name of Sophie Wykowski. Sophie was a hard-nosed Polish blonde with a striking figure who was nearly fourteen years Demetri's junior. They had met just in passing on a couple of occasions when Demetri attended meetings at the firm. At first Demetri had not been awestruck by Sophie at all and at the time he was dating another woman even though he knew he had no future with her.

On a cold December morning Demetri saw Sophie in a booth at a downtown restaurant eating a bowl of fruit and reading the Tribune. She was alone and in direct contrast to his normal timidity surprised himself by going right up to her and asking if he could join her. The moment she smiled at Demetri and said: "Oh yes please," something clicked in Demetri's head, an almost palpable 'ding'.

Sophie would not have been defined as beautiful, but she was the kind of woman men turn their heads to catch a second look at without realizing it. The way she presented herself displayed a finite assuredness that made her even more appealing. What surprised Demetri during breakfast was that they were never at a lack of things to discuss. Demetri made a point of reading the newspaper every morning and found that no matter what topic he addressed, Sophie was aware of the latest developments on the issue. Their discussion ran on until Sophie had to go to work. The matter might have ended right there if it hadn't been for what Sophie said to him when she made ready to leave.

As she was getting her things together, Demetri found himself frustrated that their little impromptu get-together was coming to an abrupt end. He struggled to find that appropriate final parting line that … that did what? Open a door for him with her? He hadn't totally figured out how exactly he felt about the girl. The truth is that if he would have had any inclination toward the girl at all, he would have never found the guts to come right up to her as he had done. It was only because he was not aware of any feelings for her that had made it so easy for him to intrude upon her breakfast to begin with.

In that short twenty minutes or so his whole attitude had shifted. He had to say something because she was beginning to slide out of the booth. "I ... enjoyed our little talk. Funny how your first impressions of someone can be so wrong."

Oh no, he thought. *How am I going to get out of that one?*

"Oh, and what was your first impression of me?" She smiled curiously and Demetri could tell that she was genuinely interested in hearing his explanation.

"Well ..." He hadn't planned on answering this question. "We really didn't speak much when I've been to your office, but I must say I guess I assumed you to be much less, what's the word, sophisticated, than I found you to be. You're a very bright gal."

Sophie tilted her head slightly and tightened her eyebrows as if trying to decide if she was being patronized. She held her smile the whole time and Demetri had the distinct impression that she was sizing him up for an equally suitable rebuttal. Then she suddenly dropped it. Her smile broadened. "I see I'm going to have to keep an eye on you, Demetri. Are you one of those guys who says one thing and means another, thinks he's being mysterious and really can be read just like the subtitles to a movie?"

At first Demetri didn't know how to take it. The question confused him, caught him off guard. He wondered if he had offended her, but then quickly realized that this was the kind of girl who wasn't easily offended and didn't give a damn if she were because she could give it just as easily as she could take it. Their discussion so far had followed all the rules of an opening volley. Proper manners at the table, fake concern about issues with which he had no interest, affirmative nods where the situation called for it, displays of supportive sympathy and understanding at all the right times, and appropriate lies like the indication he had made of how intelligent one of her coworkers was when he really thought the guy was a dunderhead.

But now it was as if they were sparing. The image of Robin Hood and Little John standing at opposite ends of the log across the river flashed in his head, but he didn't have time to dwell on it. The game was afoot.

"What do you mean by that?" Demetri smirked, pushing the cat and mouse game further, finding with every moment an enticing playfulness tickling his thoughts.

"Well, for one you're very reserved, aren't you? You'll tell the appropriate lies, but you're not half as sneaky as you think. For example, that nonsense you gave me about how you thought Richard was such a smart guy. You really think he's a schmuck, I can tell."

Demetri opened his mouth. She had caught him to the quick.

"This 'very bright gal' business. What's really happening is that you're wanting to say one thing but all you could come up with was 'You're a very bright gal.'"

Demetri had recovered sufficiently to ask "And so, what am I wanting to say?" Then he wondered if he hadn't really stepped into it by asking that open-ended question.

Sophie relaxed her smile and sat back in the booth. She wasn't quite ready to leave yet now. It wasn't that her dander was up, but she wasn't going to be finished until she was finished. "You're in a panic there, Mister Smoothie. I'm walking out of here just when you were on the brink of making a decision about me. But still too many unanswered questions like 'Am I already spoken for?' And there is our age difference to consider. You made a point of not mentioning that you were presently dating a woman that you really don't care for all that much."

Demetri again found himself with his mouth wide open. "How did you know that?"

Sophie chuckled out loud. "I told you, you read like a bad suspense novel. And now you're thinking she's leaving and the window of opportunity's closing and I need to get my foot in the door, but you're not quite sure you even like me enough yet. Might be I'm a little too brash for you … And besides that, you're really a shy guy. You're the kind of guy who's still standing on the pier while all his friends have already jumped in because you're afraid the water's too cold."

She paused for a moment, and then smirked, and then winked at him. By this time Demetri's thoughts had totally gone askew. Not only was he unable to retort, but he had already been thrown off the log. Presently he was in that panicky place you find yourself the moment you fall into water and go underneath and you don't know where you are and you can only flail your arms and hope you break the surface soon.

And the water was indeed cold.

Sophie slid out of the booth. "I'll make it easy for you. No, I'm not already spoken for. In fact, most times I'm not even spoken to. I like the opera and they're playing Puccini at the Schubert this Friday night. Oh and I like to sit close, not in the balcony. Here's my card. Call me when you get the tickets and let me know where you're taking me to dinner after the show. That easy enough for you?"

Demetri stared at the card she had given him and finding himself flabbergasted blurted out: "But I don't know anything about the opera."

And that statement put him right behind the eight ball. That stupid reply had let go an entire realm of psychological data for Sophie to scrutinize. All hopes of one-upmanship had just been stomped into the mud by that preposterous remark. That pronouncement had unconsciously confessed to Sophie that everything she had said was true and that her diagnosis of his character had been accurate. He might as well have said: 'But I don't know anything about handling a woman like you.'

Sophie swung her wrap around her shoulders and grabbed her purse from the booth. She was now officially ready to leave, but not quite.

"Well, that'll have to change if you want to hang around with me. You need to infuse a little culture into your repertoire." Then she laughed and walked off. Demetri stared down again at her card and wondered what had just happened. He felt like he had just been hit by a freight train. Then Sophie was back. "Oh by the way, thanks for picking up the check." She laughed again and this time sauntered off chuckling to herself.

Demetri saw her check sitting underneath her coffee cup. For a moment he experienced a slight bit of annoyance. He felt like a boy who had just been kicked by the bully, had swung back and gotten a fat lip for his effort. He'd been bested, but somehow his honor was still intact.

She had a lot of gall leaving him with the check, he thought. *And did she know how much opera tickets were, the good tickets? Who'd she think she was anyway?*

Then he couldn't help but smile.

When it was all over, and he'd paid the tabs, and he'd walked the four blocks to his office, and he'd gotten his coat off, there was one thought dominating his total world. His secretary told him that his nine o'clock was going to be a little late.

"That's fine," he said grabbing his coat and hat. "I got a stop to make."

The Schubert Theater was a quick cab ride away. With a little luck he could be back by nine-thirty.

He found himself actually muttering to himself in the cab, "Please don't be sold out."

Chapter 17

The Opera tickets were indeed expensive, but Demetri had not cared. They had dinner at the Como Inn and Demetri was happy to pick up that tab too. As the months went by their relationship grew into a strong bond. They came together so simply. In the past Demetri's relationships with women had been puzzling and baffling for him. He had wondered many times if he would ever find a woman that he could share his life with. In fact, by late 1953 being forty years old, Demetri had all but given up on ever having a family. The fact that he was still a bachelor really had not bothered him all that much up to that point because it allowed him to invest all his energies into the goal of accumulating wealth and security. However, now that the business was doing so well, he found his ambitions veering into other areas. The self-indulgent crash and burn days of flashing youth had curled in on themselves now and the prospect of carousing about lost its appeal. And seemingly just at that point of his life when he realized that he wanted more, Sophie had come to rescue him.

Demetri had always considered himself one of those people who couldn't bear to relinquish control of the reins of his life to anyone, but the more his relationship with Sophie grew, the more he saw how wrong he had been about that. It was not so much he was unwilling to let anyone dictate or influence the course of his life, it was just that he had never met anyone with whom he could so completely trust to handle that duty. The magnitude of importance his success was to him in terms of keeping him distanced from the always menacing alternative and allure of the globe, had cemented his resolve to such a degree that yielding a part of his life to anyone meant that the person, by definition, had to be trustworthy to a fault. This was especially true in terms of a woman who might use her wiles to lure Demetri into a point of no return where his knowledge of the globe's dangers would not be sufficient to deter him from being swayed by its magnetism.

Sophie had simply shown up, told Demetri how it was going to be, made her intentions known to him without reservation or hesitation, and shoved him out of the driver's seat. In an odd way, Demetri had never been so relieved in his whole life. Here was a competent, attractive, go-getter intent on the direction of her life who informed Demetri that he was to jump aboard and for all practical purposes, keep his mouth shut. Demetri found himself following Sophie's lead like a bloodhound tracking a scent, but the attraction was not all psychological. Demetri was head over heels in love. It had been the simplest thing he had ever done to allow her to be his social director, lover, counselor, and trusted friend and confident. By the time Sophie told him they were ready to get married, Demetri was totally hooked.

Truth be told, Demetri was not interested in directing the issues in his life he viewed as subordinate to his main goal of building the business and acquiring a certain degree of financial assistance. He was more than happy to allow Sophie to take charge of his social calendar. It didn't hurt that Sophie was the kind of girl who got around. She had a lot of friends from various walks of life that provided them many different outlets to explore. Sophie had a volunteer mentality and spent much of her free time devoting herself to the local art community, hospitals, and church organizations. As a fundraiser she could be painstakingly resourceful, as a friend her allegiance could be unfaltering, as a lover she could be tender and sensitive, and as a businesswoman she was efficient and competent. Demetri could not have wished for a more perfect partner.

However, every saint has her vices, and Sophie was no exception. There were flaws in the armor though the faults were not nearly sufficient to dilute the affection Demetri had for her.

If there was one issue that they had trouble reaching a consensus on it was children. Demetri had assumed that Sophie would want to have kids. He viewed it as a natural outgrowth of their marriage. Financially they certainly could afford it. However, if there was one virtue Sophie did not have, it was a nurturing disposition. Demetri had recognized that her assertive, self-assuredness was driven partially by narcissism and vanity. She could be a dynamo, it was true, but her forceful nature was motivated by her passion to obtain the things she wanted. Demetri had even wondered at times if her love for him was genuine or simply a necessary step for her to vault her ambitions for wealth and prestige. They had discussed children several times and Demetri came to accept that Sophie simply wasn't the mothering type. It was disappointing for him, but she had so many other good qualities that he kept his melancholy over the issue to himself.

Besides, he thought, *things could change through time. Sophie might change her mind.*

There really wasn't much else he could do. He was so in love with her by that time that there was no going back.

Demetri had his suspicions as to why Sophie was not interested in children. Sophie had been adopted as an infant. Her biological mother had been a young Polish immigrant from New York City who found herself in trouble, alone, penniless and scared. At the hospital she had taken one long look at her child and passed her on to the hospital social worker who had several families more than willing to accept the baby. Being that she was Polish, the hospital found a perfect match. The Wykowski's were a working class family in New York who had tried for years unsuccessfully to have children. The father, Gustaw, was a bricklayer and the mother, Eva, was an office secretary for a law firm. They were hardworking, good people and as often happens once they brought Sophie into their household, found themselves pregnant with their own child, Roza.

And that's when the trouble started.

It was hard to tell just who, if anybody, was at fault, but Sophie felt that once the actual biological child of Eva and Gustaw came on the scene, Eva spoiled and coddled Roza and gave her preferential treatment. Being hardnosed and driven might have evolved out of Sophie's real or imagined necessity to fend for herself. As a result an intense competition developed between the two girls from a very young age. At times the resentment and umbrage became an obstacle to Eva's natural desire to give equal measure to both her girls. Sophie became more obstinate and headstrong. Roza was not exactly an innocent bystander in all of this. She tended to use her 'protected' status to gain a greater degree of favoritism by being more submissive to her parents. Gustaw, from his 'old world' view of matrimonial duties, remained an impartial observer standing on the sidelines while Eva dealt with their children as was expected of a dutiful wife and mother.

The family held together through thick and thin however. Sophie graduated high school, took some college night classes and eventually wound up in Chicago working in advertising. As relatively successful as Sophie had become, there was a sadness and psychological wound imbedded in her soul. Sophie still 'loved' her parents and had not disassociated from them or her sister in any way. However, with her mother she had developed a particularly unpredictable love/hate relationship that was tossed from one side to the next due to the sensitivity both parties seemed to retain. Any innocent comment or remark made by Eva to Sophie could easily be perceived as an insult. Any innocuous compliment issued to Roza was construed as a further example of the favoritism Sophie had been forced to struggle against her whole life.

Some of Sophie's strongest personal traits like determination, resilience, and drive were borne out of her 'need' to prove to herself and others that, by God, she could do it on her own. That she didn't need anyone to prop her up or pave a path for her was not really the demonstration or manifestation of a confident, passionate trailblazer, but instead a desperate mission to finally receive the recognition she so desperately sought.

This convoluted, drawn-out contest served to partly dispel the notion of motherhood to Sophie. It left an unhealthy, noxious taste in her mouth. She had seen how a child could be scarred and disillusioned and how even loving parents could make mistakes causing irreparable harm.

And then there was the enigma of the biological mother she had never known. Intellectually, she probably agreed with everything her parents had told her about the girl doing the right thing in giving her up. But still she felt cheated and always wondered what kind of a woman her biological mother had been.

It was something Sophie just couldn't shake. The attitude isolated her from the normal maternal sentiment that usually developed in women. Demetri and Sophie had talked about this empty feeling many times, but the whole idea of motherhood was something she just couldn't accept.

As the years went by, they learned it was not something that either of them had to be concerned with anyway. Physically, for some reason, Sophie did not seem to be able to bear children. The failure to conceive did not deter Demetri's love and faithfulness to his wife. In all things he trusted her. He was happy to share his ups and downs with her and through the years Sophie reciprocated even adopting a less urgent need to domineer or insist on making her own way in the business world. As D & H Printing became more and more successful there was little need for Sophie to concern herself with earning a living. She had more of an opportunity to devote her time to volunteer pursuits she found worthwhile.

Their relationship progressed in trust and mutual confidence. No secrets existed between them. Demetri's sense of marital commitment even pushed him to include

Sophie's name on the safe deposit box at Guardian's Bank in case anything ever happened to him. However, Demetri made a point of keeping the key to the box with him at the office. If Sophie wanted to store some jewelry or papers in the box, Demetri always was the one who visited it.

All of their needs were being met and there was no immediate threat of any kind to either of them that even might tempt him to consider the globe. At times, Demetri went months without even thinking about the crystal or daydreaming about the possibilities it presented to him. However, sometimes in his idle moments, his thoughts would meander to what he might wish for if it ever came to that. Time had dulled the sting of the former penalties that had resulted from his prior experiences with the globe though he still held some regret for those who had been harmed. However, through the years rationalization had faded the level of guilt he had once felt so deeply. War was hell and he had no other way to get out. As for Estrella, he could barely remember the girl's face anymore, and his father's drunken rampage had not been his doing.

Demetri thanked his lucky stars things were going so well. They had money and success. Perhaps his only regret was the lack of children to share their good fortune with, but that would not have been something he would have considered using the globe for anyway because it was not an absolutely pressing need and it did not serve as a particular threat to their well-being.

As it turned out, Demetri had been right about one thing though. Sophie's desire to have children did change as the years went by. However, the reasons had little to do with the development of a nurturing spirit.

Chapter 18

3:30 pm, October 10, 1984

Tommy woke up and found himself staring at a beeping monitor. He realized someone was rubbing his head. He turned his neck to the left and saw Doctor Tim's face outlined by the light of the window behind him. He was still quite groggy and for a moment with all the brightness streaming in, he thought Doctor Tim was an angel from heaven who had come to whisk him away. Then full comprehension came and he realized he wasn't there to whisk him anywhere, but he was an angel all the same.

"Hello," Tommy said.

"How you feeling?"

"I got a little headache?"

"You've been sleeping quite a bit, I hear. That's good."

Tommy moved his eyes to the ceiling unconsciously to try and get a read on how he was feeling. His headache was milder now, but he was so loopy that he wasn't sure. "My head doesn't hurt so much as ... I just kind of feel ... dizzy a little bit."

The doctor stood up and went to the end of the bed where he grabbed Tommy's chart and started writing in it. He checked his watch and returned to the chart.

"My mom here?"

"She just left about twenty minutes ago to get something to eat. You're very lucky to have such loving parents."

"Yeah that's me. I'm like Mister Lucky." Tommy moaned as he turned to his left side a little, while the doctor kept writing. Outside the window the sky was a vivid blue and puffy cumulus clouds slowly crawled toward the east. A flying V of Canadian Geese appeared moving toward the northwest. Tommy could vaguely hear their honking, one to another, and wondered what they possibly could be talking about. Where could they be going? How wonderful if he could go with them.

He remembered something now, something his mother had recited from the Bible one night when he had asked her about death. It was funny. She had dismissed his worries as best she could and then she said she wasn't afraid to die and that no one should be. And then she read that passage, "The fish of the sea, the birds of the air, the beasts of the field, every creature that moves along the ground, and all the people on the face of the earth will tremble at my presence. The mountains will be overturned, the cliffs will crumble and every wall will fall to the ground."

That verse had given him strength like no other. The passage had nothing to do with death but everything to do with facing it. If God was that powerful, that awesome, surely he would be strong enough to be gentle and kind and good. Then his mother read another line and this he was sure she picked because of his recent infatuation with the birds in the nest outside his window: "Look at the birds of the air; they do not sow or reap or store away in barns and yet your Heavenly Father feeds them. See how the lilies of the field grow. They do not labor or spin. Yet I tell you that not even Solomon in all his splendor was dressed like one of these."

Tommy couldn't imagine how he could possibly remember those lines, but there was something so … majestic and comforting about them. No, he wasn't afraid to die, he didn't think. Maybe a little. But he knew others were very afraid for him. One of them being Doctor Tim.

"Doctor?"

"Yes," he said as he finally finished his notes and returned the chart to its clip.

"Who was Solomon?"

"Solomon? Why he was a great king from the olden days in the bible. He was very wise, very, very wise. In fact he was so wise, he threatened once to cut a baby in half just so two women who each claimed to be the baby's mother could have their share."

Tommy scrunched his eyebrows. "That doesn't sound very smart to me."

"Oh, but it was; because the mother who truly loved the boy did not want that to happen, so she offered to give up the baby to the other woman rather than have her baby killed. So Solomon knew then who the real mother was and gave the boy to her. Pretty clever cat, eh?"

Tommy looked on the counter top where flowers bloomed in a vase.

"Yet I tell you that not even Solomon in all his splendor was dressed like one of these," he mumbled.

"Wow, I'm impressed. You know the Bible."

"Something my mother read to me." Tommy paused and searched out the doctor's eyes. "I think you're smart, like Solomon. Can I ask you a question?"

"Sure."

"What do you think … happens when we die?"

The doctor's face quickly turned stony before he caught himself and chuckled. "Now why would you want to worry about that?"

"That's just the thing. I'm, I don't know, not really worried, but my parents are. I hear them talking when they think I can't hear. If I die, will you promise me something?"

"Tommy you are not going to die. Not if I can help it."

"But you're worried too. I can tell by how you are always reading my chart, talking to my parents, making jokes with me." Doctor Tim lowered his gaze. "It's okay. I want you to know it's okay. You are doing your best. I know that and I feel very good about you being my doctor." Tommy stared off through the window again. "Besides I think that when we die … it will be good. Look how beautiful today is: the sky, the trees, the birds. We live in a garden."

Doctor Tim turned away from the boy and put his hand to his forehead. There was no saving this boy and he knew it. They were able to cut a portion of the tumor away from his temporal lobe and ease the pressure on his brain. The headaches ceased, for a while anyway, but the core of the growth was embedded too far, too many entanglements with other areas of the brain. They had hoped to remove it all, but it was indeed hopeless. They bought him more time and perhaps less pain, but that was it. The cancer would continue to grow. The chemotherapy and radiation had only had limited success and did not halt the tumor's progress. Since the headaches had reappeared, the doctor didn't want to take any chances. Although now that they had him back in the hospital, he wasn't sure what he could do.

Doctor Timothy Ivins had worked on hundreds of patients with similar lesions. Some lived, some died. But never had he felt so ... determined to cure someone as he had this boy and because he was so dedicated to that cause, he found his anguish almost intolerable. He had seen many people forced to face death: children, adults and seniors and always each person had a different coping mechanism. Some, the saddest, were those who simply could not face it: those so frightened that their final hours, instead of being a slow glide to final peace, became an agonizing torture. Some accepted death with a sort of vain surrender that did not so much distill peace in them but brought out a certain disgust and aversion to the whole event. They went not so much fearfully, but angrily as if life had dealt them an unfair hand.

There certainly were those who accepted death willingly and straightforwardly. These were usually those who were secure in their faith, deeply religious. Many of them Doctor Tim had admired as they took their final journey. However, even those who were not afraid of death, whether unconsciously or not, in their final days thought of things from their perspective. The majority, even loving mothers and grandparents, became preoccupied and self-absorbed to some degree as death closed in. They certainly still had great concern for the ones they were leaving behind, but the final few bars of the song were played to themselves as would only be natural in such a crucial and momentous occasion.

And then there was Tommy. He seemed almost oblivious to death. Not specifically concerned about it so much as how it was affecting others. If he had any worries at all they were directed toward his parents: their unhappiness, their grief. He hardly gave a moment to himself. And now this Solomon business and the Bible quotes. It was astonishing. So much so that tears started welling in the doctor's eyes. Then anger jumped in. Maybe he could try surgery again, cut out even more, increase the chemo or try a different regiment. Perhaps an adjustment to the radiation technique? Maybe there was an experimental drug they had not considered. Possibly Long or Fitzsimmons might have an idea.

"It's okay Doctor Tim," Tommy said. "It's not your fault."

The doctor had not realized he had been displaying his rage so noticeably that the boy could sense it. He sighed deeply and went over to the side of Tommy's bed. He wanted to say something to the boy, how much he was trying, how sorry he was. The kid had a way of exposing the doctor's helplessness without judgment or self-pity.

"Doctor, you don't have to feel sad. I know how much you've been trying with me. You've got your whole life left, a life where you can help so many other kids, kids just like me." Tommy stared down at the IV site in his right hand and squeezed his fist to relieve some of the discomfort. His voice went down a notch. "I know you can't help me … but if it means anything to you, you've been like a … can't remember the word … like I really look up to you. If I ever do make it out of this, I am going to be a doctor like you. I want to be a part of healing people just like you." Tommy shook his head and stared back out the window. "All I've done is bring sadness." Tears started forming in his eyes. "Sadness to you, my mother, my father. I've let them down."

Doctor Tim lifted Tommy's chin and stared him in the eyes. "You haven't brought sadness to anyone. You've shown me what real courage is, real strength and faith. You're so young and yet you're so understanding and … and wise about things. The word you were looking for is inspiration. Well, you've been an inspiration to me. When I finished medical school and started my residency I started thinking about all the benefits my profession was going to give me: money and security. And I didn't realize it, but it gave me a big head like I thought I was really something special, the big Doctor Timothy Ivins. And I used to get all puffy and think I was so … so above everybody else 'cause I was a big doctor and they weren't.

"Well, when I started working with patients, it slowly came to me that the money and prestige didn't mean anything. I was holding people's lives in my hands. That realization never really dawned on me fully until I started working with you. You opened my eyes to the real work that I need to do. Your courage and grace showed me what my real place in this world is and I am never going to let that go. My real place is to work as hard as I possibly can to cure as many people as I possibly can and the heck with the money and the big name and all that stuff. If I ever save another person in my whole life, if I ever bring comfort or cure to anyone, it will have been you who had a hand in it."

Tommy lowered his eyes again and this time he started crying and the tears wouldn't stop. "I … think you're just saying that because you want me to feel good and trying to cheer me up and all that, but I'm scared Doctor. I'm so scared and I have no one to run to with my scaredness. A lot of times I wake up in the night when it's dark and quiet and I get so scared and I pray to God to not make me scared, to not make me a coward. I say, God, please help me not to be a coward. And my mother, I hear her crying and she looks so ragged like she hasn't slept in so long and that's my fault 'cause I'm so sick and I want so bad to call her and have her come to my bedside and hold me, but I don't want to wake her up cause she has to sleep. So I lay there by myself and pray to God and

I tell God how much I want to be a doctor, I want to help people just like you Doctor Tim. Just like you. And I see all the beautiful things in the world like the birds and the sky and the trees. I don't want to leave them or my mother but the hardest part, the hardest part is that my life will have been nothing but pain and sorrow and I would have helped nobody and my part would have been nothing."

"Tommy, you don't have to feel –"

But Tommy couldn't be dissuaded from finishing.

"There was a bird outside my window at home and she had a nest and she took care of her little birdies and she was so brave and if a cat or squirrel came by she would fight them off, anything to save her little babies and I was so proud of that little bird. I was so proud of that little bird and I thought how wonderful a thing that must be to be so … so driven that you would risk everything for someone else and that little bird didn't know what a … how proud I was of her. But I was jealous too 'cause of how … how strong and determined she was and I wished so hard that I had a cause like that, something I could be brave about and protect with all my might. Something that I would feel so strong about that I would risk my whole life for it if I had to. Something I would be willing to risk everything for. "

Tommy wiped his nose and suddenly felt ashamed because he had displayed the fear he had for so long struggled to keep inside, so that he would not be anymore of a burden than he already was. "I want to give my life over to helping other people, like you Doctor Tim, just like you. I wouldn't mind dying at all as long as I could know that I was a part of something good. That my life was something good … instead of just sadness."

Tommy looked up at Doctor Tim and now all reticence to say what he had been holding in for so long was gone. "If I'm scared … it's not because I want to be. And I'm trying with all my heart not to be. But if I'm scared, I mean really scared, can I talk to you?"

"Sure you can. You can talk to me anytime you want, night or day. I am going to tell your parents that we made this little deal and I will give your mom my phone number and you call me anytime you want. Middle of the night, I don't care. 'Cause I'll tell you the truth. Sometimes in the middle of the night, I wake up scared too and you know why? Because you helped me see this new direction and I don't know if I'm strong enough to do it, brave enough to do it. I don't know if I have the courage of that little bird. I don't know if I have half the courage that you have."

"You're brave, Doctor Tim. You're the bravest man I know."

"If I am, it's partly because of you." Doctor Tim leaned forward and kissed Tommy's forehead. "You get some sleep, you hear. And I'll make a deal with you. I think something good is going to happen. Something good is going to happen. And you stop worrying about all this nonsense about being a burden and sadness. You just keep thinking that something good is going to happen. Both of us will. How's that? And then we'll see. Is that a deal?"

"Okay," Tommy sniffled. "That's a deal."

"Got to go see old Mrs. Flannery now," Doctor Tim joked. "She's got the gout again, but really I think she's just got a bad case of the grumpies."

Tommy giggled.

Doctor Tim went to the door and opened it. Just before he walked through it, he turned to Tommy again. "Something good is going to happen. That's a deal right?"

"That's a deal."

Doctor Tim went out and closed the door behind him. As he stood there and thought for a moment, he heard some mumbling coming from inside Tommy's room. He put his ear to the door and listened. At first he couldn't make it out. Was it just the TV? Then he caught it. Tommy was repeating it now like a mantra: Something good is going to happen. Something good is going to happen.

Chapter 19

5:15 pm, October 10, 1984

Doctor Walter Fleming was a tall, good-natured, clean-shaven, balding, old-school physician with a wry sense of humor. His expression now was sullen however as he stared at the medical chart one more time flipping through the pages, scrunching his lips in puzzlement as if someone had played a practical joke on him. In front of him on the bed sat Demetri looking wide-eyed and rested. Outwardly Demetri displayed the calm demeanor of a rough old codger who could still handle himself in a fight with a man thirty years his junior. Inwardly his mind raced with thoughts of retribution and reckoning. Wondering when and where it would occur and who would be on the losing end of it.

"Well ..." Doctor Fleming sighed. "I'll be damned if I can figure it out. Mr Davos yesterday at this time I'd given you a thirty percent chance of survival. At the very least I thought you'd have a long road of recovery ahead for you. That fall had fractured your skull, caused blood clots on the left side of your brain, cracked four ribs and crushed several vertebrae in your back. It was unlikely you'd ever walk again. Today you wake up and are fine. Your brain function is normal, there is no swelling in your back, your ribs show only minor bruising and ... and you're just fine. In fact, you're as spry a seventy-one year old man as I've ever seen."

"Then I can go home?"

Doctor Fleming picked at his left top incisor as he often did when he contemplated an important decision. "I think you better stay overnight tonight. It's just too ... soon to trust it. I'd feel better about you staying one more night." He pulled his hand away from his mouth and returned the chart to the clipboard on the edge of the bed.

"But I'm fine. You said so yourself."

"Don't worry, your insurance will cover it. It'll be on my direct orders."

"I don't give a damn about the hospital bill. I want to go home. I have to go home."

"Can't do it. Social worker's involved too. She's got to come and finish her analysis and she's gone for the day. As much as you claim it was an accidental fall, she's not ready to dismiss it so frivolously. She's concerned about it being a suicide attempt and I can't … eh … go against that."

"But I didn't try to kill myself. Do I look like the kind of guy who would try to kill himself?"

"I don't know. I just know that I personally can dismiss you, but you can't be released until she does also."

"That's a bunch of shit, doctor."

"I appreciate the professional jargon, Mr Davos, but rules is rules. What's the big deal? Relax and watch TV. Sorry." Doctor Fleming stuck his hands inside his white smock and walked out of Demetri's room.

Quimby was standing near the door and now he moved over to the seat in the corner and sat down. Demetri curled his lip and pondered his situation. He paced from one side of the room to the other. Then he turned toward Quimby. "You say you saw her with the globe earlier in the evening, before the break-in?"

"Yes, sir, but I'm sure she never used it. It would have been impossible. I locked the door behind me and I have the only key. Besides you got well early this morning. And I know for a fact that whoever was waiting for this Passetti character made off with the globe and I am afraid that man is our good friend Andre."

Demetri went to the window and stared out. Night was falling on Chicagoland. In the distance a row of airplanes could be seen lined up in the southern sky each one in formation flying a few miles behind the one before it, waiting for their chance to touch down at O'Hare Field.

Demetri couldn't figure it out. The fact that he had gotten well earlier in the day indicated that the wish most likely was made this morning because in all the experiences he had with the globe, he knew that a wish of that nature would probably have been immediately granted. The repercussion, the price to be paid, could come later although most of the time it came on the heels of the granted wish. No doubt whatever consequence had come from the wish that had brought him to health may have already occurred. Assuming it was Andre who had taken the globe, why would he have wished for Demetri to recover?

Perhaps in his joy he just wanted to do an old friend a favor? No, that couldn't be.

Demetri went back to the bed and sat down. From the news they had gotten from the police, Vince Passetti was a second story man associated with Mizetti's band of thugs. Demetri was well aware that Andre knew Mizetti from the old days. Hell, his gambling debts to the Mizetti mob had been a major reason for the situation they were in now. Andre must have gone to Mizetti to help him break into the house. Nothing else was stolen and whoever had come in had gone directly to the closet where Andre knew the globe most likely was. There couldn't possibly be any other explanation for this whole mess. Demetri swore at himself for not returning that globe to the security of a safety deposit box as he had in the past, but he had seen how that had turned out to so he felt better about keeping it close to him.

Suddenly a wave of fear went through Demetri as a more obvious conclusion came to him for the entire riddle.

Perhaps Andre wanted to exact a specific revenge on Demetri on his own in a demented act of vengeance. Was Andre fattening him up, so to speak, so he could deliver the coup de grace himself personally? With the globe Andre could wish for anything bad to happen to Demetri. He could dream up some merciless torture of some kind like having Demetri buried alive, or stricken with paralysis or who knows what. Was his hatred for Demetri that intense? Was Demetri to be the fatted calf in this whole misadventure?

Demetri almost chuckled at the absurdity of it all. Thing was his health now was downright robust. Both physically and mentally he had never felt better in his life. Even in the touchy situation he was in right now where any number of calamities could be foisted upon him at any moment, he found himself feeling spirited, enthusiastic and confident. He hadn't felt this physically fit in years and the depression that had nearly cost him his life was now nonexistent. There was no doubting it. Someone had wished him healthy.

"Well, if I got this figured right," Demetri said, "Andre must have gone to Mizetti to help him break into the house. Perhaps he felt this was the best opportunity to grab the globe and didn't want any mistakes to occur due to his inexperience."

"But why shoot the man who brought him the globe?"

"They had to have had an argument over who was getting it. Mizetti's no fool. Perhaps he didn't know what the globe could do, but he must have sensed the thing was vitally important to Andre. Passetti might have been on orders to return the globe to Mizetti. I can imagine Andre would have been absolutely delighted with the globe in his possession and he wasn't about to let it get past him. If Mizetti got his hands on it, he would soon discover what it could do and then there would be no chance of Andre ever getting it back. With all the bad blood those two have had over the years, I can't imagine that Mizetti would have felt any remorse in dispatching Andre."

Quimby nodded his head. "I think you're right, sir. It makes sense. But why would Andre make you well? You're really the only one who can possibly stand in his way now. In fact, why would he care at all about you? He can go on his merry way now having anything he ever wanted."

Demetri laughed. "Don't you see. Vengeance my friend. He wants me to suffer for holding out on him so long. The last thing he wanted was for me to die without him getting a last parting shot at me. He knows I could have used the globe a long time ago to make him whole. He went through torturous months of rehabilitation he feels I forced on him because I wouldn't use the globe to cure him. But I just couldn't. I'd had it with that infernal thing. I vowed never to use it again. It's caused enough misery."

Quimby adjusted himself in his chair and shook his head. "This is a nasty business, sir, a nasty business. Not only are you in danger, but Isabelle, me, the whole household. If Andre's anger and quest for revenge are sufficient for him to genuinely desire harm to befall you, no one is safe. What can be done?"

"I don't know. I can't even leave this damn hospital. The police are of no use now either. They are looking for a horribly disfigured man while the truth is that probably right now Andre is staring into a mirror, admiring his restored beauty. Mizetti won't find him 'cause he'll be looking for the same thing. It'd be dangerous to try to go to him for help. God help the whole world if that son-of-a-bitch gets his hands on that thing."

Demetri then thought about what Quimby had told him about Whisper.

Could that have been the punishment that had been doled out for Demetri's miraculous cure? That had occurred during the same time Demetri was being healed. Perhaps the horse had paid with its life the price for Demetri's rejuvenation. Isabelle simply adored that horse.

In a way he was grateful. *If indeed, that was the sacrifice for his return to fitness. Better the horse than the girl.*

"How is Isabelle doing, Quimby?"

"Quite upset. I've got Amanda watching her closely. She just went to pieces when we had to shoot that unfortunate animal. Poor girl … That horse was everything to her. Victor told me he had never seen a stronger bond between a horse and a human than between those two. He told me there were times when he thought the two actually could read each other's mind. That horse was always surly and disagreeable with Victor, but with Isabelle, the horse was as meek as a lamb. It's a sad thing. I'm sorry, sir but there was nothing to be done than put the creature out of its misery."

"No, I understand," Demetri responded, shaking his head. "From everything you've said, it had to be done. But I think that may have been repercussion for my getting well. Since I reaped the benefit, it would make sense that someone in my world would suffer the consequence. I'm only glad that it was the horse and not Isabelle herself."

"True sir, true. It may have been a singularly lucky break. But what now?"

Outside a low rumble came from the west. A band of dark clouds had lined up pushing east. A storm was coming and the newly rejuvenated Demetri Davos felt as powerless as a lamb.

Andre Haskim stood in the stained bathroom of a flea-infested suburban hotel room staring at himself in the mirror, but he was not admiring his good looks. Instead he was checking his disguise. He had purchased a fake beard and moustache to hide much of his face. A large pair of dark sunglasses allowed him to remove the patch from his eye and still see relatively well. The black baseball cap on his head held the logo for a Tool and Die Company who had given him the hat way back when. By pulling the cap down low, his forehead was also hidden. It looked a little much, but still fell within the bounds of credibility.

Now there was only one question left to answer. Where the hell was he going? To the hospital? No, not at this time of day. The kid would probably not be visiting her father at this hour. Back to Demetri's house seemed the only option. The cops no doubt would no longer be prowling the grounds. However, they certainly may have stationed someone at the house overnight just to keep the house safe in case the burglars were crazy enough to return.

Andre had to be very careful. If he got caught now by the police or Mizetti before he got his hands on the globe, he would be dead meat. If the police caught him, Mizetti would be more than happy to help them out by saying that Andre had come to him wanting him to help him rob the house. Of course, he will say that he turned down the offer. How Vince and he had gotten together he wouldn't know, but anything he could do to help out the police, especially something in which he was not in any danger, he would happily do as a favor to them. A favor that could be repaid in spades by the police looking the other way as Mizetti's other nefarious actions took place.

And if Mizetti caught him, well he'd rather not think about that.

If he could just get his hands on that damn kid, all his troubles would be over. Then a sickening feeling came over Haskim, a possibility he had not considered. Would the kid have held on to the globe or given it back to her father? Or maybe back to that nosy butler who managed to ham things up. He had not considered this before, but now he thought that it was more likely than not that the girl didn't even have the damn thing anymore.

"Shit," he muttered. Why hadn't he thought of this before? It had just been a blind spot in his rearview mirror. If he thought his chances were near insurmountable before, the percentages had just gone up tenfold. Since Demetri was no doubt in dire physical straights, the likelihood was that the butler had it or at least knew where it was.

So ... what to do? Andre pondered.

He had to admit the cards were stacked against him and all it did was make him more angry and frustrated. He didn't know what to do now. The hospital where Demetri was at was not that far away. The operator over the phone had told him that Demetri was in room 511. He decided he would go by there and just see who might be sitting with Demetri. Maybe he would get lucky and find the butler there. If he did, it would be a simple matter of waiting for him to leave, grabbing him and forcing him to give up the globe. If he claimed he didn't have it, and he was to be believed, then Andre could at least use him to get to the girl and have her tell where it was.

Suddenly the whole thing seemed absurd to him and he flew into a rage. Andre swung his arm across the table top knocking the whisky bottle and glass he had been drinking from across the room. He was sick of all this waiting around, plotting, and now being hunted like an animal. After everything he had been through, why wouldn't that stupid son-of-a-bitch Demetri just have given him the globe! All he wanted was what was rightfully his. He had been forced to endure unspeakable physical pain, dig up a grave, kill a man, burglarize a house, hide out like a common criminal from not only the police but the mob, and now dress up like some damn black marauder to go out and do … what? He didn't even know where it was best to go to try and solve his problems.

Andre's anger boiled over. If he didn't get that damn globe in his hands soon, somebody else was going to die and he was beginning to not even care who that somebody was. Yes, he would go to the hospital because even if nobody was there, he might have the pleasure of shoving his damn gun in Demetri's nose and pulling the trigger. Demetri was probably of no use to him now anyway. Maybe he'd just kill the son-of-a-bitch for spite. That might be worth all the suffering he'd gone through.

Andre put on his dark jacket over the dark shirt and pants. Then he double-checked his disguise in the mirror. He looked like a villain out of a Dick Tracy comic book, an all black bad guy.

He checked his watch which read 11:07 pm. That was late enough. He went to the desk and opened the drawer. He grabbed the .38 revolver and shoved it in his pocket. He was in no mood to take shit from anybody.

He stomped out of the hotel room, a man on a mission.

Chapter 20

Andre Haskim walked into the lobby of West Suburban Hospital. An overweight, African-American guard in a blue uniform sat at an information desk reading a novel. The phone rang just as Andre entered and the guard answered it. As he spoke he spotted Andre walking across the lobby. His eyes squinted down as he looked at the odd-looking man and he held his hand over the receiver.

"Can I help you, sir?"

"No, I'm fine. I'm just visiting my wife."

"Well, visiting hours are over, sir."

"That's all right. I just left something in the room. Just want to tell her good night."

The guard stared at Andre as he continued walking toward the elevator. Andre pushed the button and waited with his back to the guard hoping the guy was not going to get serious about stopping him. From behind him Andre heard the guard tell the person on the phone to hold the line for a moment.

Please don't push this, Andre thought.

If he had thought he was going to have a problem getting up to Demetri's room, he'd have sought a different way in.

"I'm going to need you to sign in, sir ..."

Andre heard a jostling noise and a jangling of keys. The guard was getting up from his desk to try to cut him off. Just then the elevator door opened and Andre stepped in. "I'll just be one second," he said over his shoulder. For a moment that seemed to satisfy the guard who stopped in his place. The elevator door closed.

"Dumb son-of-a-bitch ..." Andre muttered.

The elevator went up to the third floor and stopped. When the door opened two heavyset nurses, one unwrapping a Mounds bar, stepped into the elevator. They had been chuckling to each other when the door opened, but one look at Andre and their chuckling stopped abruptly. One looked directly at the tall bizarre man standing in the corner of the elevator and gasped for a breath. Her eyes widened before she caught herself and moved quickly over to the right. She pressed four and then held her breath waiting for the elevator to go up one more floor. The women said nothing as the elevator rose. When it reached four, they scuttled out quickly, but not before shifting a quick eye back at Andre who stood motionless.

Andre snickered to himself. No doubt he looked strange, but he didn't care. Something had happened to him in the last hour or so, ever since he had that epiphany at that flea-infested rat trap he was staying at. He was done playing around. He would kill anyone who got in his way now: man, woman or child. Never before had it dawned on him so clearly that his entire future rested on the mission he was on now. There was nothing else to live for but that globe. Without the ability to wish himself whole, both physically and financially, he would live the rest of his life out as a miserable wretched creature hiding in the shadows or rotting in some prison cell: a scorned, detestable scar of a human being.

Andre looked down and realized his hands were trembling. He tried to grab hold of himself. He had to be careful too though. There would be few, if any, opportunities left.

"Be smart," he mumbled to himself as the doors opened.

He stepped out into the corridor and saw that it was empty except for a nurse's station at the far end of the hall. From down the other end of the hall, the sound of a television broke the stillness. The lighting in the hallway was dimmed to allow the patients a better chance of sleeping. Andre looked to his right and saw that the first room was 525. Slowly and cautiously he moved down the passageway. The numbers were going down now: 523, 521, 519. He came to the end of the corridor and looked to where it turned to the left. He counted the room numbers and cursed. Room 511 was a short distance down the hall but directly across from another nurse's station. The lights there were much brighter than the rest of the hallway. Andre peeked around the corner enough to see that there were two nurses at the station. One was seated right up front to the counter bordering the hall. Another was seated further back along a table making notes into a chart. They were speaking to each other, but Andre was too far away to hear what they were talking about.

Andre didn't want to go past that desk for fear that he would be stopped or at least questioned. He certainly did not want to be confronted directly outside Room 511 where Demetri might instantly become aware of his presence. However, if the man was in as serious a condition as he was led to believe, he probably would not be mindful enough to even notice his presence.

Suddenly the elevator dinged. The doors would soon open and someone would come out. What if it was that nosy guard? Andre panicked for a moment before deciding on a plan. He would turn the corner and as quickly as he could walk past the nurse's station as if he were on his way further down the hall. Chances would be the nurses would not stop him if he looked as if he were on a mission. He would scratch the side of his head as he walked by so they could not get a good look at his face and as he went past Demetri's room he could glance inside and see what he could see.

As Andre heard the elevator door open a clattering of noise filled the passageway. A man pushing a huge supply cart began bumbling his way out of the elevator. Andre took off.

He rounded the corner and kept close to the side wall so that the nurses at the station would not see him until the very last possible moment. Thankfully the door to Demetri's room was wide open. He walked as quickly as he could. Neither of the nurses even looked up as Andre sped past. Seeing that they were not interested in him, Andre ran his hand to the other side of his face to shield it from the open doorway of Demetri's room. As he went past, he peeked through his fingers and was astonished at what he saw. Quimby, the butler who had nearly shot him dead, was seated in a chair resting his head on his arm, his eyes locked on the TV set overhead. But that was not what took Andre by surprise. Standing in the center of the room, arms folded across his chest seemingly staring a hole in the wall was Demetri. He began speaking to the butler just as Andre went by.

"No, he wouldn't do that ... too many ..." And then the words were lost to Andre as he rushed past the room.

When Andre got to the end of the hallway, he ducked into the men's room, went into a stall and tried to figure it out. Demetri looked fine. Fit as a fiddle. How could he be standing up? The paper indicated the son-of-a-bitch was near death.

"What the hell's going on?" Andre muttered. "Now what?"

If nothing else, he thought, *he could hide out in the bathroom and figure out his next move.*

Demetri was well, that was obvious. So either the paper had it wrong, which was unlikely, or Demetri had made an almost inexplicable recovery or ... of course. Someone had used the globe to cure him. That meant that most likely either the girl, Demetri or Quimby had the globe. However, he had basically known that anyway. So he was right back where he started. In fact, he was worse off because now a healed Demetri represented a renewed obstacle to him. With him on his deathbed, Andre would have only had the butler and the girl to worry about. Now Demetri was back in the game and he knew Andre better than anyone.

Where was the globe now? Andre wondered. *Could be right here in the hospital in that very room he had just passed.*

Maybe his best bet was to go to the room right now, shut the door and face off with the two men. What would happen? No doubt they would deny the globe was in the room and then what? He could certainly search the room, but it was all just too dangerous with the nurse's station right there. If the globe was not there, he would have to take them both out of the room at gunpoint and head back to the house. Logistically that would be hard to pull off. One loud word, one suspicion on the part of the nurses and he would be done. Andre realized it was too perilous.

He would need to eliminate the possibilities, one by one, using the least risky methods at his disposal. The fact that Demetri was still in the hospital most likely meant he would be here at least until morning. The butler would no doubt be leaving soon though. When he did Andre would follow him out, confront him in an isolated spot and take him back to the house. There he could be more in control. He could search the house, the grounds, wherever he thought the globe likely to be. He could force Quimby to rouse the girl and question her. A gun to Quimby's head would no doubt get her to fork it over in a hurry if she had it.

And if all else fails, if he couldn't find the globe at the house, then what? Then he'd do what he had to do at the house and return to the hospital and confront the only other possible person who would know where the globe was.

Whatever was going to happen, before morning he would have that globe in his hands. And he'd kill anyone who got in his way.

Suddenly the door to the bathroom opened and someone walked up to the urinal and unzipped his pants. Andre looked down at the shoes. He was almost sure it was Quimby. Providence had delivered his bait right to him.

Andre left his stall and looked at the man from behind. It was Quimby.

Quickly he returned to the stall and fumbled with the toilet paper roll to make the man think he was still busy. Quimby finished and went to the sink to wash his hands while Andre waited. Then Quimby left the washroom. Immediately Andre followed him out and checked which way he was going. The man was headed toward the elevator. He was leaving.

For once, Andre thought, *luck was on his side. Maybe he could pull this damn thing off after all.*

Then the fuming anger came rolling back. It was all so simple. If he could just get his hands on the globe, everything would be fine. Even more than ever before he hardened himself to his goal and realized, in all likelihood he may have to kill someone tonight. Maybe more than one someone. So what? He had already killed one man. Jekyll had turned into Hyde in that hotel room of his when he had that outburst of anger. From that moment on, Hyde had taken command and Jekyll would never return until all of this nasty business was done.

Andre waited at the bathroom door until the elevator dinged. As soon as the door opened and Quimby stepped inside, Andre ran out and slid into the car. Quimby eyes were focused on the floor and he did not even glance up at Andre. Then the door closed and the elevator began to descend.

Quimby looked up and his face went cold. Andre pulled out his gun. "I'll kill you, I'll kill Demetri, I'll kill the whole lot of you. I don't care. I've already killed one man because of your boss's pig-headedness. Where's the globe?"

Quimby leaned into the corner of the elevator as if he could get away from Andre.

"The … the globe? But I thought …" Quimby's face showed confusion.

"You thought what?" Andre stared at Quimby trying to read the astonishment in his face. It appeared genuine. The elevator had four more floors to go. Before he could follow up on their conversation, Andre became distracted by the possibility of the elevator stopping before they reached the first floor and of the nosy guard at the desk.

"Listen to me. We are going to walk out of here, nice and neat. No tricks. If you try to alert the guard, I'll shoot you down. I don't care. You understand?"

Quimby nodded. He was convinced of Andre's intent.

"When the door opens, we walk right out. We go to your car. Understand?"

Quimby nodded his head again.

The elevator door opened at the ground floor. Andre motioned for Quimby to go first. As they left the car, Andre spotted the guard off to the right fiddling through a pile of magazines on a table. The guard looked up.

"Thanks. Found my ride home," Andre said with an upbeat tone. The guard said nothing and the half smile on his face turned to an expression of uneasiness. Something wasn't quite right. The man in front of the weird one looked overwrought and uneasy as they made their way out the door.

The guard thought about it for a moment. He had seen people leave the hospital upset before. Worry over a loved one, no doubt. He turned back to the magazines. Then he raised his eyes one more time as the two men walked out of sight. He just couldn't dispel the odd feeling he had.

"The car's in the lot across the street," Quimby said.

"Okay, let's go," Andre replied. "Now, where's the globe?"

"But ... I don't have it? I thought you stole it the other night."

"No. That damn kid snatched it up. Then you showed up and I had to make a quick departure. She gave it to you or Demetri, didn't she?"

"No ... no honestly. I thought you had it." It was becoming clear to Quimby now. Isabelle had wished Demetri well and the horse had been recompense for it.

Why hadn't he seen that before?

Andre mulled it over in his head as they moved through the dark parking lot towards the Cadillac. Quimby could be telling the truth. The girl could have very well been the one who had wished Demetri cured. If that was true, it should be easy enough for them to go to the house and force the kid to give them the globe. Andre's hands began to shake. He could very well have the globe in his hands in matter of minutes.

When they reached the car, Andre sat in the front passenger seat and instructed Quimby to drive to the house. He thought he would try to appeal to Quimby's senses.

"Quimby, I don't wish to cause you or anyone else any harm. I simply want what I am owed. You help me get the globe and I promise you no harm will come to you or Isabelle or Demetri or anyone. I will simply take it and be on my way. Gentleman to gentleman, I give you my word."

"Andre, you know I can't do that. Even if I take you at your word on that, you'll take that thing and wish upon the stars. Who knows how many people will be hurt. Look at what's happened already, who's been harmed. Sophie, Isabelle, Demetri, yourself. The thing's accursed. You of all people should realize the danger."

Andre smiled. "Oh I'd be sensible about the thing, Quimby. I just want my health, wealth, and youth. How bad can that be? Then I'll tuck the thing away for a rainy day. A rainy day that may never come again."

"Yes, until you have a heart problem or develop cancer or run into any inconvenience whatsoever. It's your actions that brought us to this in the first place, Andre. Your greed, your selfishness."

Andre rolled his eyes to the ceiling feeling more and more comfortable in his position. "I'm no saint, it's true. But then again, we all have our faults, don't we. Nevertheless, Quimby, I mean to have that globe and I won't be dissuaded. It's too late for that now. Unfortunately you're right. My actions have brought us to this. I've got the police and the mob on my tail. I have no other recourse. There is no other avenue available to me. Even if I wanted to give up the whole chase, I couldn't 'cause I'll wind up dead or in jail. So there you have it. My hands are tied as much as yours. The smart thing is for you to cut your losses and give me the globe. At least then I leave the family alone. I actually do give you my word on that. I just want the globe, nothing more. And then I'll be on my merry way. Think about it, Quimby. After all, I will kill you if you try to stop me. I give you my word on that also."

Quimby stared at the stripes in the road as they went streaming by. He had known Andre for many years. He almost felt he could trust that if he gave him the globe, he would simply leave and not harm anyone. It was tempting. Any man in his position would be a fool not to consider it. He did not want to die. Nor did he want harm to come to Isabelle or his master.

What were his options? And then it became obvious to him. No, he did not want to die, but Andre had forgotten one thing. Quimby was a trained servant, a dedicated butler devoted to the calling of his rank. The creed he was sworn to went all the way back to his childhood days in England where he grew up the son of an aristocrat's lady and her butler husband. Together they raised him up in the ways of an established servant. Staunch loyalty to his gentleman, steadfast dependability, and a sheer disregard for selfish pursuits that went counter to the safety and security of the household were the basis of his craft. Diligent and dogged fastidiousness and meticulousness to detail were the trademarks of his profession. To let Andre anywhere near the house would be tantamount to a breach against everything his mother and father had stood for in their lives of servitude.

Quimby looked down at the speedometer. They were traveling on a side road at forty miles an hour. Up ahead was the entrance to the expressway they would take west. The speed limit on the expressway would be fifty-five miles an hour. He could most certainly get the car up to at least sixty-five. There would be bridge abutments that would serve his purpose well. All he had to do was remain calm and committed. Calm and committed.

Quimby whispered a prayer and thought about his deceased parents. He offered up the action he was about to take to their legacy.

"Andre, I understand why you feel like you have a right to the globe. I give you my word," he said as he pulled into the merging lane of the highway, "that you will get what you are owed."

Chapter 21

August 9, 1968

Sophie picked up the phone on the second ring. "Hello".

"Hello honey, wanted to make sure you knew my plans." Sophie recognized her mother's voice immediately. "I'm leaving on the afternoon train and expect to get to Cleveland by nine. Roza and the kids are going to pick me up if it isn't too late for them. Can't wait to see them. You should come with me. Been a while since you seen Roza and Jack and the kids too."

"I don't know mother. I'm kind of busy right now. Really can't afford to get away right now." It was a lie.

"What do you got to do Sophie? You got no kids to hold you down. Not like Roza. Now I could see how she might have that for an excuse. But not you."

Sophie gritted her teeth. More of the same. Since Roza had her third child, Amos, her mother's needling, whether unintentional or not, had gotten downright disparaging.

"Do you do that on purpose, Mother, or is it just that you can't help yourself?"

"Well ... what do you mean?"

"You know that stick in the ribs you constantly give me. Roza's kids this and Roza's kids that. It gets a little annoying. We just bought this property mother, new house and all. I got all kinds of things to do to fix it up. Repair men are here all hours of the day."

"I know you must be busy with the house, Sophie. I'm just saying that you don't have kids to tie you down like they do, that's all. You're free to come and go. You're not working all that many hours now. In fact, I'd quit that darn job all together. I mean now that you got the ... the house and everything."

Sophie's Mother, Eva, had not said it, but those last comments had nothing to do with quitting her job or being busy with the house. Busy starting a family is what she meant. Sophie let it go.

"Well, now that Roza's got Amos I want to spend more time helping her out. Josh is starting third grade this year and Mary's in first. She's got her hands full. You know she's only a couple of year's younger than you. Have you talked to the doctor anymore?"

"Yes, Mother I have talked to the doctor. I've told you before. They don't know what the problem is. Besides, I'm very happy not having children." Sophie took a deep breath to try to keep her anger at bay.

"Maybe you should try a different doctor. You know they got fertility drugs now. If you don't hurry dear your time's gonna be up and then what …"

"Then my time will be up, Mother! My time will be up."

Silence held for a few moments while Sophie's outburst settled.

"Yes, well I'm going to get going, Sophie. Can't miss my train you know."

"You know, Mother I've got a lot of decisions to make here on the house. You could help me with the color schemes and furniture. I wouldn't mind you being a part of the decisions."

"Oh, they've got interior decorators for that kind of stuff honey. Let them handle it."

Sophie sighed. "Okay, Mother. Give Roza and the kids a kiss for me."

"Sure dear. My best to Demetri."

Sophie hung up and stared out the window. Then the tears came again. "Damn!" she muttered.

She went to the kitchen and poured herself another cup of coffee. Outside laborers were working on building the barn at the back of the property. Since they had bought the acreage, Demetri had started on his big plans. He loved horses and wanted to have a few of his own. The barn would hold several stalls where the horses could reside. Their property was nestled among woods on three sides and the trails they could ride through would be numerous. Sophie herself had no particular experience with horses, but she liked them. Especially if they were going to be able to hire help right on the grounds to care for them, clean their stalls and manicure them. She was actually looking quite forward to the following weekend when they were going to go to a horse show at the Illinois State Fair and perhaps buy one or two.

Sophie finished off her coffee and went upstairs to get dressed. She had not told her mother, but she had already quit her job. With the new house and everything, she had plenty to keep her busy. That afternoon, in fact, she had an appointment with Arthur at the furniture store. So why hadn't she just told her Mother she quit her job? Some kind of damn spite or … something. Just the thought of agreeing with her, knowing she would give her the, 'Glad you took my advice' line or whatever would have came after that, would have been too much to bear.

Then she started to cry again. Sophie cursed herself for this weakness in her. She was smart, confident, accomplished in her own way. So why could slights from her mother bring her so much heartache? It was all about those damn kids of Roza. Nothing would ever match up for her in her mother's eyes like Roza's kids.

The truth was she had been trying to have a baby all along. Ever since she realized nothing would ever stack up for her in her mother's eyes except a child, Sophie had been secretly hoping she would get pregnant. She had spoken to Demetri about it, and he was all for it. In fact, she had been to her gynecologist regularly trying to figure out what might be the problem. It seemed she had a severe case of endometriosis that was causing blockages in her Fallopian tubes and growths on the walls of her uterus. She had even gone through a procedure to scrape some of it clean but that did not appear to have helped. At least not yet. She was now on some new medication she hoped would work.

Sophie sat on her bed and tried to psychoanalyze herself. Personally, she didn't even want kids. Truth was she was now forty-two years old. If she hadn't gotten pregnant by now, it wasn't going to happen. She had even seen it on her doctor's face after they had no real answer for her after her operation. Why did this approval from her Mother mean so much to her? All her life she had been trying to measure up in that woman's eyes and it had never been good enough. No matter what she accomplished, there was always Roza. Her business successes were always viewed by her parents as a kind of embarrassment because that was something men did, not something a woman ought to be striving to succeed at. Her parents only begrudgingly supported her through college because what did women need with a college degree? Roza's disastrous first marriage to a shoe salesman was attributed to that "no good son-of-a-bitch", even though Sophie had known that it was Roza all along who had wanted out because of the things she confided in her that she never told her parents. No fault had ever been attributed to Roza.

It went back to her being adopted. It had to be that. They would never admit it, but that was it. And if she became president of the United States it would still be secondary to the fact that Amos had gotten his first tooth or something equally as trivial.

Sophie dried her tears and continued unpacking boxes. They had moved from a medium sized home in a very established neighborhood on Chicago's south side to their new place in Long Grove. They would need much more furniture and artwork to fill up this place, but first she had to get through their former possessions.

It was while she was going through one of the boxes of important papers that Demetri had packed that she found it. She had nearly forgotten all about it. Demetri had made a point of telling her to let him deal with this particular packed box as it was papers from the business that he usually handled, but Sophie wanted to get as much done as possible.

Sophie stared down at the key in her hand. She pulled out the letter from the envelope she had found it in. It documented the existence of their old safety deposit box at First Guardian on LaSalle in Downtown Chicago.

In going through their things, packing and now unpacking, Sophie had come across several items she thought should best be kept under lock and key in their safety deposit box.

She had to go downtown sometime in the next week. She would get together those things she wanted locked up and would go to the bank.

No need to bother Demetri, she thought. *He's busy enough.*

Chapter 22

August 13, 1968

When Sophie got to the bank, she identified herself, produced her key and soon found herself being escorted down the hall by a Mr Willingham to where the boxes were kept. A guard sat off to the right reading a magazine and came over jiggling his keys when he noticed Mr Willingham leading the woman toward the barred off area.

"Rodney, Ms Davos wants to use her box, 389, can you help her?"

"Sure, how are you, ma'am?"

"Rodney here will help you out. Thanks again, Mrs Davos." Willingham walked away while Rodney searched for the correct key to the cage.

"I just need you to sign the card." The guard opened the caged area and walked Sophie through an open doorway that led to a large metal door. Rodney used another key on the lock and then slowly pulled the heavy door open.

"Follow me, ma'am." Rodney led Sophie to a small desk where he fished through a series of cards. "If you'll sign right here ma'am."

Sophie signed the card.

"Okay follow me. Now you're 389 so you just follow the numbers and three hundred is in the third row all the way around to ... here." Rodney walked to an area against the right hand wall where the numbered boxes ran from 360 through 399. He used his key then stepped aside to let Sophie use her key.

"And I'll be right outside the door if you need anything. Take as long as you need, ma'am."

"Thank you, Rodney."

Rodney walked out and Sophie pulled the box door open. She lifted out the bank's inner metal container and carried it to one of the small viewing rooms and set it on the table. Inside there was a wooden box containing a batch of papers and a black sack concealing a circular object. Sophie had no idea what it was. Almost cautiously, she unfurled the bag and pulled out the globe. The crystal was black except for a tiny piercing light that shone from the middle of the glass.

What could it be? she thought. *Was it some kind of huge gem? What possible reason would there be to hide it from her?*

Sophie picked it up and stared into the center. As she did her thoughts began to swirl almost making her dizzy. She placed the globe back on the table and pondered it some more. She would need to confront Demetri and find out what it was all about. Was it some kind of old family heirloom she didn't know about? A surprise of some kind?

She was just about to place the globe back in the bag when the yellow light in the center began to softly pulsate. She stared at it some more and now her thoughts began to sharpen. Things she desired, things she needed crystallized in her mind.

The globe began to glow brighter.

Chapter 23

April 21, 1969

Sophie was due in three weeks. She had been to the doctor the day before so he could continue to monitor her fluctuating blood pressure and the manner in which her body was retaining fluid.

Sophie felt flushed and tired. Her mother had finally come to visit. Even though she was now pregnant, Sophie found their relationship had not improved as much as she had envisioned. She thought her mother would be gloating over the whole thing, calling Sophie constantly, visiting her in Chicago numerous times, going with her to the doctor and, all in all, making a fuss like never before. But that's not exactly how things had progressed. Yes, her mother was paying more attention to her, but it almost seemed forced, as if her mother felt obligated to spend time and energy on Sophie.

Truth was Sophie was worried about being a mother. Motherhood had never really been a goal for her. What she had really wanted was her mother to treat her with the respect she felt she deserved. She thought a pregnancy would do that. She thought it had been Roza's kids that had made the difference in the treatment she got from her mother. But now she was seeing that really was not true. It was obvious that Eva still favored Roza. Even with the hubbub of her pregnancy, Sophie saw it for what it was.

She was adopted and Roza was not. It would always be that.

Sophie excused herself and went to the washroom. She stood in front of the mirror and started to cry. Her plans were not turning out as she thought they would. She would have to understand that her mother would never love her as she would Roza. And maybe it was not Eva's fault. Maybe she couldn't help herself. Who knows, maybe Sophie would have felt the same way in her place. She was going to have to face reality and be the bigger person here. Demetri was happy. Sophie knew she must concentrate on that.

"Let it go," Sophie mumbled as she lowered her head. "Why can't I just let it go?"

Sophie looked at herself in the mirror again. She felt fat and ugly. Her face was more rounded and puffy now due to the pregnancy. In addition, she had not felt all that well in the last couple of months. Besides her fluctuating blood pressure that the doctor had a hard time controlling, her ankles and feet would swell sometimes for days at a time. Sometimes terrible headaches would visit her. They told her she had a touch of Toxemia. The condition could be dangerous if not watched. In the last couple of days, the swelling in her feet had started again.

Sophie wiped the tears away from her face and took a deep breath. Today had not been a good day. Her back ached and she had felt a lightheaded dizziness on and off as the afternoon wore on. However, she did not want her mother to know she was feeling poorly. That would just make things worse.

Suddenly Sophie felt on odd feeling in her belly as if the baby had moved very suddenly. Then a kind of release followed. When she felt warm fluid running down her leg, she screamed for her mother.

Demetri sped to the hospital going through two red lights on the way. His mother-in-law had called him from there once they had arrived and the emergency team had taken control. Her water had broken, that was obvious, but it seemed to Eva that Sophie had lost an unusually large amount of blood. She immediately called an ambulance not wanting to take any chances. When Demetri finally arrived, the doctor had just come out to fill them in on her condition.

"Doctor, I am Demetri, Sophie's husband. Is everything okay?"

The doctor's smock was smeared with traces of blood. Demetri did not like what he saw.

"Your wife is fine for the time being. We've stopped the bleeding I think and she's stable. Having a little trouble keeping her blood pressure from fluctuating though. We think it best to go in and take the baby now. This much bleeding, there's no reason to risk anything. She's certainly far enough along that the baby should have no trouble at all. We're going to take her to OR in a few minutes."

"You say she's stable. Can I see her?"

"Sure, for a few minutes anyway. They'll scoot you out when they're going to take her. Third door on the right. She's sedated so she might be a little out of her head." The doctor pointed to the room and went off down the hallway in the other direction.

"I want to go see her, Mom. By myself, okay?"

"Sure, sure," Eva agreed.

Sophie was lying in the bed, her head partially raised. Her eyes were closed. An IV tube was inserted into her left hand and she seemed to be resting comfortably. Demetri went up to the side of the bed.

"Sophie, it's me."

Sophie opened her eyes and stared at Demetri. "Is the … baby … is the baby okay?"

"Yes, everything's fine. You've been bleeding a little too much so they want to take the baby now. But the doctor tells me that's fine. The baby will be fine. So don't worry."

"Demetri, I'm so … my head aches terrible. Can they give me something for my headache?"

"I don't know, honey?"

"Demetri … I'm sorry for not trusting you."

"Not trusting me? What?"

"I'm afraid. I'm afraid something bad is going to happen to the baby."

"Why? Everything's fine. The doctor says everything's fine. Don't worry."

"But the baby ... I'm afraid for the baby."

"Why? I told you everything's all right."

"But ... Demetri ... what ... I was scared. I went in the safety deposit box at the bank and I found that ... that glass globe and I didn't understand, but something weird happened. I wished for the baby but not because I wanted the baby but because of my mother so she would ... love me more. I'm scared. I can't stop thinking about that glass. I don't know why I didn't tell you. I was scared. I don't know. Something kept me from telling you. I'll be a good mother though, you'll see."

Demetri's heart sank. "Tell me Sophie. What did you do with the globe?"

"It's still in the safety deposit box."

"But what did you do when you found it?"

"I wished ... I made a wish for the baby. What is that thing? It's like it swallowed my thoughts and I wished for the baby but, it was wrong I think. Demetri, I don't understand it. What is that thing? I'm scared for the baby."

Demetri's hands began to shake. "Don't worry. Don't worry about that now. You just rest, just rest. They're going to come and take you and take the baby and everything will be fine. Just rest. I'll explain it to you later."

"I'm tired. I'm so tired. I'm so warm."

"Just rest, honey. Just rest."

Sophie shut her eyes as Demetri pulled away from the bed and stood back a distance. A tremor of fear rose in his brain. He never should have hid the globe from Sophie. He should have explained it to her. Now there was danger. If she used the globe to wish for the baby, some terrible repercussion might very well follow.

Two nurses came in and instructed Demetri to leave. He went out into the hall, a dull, expression on his pasty face.

"What's wrong, Demetri? Eva asked. "Is everything all right?"

Demetri brought his hand to his forehead and rubbed at his eyes. "Everything's fine. Everything's fine. She's a little groggy, but I think she's fine." Demetri walked over and sat down in a chair. He didn't want to think now about what could go wrong.

The baby would not live, he thought. *The baby would not live.* In his heart he knew it. Whatever happened now would be on his head. Demetri kept up an expressionless face for his mother-in-law, but inside his guts were squirming.

It was too late now to change anything.

What would happen? Demetri prayed for the baby's health, but in his gut he feared what the future now would be. The nurses wheeled Sophie out of her room and they watched as the gurney was led onto the elevator and the doors closed.

Demetri paced nervously from one side of the room to the other. It had been three hours since they had wheeled Sophie away and he was nearly out of his mind. Suddenly a doctor came from down the hall asking for a Mr Davos.

"Here," Demetri said. "Is the baby all right? Is everything all right?"

"Please, let's go in here and I'll explain things to you," the doctor responded. The doctor's face was muted and blank. It was impossible not to see that something was amiss.

As soon as they got into the room and shut the door, Demetri was on the doctor again. "Tell me, doctor. Is everything all right?"

"Mr Davos your baby girl is just fine. She's about seven pounds and she seems just fine. They'll be able to let you see her in just a little bit."

"Thank God," Demetri said, as he nearly collapsed into a chair. Perhaps he was wrong. Perhaps there would be no repercussions to Sophie's wish. After all, how could wanting a baby ever be wrong? It hadn't even dawned on him yet. He had a baby girl.

Demetri gathered himself together and wiped his eyes with his handkerchief. He felt so relieved. "When can I see my wife?"

The doctor stared at Demetri and then looked away. He went to the other end of the table and sat down. He looked up at Demetri again and then rested his eyes on the floor. "I have some bad news for you, Mr Davos. Sit down, ma'am," he motioned to Eva to have a seat beside him.

Demetri's stomach turned in on itself. How could he have been so foolish as to think there would not be a price to be paid? His whole body went limp and his mind dulled until all that was left was emptiness and blackness and fear.

"Your wife has suffered a stroke. This sometimes happens in childbirth. It's known as Eclampsia. Usually it occurs in the weeks following birth, but not always. As you know your wife has had an ongoing problem with her blood pressure throughout her pregnancy. We'd spoken about it before. The headaches, the swelling, the protein in the urine were all symptoms of this type of condition. Sometimes, in these cases, in the act of giving birth spasms in the blood vessels can cause an artery to burst. In some cases, the stroke is not severe and the patient, after a short recovery period, returns to normal." The doctor paused and took a deep breath. "In some cases, the stroke can be more … life threatening and more serious in nature where the part of the brain damaged does not heal or heals only very slowly over time."

Demetri stared at the table before him. The beacon from a street lamp across the street reflected off the shiny surface in white stripes mirroring the venetian blinds through which it shown. A pale and emotionless expression lined his face while Eva sat next to him crying into a tissue.

"Is my wife dead, doctor?" The voice seemed to come from out of the ground.

"No. She's alive, but I'm afraid the stroke is serious. It's hard to give you a prognosis at this time. We'll know a little more as the days go by. We'll see how much she improves."

"She's going to die, isn't she?" This time Demetri's cold eyes met the doctor's.

"No, I don't think so. But she may need some … aftercare."

"Aftercare? What does that mean?" Eva asked.

"She may not be able to care for herself. Things may not come back to her easily: how to eat, how to talk, to walk. Again it depends on the severity which we really can't decipher quite yet."

"Nursing care, is that it?" Demetri asked.

"Yes, I think there will be a need for that for at least a few weeks. By that time … we'll know more." The doctor rose from his chair and went to the door. "I'm sorry, folks." Then his face lightened a little. "Your baby girl is beautiful though, Mr Davos. She's a little angel."

The weeks went by and they brought Sophie home from the hospital. Demetri hired an around the clock nurse to watch over her and Amanda to care for the house. Quimby had already been in Demetri's employ before the birth of the baby. Demetri named the baby Isabelle. She was a joy from day one, always happy and bubbly.

The months went by and Sophie's condition only improved slightly. She was bedridden all the time, could not speak and could not feed or care for herself properly. Amanda and the nurse saw to her personal needs. A somber pall seemed to fall over the house in those early years, an eerie drabness that was broken only by the joyous chirping of Isabelle. By the time she was three she was beginning to understand her mother's condition. As strained as some children might have found trying to comfort an invalid such as Sophie, Isabelle loved to spend time with her mother. She would use her mother's bedroom as her own on many days lying on the bed coloring and playing with her dolls. At the time they had a small black poodle by the name of Smoky whom Isabelle loved and who served as good company for both mother and daughter.

During this time Demetri's normal exuberance and business

acumen declined. It was as if a dagger had been thrust through his heart which he could not remove. Guilt and sorrow wore him down until he spent many of his days at home leaving the day to day work at the shop to Andre. Although Andre was not as insightful or shrewd in his business dealings as Demetri and certainly not as responsible or accountable in juggling the finances, the truth was that they were both well off now and they no longer had the necessity of scrutinizing every nickel and dime on the accounts payable ledger. For several years Demetri took a hiatus from the drudgeries of work, content to simply receive his share of the profits as they came in and comforting himself with the luxuries offered by his estate.

When Isabelle was seven he started her on dancing lessons and riding lessons. He embraced her love of animals by buying several horses which they kept on the grounds and giving home to every stray dog or cat Isabelle found wandering the woods or cornfields around their home. He spoiled her as he would have wanted to spoil Sophie. Everything he gave to Isabelle was in essence a gift to the woman whom he could no longer liberate from her frozen mind. The culpability he felt seemed to drain away all the other gratifications his life truly provided. His mission in life now, to the almost exclusion of all others, was for Sophie's and Isabelle's comforts. Victor was hired on to care for the grounds and between Sophie's nurse, Amanda, Quimby and Victor, all was taken care of as it should be.

Demetri began to retreat more and more into a world of isolation. His zeal for business simply dissolved into the despair that was beginning, more and more, to become the only identity left to him. His loneliness and solitude became a blanket for him. His loss of composure loosened his tongue also and to Quimby he confessed the whole anguished tale of the globe. Many nights in the throes of depression and regret, he sought out the globe which he had retrieved now from the safety deposit box and sat staring at the spark of yellow light deep in its center. Many times he struggled with his will dangerously tempted to wish away the penalty weighed on Sophie. But he dared not risk it. The connection to Isabelle, he worried, was too strong. If he wished for the return of Sophie's health, surely some terrible fate would claim Isabelle. Even if no harm came to Isabelle, some misfortune might visit him and he could not gamble on that possibility. It was very important now that he stay well because both Isabelle and Sophie counted on him for their well-being and future needs.

In those dark days, Quimby was his only comrade. His butler tried over and over to reason with his master to return to some semblance of normality. He urged him to take back more of a role in the business and not leave its management to Andre, whom Quimby did not trust nor felt was as qualified as Demetri. As for Andre, his visits to the house became less frequent and his consultations with Demetri over the everyday dealings of the business more seldom and less crowded with details and complexities. Quimby sensed that in a way Andre was not bothered with his new role as sole arbitrator and authority of D & H Printing. His master's failure to follow up on important issues confronting the company did not sit well with Quimby because he recognized the weaknesses in Andre and he knew the company's history and how its success had truly been built on the studiousness and tireless efforts of Demetri. Now that the business was sailing along, most anyone could have kept it afloat. However, Andre did not have half the resolve or self-discipline that had made the business such a success and Quimby knew it. It would not take much for an undisciplined administrator to turn the business on its heels.

But Quimby could not convince Demetri to take a more active role. He was content to live semi-retired naively trusting that the success of the past would remain a constant for D & H Printing.

And so many days, with the sun setting in the west crawling slowly across Sophie's bed, Demetri would be content sitting in his easy chair while Isabelle snuggled with her mother and read to them from the great novels that would deliver them to a different place and time where beauty still held court and a certain hallowed sanctity blocked out even the remotest notion of misfortune. The late afternoons would be filled with tales like Gulliver's Travels, Ivanhoe, Treasure Island, Little Women and The Call of the Wild. Demetri would read on as the day grew long until finally he heard the muted snores of his child whose head lay on her mother's leg. Exhausted, his head would nod down to his chest and he would surrender the estate to the services of his staff, the beckoning dongs of the grandfather clock in the foyer, and the soothing blanket of night.

Chapter 24

July 11, 1980

Andre Haskim sat at the bar at Stevo's Steak House on South Wabash Street trying to make time with the shapely bartender who had just poured him another scotch and water when he noticed her gaze shift to the right and her face go icy cold. Andre half-turned on his stool to see what had caused such a response in the girl. Beside him stood a big, burly gorilla of a man with dark curly hair, wearing an outdated, golden Italian knit shirt that was a size too small. Behind him was a shorter man whose face bore the traits of a former boxer. His nose was misshapen as if it had been broken several times. No one would have considered his dull stare and glassy eyes to be those of a mathematician or physics professor.

These boys were not collecting for the Policeman's Benevolent Association.

The big one spoke as he leaned in close to Andre. "Hey Andre. How ye' doin'? Jimmy Vitello." He held out his hand to Andre.

Andre sighed. "I know who you are."

"Came to have a little talk with ya'. Watcha drinkin'?"

"Nothing you're buying me."

"Hey be nice. I'll be nice, you be nice."

Andre leaned back and looked at the second man. "And who are you, as if I care?"

The man scrunched his shoulders and waved his thumb toward Vitello.

"I'm wit' 'im."

Andre nodded. "You're with him, eh. You should pick better friends." Andre swallowed down the last of his scotch and water. "Well, if you're going to buy, start buying."

The big man motioned to the barkeep. "Hey honey can you fill him up? I'll take a CC on the rocks. Freddie?"

"Bottle of Schlitz."

The bartender got busy and Jimmy nestled himself down in the seat next to Andre. His breath smelled of stale cigars. "So, we haven't seen ya' for a while, Andre. You havin' a problem?"

"Yeah, you," Andre smirked.

"Leo wants to help when our people have a problem. That's why I'm here. I'm kind of like Leo's customer satisfaction representative."

The waitress brought over the drinks and Jimmy threw a twenty down on the bar. "Thanks, honey," he said as he handed Freddie back his bottle of Schlitz.

Jimmy directed his attention back to Andre. "Talk to me, Andre. Where we at?"

Andre dropped the sarcastic tone. "Jimmy, I got a business, you dig? I got payrolls to make, supplies to buy, customers to please. You know sometimes the money ebb and flow ain't as consistent as one would like."

Jimmy nodded. "I understand. That's why I ain't been here sooner. But your tab's a little high. Normally if it were small potatoes ... we can wait. But you gotta' make an effort. Leo don't see no effort. So that's why I'm here."

"Look I'm good for it, okay. Yeah I'm a little late. I'm in the printing business, Jimmy, the typesetting business. You know anything about the typesetting business?"

Jimmy shook his head.

"Well, you see there's a change coming through in the last few years. Computers, you heard of computers? Well, typesetting was always done by making the letters with metal. It went all the way from melting down the metal, filling up the typesetting machines and having the type made from the metal, letter by letter. Those machines are expensive and troublesome to maintain. Well, now with all that investment in those machines, computers come along and the things that took a lot of time and energy and cost on the old machines can be done bing, bang, boom on computers. So now to keep ahead, we got to invest in computer technology. I got to hire a different kind of person. Used to be a big lug like you with a wrench and a screwdriver could run my machines and get the type out. Then my typesetters, a little higher up on the evolutionary scale from the apes I got running the typesetting machines, position the type, get it all lined up, etc" Andre noticed the frown beginning to grow on Jimmy's face. "Am I moving too fast for you, Jimmy?"

Jimmy looked as if Andre had been reciting Shakespeare.

"Then once the type is all set up in the right columns, etc, it's passed on to the pressmen who actually run the presses and print the type and then it's nicely printed out and sent to the customer. Now that whole process can be done by one man at a machine, some jamoke with a college degree in one hand and his palm open in the other. You see the problems. I got a whole new level of investment to make. I got to train apes like you to run a computer or else hire on some young punk from the University of Illinois and I got to figure out what to do with all the outdated equipment I got without taking a beating on it. I got the unions on my ass who want me to pay more money to employees I don't really need anymore. I'm a business man, Jimmy. And right now I got troubles. Right now I'm a little short."

Jimmy nodded his head up and down several times and took another sip of his whisky. "I can see ya' got troubles, Andre. But maybe if you didn't like the horses so much, I wouldn't have to come talk to ya' and take Freddie away from his new girlfriend."

"Yeah well tell Leo I ain't going nowhere. He knows where I live. I just need a little time right now. Okay?"

"If it was up to me, I got no problem," Jimmy said.

"Yeah, but we ain't the ones giving the orders," Freddie jumped in.

"Oh, so he can actually put more than two words together eh?" Andre said to Jimmy.

"Yeah I'm training him. I don't like doin' this shit anymore. Getting' too old to be chasing schlups like you around the block. Got a rotator cup problem now too doctor says. Can't throw my right like I used to."

"That must be a real problem for a guy in your profession. Mizetti got a pension plan set up for his muscle?"

Jimmy burped, swallowed down the last of his drink and pulled himself off of the stool. "Look, we gave you some time. And maybe in the future we can give you a little more time here and there. But right now Leo says four large by next Thursday or then I got to come see ya' again. Sorry that's what I got to go by. And if I got to come see ya' again, I'm gonna tell you four large by Saturday. And then if Saturday rolls around, then I gotta stop asking and Freddie's got to pay you a visit. Ya' dig, ya' friggin', Hungarian. Let's go, Freddie." Jimmy turned and walked away. Freddie stayed where he stood for a few moments after Jimmy left just to make sure Andre didn't do something stupid. He didn't.

"Lester, we're going to have the equipment up and running just as soon as possible," Andre said into the receiver.

"I'd like to help you out, Andre, but I got my overhead to consider. Cartwright can give me what you can for a third less and faster. Now we still got four jobs with you that were due Thursday and I got to say I got them late and they were a little shoddy. I talked to the others about it and they're adamant. You get modernized and come back to me with an offer and I'll see what I can do. But right now, I don't know what else I can tell you."

"You been with us how long Lester? Eleven years … Cut me some slack. I'll make it right."

"I … I can't help you right now. What about Demetri? Did he sell out to you or what? Don't hear from him."

"No, Demetri's still half owner. Just semi-retired. He's got family problems."

"Well … if maybe he was a little more involved, things might be different. Richard and some of the others like him. I tell you what. Have Demetri call Richard. That's your best shot. Maybe he can sway things your way. Other than that, I don't know what to tell you."

"Okay, Lester. Piss on it then you want to be that way, you want to throw away years of loyal business, fine. But when Cartwright starts raising his tab on ya', don't come crying to me!"

"Now there's no reason to get like that, Andre. Business is business."

"Yeah, bullshit, Lester." Andre hung up the phone and rubbed his hand over his face. He was sitting in his office on Federal Street with a series of spreadsheets in front of him. The troubles he had been avoiding by robbing Peter to pay Paul were skyrocketing out of control. Through the previous few months, they had lost several of their most valued customers like Derrian Advertising, J & W, and Holcomb and Associates. Now Shanada Inc. was pulling the plug. Part of the reason for the mess he was in had to do with what he had tried to explain to Jimmy, but some of it had to do with Andre's personal management style. He had made promises to companies and failed to keep them. In the case of Williams and Williams, he had insulted Gordy Williams inadvertently because, truth be told, he couldn't stand the son-of-a-bitch. He had been late in starting the upgrading process that was necessary for D & H Printing to stay on top and now that failure was beginning to affect business. But those weren't really the main reasons for D & H's troubles.

Once Demetri had turned the reins of the company over to him, Andre Haskim ran things fairly well. The company was on the right track and as long as he didn't do anything too stupid, things would continue running that way. However, slowly he had started getting something of a big head. A mistake here, an insulting comment there, a bad business decision made on top of an unfortunate string of bad luck and before you knew it, D & H was in trouble. Andre's employees did not like him as much as they did Demetri and he knew it. So he tried to make up for it by giving them raises. The company was doing well at the time so it was not a big deal, but now overhead was killing him. As he took charge of more and more of the daily responsibilities, which was never his strong suit anyway, he had less and less time to devote to what he had been good at, schmoozing and drawing new customers.

Andre rose from his chair and went to the window. The bright lights from downtown Chicago lay a haze of pale light above the skyscrapers in the distance. Even with the problems he was having, D & H had still been doing okay. He always made sure that Demetri got his fair share because he didn't want to let on to him that they were having cash flow problems.

There was the real problem and Andre knew it. The cash flow problems had more to do with his extravagant lifestyle more than anything else and the gambling problem that he had developed. He was living in a condominium on the gold coast that was costing him an arm and a leg. He always liked the horses and Mizetti's crew was always happy to serve as bookie to him. Then he started in with football, betting heavily each Sunday on the NFL games. He had purchased season tickets for the Chicago Bears that he figured would serve as a write off, which it did, but still cost him a pretty penny. He was drinking more too and that wasn't helping anything. He would get drunk and the depth of his gambling would increase with every scotch and water he consumed. His socializing with the ladies had gotten out of hand. He'd purchased expensive bracelets, rings and lavish trips to keep the three girlfriends he juggled happy.

And then when things starting getting tight, he resorted to financial chicanery. He took a little from here and a little from there. He shifted some from Column A and put it in Column B. The trouble was he was not an accountant and all his moving funds from here to there had turned the books into such an awful mess that at last tax season Gilbert Haas who normally did their taxes every year grew suspicious and told Andre that he would no longer be willing to look the other way on documents he was required to put his John Hancock on. Truth was the books were not in order. The IRS was hounding them now. D & H owed back taxes.

And the last thing he needed right now was Jimmy and that dumb shit Freddie threatening to break his legs.

Andre went to the bar he kept in the corner of his office and made himself another drink. He was at his wits end. How long was he going to be able to keep this up? Oh, he'd get Jimmie his four grand by Thursday, but what about next month's grease? He didn't dare go to Demetri with his troubles. Son-of-a-bitch might start demanding compensations they didn't have.

Well, hell with him, Andre reasoned. He'd left Andre holding the bag so the least of his worries was being a disappointment to him.

Andre downed his drink, muttered to himself, and poured himself another one.

Chapter 25

August 27, 1980

It happened on a Wednesday morning. Amanda woke Demetri up early and told him she was concerned about Isabelle. Something was not right. She was sitting in the barn petting Blackie and wouldn't respond to her. Demetri quickly rose, threw on his robe and went out to the barn. Isabelle was in one of the stalls brushing Whisper. She had a dull expression on her face.

"Isabelle, Isabelle honey, what is it?" Demetri turned the girl around and waited for a response. It was almost as if the girl was in a trance of some sort.

"Isabelle, don't you feel well?"

The girl just stared blankly at Demetri. Demetri thought he sensed frustration in her gaze and confusion, but there didn't appear to be any recognition, reaction, or indication whatsoever that she was receptive to his words. Demetri took his hands away from her shoulders and the girl went back to brushing Whisper immediately. From the look in her eyes, it was as if she was listening to something in her head. She seemed to be paying particular attention to Whisper who would turn his head occasionally and widen his eye at the girl. Blackie came bounding into the stall and wiggled his way through Demetri's legs until he was facing Isabelle. He stared up at her and started barking. Isabelle leaned down and curled her hands around his head and began rubbing his ears. The dog tilted his head slightly as if attune to some communication or confused by a sound he heard. Then he got bored and went sniffing around the barn.

"Amanda, call Doctor Blaine. Get him out here right away."

Demetri and Quimby sat waiting for the doctors to come out. They had been at the hospital all day. A specialist from Loyola was called in and had arrived several hours before. Demetri was near hysterical. He had told Amanda to go home. She had insisted on staying, but he wanted to ensure that Sophie's needs were being met.

Doctor Blaine came down the corridor and asked the men to follow him. He escorted them into a conference room at the end of the hall. Seated at a table were two other doctors.

"Demetri Davos this is Doctor Hendel from Loyola and Doctor Wyatt from our staff. Doctors, this is the child's father, Demetri, and his aide, Quimby. Gentlemen have a seat."

"Doctor, what's wrong with Isabelle?"

"I know you're concerned, but can we start by having you answer a few questions?"

"Sure."

"Now I have examined Isabelle several times through her life and never found anything remotely wrong with her in terms of development, physical maturation, intelligence, etc. She's received all the normal inoculations that all school kids get and never had a reaction to any as far as I know. Is that true? Have you ever noticed any type of adverse reaction to any shots she may have had? Anything out of the ordinary?"

"No, not that I know of."

"The last time I actually gave her any kind of physical exam from my records is last year and my write up shows no problem whatsoever, so I have to think that whatever the problem is had to develop recently. In the last few months have you noticed any ... strange behavior of any kind?"

"Strange behavior ... like what?"

Doctor Hendel spoke. "Any type of atypical staring or rocking herself to sleep or angry outbursts or tantrums?"

"No. I've never witnessed any and I'm sure if Amanda, she's my house lady, would have noticed anything I would have been alerted."

"How about her interaction with children at school? Have any of her teachers ever complained of isolationism or trouble relating to other kids, that kind of thing?"

"No." Demetri's patience was wearing thin. "Look, as of this morning Isabelle was a perfectly healthy, sound, loving child. Her grades are fine. She was always talkative and generally as compliant as any other kid. What's going on here?"

Doctor Blaine rubbed his nose and looked to the other doctors for help. Doctor Hendel spoke again. "Mr Davos, the things we've been asking about have to do with autism in children. Many of the symptoms she is displaying are similar to those displayed by children suffering from an extreme case of autism. However, autism is not some … disease that comes on over night. It's genetic in nature and except for rare cases the symptoms always surface by the time the child turns three. Autism does not surface in this severity overnight."

"All right so what else?"

"We have given her a general physical exam: reflexes, hearing, vision, brain scan, etc. So far we haven't been able to pinpoint anything. Physically she seems fine. A possibility certainly that we want to explore further is that of stroke. I must admit she doesn't seem to display any general signs of that, but there are more tests we need to conduct. At this point we just have to wait and see what the results of more testing show. We'll need to keep her a few more days at least."

"One thing I wanted to ask," Demetri said. "You're aware of her mother's condition. She's bedridden due to a stroke that occurred when Isabelle was born. Could this be any kind of, I don't know, mimicking behavior of some kind? Could her mother's condition be like some kind of catalyst that might cause her to revert to that kind of behavior?" Demetri shook his head in exasperation. "I don't know. I'm just throwing things out there trying to understand this."

"We're aware of your wife's condition, Mr Davos," Doctor Hendel said. "But we don't think, at least right now, that her condition has anything to do with this."

Demetri took a deep breath and sighed. "I didn't think so."

Quimby drove Demetri home through a light drizzle. The day was as drab as the feelings running through the two men as they made their way home.

"She must have gotten her hands on that globe. It's the only thing that can explain this whole business." Demetri sighed. "Good God, Quimby, what have I done?"

"You haven't done anything, sir. We're just going to have to see how this plays out. Maybe she'll get better."

Tears were welling up in Demetri's eyes. He had not used the globe to cure Sophie because of the harm that might have befallen Isabelle. But now this. "What do I do now, Quimby? What do I do now?"

Demetri stared out the window at a pond they were passing. On the shore a group of ducks were plucking the ground for food while a few others meandered about the water floating effortlessly about oblivious to the world around them. Demetri envied the peace of mind they seemed to display that was in direct contrast to the pain and misery he felt now.

"Maybe you're right, Quimby. I don't know what to think anymore. Maybe she'll get better."

But Isabelle did not get better. Her focus remained aloof. She did not speak and did not react when spoken to. Her eyes were not dull however. They were still alive, vibrant and alert. It seemed to the doctors that there had not been a loss of intelligence or awareness so much as a loss of the ability to communicate. Demetri often sensed frustration in Isabelle's eyes as if she desperately wanted to communicate but just somehow had lost the faculty to do so. Neurologically she was examined head to toe. She could still hear, see and there appeared to be no damage to her vocal chords. At times of excitement, Isabelle produced sounds such as moans and incoherent yells, but language simply was not there.

Over a two year period Demetri had her examined by every specialist he could get his hands on. He had even sent her to a home for autistic children for awhile, but that experiment had not worked out. Isabelle became combative and unhappy. Demetri hired private tutors who came to the house on a daily schedule and still no progress was made. It seemed that Isabelle was happiest just being back on the estate hanging around the barn mixing with Whisper, Prado, Blackie and all the other animals who made their homes on the ground.

Between Isabelle and Sophie, Demetri's interests stayed even more focused on the estate. Andre Haskim's control over D & H Printing became more and more prominent, not so much because he wanted more control, but just because it fell to him. Demetri basically gave Andre carte blanche to run the company as he saw fit. He was still consulted whenever important decisions needed to be made, but for the most part he sank further and further into the background.

And so the readings continued late into the nights with Isabelle lying beside her mother and Flip the cat, curled up between them. Demetri took from his library all the books he thought might get through to his unreachable family: Charlotte's Web, The Old Man and the Sea, Alice in Wonderland, and others. The words of the great books rolled off Demetri's tongue to a wife who could not hear him and a child who could not understand him. And yet it was one of the few times he found peace in his mind and heart. At least he could offer them his presence, his care, and his concern.

Chapter 26

September 1983

It was no secret that Sophie's condition was getting worse. She was no longer accepting food. Bedsores, an ongoing problem, had become severe enough that she had to be hospitalized several times in an attempt to get them healed. Things began piling up. Her kidneys started malfunctioning. Of course, the lack of exercise had atrophied her muscles. They had resorted to a feeding tube and not long after that infection set in that seemed to take her down even further. She was now in the hospital being cared for as best they could, but the doctors had admitted to Demetri that they didn't feel there was much more that could be done.

As Sophie slipped further and further away, so did Demetri. His concentration waned and he slid away from his responsibilities even further. He hadn't spoken to Andre in months. He simply assumed things were being run satisfactorily at D & H and didn't pay it a second thought. His monthly checks from D & H continued rolling in without a hitch. In conversations with Andre, his partner assured him that the business was running soundly. They had run into some troubles here and there trying to keep up with the switch to the computer world that the printing business had been forced into, but slowly the tide was turning and even though they had lost some of their best accounts through the years, they had picked up others which kept the company firmly in the black.

Seemingly assured that all was well, Demetri turned more and more to the bottle. His main preoccupation with Isabelle's care even began to take a back seat to his afternoon drinking. Demetri was confident that between Victor, Amanda and Quimby, Isabelle did not have a care in the world. When summer came, she returned to her habit of sleeping in the barn. Demetri made sure that Victor set up a stall right next to Whisper's to serve as her bedroom. Her dedication to the animals on the property and the way they seemed devoted to her in a way that was truly unique mystified Demetri. Victor had related to him times that he could have sworn Isabelle could communicate directly to the animals, Whisper and Flip especially.

Knowing Isabelle's love of animals even before she changed, Demetri suspected that she had made some kind of wish that she be able to communicate with them. His suspicions were borne out to a degree when he summoned Amanda to bring Isabelle to his room. After Amanda was dismissed, Demetri produced the globe and gauged Isabelle's expression to it. When Isabelle saw the globe, an unmistakable reaction overcame her. Her alarmed expression could not disguise the fact that she recognized the thing and knew the potential it held. That acknowledgment could only have been present if she had seen its power demonstrated in the past. Otherwise it would have simply been an interesting artifact and would have produced no appreciable reaction in the girl.

After a while, Quimby became annoyed at the decline in his master's interest in all areas of his life that truly mattered. When he could hold his tongue no more, he came to him one night while Demetri nursed a glass of wine and puffed on a cigar on the back patio.

"Sir, may have a word with you?"

"Certainly, have a seat," Demetri motioned toward one of the other patio chairs facing the back woods of the property.

"If I may say, I think you need to take more of a role in the things going on both on the grounds and at your business. Until recently your devotion to Sophie and Isabelle has been quite admirable. You had quite a bit on your hands and I felt you did your best to align your priorities appropriately. But now since Sophie's decline, how should I say, you've slowly slipped into a malaise that I am getting a little concerned with."

"Been drinking too much, eh?" Demetri brought the cigar to his mouth and took a puff. "You're right you know. Even I realize that."

"Sir, if I may, I realize what a jolt Sophie's condition is to you, but I think you need to reassess your situation and maybe … maybe make some changes."

"What changes do you suggest?"

"We need to face facts. Isabelle and Sophie still need your attention. And may I say that if you don't want to commit yourself to the business anymore, talk to Andre and have him buy you out. You've basically given the reins of D & H over to him anyway and, as you know, I don't trust him. I have a suspicion that things aren't as rosy as he might be leading you to believe. Your share would most likely keep you solvent for the rest of your days and ensure that there would be enough money to set up Isabelle's care should anything happen to you. I think at this point in your life, you don't need D & H anymore. Be done with it. As for me, I'm with you no matter what. I want you to know that."

"Thank you. I can't tell you the help you, Victor, and Amanda have been. Without the loyalty and support of you … I don't know where I'd be." Demetri looked out toward the East and his eyes fell on a large plot of empty farmland recently plucked clean of its corn so that only broken stalks remained. Quimby was right. He'd let D & H go almost completely. Perhaps there was no sense holding on to it any further. From the few discussions he'd had with Andre, he knew the business had fallen on a little hard time. He didn't have the energy to get involved. He hadn't really since the change had come over Isabelle. Now that it appeared Sophie would soon be leaving him, his energy had diminished to such a degree that getting up in the morning was sometimes more of a chore than he cared to admit. Maybe the time was right to cash in his chips.

"Oh Quimby," he sighed. "I've made a mess of things."

"Sir, we'll get through this. You'll see."

"I'd give my very soul to make things right for Isabelle, for Sophie. But I can't use that globe again. I can't trust what might happen." Demetri gazed at the dark woods and brought the cigar to his mouth. He didn't give a damn what happened to him anymore, but he wanted to make sure that Isabelle was cared for the rest of her life secure in the protection and shelter of his trusted servants. Any wish he made for her could backfire. Any wish he made for Sophie might impact Isabelle. She could be made worse off than she was now.

"I can't use that globe again," he muttered. "I can't." This time he spoke the words to himself. And he wasn't quite sure if he was declaring it as an absolute or trying to convince himself of his sincerity.

Quimby ushered Andre into the study and informed Demetri that he had arrived. Demetri came down and greeted him.

"Thanks for coming, Andre. Have a seat. I want to talk to you about something."

"How you been, Demetri? I see so very little of you."

"I'm fine, fine."

"And Isabelle and Sophie?"

"As for Sophie, I'm not sure her body will hold up much more. She's in the hospital right now on a feeding tube, but she had infection problems, bed sores, a whole mess of complications. The doctors have told me that it probably won't be long."

"I am sorry to hear that. I always liked Sophie. It was a bad knock she got."

"As for Isabelle … there's no change really. Doctors can't figure it out. I've got a tutor trying to work with her but … just nothing there to work with. All she wants to do is be with the animals. She's even gone to sleeping in the barn in her horse's stall. Actually she's part of the reason why I've called you here today. Do you want a drink?"

"Sure," Andre replied as he went to the couch and sat down. He did not know, as of yet, why Demetri had called him to his house, but the fact that Demetri had asked him to bring the ledgers with him had made him nervous. If he wanted to now go snooping around into the books, Andre would not be able to conceal the desperate situation they were in. In the last few months, things had gone from bad to worse for D & H. Andre was nearly at his wits end. He had half a mind to confess the whole thing to Demetri and tell him they were facing bankruptcy, but he hadn't had the guts. He kept thinking things would turn around, but they hadn't.

Demetri was fixing the drinks and facing the wall away from his partner. "Andre, with everything going on here, I've come to the realization that it's not fair for me to devote my energies to anything but the girls. Now with Sophie so sick, I … well I just don't have the motivation and drive I used to. It's unfair to you too. I've left you holding the bag pretty much at D & H. That Ken Grimes you hired for a manager seems to be working out well. Bottom line is you really don't need me anymore. I've basically been an albatross around your neck if nothing more." Demetri brought over Andre's drink and handed it to him. "I want you to buy me out."

Andre's hands began to shake. "Buy you out?"

"Yes. I'll sell you my half at a reasonable, fair price, seeing as you been the responsible party for the last few years and then you can have full autonomy with the business and handle it as you see fit. Maybe Grimes might want to kick in with you. He's a good man."

"But … I really don't want to buy you out. I mean … time's just not right for me …"

"We can work it out any way you want. An installment like situation, half now, half later whatever. I promise I'll be reasonable with you. I'm not looking to make a killing here. I just want to devote all of my time to what's really important for me."

Andre used both hands to grip his glass and bring it to his lips.

How was he going to wiggle out of this?

"Aren't the regular monthly amounts I've been supplying you meeting your needs?" Andre asked.

"Yes, that's been fine. But my thoughts and energies have been far away from D & H for a long time and I want to just move on."

"I … I'm afraid I'm just not in a position right now to … to buy you out. Besides I don't want to. We've been partners for a long time. We should stay that way."

"I appreciate that, but I've made up my mind I'm afraid."

The jig was up. Andre was backed into a corner and he knew it. He took another sip. Then he looked up at Demetri. "I'm afraid I've got some bad news for you, Demetri. I'm in no position to buy you out. The bottom line is we're broke."

Demetri's expression turned into a scowl. "Broke? What do you mean broke?"

Andre went on to explain the whole sordid mess to Demetri. The loss of customers, their lack of foresight in moving toward computer technology, the outdated equipment, the loans he had taken out on his own to try and shore up the business, the taxes owed. While he explained the sorry state of their affairs, Demetri sat there stone-faced.

Once Andre finished, Demetri went to the books and poured over them for nearly twenty minutes asking Andre questions as he came across confusing or inconsistent information. It was obvious the numbers had been smudged. Funds had slipped out the side door, expenses had not been paid promptly, and the taxes, that was a whole other problem. After he had sorted through the mess, he looked up at Andre.

"Why didn't you come to me sooner with this? Do you realize the seriousness of this situation? Why didn't you tell me that we lost the Bancroft and Whittaker accounts, J & W, the others? Did you think I would not find out eventually?"

"I was going to tell you in time, but I kept hoping things would turn around."

"There's more here than meets the eye, Andre. You've been pulling out monies that seem to have not gone into paying bills or for reinvestment. Thousands I'm seeing just at a glance. And the taxes. What I signed last year showed us in the black."

"The tax papers you signed were fakes. I couldn't let you see the real thing. The year before too. Truth is I been busting my nut just to get you your payment every month."

"Son-of-a-bitch, Andre. You've been stealing from D & H, haven't you?"

Andre remained silent.

"Haven't you!" Demetri screamed.

Finished with his mea culpa, Andre suddenly no longer felt remorse or shame. Instead a sarcastic insolence took its place. He was glad it was out in the open now. It served Demetri right for laying the whole company on his back. If he wanted to be upset, fine. Yes, he had stolen. Yes, he was caught with his hand in the cookie jar, but he didn't care. Let Demetri be angry. It was his problem now too.

Andre walked over to the bar and began fixing himself another drink. He suddenly felt cocky and smug. "Yes, Demetri. I'm afraid you've caught me red-handed. But the truth is we're broke. I've been sending you monthly payments just to keep you off my back and make you think things were coming along hunky dory. But where were you those late nights when I had to make decisions and try to keep customers satisfied? Where were you when receipts starting getting light, when I had to use my ingenuity to try to keep the damn place afloat? Where were you when the unions were busting our balls with wage concessions and demands for more benefits? Where were you, huh!"

Demetri lowered his eyes and went to the couch to sit down.

"I'll tell you where you were, you sorry for yourself son-of-a-bitch. You were here reading … frigging Shakespeare to Sophie, crying in your whisky, letting me do all the work, leaving me in the fucking lurch. And what did I do? I tried to protect your sorry ass, tried to keep you out of things so you could go on with your … your damn requiem."

"You're full of shit," Demetri responded. "You intentionally led me on to believe things were fine. Truth is you didn't want me anywhere near the business, not while you were helping yourself to the apples. How could you do that to me? Steal from me?"

"Steal from you, huh. Well, fuck you. Yeah I stole from you, I shorted the books. I was owed it, I was owed for all the extra time I was putting in while you were … playing nursemaid over here. You with your maids and your butler and your handy man." Andre raised his voice mockingly. "Oh, maybe I'll go for a little jaunt on Prado today. Maybe I'll walk through the gardens, pull some weeds, take a nap." Andre sat down and put his feet up onto another chair in an act of self-righteous mockery. "Don't give me your holier than thou shit. It don't work with me. We're broke friend, partner. We're broke. Buy you out, huh! That's a laugh. You'd have to pay me thousands just to make up for the hole we're in."

Demetri stared at Andre and was about to speak, but then just lowered his head. He was as angry as a hornet, but there was some truth to what Andre had said. He had left him holding the bag. He hadn't pulled his weight. He thought about all the concerns Quimby had discussed with him through the years: how he didn't trust Andre, how he was not half the business person Demetri was. Why hadn't he listened? He should have known better.

Andre spoke again this time in a derisive tone "As far as I can tell, we owe the IRS more money than we got or are gonna have in the near future. Our creditors are just about busting down our door and, oh by the way, don't be expecting your monthly check that I been so good at providing you. I ain't playing that bullshit game anymore. So I guess there's only one question left for me to ask. How about you spotting me several grand? You see my bookie's a little pissed at me. I've missed a payment or two in the last few months."

"That's what it is, is it? Your gambling habit! I always knew you were unlucky Andre. I guess I didn't realize you were so stupid too."

Andre quickly rose from his chair and downed the last of his liquor. "I'll take your proposition under advisement. Me buying you out that is. I'll go home and think of a fair price. Maybe you paying me several tens of thousands of dollars might be sufficient to 'buy you out' of our little mess." Andre took a deep breath. "You know I'm almost glad this all came out. I was getting a little tired of all the sleepless nights and what not. Now you can have some." Andre stared hard at Demetri. "It's a real pleasure for me to finally tell you what a sniveling coward I think you are. I feel so much better. I'll let you keep the ledger book there, Mister all high and mighty." He paused as he reached the door. "Oh, no need to show me out. I think I can find my way."

Chapter 27

The night had closed in and Demetri's room was dark and quiet except for the sliver of yellow emanating from the center of the globe. The spark of light illuminated the walls in an eerie glow. The ball sat on the edge of the bed while Demetri stared at it in silence. The news that Andre had disclosed concerning their financial situation came at a great surprise to Demetri. How stupid could he have been to not keep his eyes on the financial coming and goings of D & H Printing? Quimby had warned him and he had disregarded his feelings. Demetri had been a friend and partner of Andre for enough time to know the man was not always reliable and was susceptible to temptation, but he was not an ignoramus when it came to business. In reality, the first couple of years that Demetri had taken a back seat to the business affairs, he had been diligent in monitoring how the company was doing. When he had seen that Andre had been quick to pick things up and was satisfied he was able to handle the affairs of D & H, only then did he walk away assured that all was in good hands.

Now he saw the mistake he had made. He been so caught up with Sophie's care and with raising Isabelle that he had failed to recognize the danger right in front of him. How naïve he had been? Demetri looked over at the globe and saw the spark of light oscillating slightly, changing in color from yellow to red to orange. There was no way he was going to allow his finances to be plundered now at this point in his life. He had Sophie's and Isabelle's futures to consider. He didn't give a damn now what happened to him, but he had to make sure that their needs would be met for the rest of their life. Through the years Sophie's condition had been getting worse and worse and he knew, sooner or later, she would leave him, so he was not as concerned about her care as he was Isabelle's.

Demetri had always been a good investor and did have a decent amount of funds in savings in various forms. He had money in the stock market and money in different funds which, through the years, had not done badly for him. However, the amount of money it was going to take to bail D & H out was substantial. As if that were not bad enough, the loss of monthly income he had been receiving from what he thought was a thriving business meant he would have to live on what resources he had left and that simply would not be enough to maintain the property and the care Isabelle would require. He'd be damned if he was going to sentence her to life in a nursing facility. He'd seen and smelled those places and Isabelle was not going to be doomed to live out her days in a place like that.

Demetri had taken the globe out because he was considering doing something he never thought he would do again. Suddenly finding himself in dangerous financial peril, Demetri was confused. This was why he had never ridded himself of the infernal thing in the past. If ever he found himself with his back against the wall and no where to turn, the globe would always serve as a last avenue of escape.

Demetri considered what might happen if he wished for a sizable amount of money. Something even more horrible than had already befallen Isabelle could happen again. He didn't fear for Sophie as no matter what, at this point, she could not possibly hold out for very much longer. He could lose his life, but he didn't care about that. After all he'd been through, all the mistakes he'd made, he would gladly die to know Isabelle would be cared for. The problem was if he made the wish, he could never be certain where the ax of reprisal would fall. If only he could know that the repercussion would befall him, he would gladly wish for the money, but there was no way to be certain.

Demetri tried to reason through the past. The relationship between the beneficiary of the wish and the recipient of the punishment was not always consistent. In the case of his father, people in town had died. Demetri himself had benefitted and not been hurt. With Estrella, it was she who paid the ultimate price. Again Demetri was left unscathed. When he escaped from France, the British sailor and perhaps Antoine had been sacrificed. However, the same was not true in terms of Sophie. Sophie had wished for a child and gotten it, but was left bedridden and useless to herself. In her case she reaped not only the benefit, but the terrible result. And Isabelle, Demetri did not know what to make of that situation. It was hard to understand exactly what the girl had wished for. His best guess was the ability to communicate with animals. In her case she seemed to be the beneficiary of the gift and the recipient of the resultant penalty. Was it possible that her condition was not related to the globe? Could Demetri be wrong in assuming that the globe was the cause of her breakdown? Could she simply have developed the condition on her own?

No. He wasn't buying any of that. It had to have been the globe.

In actuality, it made no difference. The uncertainty was too great. He would never know just who would pay the price. To make the wish himself represented too dangerous a prospect for his household. If at all possible, he had to avoid being the one making the wish. He needed to be alive and well to see things through and make sure Isabelle came out of the whole nasty business secure and safe.

But how could he get anyone else to wish good financial health on himself?

Then it became as clear to Demetri as glass. Andre had brought them to this point. His recklessness, his treachery, his lack of self-control was the major reason they had been brought to their financial knees. That was the answer. He would show Andre the globe, explain it to him and let him make the wish. Chances are the only one in his family who could come to some harm was himself. Isabelle was too far removed, the connection was too weak. And Sophie, what more could possibly happen to the poor woman. Having

Andre wish for the money might bring death or damnation on himself, but he would have to take that chance.

And if the vengeance fell on Andre, so much the better.

If he showed Andre the globe, he would no doubt be seduced by its magnetism. Andre could make the wish. Perhaps, to make it work all the better, Demetri could not point out so vividly that for every wish a price had to be paid. With a little luck, they would both get what they needed and whoever suffered the price ... well, there was no way around it. It was the only salvation left them. He simply could not allow financial destruction to jeopardize Isabelle's future. Her safety was all that mattered now.

Demetri would tell Quimby of his plans. He would make sure all his affairs were in order. That way, in case anything happened to him, Quimby could follow up and make sure Isabelle was cared for.

It would work. It had to work. And then, perhaps, when it was all over and their future was secured, then maybe he would find the courage to destroy the damn thing once and for all.

Demetri got together with his lawyer, Alvin Rothman, and made sure all his affairs were in order. Once that had been accomplished, he called Andre and asked that he come to the estate for a meeting. He scheduled their meeting for a night when both Quimby and Victor would be off. He arranged for Isabelle to be gone also, allowing Amanda to take her overnight to a hotel. Sophie was still in the hospital, slowly slipping away. Demetri would not have any distractions getting in the way.

At first, Andre was suspicious when Demetri contacted him and asked him to come over. But when Demetri told him he had the answer to all of their problems, Andre agreed to meet with him.

Several days had passed since their last meeting. An early taste of fall had come to Northern Illinois. An unusually cool breeze for September billowed in from the West bringing with it a light drizzle that knocked some of the drying leaves from their branches. The sky flickered now and again with the flash of lightening and a rumble of thunder occasionally sounding in the distance.

Andre pulled up to the circular drive, trotted to the protection of the covered archway and knocked on the door. In his normal customary manner, he was late.

Demetri opened the door. "Come in, Andre," he said, closing the heavy wooden door behind him as he entered.

"Quimby and Amanda off tonight, Demetri? Usually you have one of your minions greet me at the door and usher me in to see the great master of the house." Andre's words bore a mocking tone. It was obvious to see that he was in a cynical state of mind. His predisposition to their meeting seemed to match the distrustful and sarcastic mood he had last left with Demetri.

"If you think your derisive tone is going to anger me, you're wrong. I believe that when you leave here tonight, you will be of a different mood. A more pleasing one, I suspect."

"If you think I'm going to bow on my knees and ask your forgiveness, you're wrong also." Andre said the words almost in self-defense not knowing what it was that Demetri was up to.

"No bowing or kneeling will be required tonight."

"I don't like the fact that it seems that all your usual domestic help is gone. Are you planning to do away with me tonight, my old friend?"

"As pleasing as that consideration may seem to me, no I am not planning to do away with you. You are perfectly safe tonight, Andre. Let's go into the study."

Andre followed Demetri into the study where a couple of dim lights lit the dark brown bookshelves. Three great windows provided a panoramic view of the back of the property that was for the most part shrouded in darkness except for the occasional flash of lightening that lit the rolling hills and woods beyond.

"Whisky, Andre?"

"Please …"

Andre went to the windows and peered out into the darkness. He had no idea why exactly Demetri had called him here tonight. His first inclination was that Demetri was going to turn the tables on him and make him an offer to buy him out. Perhaps he had intentions of reinvesting himself into the business and hopefully resurrecting it from its dismal state. If so, Andre had half an ear to hear such a deal. He didn't want to show Demetri just how truly desperate he was. If he knew the amount of money Andre still owed Mizetti, he would have the upper hand. As it was, any kind of lump sum now might be sufficient to bail Andre out of his precarious state and allow him, modestly, to resume some sort of life again.

Demetri brought Andre's drink to him and bid him to sit down.

"Be a pity for you to have to divest yourself of your estate here, Demetri. I don't know exactly how well you've done with your investments through the years, but unless you've been lavishly creative and lucky, my guess is there will be a for sale sign in the yard soon. That would be unfortunate. I always liked your place."

"I don't have any plans to sell the property quite yet because I have an idea I won't need to."

"I can imagine you have gone over the books with a fine tooth comb since we last met. If you have, you know how dire the situation is. It serves you right for sitting around here all these years leaving me holding the bag, acting like some damn aristocrat."

Demetri ignored Andre's surly comments and went and sat behind his desk. In the closed drawer on the left side of his desk sat the globe in its black velvet pouch.

Andre took a long sip of his drink and laid his foot on the edge of an end table slouching himself deeper into the rich leather upholstery of Demetri's couch. "If you called me here to commiserate about the old days or try to appeal to my better nature, my former friend, you're wrong. You said you had a way out of this, for both of us. So let's hear it. Be perfectly honest with you since the other night when we had our little spat, I've felt a whole lot better. I feel sorry for only myself. Not for you or your mute kid." Andre chuckled. "How's that for being a gracious guest?" He laughed louder.

Demetri leaned back in his chair and ignored the inhospitable tone of Andre's words. "I'm going to tell you a story Andre, and when I am done with this tale, I suspect your imagination will be on fire and you will be considerably more humble and congenial."

"I know this one. Does the story start out something like 'I'm going to sue you for everything you have or else have the authorities on my ass'? Something like that? Go right ahead. 'Cause I can tell you what the climax of that story will be. I've got nothing right now, but I tell you what. You can have half." Andre chuckled and swallowed down the last of his drink. "You know for such a gentleman you hold yourself out as being, your liquor is of an ordinary variety."

"Enough of your tongue, please. I beg your indulgence to shut up and let me finish. Go make yourself another drink. You'll need it."

Andre went to the bar and began filling his glass with ice as Demetri began his long tale. It began way back at the wagon of Zarpello the Great. It ran through the vicious circumstances of his father's death, the tragedy of Estrella, the drunken British sailor who so unfortunately hit his head, Isabelle's birth, Sophie's physical decline and Isabelle's mysterious malady. It ended with two old partners seated in a study listening to the rumble of thunder off to the West trying to figure out how to uncoil themselves from a precarious situation.

When he finished, Demetri looked over at Andre who had returned to his seat on the couch. For a moment no words were spoken. Then Andre burst into laughter.

"Demetri ... it appears that this financial setback you have incurred has jostled the remaining functioning parts of your mind. Do you really expect me to believe such rubbish?"

Demetri leaned down and opened the drawer. He lifted out the black pouch and placed it in front of him on the table. Slowly and carefully he removed it from the bag. The glass was glistening red and yellow, the light oscillating vividly. Andre's sarcastic look froze for a moment and then solidified into an earnest regard. He held his gaze for a moment in a dumbfounded stare before his mouth curled into a wry grin. "Where'd you get that thing, the local five and dime?" He brought his drink to his mouth and slurped a swallow.

"Come look at it closely, Andre. Usually I keep it tucked in my closet upstairs. Odd how the light works on these dark, paneled walls."

For a moment Andre did not move. In his head he was thinking either Demetri had really lost his mind or there was something truly here. He'd known Demetri for many years and as misshapen as their friendship now may have seemed, he always considered the man level-headed and composed. His sanity was never in question.

Andre rose and came to the desk. He picked up the globe and stared deep inside. It was warm to the touch. At once he felt the pull as if his mind was being teased. The sensation mirrored that of temptation.

In laying out the tale to Andre, Demetri had not accented the fact that for every wish granted, a price was demanded. His intention was to lure Andre to his cause, have him do the dirty work and he didn't want the veracity of the globe's true nature to jeopardize his mission.

"You feel it, don't you, that certain pull, that tempting allure? It's there. What I tell you is the truth."

Andre's eyes were glistening as he peered into the globe. He was being led hook, line and sinker. But Andre was wise enough to know a dupe when he saw one. He cautiously placed the globe back on the desk and stared at Demetri.

"If it's that easy, why haven't you wished for money, women, fame ... through all these years?"

Demetri would venture the answer to Andre because at this point he suspected that nothing he said would dissuade Andre from making a wish. The allure would be too great. He did not have the willpower that Demetri commanded. Demetri felt indeed that he was the more disciplined of the two and he knew how hard it had been through all these years not to be seduced by that yellowish haze and dreams of grandeur. No, Andre would not walk away from this tease no matter what the perceived danger.

"I have wished for things. I told you. I didn't wish my father dead, only for me to be rid of him. Estrella I loved. I thought my wish a genuine good, but I realized too late how greedy and self-centered it was. I was a child. In France, I felt I had no choice. People were dying all around me. I knew what would happen to me if I did not escape. They were killing Jews. No, Andre, I have wished for things in my life. And I would wish for the money myself, but you see what it has brought my family. I won't do it again."

Andre squinted down one eye and brought his hand up to his chin. "Yet you want me to do this?"

"It's your choice. I'm not forcing you to do anything. But let me ask you this. Are you willing to hide in the gutter like a rat for the rest of your life? You think I don't know how deep you're into it with Mizetti?"

Andre's eyes flashed wide.

"Yes, he sent one of his fellows to talk to me once. Tried to get me to work with him to persuade you of his ... how should I say, sincerity. They don't like getting rough with people anymore. Those were the old days. They're businessmen. I told him I wanted nothing to do with it. Surprisingly that was just a few days before our little talk the other night. I was going to speak to you about it, but we had other matters to discuss, as you are well aware."

Andre stared down at the globe. As he reached down to pick it up again, Demetri quickly snatched it away. "Your wish must be for the wealth of both of us, Andre. The both of us." And here Demetri laid a bluff. "You see there is one other secret about the globe that I haven't told you about. It has to do with the nature of the wishes made. I will tell you this. If your wish is for not only yourself but someone else's benefit, then this secondary danger will not be a problem for you."

"What secondary danger?"

"A secondary danger that I have learned through the wishes I made. Whenever the wish made is one-sided, for one person's benefit only, there is an added ... risk. Don't be alarmed about it. It is of no real significance to you whether you wish yourself alone a way out of this mess or for both of us to escape. Six of one, half dozen of the other. Trust me. It will behoove you to include the both of us."

"And I wish what? To be rich?"

"No. I would be careful about that too. The degree of your wish is generally symmetrical to the price that will be exacted. If you wish for untold wealth, you may be wishing yourself untold peril. I would simply wish for the financial resources sufficient to get us both out of our particular fixes. Yours would be full payoff to Mizetti and enough money to be comfortable. Mine is a guarantee that long after I am gone, Isabelle will be secure for the rest of her life. Besides, there appears to be no limit to the number of wishes that can be made. After we've wiggled off this hook, we can move on, perhaps, to the next troublesome aspect of our lives that may need mending."

Andre suddenly strutted back a couple of steps. "This is bullshit! This has got to be bullshit."

Demetri reached out the globe to Andre. "Here. Take it. Take it and go sit down with it."

Andre came forward, took the globe carefully and walked back to his seat. His gaze was concentrated on the glass. It was sparking out shards of color now, growing more intense.

Andre's eyes widened. He was feeling the magnetic pull now. He would have considered the whole thing a ruse if it wasn't for that magnetic allure he felt. The globe glowed ever brighter. Now the glass was almost flaring like a ball of flame. With each moment it became brighter and brighter. Andre was hooked now, his entire being mesmerized by what lay on his lap. Up until now, Andre had been skeptical, but now that he was truly feeling the globe's allure, he became convinced that something miraculous was going on.

"You feel the pull, the magnetism. It's true, Andre. Your mind is on fire, isn't it? Temptations rising and falling, visions of magnificence and splendor spinning around that little brain of yours. What I say is true. You know it now. But remember what I said, both of us and just enough to pull us out of this mess. Don't get too greedy."

Andre's mind was indeed on fire. He had never experienced such an odd grappling of wants and desires streaming through his head as they did now. The globe was truly something … powerful. Andre let his mind wander aimlessly and let the thoughts and wants carry him in whatever direction they would. He surrendered his will and released any inhibitions he had left. The globe flamed wildly sending streams of violet, green, yellow and red light around the room in a strobe like effect. The glare was nearly blinding.

Andre closed his eyes and thought about what Demetri had said. He would play along. What could it hurt? Something was certainly going on here. He would wish for the both of them, just enough to get them off the hook. He curbed his greed and surrendered himself to the globe. For a moment the intensity rose until the entire room was nearly devoured by the light. Then the glare receded, the brightness dimmed and slowly the sparking shards of light dissipated until the globe returned to normality showing only the yellow beacon at its center.

Andre sat almost stunned for a moment. A profound look of astonishment had taken the place of any skepticism or doubt he may have still had. He brought the globe back to the desk and laid it back on the table.

"It's quite something, isn't it?" Demetri asked.

Andre stood dumfounded for a moment trying to recover his senses. "What happens now?"

"What happens now? Now we wait. Something will occur that will deliver us both from our troubles."

Andre turned and walked toward the door. He was befuddled and bewildered. He turned back to Demetri. "What is this bullshit Demetri? What's going on here?"

"Let's just let things play out now. Just be a little patient. Let's see what happens."

"I don't know what kind of ... trick you're playing here. Did you get that thing from some magician or what?"

"Just be patient."

Andre stared at Demetri not knowing exactly what to think. Then he simply walked out to his car and left. Demetri went to the window and watched him drive away. A surge of fear coursed through his brain as he watched Andre's headlights recede into the distance.

"God help us now, Andre. God help us now."

Chapter 28

Two nights later, at twenty minutes to midnight, Andre Haskim was stirred from his slumber by a thumping noise. He was sleeping on the couch in his office at the Federal Street building that housed D & H Printing. Since their initial start, the business had expanded further and now Andre and Demetri owned the entire building, all five floors.

Andre's worries about money were waiting for him when he awoke. They could try to sell the business and the building, but times were tough all over and they wouldn't get a fair price for either. It was a shame because it was prime downtown property.

Andre had been working late trying to figure out where he could stretch some funds to keep the business afloat. He had spoken to Demetri today and asked him why their supposed salvation had not come through. Demetri had told him to be patient and Andre had told him that he was fucking nuts and that his story was bullshit and that they were ruined.

Demetri once again told him to be patient. Andre screamed at him and hung up the phone. If the dumb son-of-a-bitch wanted to just sit there and let the sword of ruination chop his head off, then the hell with him.

Andre had been going through the books trying to figure a way through their dilemma, and all he got for his trouble was a headache. He had lain down on his couch several hours before and took a nap, but had not meant to sleep as long as he had.

Andre got up and returned to his desk where a slew of papers were spread out. He pulled out a cigarette and lit it up. He stared down at the numbers. The problem, as he saw it, was all this damn equipment they had. Although they owned a fortune in all types of typesetting machinery, most of it was outdated and worth nothing on the open market, because of the trend toward computer equipment that was now overtaking the industry. It was worth a bunch of money on paper, but in practical terms it was nearly worthless.

The thumping noise that had woken him up sounded again. It appeared to be coming from below him in the basement. A knocking rattle rang through the floor.

"What the hell is that?" Andre muttered. He went down the hallway and took the stairs to the basement. At the bottom of the steps he turned on a light and walked down the hallway listening intently. He heard it again, this time coming from the room where the central furnace was located. It almost sounded like a trickling sound, like water running or air rushing. Andre went to the door of the furnace room and listened intently. He didn't hear it now but now something else had him worried. He detected the slight scent of gas in the air. To be safe, he took a last drag off his cigarette and stubbed it out on the floor.

Then he opened the door. Immediately the strong smell of gas overwhelmed him. He flicked on the light. When he did, a huge fireball ripped through the room, blowing Andre into the wall. His head struck the metal piping and he was instantly rendered unconscious as the flames ripped through the basement gobbling up all the available oxygen and shot down the hallway and up the staircase.

If anyone in the building survived, it would be a miracle.

Quimby woke Demetri in the middle of the night. "Sir, phone call. Someone from the fire department. There's been a fire at D & H."

Demetri couldn't quite absorb what Quimby was saying, but he picked up the line next to his bed. A spokesperson from the fire department told him about the explosion and fire. Demetri processed the information as best he could and hung up.

"My God. There's been an explosion on Federal Street. The building's on fire."

Quimby immediately went to the closet and provided clothes for Demetri. As he dressed, Demetri thanked God the accident had happened at night. During the day who knew how many might have been hurt or killed. On the way downtown Demetri began wondering how this happenstance might have been part and parcel of the wish Andre had made. He couldn't think how it could, and then he remembered the insurance. The business and the building were heavily insured. On paper the equipment at their facility may have been worth a significant amount of money, but in the real world it was nearly worthless. They could have never sold that equipment to anyone, but the insurance company would have to pay its full worth. In addition, the business itself would reap a financial reward. If indeed the building was a total loss, they would most likely be reimbursed a handsome sum from their insurance company. It would not make them independently wealthy, but it just might be enough to clear their debts and provide them with just enough funds to get off the hook.

Quimby drove them downtown and pulled up a block away from the site where the police had cordoned off the street. Both of them hurried up the sidewalk where they could get a good view of the building. It was a total loss. An entire side of the structure had caved in and angry flames shot through the roof spitting sparks and billowing smoke up to the heavens.

Several ambulances were parked at the scene, but Demetri did not see any activity around them. If they were lucky, perhaps no one was hurt. Suddenly the west wall of the building crumbled down. Fireman scattered trying to avoid the avalanche of flames and splintering wood. Two firemen were pulled out of the wreckage while others tried valiantly to reach another who had been caught in the collapse.

It would later be learned that Wes Halman, a fireman of sixteen years with a wife and two children, had fought his last fire.

While panicked firefighters struggled to rescue their partner, two other firemen came hustling out from the side of the building. They carried between them a figure whose body was nearly naked. The clothes that remained were badly singed. They laid him on a stretcher and the medics took over. As they worked on the man, Demetri wiggled through the crowd to get a better look. He got close enough to catch a glimpse of the victim when one of the medics moved aside. Demetri saw a horribly burned man, the body scorched black from the burns and soot. Demetri could not be sure, but he thought the body type resembled Andre's. A moment later they hoisted the gurney in the ambulance and sped away.

Demetri walked over to the far sidewalk and peered back toward the back of the building to the parking lot. There sat a lone vehicle parked beneath one of the streetlights. It was Andre's Cadillac.

For a month Andre remained in critical condition. Eighty percent of his body had received second and third degree burns. The doctors were amazed he had survived. Andre endured eleven operations over a seven month period, but there was only so much the doctors could do. The horrible scars would remain, the deformities could not be rectified, but the man would live.

In the meantime Demetri handled everything with the insurance company who paid handsomely for the damage done. He sold the ground to a company interested in constructing an office building on the spot. The sale brought more money than Demetri had imagined. With the money, he reconciled all the debts D & H had incurred. He even went to Mizetti and paid off Andre's gambling debt. When Mizetti heard of Andre's accident, he begrudgingly respected Demetri's plea and agreed on a lesser amount than was required to settle the account. It appeared even Mizetti had a heart buried beneath those layers of fat although he did tell Demetri to make sure Andre understood that his sympathy was not a character trait that could be counted on in the future.

While Andre began the long, arduous task of healing, Sophie's condition deteriorated to such a degree that the doctors could do nothing more. Demetri took his wife home, hired additional round the clock nursing care and waited for the end. On Christmas Eve night, Isabelle lay snuggled up against her mother's side cradling Flip in her arms while Demetri read from Dicken's Christmas Carol. As a light snow fell from the sky bringing a white Christmas to Northern Illinois, Demetri's eyelids grew heavy and he fell asleep. While Isabelle, Flip and he slept, the angels came and on that most silent of nights, escorted Sophie to a new home.

Sophie's death stung Demetri even more than he had imagined. The occurrences of the last few months had aged the man considerably. His step seemed to slow a bit and his energy level decreased markedly. Demetri continued to visit Andre feeling somewhat responsible for the condition the man now found himself in. He told him that his bills had been paid and that there would be money left over for him when he finally was released. During Andre's convalescence, he repeatedly asked Demetri to bring him the globe so he could wish himself well. Demetri refused. He had enough and had seen enough. Although he felt a certain degree of empathy for Andre, Demetri could not dismiss the image of Wes Halman's wife and children huddled together at the graveside of their beloved husband and father.

Andre's requests turned to demands. Demetri continue his refusal. Eventually Demetri lied to Andre and told him he had buried the thing with Sophie. He wanted nothing more to do with it. Andre wasn't sure he believed him. As time progressed, Demetri's visits to the hospital and later the convalescence center became unpleasant and distasteful. Andre simply would not let it be. Demetri finally told Andre that he could no longer continue visiting him. Their relationship had concluded. Their bills were paid and once released, Andre would have enough money to begin a new life.

Demetri wished his friend luck and walked out.

Chapter 29

11:35 pm, October 10, 1984

Quimby pressed down on the accelerator as the Cadillac merged left onto the expressway. A tear had come to his eye as he realized how much he would miss all the people he had worked with and served through the years. He thought of Isabelle and for a moment wished that he had the globe with him at that very second so he could wish her health and a long life. He hoped that she had hidden the glass well so that if by some freak chance Andre survived the crash, he would ultimately never be able to find it.

The Cadillac had reached sixty-seven miles per hour.

"I was thinking, Quimby, in all these years, you knew about the globe. Demetri told me. Why haven't you used it for your own personal self-aggrandizement?"

"I've been very lucky in my life, I guess. Seems I already had everything I ever wanted."

"Foolish of you really."

Quimby sighed deeply. "Yes, I guess I'm just an old fool." Quimby swerved the wheel to the right and aimed for the abutment of an avenue that crossed the highway. For a moment Andre did not react. Suddenly realizing what Quimby intended to do, he reached over and tried to force the wheel back to the left, but Quimby held firm.

"You'll kill us, you son-of-a-bitch!"

The car began riding up the grassy slope as Quimby aimed for the concrete wall. As the car angled up to the embankment, Andre's body slid down the seat up against Quimby. By that point it was too late and Andre knew it. To protect himself he laid his head down as low as it would go just as the car collided with the concrete. The force of the crash spun the car violently to the right causing the passenger side of the vehicle to slam sideways against the abutment. The vehicle then spun again until the trunk was facing down the slope. Gravity pulled the Cadillac back down the hill until it came to rest on the shoulder of the highway.

When the car came to a halt, Andre's first thought was that he was alive. He took a moment to let the shock wear off and to just wait to get his bearings. His head was resting on Quimby's lap. Slowly he raised himself up. A warm trickle of blood was oozing down his face. He checked his head and discovered he had a laceration above the right temple but he did not seem to be suffering any ill effects from it. Slowly he sat straight up. He then felt a pain in his thigh which had smashed up against the bottom of the dash. Andre looked over at Quimby. The butler's head had slammed into the side window which was smeared with blood. Andre checked his arms and mid-section. Except for the pain in his thigh and the laceration to his head, he did not appear to be seriously hurt. He did notice some dizziness as he crawled out of the passenger side window which had burst during the crash.

Someone yelled: "Are you all right?" Andre fell to the ground and turned to his right. A middle-aged woman with glasses was asking him questions from the front side of the car. "Are you okay? Can you walk?"

Andre turned back to Quimby. He began moaning. Up until that point everything had seemed to be going in slow motion. And then suddenly Andre came to his senses, realized the situation and started to stand. He felt pain in his right ankle now that he had not noticed before and he wondered if it was broken. The woman helped him up. When he finally straightened out another wave of dizziness came over him. He sat back down again in the grass and began reexamining himself. His ankle was indeed sore and something was out of place in the joint.

Other people had arrived and were trying to get at Quimby. Several cars with their engines running were parked haphazardly on the shoulder of the road. Andre lurched to his feet and paused for a moment to get his bearings. Except for his ankle, thigh and bleeding head, he felt he was good to go. He checked the inside of his jacket. The gun was still there. Slowly he walked over to a red Buick and leaned up against it while the others still tried to tend to Quimby.

Andre waited for the right moment, walked over to the driver door, and got in. The owner of the Buick saw him seated in the car and thought nothing of it. Quimby began moaning again. The man turned his attention back to him.

Suddenly the red vehicle pulled out into the right lane and sped past them.

"Hey! Hey!" the man screamed, his yells uselessly funneling up into a star laden sky.

The house was quiet when Andre pulled up the drive. He shut off the light and got out being careful not to slam the car door. On the ride over, he had felt a little woozy and disorientated, but was in total command of his senses. His ankle hurt especially because he had to use it to drive. By now his thigh was aching so badly he had to limp along.

Andre hobbled out of the car and went around to the side of the house. In the distance was the barn. He knew the girl liked to stay out there sometimes and before he went for the more dangerous avenue of checking the house, he figured he would try the stalls first. For a moment he stopped and thought. He wanted to make sure he wasn't forgetting anything. Demetri had no idea he was here. Quimby was now out of the picture, so he had nothing to fear from him. As far as he could tell, no one had any reason to believe he would be coming to the house. The stolen car he came in was of no consequence. He was free to take his time and get this right, once and for all.

Limping across the grounds to the barn was not as arduous a task as Andre had feared. He opened the barn door and went in. It was pitch black and he cursed himself for not first searching the car for a flashlight. A noise off to the left startled him. Slowly he moved forward until he came to a stall where a horse turned its head and stared at him. The animal did not recognize the man.

Andre could barely see. Perhaps there was a flashlight in the car. He decided to double-back to the vehicle and see if he couldn't find one.

Suddenly in the far corner of the barn, Isabelle stirred awake. It was Prado. Something had alarmed him.

Probably a mouse or something, Isabelle thought. But then she realized Prado was concerned about an intruder. The thought came and went in the horse's mind and he was no longer alarmed, but Isabelle knew he had seen someone. A vision of the monster man sparked in her head.

Amanda picked up the phone in her bedroom and called Demetri at the hospital. She was concerned that Quimby had not returned to the house yet, and she didn't want to go to bed until he was home. Demetri was just about to put on his pajamas when the phone rang.

"Hello."

"Demetri, is Quimby still there?"

"No, he left awhile ago. He should be home by now. Isn't he home yet?"

"I don't believe so. Let me check again."

Amanda walked across the room and looked down into the driveway. She saw a Buick sitting on the edge of the gravel. "The Cadillac is not here, but there is another car, a red one in the drive. Did he take … a different car or something?"

"Not as far as I know. He should have the Cadillac."

"Well, then I don't know whose car …"

Demetri was glad Amanda had called. Ever since he heard the news about Whisper, he had been worried about Isabelle. "How is Isabelle doing? How's she holding up about Whisper?"

"She's been quite upset. It was quite a blow to her."

"Yes, I can imagine. I still can't figure out what would have made that horse react like that. Whisper was such a gentle creature."

Out of the corner of her eye, Amanda spotted a figure hobbling back toward the car. She recognized him immediately. "Sir ... are you expecting Andre to be here?"

"Andre? No why?"

"Well ... I believe it's him who came in the other car. He's looking in the back of it right now. I couldn't mistake that poor man's features."

Suddenly, it all became crystal clear to Demetri. His cure had come from Isabelle. Whisper had paid the price. Andre didn't have the globe, he couldn't have the globe or else his disfigurement would be gone by now. Isabelle had the globe!

"Amanda, get Isabelle and lock the doors. Don't let Andre in. I don't care what he says. Don't let him in!" Demetri quickly hung up and ran to the elevator. In a matter of moments he was in a cab ordering the driver to step on it.

Amanda hung up the phone and moved aside one of the blinds and watched Andre search the car.

What was going on? she wondered.

Andre cursed. There was no flashlight in the vehicle. He gave up the search and began hobbling back up the lane. When he reached the barn, he slowly moved down the open path in the middle that was bordered on both sides by stalls. Four stalls ran on each side. A stirring and then a deep, low growl came from the stall to his right. A dog was standing there intently staring at Andre, its growl becoming louder and louder as he made his warning clear.

Blackie's apprehension came to Isabelle in a wave of emotion. The danger in Blackie's thoughts was undeniable. Now she heard the animal growling too. She swung her legs out of the bed and walked silently to the edge of the stall. Peeking out she saw the black silhouette of a man against the backdrop of the courtyard light that lit the grounds at night. Blackie was holding the man at bay, growling deeply, standing his ground cautiously. Suddenly a bright light flashed and a loud shot reverberated through the barn. The thought pattern Isabelle was receiving from Blackie instantly fizzled. The dog fell over silently.

The shot terrorized Isabelle. In the flash of light from the gun, she recognized the ugly face of the monster she feared. A wave of panic flooded her senses. She turned and stared at the stall trying to figure out where to hide. There was only her cot to shield her, so she crawled under it and waited. From beneath the bed she was able to see the man approaching her stall. He came up to the door and paused. Isabelle's whole body trembled and she tried as best she could not to cry or whimper.

Amanda had searched the house and not found Isabelle. She opened the front door just as the shot rang out. At first, she thought something had just fallen over in the barn making the loud single report, but a cold apprehension came to her. It had sounded like a gun shot, but there were no guns in the barn. What was going on? Amanda stood and did nothing for a moment listening for whatever might be next. Something was not right. She turned and ran back into the house. A moment later she was on the phone to the police.

Andre scanned the stall. His eyes were still getting accustomed to the dark. He didn't see anyone so he moved further down the lane. He reached the end of the barn and saw no one. Several goats came up to him thinking they were going to be fed. Andre shooed them away.

The barn door at the other end of the corridor screeched. Someone had opened it and was standing against the light, his shadow laying a long trail into the barn.

"Isabelle ..." Victor called out from the doorway. "Isabelle, are you all right?" Prado rustled in his stall and kicked at the wooden boards as Victor came walking forward. Andre sulked back into the shadows and waited.

"Isabelle ... where are you?" Victor stopped for a moment and listened. Andre held his breath. For a moment the three people in the barn all waited in fear for the next thing to occur, whatever that might be. Victor spotted something black lying in a heap off to his right. Slowly he ventured toward it. Only when he came right on it, did he realize it was Blackie. He bent down and rolled the dog over. His hand came away caked with blood.

"Blackie ..." The dog made a soft whimpering noise. Victor laid him down and raised his eyes. It had been a gunshot he had heard. "Who's there?"

The sound of a goat munching hay was the only response. Isabelle quietly began crawling out from under the bed as Victor cautiously came forward. "Isabelle, are you there?"

Isabelle scrambled up and ran into Victor's arms as he entered the stall. He hugged her close and then turned to leave when he saw the figure standing in the doorway. He recognized the distorted face and the patch over the eye immediately. In the darkness, he had not noticed the gun in the man's lowered right hand.

Confused, Victor moved toward Andre. Andre raised the gun and shot Victor in the belly. He fell over and slid across the ground. Prado began kicking and chortling, his snorts and bellows reverberating through the barn. He kicked at the door in his stall once again.

Isabelle did not move.

Andre blocked the doorway and stared at her.

He took a deep breath and sighed. "Now ... Isabelle, where is the globe?"

Isabelle did not understand the man, but she knew what he wanted. She knew it the moment she had seen him. The man's face terrorized her. Prado continued to cause a ruckus in his stall. The shot had terrorized him also.

"Give me the globe!"

Isabelle spoke to Prado and told him to kick open the door of his stall. It was never locked so a simple kick or two would open it. Prado complained, but sensing the urgency in her command began kicking furiously until the gate gave way.

The animal came bounding out of the stall. Isabelle told him the man was an intruder and that he must attack it. Prado neighed and bucked and then reared up trying to kick the man. Andre ran inside Isabelle's stall and shut the gate behind him. The horse kicked and bucked at the door but was helpless to do anything further since the gate could only open out.

Assured that he was safe from the flailing animal, Andre turned his attention back to Isabelle.

"Now, Isabelle, before we are interrupted again, where is the globe?"

Isabelle just stared at him. She told Prado to relax as she knew there was nothing the horse could do for her. The globe was still where she left it, under the bed she had just crawled out from under, but she knew how valuable it was, the power it held. She needed the globe now to help Blackie and Victor. She wasn't going to just give it up.

Victor moaned and curled his body holding his stomach.

"Where is the globe?" Andre screamed.

Isabelle hands began to tremble. She was terrified, but she was not going to give up the globe. Not while she could cure Victor and possibly Blackie.

Andre cocked the gun which made a loud metallic snap. He was so close, so close that he could almost taste salvation. It all rested on this mute's shoulders. He knew he couldn't kill her. If he did he might never find the globe. No, he couldn't kill her, but he sure as hell could terrorize her. Andre rushed forward and slapped the girl hard across the face sending her reeling. The blow nearly knocked Isabelle out. Her mouth was bleeding and her head ached. Slowly she got up and leaned against the wall. Andre came forward again and kicked her in the left shin as hard as he could. Isabelle collapsed in agony. The pain was like nothing she had ever experienced. She didn't know what was more terrible, the pain or the apprehension she had for the next blow to come.

Andre's mind was on fire. He could tell by the girl's demeanor that she was about ready to give it up. Perhaps one more blow would be all it would take. He moved forward raised his arm but then suddenly stopped when a flicker of light caught his eye from beneath the cot to his left.

Andre's search was over.

He scrambled to his knees and reached under the cot pulling out the velvet sack. The ball was glowing so wildly that some of the light was glistening through the small pinholes of fabric. Isabelle got up and circled around Andre who now paid her no attention at all. Andre sat down on the bed and pulled out the globe. It was glistening red, yellow and white, sparks of light revolving around the dark corners of the barn. Andre's face glowed in the illumination as the ball grew brighter and brighter.

Isabelle ran from the barn.

Chapter 30

Tommy woke up startled by a nightmare. He turned to his right and saw his mother sleeping in the chair on the other side of the room. He straightened up again and thought about his dream. The girl he had seen the other day was running down a long dark corridor away from some sinister thing he couldn't quite make out. An ominous ringing resounded in his head, like a gunshot, and that had been the thing that had woken him up.

What did it mean? he wondered.

Tommy thought back to his experience with the girl in the hallway. He had just been sitting there minding his own business when it felt like someone had just entered his head. It was like that odd feeling he had every once in a while that he was being watched. But this was different and Tommy had never experienced anything like it before.

He rolled over on his side careful not to disrupt the IV running through his hand. He had been awfully upset on that day when he had seen the girl. Worry about his mother and his condition had consumed him. When Doctor Tim came by it heightened his spirits somewhat and whatever communication he felt with the girl seemed then to dissipate.

For a moment his thoughts drifted from the girl to Doctor Tim. Why did he feel the way he did toward the doctor? The truth was he loved the man. He loved his dedication, his caring nature, his medical ability. The man represented everything that Tommy held dear and everything that Tommy would most likely never have an opportunity to accomplish. Imagining all the good Doctor Tim would do in his life made Tommy envious.

A wave of nausea ran through his stomach again. The medicine they had him on now was strong. Doctor Tim had warned him that he might feel sick to his stomach at times.

Tommy stared at the ceiling and began praying. Prayer helped calm him when he was scared or bitter about his illness. In his prayers he thanked God for giving him Doctor Tim and for showing him the little sparrow that had made such an impact on his consciousness.

Then a heartbreaking thought came to him, something he could not figure out. He was so thankful to God and yet so … frustrated. Why would God demonstrate to him Doctor Tim's dedication, illustrate to him the true nature of commitment through the gallantry of a tiny bird, instill in him an insatiable desire to emulate their behavior and to do good in the world, and then simply snatch away his opportunity to act on it.

Fear rose in his chest and he began to cry. He desperately wanted his mother to come over and hold him, but she needed her sleep. He would not wake her up no matter how tough the night got.

He closed his eyes and thought about it some more. No, God would not do that. He would not have the wisdom to show him such bounty without a purpose. Something good was going to happen. Something good was going to happen …

Chapter 31

Demetri sprang from the cab and ran to the house. Amanda met him at the door and told him Isabelle was upstairs safely in her room. She didn't know for sure but thought Andre was in the barn. Demetri told her to go upstairs and lock themselves in her bedroom. Then he went to his den and got his shotgun. He made sure both barrels were loaded and went back out the front door.

The wind had picked up some and a wild breeze was bending the limbs of the tall oaks on the property. Leaves skittered across the gravel as Demetri cautiously approached the red car. His concern was that somehow Quimby was inside hurt or worse. When he discovered the vehicle was empty, he turned around and faced the back of the property. The night light from a pole dimly lit the grounds. As Demetri began walking toward the barn, a burst of colored light blossomed from deep within the barn. Shards of light sparkled out from all the cracks and crevices in the wooden planks. The eruption of light grew like an expanding plume of flames. It peaked for a moment and then slowly receded in intensity until the fading glow dissolved totally.

Demetri cursed. The son-of-a-bitch had done it. Who would pay the price for this act of selfishness?

Demetri's anger bubbled over. Now that the bastard had the thing, there was no reason to fear him. Demetri reached the barn and swung the door open wide.

"Andre! Where the hell are you?" Demetri looked down and saw Blackie on the ground in front of him. He bent down and raised the dog's head. Blackie was dead. Demetri stood up again, cocked the shotgun and moved forward.

"Andre, where are you?"

"I'm here, Demetri."

Demetri swung around to the voice and saw Andre seated on Isabelle's cot. Looking down he saw the body of Victor sprawled in the dirt. He raised the shotgun and held it up to the dark figure. "Come out into the light." Demetri stood back and watched Andre rise from the cot and step out into the middle of the barn.

"Certainly I will, Demetri. There's no need for the gun now, my old friend. I've no desire to harm you." Andre turned his head so that the dim light from outside the stall fell upon his face. Demetri took a step back. He was looking at Andre as he looked thirty years before: tall, handsome, well-defined, his hair dark and full. The ravages of the fire had disappeared.

"How do I look?" Andre suddenly moved forward to a glass window and caught his reflection in the light. He began to laugh raucously. "My, but ain't I one beautiful son-of-a-bitch, eh?"

Andre started dancing a jig, hamming it up to an old Al Jolson number, *I'm Sitting on Top of the World*.

Demetri turned back and saw the globe sitting on the bed, a small single spark of yellow light dimly shining out. He went to Victor and bent down to examine him. He checked for a pulse and found none. Demetri bowed his head and sighed. Suddenly the sound of gravel spinning off of tires and the screeching of brakes came from the driveway. Demetri heard Amanda's voice calling out and then the far door of the barn swung back open. The silhouette of two police officers standing at the door became visible. Demetri looked up at Andre. His face suddenly soured. He looked at Victor and realized the trouble he was in.

"Come out of there, now. You here!" Demetri recognized the Irish brogue of Mike O'Malley one of the local police officers.

"Mike? It's Demetri. I'm coming out, Mike." Demetri looked up at Andre. It was obvious to the both of them what the repercussions of Andre's regained youth would be.

"No, you're not going out there," Andre said desperately.

"Give it up, Andre. Give it up."

Andre's face curled into a menacing sneer, as ugly as the scars that had previously riddled his face. His anger fumed over. He raised his gun and pointed it at Demetri. Then his hand began to quiver as the full weight of what the police could do to him became clear. He'd be locked up for the rest of his days. And now that he was healthy and springing with youth and energy, who knew how many years that would be.

"Demetri ... is that you?"

"Yes, Mike. Give me a moment."

"You got to come out now!" The policemen moved to either side of the corridor that ran down the middle of the barn positioning themselves for a better shot in case of a shootout.

The expression on Andre's face drifted from anger to loathing to disgust and finally to a desolate admission of defeat. Then suddenly his face brightened. "Move away from the globe, Demetri."

Demetri realized what Andre intended to do. He held his shotgun up at Andre. "No."

"I'm warning you, Demetri. Move away!"

Demetri hesitated. He didn't know what exactly to do. He figured that Andre wanted the globe so that he could quickly wish to be whisked away to some safe place. Demetri could not allow that. If Andre got away with the globe, there would be no end to it. No end until perhaps finally the resultant penalty for one of Andre's future wishes would be his own demise.

"Get away now. I'm telling you, Demetri. Get away!"

"No, Andre." Had it come to this? Did he need to murder his once best friend? Demetri put his finger on the trigger. Only remorse, regret and repentance prevented him from pulling the trigger.

"Demetri, we're coming in," O'Malley yelled.

Andre knew he could wait no longer. He shot Demetri in the leg. Demetri crumbled to the ground and the shotgun fell to the floor.

Andre jumped past him and grabbed the globe while Demetri sprawled in the dirt. Andre put the globe in his lap and quickly funneled his thoughts. Demetri tried to turn himself in the dirt so he could reach up and try to stop Andre.

"Demetri ... Demetri?" the cop yelled out.

Panic ran through Andre's head. He heard the policemen coming closer to the shed. They would be there in several more seconds. He had no time to waste. Quickly he concentrated on the globe and wished himself away from there. A vague, yearning arose in his scattered, panicked mind. He craved to be away, to be miles away, free from the cops, the estate, the arms of the law ... away.

The ball glowed wildly spinning colors and strobe lighting around the barn. Demetri grimaced in pain as again he tried to boost himself up and pull the globe from Andre. The pain was too great. Demetri fell off to the right and passed out.

In a burst of light and color, Andre desperately wished himself to be miles away. In the final flash of light from the globe, he disappeared. The globe fell to the mattress and rolled up against the pillow. Only the tiny yellow flicker in the center remained.

Andre Haskim suddenly found himself floundering in Lake Michigan. Immediately he realized the terrible mistake he had made. The water was freezing cold and the waves were lapping around him. He was shrouded in absolute darkness. In the distance a blinking red lamp shone from the top of a lighthouse. The huge searchlight at the top slowly twirled sending a stark white ray of light out against the blackness. As the beam fell on Andre, he thrashed about in a wild panic trying to keep his head above the cascading waves.

The beacon illuminated him for a moment and then slowly spun past him on its never-ending journey. When it made a full rotation on its axis and returned to the spot where the struggling man had been floundering, it revealed only the dark, ceaseless waves.

Chapter 32

9:30 am, October 11, 1984

Isabelle sat quietly in the chair and watched as Amanda helped prop up her father's pillow to make him more comfortable. When the emergency room people had stabilized Demetri, he was brought up to a room on the third floor. His former room had been on the fifth and Isabelle wondered how she was going to get back up there.

It had been a long night. Police had been all over searching the grounds and the barn while emergency personnel tried as hard as they could to help Victor and Demetri. Demetri had been whisked away in an ambulance. They had finally carried Victor out on a gurney with a blanket over his face. Isabelle knew what that meant. Isabelle had wondered what had become of Quimby and only when Amanda had taken her to a different room on the fourth floor did she see that he was also in the hospital. They had visited him for a while before coming down to see her father. Quimby was awake, but his head was bandaged and his speech slow and slurred. Isabelle did not know what had happened to him, but she assumed it had something to do with the monster man.

Isabelle looked down at her feet where the big purse she had insisted on taking to the hospital leaned up against the foot of the chair. In all her excitement and nervousness, Amanda had barely noticed it when she loaded Isabelle into the car for the ride to the hospital. A nurse came into the room pushing a cart that contained several different items on it. She spoke quickly to Amanda who then looked at Isabelle and nodded her head. She walked over to Isabelle and indicated that she needed to leave the room. Isabelle understood, grabbed her purse and let Amanda lead her down the hall to a room where a television set in the corner showed a Tom and Jerry cartoon. She made Isabelle understand she was to stay there until she came back. Then she went hustling back down the hallway to Demetri's room.

Isabelle thought about what had happened when the police finally took control of the situation the night before. Once she thought it safe, Amanda had run out to the barn. Isabelle followed her out the door but went around the long way to approach the barn from the rear. Through a window she saw the men working on her father. It seemed he was very groggy but other than a wound to his leg which they were busily wrapping, he seemed okay. They had taken him out to the corridor once they had secured him on the gurney and stopped the bleeding. Isabelle saw the globe lying on the bed hidden partially by a pillow. Once they led both Victor and Demetri out, Isabelle snuck in the back door and hid the ball once again beneath her bed.

While the cartoon blared from the TV, Isabelle grabbed her purse and walked across the hall to the elevator. She pressed the up button and waited for it to arrive. No one seemed to be paying any attention to her. The elevator came and she boarded. An older couple was standing in the car and they smiled at the girl. They began speaking to her, but Isabelle could not understand what they were saying. She just smiled and waited for the door to open on the fifth floor.

Quickly she made her way down the corridor until she came to the room she wanted. Slowly she pushed open the door and peeked in. The boy was sitting across the way in a chair staring out the window. His view faced the west where the last of the overcast cloud layer was slowly moving toward them exposing a bright blue sky.

Isabelle stepped in, closed the door and walked over to the boy. Tommy had been napping but awoke when the girl reached him. He sat up straight and stared at her for a moment.

"Hi," he said.

Isabelle did not respond, but smiled.

Tommy looked at the girl and wondered who she was. She obviously must have been a patient, he assumed, though he wondered why she was not wearing the usual hospital garb.

"Are you sick, too?" Tommy asked with some hesitation.

A look of frustration came over Isabelle. She so desperately wanted to understand what the boy was saying and respond to him, but of course, she couldn't. Tommy asked again, but Isabelle just looked at him with a smile on her face. Tommy assumed there must have been something wrong with her throat. He put his hand up to his mouth and throat as if to ask her if it hurt. Isabelle just stared at him. Tommy didn't know what else to do so he reached over and grabbed Isabelle's hand. Isabelle grabbed it back and together they smiled at each other.

Tommy turned back toward the window. It didn't matter much. He was glad for the company. His mother had to leave earlier to run a few errands. He'd been having a bad day. The dizzy spells had returned and so did the nausea. He had a small hospital pan next to him just in case he threw up again. All morning Tommy had felt disheartened and alone. He tried to keep up his courage, but it was waning. He had been repeating the phrase to himself all night, that something good was going to happen, but then he had a visit from Doctor Tim after his mother left. The doctor seemed different. It was almost like he was apologizing to Tommy without saying so. He looked at the charts and had a discussion with the nurse. Something she had done brought it all clear to Tommy that all hope was lost. Doctor Tim had taken her aside and was whispering to her. Suddenly in the middle of a sentence he bowed his head slightly and the nurse latched onto his arm and squeezed it. They didn't think Tommy had seen it, but he had.

It was unmistakable. Doctor Tim had withered himself to the bone trying to figure out what else to do. He looked like someone had kicked him in the guts. Before he had said they might operate again when the tests came back. The tests had come back and he had not mentioned surgery again.

That one moment when Nurse Simmons squeezed his arm and looked at him when they thought Tommy wasn't watching had said it all. There was no hope. He was wise enough to know that now. His mother would be crushed, his father too. Doctor Tim, Nurse Simmons, all of them. All his sickness had done, his whole life, nothing but unhappiness and disappointment to everyone.

Tommy raised his head and stared out the window. A flock of birds in a churning swarm swirled up from a nearby roof and went fluttering off. They would go south, mate, come back north, have their babies, protect their nests, and be a great part of the swirling, wonderful magnificence of the world. But he would not. He would not have a chance to be dedicated to a cause like Doctor Tim, like his mother, Nurse Simmons, his father, the birds. Again a tear welled in his eye and he felt disgusted with himself. He was the lowest thing there was on the earth, a drag on the whole inertia of energy and power and majesty that was the world. His life had no meaning, no purpose. When he was gone, he will have left behind to anyone who loved him only regret, grief and financial loss. Any skills he had, any supposed brains he had that his teachers had all told his parents about over and over were nothing, a waste. His existence had aided no one, provided help to no one, comforted no one, and benefitted no one. That desire to commit his whole mind and body to some ... great cause, some great good, was nothing but the useless dream of a sick kid who served only to drain the resources of everyone around him.

Tommy lowered his head in shame. *God forgive me for my wasted life,* he thought.

Isabelle squeezed Tommy's hand again and he looked up at her. For a moment he had forgotten she was there. Why did he feel such a bond to this girl? He didn't care now. He had surrendered the last possible ounce of resolve and will he had left. It was just unfortunate for her that she had to be there to witness it.

Isabelle reached down into her bag and pulled out a black pouch. When she opened it at the top a ray of bright light streamed out. It was oddly colored, red, yellow and white. She pulled out the globe and suddenly the room lit up even more brightly. Streams of pulsating light came dancing off the thing, spinning, swirling, curling. Isabelle knelt in front of Tommy and placed the ball on his lap. He put his hands on the globe and felt soothing warmth coming off of it. Whatever the thing was, it fascinated Tommy.

A swirl of colors and thoughts started whirling in Tommy's head. At first he thought he was suffering from another dizzy spell that had been coming more and more often, but no. He began dreaming, seeing himself a doctor like Doctor Tim, helping children, helping people, serving others. He wanted that so bad, to be of service. He found himself almost carried away by that wish. His head filled with promise and optimism and hope. He saw the tiny sparrow again and suddenly found himself wishing as hard as he could for his health to come back. Together Isabelle and Tommy closed their eyes while a flood of light and warmth enveloped the room in a wash of swirling, oscillating colors.

Then the warmth of the globe began to recede. The brightness began to fade, slowly down into itself. The color waned and dissipated and drained away until all that was left was a tiny yellow dot in the middle of the ball. And then suddenly it winked out. The globe went black and cold. Tommy suddenly noticed that the dizziness he had been feeling all morning had lifted. His mind was clear, clearer than it had been in weeks. He suddenly felt hungry too. In fact, he was famished which was odd because he hadn't had much of a stomach for anything the last several days.

Isabelle rose from her knees and picked up the globe. She walked over to the garbage can and dropped it in. It would be of no use to anyone now. She went back to Tommy and placed her hand on his shoulder and squeezed it softly. She needed to be going. Amanda was going to be missing her. She gave Tommy a smile and one more reassuring squeeze and then turned to go.

Totally confused, Tommy turned to her. "Thank you …" he mumbled. "Thank you."

Isabelle turned back to Tommy. "No, thank you," she said.

The End

Also Available from BeWrite Books

The Harrowing of Ben Hartley
by Steve Attridge

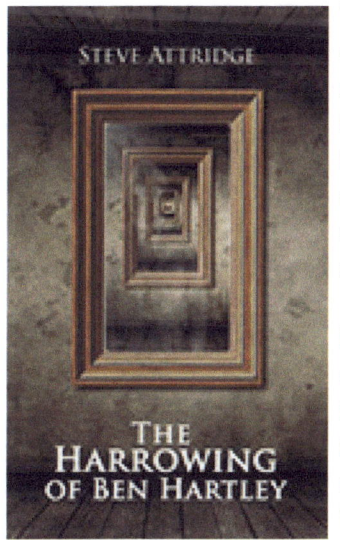

Timid Ben Hartley's life is not easy. His mother's boyfriend is a malevolent bully. School is a friendless ordeal. His sleep is increasingly hijacked by strange dreams ... and things begin to seem more real when he is asleep than when he is awake.

But when his mother takes him to a psychiatrist, things only get worse. Dark figures from his dreams start to leak into waking life, including the strange and uncompromising Wolf.

Ben learns that he has been assigned a seemingly impossible task requiring courage he does not possess. And when people around him start disappearing and dying, he must face the greatest ordeals of his life.

His enemies are legion – the Nomads, the Hunters, and the vague and destructive figure that is always just on the blurred edge of vision. His own friends and family are not to be trusted either.

Ordinary life is threatened by its mirror image, and as everything he knows crashes and collapses, Ben is forced to make life and death decisions to save humanity from being drawn into a hellish twilight world where nightmares are both real and everlasting.

Award-winning screen writer and novelist Stephen Attridge's 'The Harrowing of Ben Hartley' fantasy thriller reveals how the surreal dream world of an asthmatic, solitary and frightened teenager becomes terrifyingly real – for everyone.

Paperback ISBN: 978-1-927086-87-2
eBook ISBNs: EPUB: 978-1-927086-88-9
MOBI: 978-1-927086-89-6
PDF: 978-1-927086-90-2

The Marsh People
by Valentine Williams

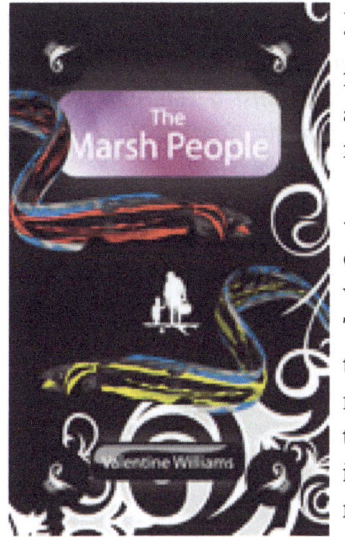

In a post-industrial age, the last 'free' humans cower in hiding from the mysterious Masters and struggle for life in merciless marshlands.

The Masters – human or alien – are never seen but rule the crumbling cities they dominate with fiendishly trained, dogs. The ferocious mastiffs are also the near-feral police force that raids pitiful villages and herds their occupants like sheep into inhuman city slavery and mindlessness.

But city slave Scummo finds his latent humanity stirred when an orphaned child comes into his care ... and they go on the run into the boggy wastelands, living rough, starving but skirting scattered tiny villages in constant fear of 'the herdings' by packs of pitiless hunting dogs, electronically programmed by the Masters to enslave or cull village-dwellers.

Scummo and his young charge, Kelpin, re-learn long-forgotten survival skills from Bethyl, the fiercely independent female leader of one Marsh People group.

But in the bloody struggle to survive against desperately competing wandering human bands, can Scummo and Kelpin avoid a return to primitive brutality, dehumanizing ignorance and even cannibalism or hope to replace the building blocks of civilization before it's too late?

And are the mysterious Masters secretly monitoring their every move, ready and able to destroy the last ragged vestiges of human liberty by unleashing the dogs of final war?

In Scummo and Kelpin's hair-raising odyssey of life as outcasts in a terrifying marshland, alive with both human and unworldly predators, Valentine Williams prompts us to ponder just how thin the veneer of civilization and humanity might be. Would mankind band together against a common enemy or would it turn on its own ... just as the dogs so quickly became man's worst enemy rather than his best friend.

paperback ISBN: 978-1-927086-62-9
ebook ISBNs: EPUB: 978-1-927086-63-6
MOBI 978-1-927086-64-3
PDF 978-1-927086-65-0

Brotherly Love
by Peter Tomlinson

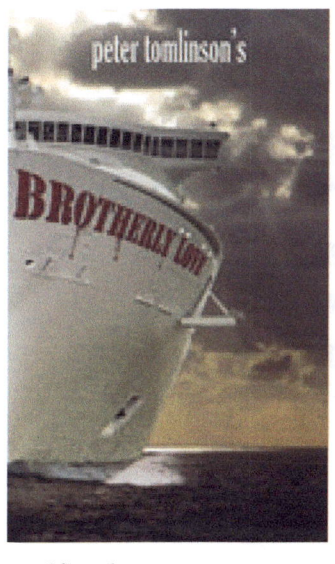

'Brotherly Love' is the mighty flagship of the renowned Mercy Fleet, financed by one of the richest men on earth to bring emergency relief and medical aid to crippled countries ravaged by poverty, drought, famine and disease ... at least that's what the world believes.

But love and mercy are far from the true mission of the 'Brotherly Love' and its angelic armada. And aged multi-billionaire Vival – internationally praised for his philanthropy – is anything but a selfless humanitarian.

Nearing retirement, Ralph Collingwood has his quiet life in a peaceful English village torn apart when he's ordered by British intelligence bosses on a last desperate international assignment ... to risk his life in a bid to expose what the cargo of the 'Brotherly Love' really is ... misery, torture and death ... and the Mercy Fleet's sinister mission ... to rip the civilised world asunder.

Tomlinson's race-paced thriller spans the wild seas and desolate peaks of the world and of the human spirit as actual brotherly love strives to expose Vival and his Mercy Fleet's sinister plans for the horrendous evil they are.

ebook ISBNs: EPUB: 978-1-927086-18-6
               MOBI: 978-1-927086-19-3
               PDF: 978-1-927086-20-9

BeWrite Books